THE SEA OF
LIGHT

THE SEA OF
LIGHT

JENIFER LEVIN

A DUTTON BOOK

F

3-93 BT 21.00

DUTTON
Published by the Penguin Group
Penguin Books USA Inc., 375 Hudson Street,
New York, New York 10014, U.S.A.
Penguin Books Ltd, 27 Wrights Lane,
London W8 5TZ, England
Penguin Books Australia Ltd, Ringwood,
Victoria, Australia
Penguin Books Canada Ltd, 10 Alcorn Avenue,
Toronto, Ontario, Canada M4V 3B2
Penguin Books (N.Z.) Ltd, 182–190 Wairau Road,
Auckland 10, New Zealand

Penguin Books Ltd, Registered Offices:
Harmondsworth, Middlesex, England

First published by Dutton, an imprint of New American Library,
a division of Penguin Books USA Inc.
Distributed in Canada by McClelland & Stewart Inc.

First Printing, January, 1993
10 9 8 7 6 5 4 3 2 1

 REGISTERED TRADEMARK—MARCA REGISTRADA

LIBRARY OF CONGRESS CATALOGING IN PUBLICATION DATA:

Levin, Jenifer.
    The sea of light / Jenifer Levin.
        p.   cm.
    ISBN 0-525-93562-2
    I. Title.
  PS3562.E8896S43   1993
813'.54—dc20   92–18596
                                                                    CIP

Printed in the United States of America
Set in New Baskerville
Designed by Leonard Telesca

PUBLISHER'S NOTE
This is a work of fiction. Names, characters, places, and incidents either are the product
of the author's imagination or are used fictitiously, and any resemblance to actual
persons, living or dead, events, or locales is entirely coincidental.

For Julie DeLaurier

You will experience a glimpse of blinding light, subtle, sparkling, bright, dazzling, glorious, and radiantly awesome, like a mirage moving across a spring-time landscape in one continuous stream of vibrations. Be not daunted by this, nor terrified, nor awed. This is the light of your own true nature. Recognize it.

—from *The Tibetan Book of the Dead*

Angelita

🐬 🐬 🐬

Rescue helicopters hovered over the water like great metal dragonflies. Below bobbed fragments of the 747 that had gone down more than two days ago, filled to capacity and carrying with it all the members of Southern University's top-ranked NCAA Division I swim team. No one expected survivors.

It had been one of the worst storms to hit the Triangle in years. Winds gusted to 150 miles an hour and more, swells rose higher than eighty feet, the ocean turned a savage gray color. Meteorologists dubbed the storm Angelita—Little Angel.

Now, though, turquoise swells rippled mildly below, capped with white froth. It was as if this bright calm covered the entire surface of the earth, as if green-blue ocean had always spread everywhere like an undulating mirror of tranquility and always would. Sun seared the tropical sky unbroken by a single cloud. It was hard to believe in Angelita today.

There wasn't much left of the airliner: a few decimated wing parts, some salt-ravaged chunks of material that appeared to be seat cushions. U.S. Patrol ships cruised the area in their own search. Sometimes they'd launch an inflatable. Navy frogmen went off the sides backwards, hands gripping face masks, lead weights circling their waists. If there'd been survivors after the crash, chances were they wouldn't have lasted an hour in the chaos of Angelita, with or without a flotation device.

But the airliner's demise had made headlines for two nights running, *and, back on the mainland, scores of relatives clung to a hope that wouldn't die.*

"Gringo to Chico. Over."

In his hovering bubble of glass and metal, Alonzo sighed. "What is it, Stu?"

"I got news for them down there." The voice crackled harshly from the instrument panel. "No fins, no bodies. Those Navy boys are a bunch of bozos. They say hammerheads got brains the size of a pea. But how much you want to bet, a hammerhead at least knows where to look? Listen, you want to hear a story? Over."

Alonzo's eyes searched the blue swells. "Not really," he muttered, but audio never picked it up. Something tugged at his insides. Nausea, maybe, mingled with an odd sense of expectation. Overtired, he told himself. Too many searches futile, too many end in failure, a bad storm at sea is indeed death's little angel—no more, no less—but lately this thought had pierced his logical armor, led him through increasingly frequent moments of black nothingness. These moments had gone un-named until a recent night when he'd woken in a bath of his own sweat, suddenly knowing the name. Now he scanned the waters below, hot with useless hope.

"Ever hear the Chinaman's advice to beginning divers, Chico? Over."

"No, Stu. I never did."

"Confucius say, always dive with buddy and always carry knife. If you see shark, take out knife. Stab buddy. And beat it the hell out of there. That's an old proverb, señor. You can tell that to your mama-san. Over."

Sunlight streaked the water a shimmering platinum. It burned Alonzo's eyes and he nosed the chopper down by instinct. One of the inflatables had edged close to something. A piece of material, discolored beyond recognition—one of those flotational seat cushions—he was sur-prised it had lasted so long. No, it wasn't a seat cushion after all but something that resembled a bloated mannequin, stiff and crusted white with salt. The divers had gone crazy, surrounding it. They'd even sent in a couple of guys with electric prods to buzz off the man-o'-wars. Encased in his bubble, he watched them ease the thing over the inflat-able's edge. He thought he saw it flail an arm faintly, thought he saw it kick. But it was barely recognizable as a human body. Scraps of colorless clothing hung from it, the lips were big as balloons and the eyelids swollen completely shut, the limbs withered to a clawlike shape. He followed procedure and kept all frequencies open. Seconds passed. The panel crackled silence.

Then, "Jesus," he heard. "Jesus fucking Christ."

One of the Patrol clippers had veered close. The inflatable rocked in its wake, filled with frogmen and the crusted white mannequin thing.

"God," he heard, "is there a doctor in the house?"

Then: "Sure thing, Tarzan. Jesus. Jesus Christ. It's a girl."

Terror 101

≈ ≈ ≈

(B R E N)

Terror 101: An Introduction to Adult Life. It's this course Kay and I conjured up once over too much birthday champagne.

Not that we were big drinkers. Not that the terror was present then. But here we were, in the place she used to call Pretty Land—State University country. Among the folks she called Straight White People, the ones we both worked with in our different ways.

Drive along Route 3 past clusters of dormitories, frats, classroom and administrative buildings, labs, greenhouses, a natatorium complex, soccer field, outdoor track—there they are, everywhere. Keep going into the light and you'll see the apple of their collective eye: a new stadium, rising before you, blocking the sun. *Pride of the East!* is their motto. Football gets more important here every year, stirring up enough revenue to pay for the lavish spread of fieldhouses, tracks, pools.

The place is big on basketball, too, and ice hockey, cross-country, track and field. Swimming, winning. That's where I come in.

Super Coach.

The title Kay gave me. She was like that, an English prof, quick with words.

Sweetheart, she'd say, when things started to get bad, *my baby. Why don't you cry?*

Because I'm the coach, I'd tell her. Then try to smile. *Super Coach.* Try to laugh. But it wasn't funny.

Super Coach has seen athletes do wonderful things to win, things that change them in positive ways for the rest of their lives. Some of the other things they do to win, though, go shamefully unmentioned. You don't even want to think about it.

But here—between the wonder and the shame—sheer luck, and the thing Kay always called my Great Protestant Work Ethic, have been pretty much on my side. Six years ago their women's team was at the bottom of the division, and all the yahoos and hotshots over in Administration were busy trying to explain things to a bunch of angry alumni tying purse strings into vicious knots. Since hiring me they've been winning more than losing. That's the truth. The kind they call incontrovertible.

It's just my job—winning, I mean. Not truth. Although there is some of that in me, too.

To her everlasting credit, Kay abstained from commenting on most of it—the job, collegiate sport, truth, winning, me. Except for an occasional stab or two: *Yes, love, there is life after the short-course season!*

Fine, Kay, so what do you want me to do about that? Read the classics?

Well, I'd think it, but never say it. That's the way we handled most of our sore points, for better or worse, by sort of neglecting them. A lot of nastiness went unspoken. Bumps in the road avoided. Saved plenty of dishes from smashing against poor unsuspecting walls.

And anyway, I loved her.

Everyone's got rituals. People of discipline, more than most. Spit in the left goggle first, tap toes twice with your favorite bat, tie on a pair of good-luck track flats, pray to the gods of the javelin throw for a perfect tail wind—just hang around people sweating to win and you'll notice a million rituals.

Coaches have rituals too. And not too long ago, I'd certainly have described myself as disciplined. Now, though, what goads me out of bed isn't discipline, but fear. Remembering this dream from last night. Makes me think of Kay, I don't know why. Very weird: a bunch of naked young women in a cavernous, hollow-seeming big gray place shaving all the hair from their bodies, thighs, arms, together, like in a synchronized slow dance. Shaving their heads methodically, almost lovingly. Razors caressing broad lines above each ear. Around the temples. Over the crown of the head, across each nape of neck. Then they all slip easily, slowly, into identical racing suits, our team uniform. And disappear. Except for one—one kid. Who stands there in the strange gray emptiness staring silently at me, shaved and clean and raw. Something terrible is about to happen. I don't remember what. In the dream, though, both of us know. We are both afraid.

"Fear," DeKuts used to yell, "is always physical. Fear is in the body, and the body tells no lies." He'd go into his spiel then, throw a kickboard at you if he thought you weren't listening. Sometimes he'd miss and the board would bounce off a pool gutter, skim pastel blue water like a manta ray's fin.

"I want you to be afraid when you swim for me. Healthy fear of the pain it takes to win and a deeper fear of losing, and a much much deeper fear of me."

He'd stalk past every lane, his bare toes just missing your fingers as you hung on, his eyes glittering like brown, mean little bugs. "I want you to be afraid of ease and comfort, I want you to feel like if you stop or let up for a second you will die. I want you to work and I want you to race like your lives depend on it. If you do all that for me, you will earn my respect."

Once, the toes stopped near the wet gutter space between my thumb and forefinger. They were big, warped, specked with shiny black hair. They lifted with the foot, and his callused heel came down on my wrist, trapping it and me, sent a cold line of pain up to the elbow. Chlorine and a sour fleshy smell mixed in my nostrils. I felt tears about to spill, resolved not to let them.

"You!" he shouted, "I'm talking to *you*! No talent. So show me some guts. Use your fear. Maybe you can swim with the big girls some day. Then you and I can be friends."

He made me do an extra set of 200s that day—ten on a short interval, and when practice was over I puked in the locker room sink. When my wrist swelled I wrapped an Ace bandage on. The fear settled deep down in a dark, living, inside place I couldn't touch. I needed it. I got used to it. Like I needed him, got used to him. Dreamed of beating him to death. But wanted, more than anything, to be his friend. And found that, after all, having the terror inside is a useful thing. Toughens you for the rest of life.

Getting used to it can be deceptive, though—you tend to forget it's still and always there. But crisis never fails to remind. The day of Kay's diagnosis I felt it flare up again, chilling and bright, vomit bubbling around in my throat and the sweat suddenly sliding over my forehead, down my belly, just like old times. Later we took a walk. It was right before New Year's and things were sunk in ice-sheeted snow. We wore boots and sweaters and long coats and hats, I'd made her put on a couple of scarves, too, because of the fever. We walked with one of my arms around her shoulders, the other across her chest so I kind of staggered along sideways, shielding her from the wind. Neither of us talked. Until she said, very quietly, *Baby, why don't you cry?*

It was late afternoon. The air was red-tinged gray and wet, tasted like more snow.

Because I'm the coach, Kay, I replied—for the first time, though not the last. *Super Coach. Remember?*

I wanted to cry, but didn't.

A lot of things happened that winter. Second opinions. Bad prognoses. The weather was particularly severe worldwide: plenty of frost, orange crops ruined, old folks freezing next to kerosene heaters, ice storms and airlifts in Alaska and, farther south, the storm they called Angelita—worst Gulf hurricane of the decade—and the 747 disaster. A banner year. I spent most of our savings on a new car with deluxe heater. Kay had these chemotherapy appointments twice a week, felt cold most of the time.

And I thought getting tenure was rough, she said. *Great way to spend a sabbatical, huh?*

In the midst of all this, my team started to win. Really win. I sort of watched it happen out of the corner of my eye. Afraid that at any moment they'd find out what a hoax I was—for all intents and purposes out to lunch, gone, kaput, busted up like no one ever told me I'd be, not even DeKuts. I flew on automatic pilot, put them through their paces twice a day. Shifted into an unearthly kind of gear and sewed together perfect training schedules. Bugged them at workouts, made them dread the sound of my voice and my footsteps. Reminded them that I'd recruited them, each and every one. That they weren't exactly the cream of any crop, weren't exactly the stuff Industry Hills senior meets are made of, that they owed their barebones little college scholarships to me, and if they wanted to keep what I'd given them they would damn well cut out the crap and work hard. Because they were mighty short on talent, I told them, and if they won they'd win on guts and work alone. Forget all your Olympic medal fantasies, I said. Forget your dreams of Pan Am gold. The world's not waiting for a single one of you. Better start thinking about survival.

They wondered what was wrong, but didn't dare ask. Hated me, but didn't dare express it. So while Kay was dying, and the deep-down living terror kept boiling up from inside until my skin felt pale and slimy and I responded to every hello with a punched-out vacant look, those kids swam their guts out—and they won, and won, and kept on winning. Until, in the Division II land of the Straight White People, I became a rising star.

WASPs, Kay said. *Never a tear. What on earth is wrong with you?* Kay was Jewish.

Our private life centered more and more around stained beds that winter. Around tubes like tentacles filled with colorless liquid, sick blood.

I don't have a lot of friends, and I was pretty busy worrying about all those tubes, and about fending off her relatives—with whom we had always coexisted in a state of mutual dislike—and about the insular whirlwind of athletic triumph at work that had placed me at its core. But I did keep in touch with Chick, calling once in a while to say how things were going. She came up to visit quite a lot at first. Then Kay got depressed and asked her not to any more.

Once, just before spring, I called DeKuts. It had been years. He answered with a cough so hard and thick I thought his guts would spew out in chunks through the receiver. When he could breathe we talked swimming for a while. This and that. He congratulated me on the program I'd built at State. Said he'd done right to get me into coaching, hadn't he? A mediocre swimmer, never go All-American in any division, nothing but a hammer with one talent, one talent only: to persevere. Outlast hope itself. A workout king. Queen. Some ability to organize, too, sniff out the talent in others. Still, girl coaches wouldn't go far, not in the big clubs. Never coach a national team. But college sports, Division II—yes, that was right where I belonged. He laughed and the coughing wracked him. His voice was half of what it had been, though there was still that unmistakable hard-driven rage in it fueling the cruelty he'd use like a tool. Finally he asked why I'd phoned. What did I really want? I told him I was afraid.

"What a coincidence," he said, "I am too." Then started to cough again and I knew it was true. "They opened me right down the middle, Bren. Took out everything they could lay their hands on, zipped up the zipper. Told me, Mr. DeKuts, you'd better go home to die. So here I am. Interesting that you called. Say your piece now, though. We won't talk again."

I was quiet and the receiver sweated in my hand. Then these words popped out of me—I meant them to be cruel, to pay him back then and always—but for some reason, I don't know why, they came out very gently.

"Is it the worst fear, Jan?"

"Sure," he said, "but that doesn't really matter."

There were many states between us. His throat rattled, long-distance, while he tried to keep breathing.

September 1st. What wakes me is fear and the dream. And Boz planting crusher paws on my chest, pink pit bull tongue dripping everywhere. Ugliest dog in the world. Kay's choice, two years ago. Even then I knew I'd regret it.

"Boz, cut it out."

Dawn sifts through the living room blinds. I remember everything with a big sick rush that seizes my throat again like a prison guard moving in to stay, so for a moment there's nothing I want any more, not really, least of all to wake up.

Personally, I adore pit bulls, Kay said. Putting her foot down. *And I will have one, Bren, an albino, pink-eyed, rat-eared, Roman-nosed as can be. The ugliness is noble somehow, don't you think?*

No, Kay, I think that's bullshit.

Another thing that never got said. But I loved it when she put her foot down. Her eyes blazed wide and deep, you could see the flush begin around her ears. It would just about decapitate me.

"Come on, Boz."

He twists his thick body like a corkscrew. Starts doing what Kay called The Morning Dance, half-growling, half-whining, be-seeching with tongue and whirling tail. Breakfast time. So without quite realizing it I'm off the couch, heading for kitchen and can opener, contemplating the upcoming hypocrisy of goading a bunch of college kids to set their alarms for six a.m. workouts when Super Coach herself has trouble finding any real reason whatsoever, these days, to crawl off the living room sofa at day-break. Bless Boz, the living alarm clock. Who has probably become my reason for being—what Kay would call, in this beautiful academic French accent she could muster at will, a *raison d'être*.

Not that I will ever let on to the kids about that. Or about anything.

"Okay, pal, here. Here's your food."

He dances, toenails clicking the floor tiles in a frantic shuffle, eats with fierce gulping sounds while I refill his water bowl.

Now the twisted tail's flagging air again and Boz has that hope-ful head-cocked look. Maybe uncertainty has crept into whatever his consciousness is. Maybe he misses Kay, expects her back any minute now, any day.

"You want to go out?"

I let him bite the ratty hem of my robe and drag me to the door, watch him lope across the lawn. Breeze ruffles the tips of grass, turning them over like thousands of tiny spears shim-mering green, then silver, in the morning. He burrows through pine cones, dandelions, disappears behind some trees. I lean against the refrigerator and close my eyes. Then the handle springs. The fridge door flies open. Half-finished bottles of salad dressing and soda rattle dangerously, an opened tin of sardines splats against my bare feet while the fish oil spreads.

Cleaning things up on my knees on the floor, I cannot help it: ripples surge along my spine, shock waves of memory. *Come here, sweetheart.* Her mouth moved in the mess of tubes. *I'll tell you a secret.* I stepped in, then, toward the bed. Willed myself to lean closer. Saying this is your lover, Coach, and you must, you must.

*   *   *

You're so damned obsessive-compulsive! she always told me. Exasperated. Resigned.

Yes, love. Yes.

I go through the house straightening edges and surfaces. Obsessively-compulsively—is that a word? Kay would know. Checking everything twice the way I usually do. Avoiding the bedroom. I shower, dress in the hall, toss cosmetics into a purse and sweat clothes into a gym bag, examining my face in the bathroom mirror from a variety of angles to see what, if anything, can be done. Boz watches, curious. Either it's real loyalty, or just habit: to sit patiently, good-natured, ugly pink eyes noting every move, tough paw pads scuffing rugs and tiles and wood as he follows.

"You and me, dude."

He thumps his tail.

Powder under the eyes, dribble a little Visine in to clear the red. There's this glossy lipstick Kay liked. *When all else fails, bright lipstick, Bren.* I took careful lessons from her, the veteran of countless departmental meetings and tenure committees. She was older than me, more familiar with the Straight White People, knew better than anyone how to spiff up an act.

I pull my briefcase together.

Obsessive-compulsive makes for good coaching. Maybe it's a survival mechanism, too—not necessarily the best, or even the most appropriate—just what I have at hand, practically speaking. Kay would have agreed: I am nothing if not practical. And there are all these things to do. Partial scholarships. Team cuts. Big interview with a prospect this morning.

Suddenly I understand about the dream, and about waking up afraid. At first glance, there is shocking similarity in the appearance of a shaved-down swimmer and a hairless chemotherapy patient. They are both creatures in limbo somehow—recognizably human but oddly so, poised on a starting block or the edge of a hospital bed in some transitional place between effort and finality.

Cry, sweetheart, she told me, holding my head in ruined hands. *Please, baby, let it out. You'll feel so much better if you do.*

Yes, I said. *Yes, love.*

But I couldn't.

Inner things came to me, things from the past. Images. Snatches of almost-understanding.

A cold drink of water. Splashes of chlorinated powder in full basins. Showers. Steam. Whirlpool on damaged shoulders and knees. I have been around this stuff most of my life. First out of love, then out of fear, until it became a meal ticket for me, just work, obsession, nothing more. But it got so intertwined with the other things—the water did, I mean, and the swimming and coaching—that it wrapped around a stuck-deep root inside and meshed its genes with that root. The way the love did, and the fear. The way Kay did from the first time I met her. So that, now, I could not stand to lose it.

I stepped in closer to the bed, plucked a tube aside. There were sores on her mouth and I put my ear to them. Something jangled in my head, a tangible rattling sensation. It made white and gray waver in front of my eyes and I knew that if I remained standing I'd faint. So I sat on the side of the bed, fighting it. She wanted to tell me something—her hands shook, beckoned— to tell me a secret. I was all weighted with heaviness inside, then I just lay down next to her. My ear pressed her mouth again while she whispered.

What she said, I must not tell. But I know that after she'd said it the heaviness burst out of me like fever, so I was covered with sweat. I lay there pushing tubes aside and held her. Our heads rested together on the pillow, calmly, easily.

Did I say I held her? That's wrong. Because the tubes held her, held her up, and she held me. She was so light, hardly there at all. When I opened my eyes things looked different for a moment—like they were dissolving, losing shape and form, and beneath the shape and form they were losing was a bright white heat that burned.

Turn off Route 3, continue along past the stadium and you arrive at what Kay used to refer to as Bleaker Land: government-sponsored project areas, the buildings fenced off, access granted only to people with security clearance. And there are other places, places where they do things to animals.

But all that is out in the sticks. From central campus, it's impossible to believe anything exists except the morning. The sun's always splendid when it shows, a sudden light over tree tops that obliterates dawn. Pure, sweet, wet-hot. Sometimes it brings tears to your eyes.

It would be nice to believe that there's only this: leaves not quite ready to turn, lush hills to the west, fonts of knowledge overflowing, handsome young people playing to win.

Defeated whimpers sound somewhere else altogether. At least that's what most of the kids seem to think. Which is just as well. They don't know what they're in for later—and why should they? Give them a few years to agonize over midterms, or over how to pull off a good 200-freestyle. It's all practice for when the shit really hits the fan.

For now, no Terror 101. Just research papers, final exams. Football tickets. Swimming meets.

The Department of Athletics and Physical Education has been renamed several times. They keep renaming the Phys Ed degrees, too, to make them sound more scholarly, and the buildings are all set apart from the centers of academic research.

It's the mind/body split, sweetheart, Kay said once.

I resented that a little. Wordlessly, of course.

To get there I turn west, skirting central campus and the graduate library where she'd had a fifth-floor study booth reserved, its table spilling over with books about Hawthorne and Melville, pass early-morning joggers along the road to the natatorium complex, and park in my spot, queasy at the thought of running into any of the kids I coach. As if I'd owe them an explanation.

The building's angular, clean, new. There's something vaguely cruel about it, as if it could swallow you whole and alive—mash you up thoroughly, send pieces of you whirling into the pool, the diving tank, the sauna, weight rooms and equipment rooms and first-aid rooms with training tables—like that big white whale Kay was always going into philosophical rhapsodies about.

This interview is at half past ten.

Serendipity. But I'll believe it when I see it.

There are unopened envelopes everywhere, letters requiring my signature, folders unfiled, a mug emblazoned with the name of the university that tips over when I sit, spilling pens and a chain of rusting paper clips onto the desk blotter. The lamp's working, anyway—one of those full-spectrum things recommended for relieving competitive stress. Which is fine as long as you stay near the source of light. But I forgot to lock the door, and McMullen's head is a ruddy, balding egg poking into the office, his eyes blinking cheerfully like twin beacons of primitive mischief.

"Heard about your coup, woman. When do I get a peek?"

I wonder what it is about him that makes me want to stuff an air conditioner up his nose.

He settles into my swivel chair, grinning. "Don't hold out on me, Bren, for Christ's sake, I deserve some good news. These kids are a bunch of maniacs. You know the headaches I've got? Remember Canelli, my sophomore, All-American last year? Well, he decided to do some spelunking in New Mexico this summer. Great idea, huh? Spe*lunking*, for Christ's sake. Anyway, he broke both his arms and gained forty pounds. So after serious discussion with yours truly he decided to redshirt the year, and that's swell, but it leaves me shoveling shit up an alleyway when it comes to my medley relay." He plants both elbows in a pile of memos. "You girls have all the luck. Delgado—she could've made the national team."

"*Could* have."

"Look, when they're good they're good. You're going to have to steal a free ride from somewhere, aren't you?" The tiny eyes glitter. McMullen makes no bones about his nosiness. But, like an infant, he lacks perception—and this, the cornerstone of our relationship, is a saving grace. I still hate lying to him, though. Makes me feel like an ingrate. On the other hand, I was the one who came along and saved his butt. When I give him the nod his big face lights with triumph. "I knew it! Take my advice and buy her a damned Rolls-*Royce* if she wants one, never mind what kind of shape she's in. You'll have to come up with some dough, lady."

"I know."

"Lots of dough."

"Okay, Pete. But promise me you'll try to be a little low-key, all right? She's been through a lot."

"No kidding." For some reason we're out of my office now, heading down the hall, and I can feel the comfort of the specially recommended stress-relieving light fade away. I've let him take my arm and lead me along, like he's got somewhere important to lead me to. McMullen is a salesman at heart—someone who gives you the feeling that he's comfortable around snakeskin, bad real estate, phony ID's. But exposure to genuine quality

unnerves him. "Hear anything about the other kid, Hedenmeyer? Now *he* was a big animal, that boy would've dark-horsed
it at the Trials. They say nowadays he can blink okay as long as
they don't unplug him. If you ask me it's a crime they kept him
alive in the first place. They removed a lot of that kid, just to
keep him going on some fucking machine." At the water fountain he drinks, splashing his chin and shirt front, talking all the
time. "But the girl pulled through okay, didn't she? Or is that
what we're waiting to find out?"

"*We?*"

"Well excuse *me*! Look, Bren, I'd have given my left molar for
Kenny Hedenmeyer. Shit, I'd have given my jaw bone for either
one of them. But if I'd done that I'd be in a different division,
and I wouldn't be able to talk the ears off these fucking delin-
quents I've got swimming for me here. Anyway, let me know
how it goes."

"I will."

"Do that, girl. Let me know."

He storms down the hall, pounds on doors to annoy people.
Out of one flies a paper airplane, aimed perfectly at the bald
spot on his head.

I duck through an exit, sit on the landing that smells unused,
faintly damp with leftover summer and sweat. An image of Boz
mouthing silent yelps against the living room window as I drive
away rises up inside so that, for a moment, I want to say it out
loud: *May I stop now, please?* But there's this interview. I head
down a flight.

Bob Lewison's door is open, the walls trophy-cluttered, Lewison himself sunk deep into some text propped amid the mess
on his desk. Everything in the room is askew. Not like the neat
and orderly lines of an obsessive-compulsive's office. Everything's
a little too large for the space—unlike Lewison, who is slight and
rail-thin. An economy model, McMullen calls him, snickering.
An economy model of man, old Bob.

They've never really liked each other.

"You look tired, Bren."

"Thanks. That's the nicest thing I've heard all day."

"Rough summer?"

"Something like that."

He closes the book, pats it like a shoulder. "Tell me about it. My cross-country squad's in leg casts. Last month I missed an alimony payment. My kids aren't talking to me. And MasterCard wants five thousand bucks. That's the good news."

Our hands meet across the desk, squeeze. I mumble the thing I always mumble with him: Poor Bob. Ah, business as usual, he tells me, what about you? and then I'm stuck. Hoisted on my own petard of lying secrecy—*privacy,* Kay called it, but that was a euphemism.

It's been a hell of a time, I say vaguely. Family business.

"Anything I can do? Just let me know."

But I shake my head. Then grin the weary, wary grin that lets him off whatever hook is always swinging there between us, the grin Kay told me was handsome and bright and full of warning.

"You know, you're a good-looking woman. You're good-looking even when you're tired." It's shy, kind. Ancient discomfort, a mix of regret and panic, makes me pull my hand away. Say something diplomatic now. For all the boys and men in my life— well-meaning, virile, clumsy—whom I could not and would not love. Spilled beer suds, graceless dancing. Kisses and caresses that, after a while, I no longer even attempted. He's trapped there in the too-long silence. Again I set him free of the hook, saying, Well, *that* is definitely the nicest thing I've heard all day.

Bob lands with alacrity. On his feet, and smiling.

"Since I'm scoring so many points, then, would you mind me making a suggestion?"

"Go ahead."

"Before this girl shows up, gag McMullen and shove him in a closet somewhere."

"Does *everyone* know?"

"Pete's been intercepting your mail for weeks. But I'm rooting for you. And another thing."

"What, Bob?"

"Get some rest," he says, so gently it's a surprise. "Get some rest, quit driving yourself. None of this stuff is that important. You're on a roll around here, enjoy it. Don't you think there's a critical point to it all? Winning maxes out after a while, you know. It does. Then you've got to say, Well, fuck the whole bunch of you, I guess I've won enough. And you sit back a little, you smell the daisies."

He reaches for my hand again when we stand, presses it with affection. We're about the same height. Our eyes meet perfectly. I decide to avoid him from now on—a shame, because he's been an ally, almost a friend. For now, though, I will just shake hands.

"Good going, Bren. The girl—"

"Delgado."

"Right. Well, listen, there's money around here somewhere. I'll back you up all the way."

"Thanks."

"Don't mention it. Just ghost-write a couple of proposals for me later on this term. And good luck. Good luck raising the dead." He pales slightly, then blushes. "I mean the idiots in Budget Accounting—not the kid."

Back upstairs I pass McMullen's office on the way to mine. Luckily, he's on the phone. Haranguing. Someone else is getting it now and, despite myself, I smile. His voice booms down the hallway.

"I don't mind telling you, pal, this place is going to hell in a handbasket! They keep pouring money down these kids' throats and it keeps coming out their rear ends! And guess who has the honor of mopping it up? Yours *truly.*"

The girl is prompt. McMullen's secretary buzzes me at twenty-five past and I head out to meet her. She's the kind we don't see much of around here: big-framed, five foot ten, once lean but carrying too much weight around now. Taller than me, when she stands she comes close to taking over the room. We shake hands.

"Ms. Delgado."

"Um—Babe."

"Bren Allen. How was your trip?"

"Okay. I mean, fine."

"You didn't have any trouble finding us, I hope?"

"No!"

It sounds like panic. The kid's very pale—there's something vaguely upsetting about her presence when we head for my office—an awkwardness of the body. Nice-looking face, a little puffy yet ragged somehow. Like a thoroughbred beaten and lamed—maybe the bone sets, but the animal never runs the same.

Then I'm ashamed to evaluate her so coldly. Even though it's part of my job, to evaluate coldly—it seems inappropriate now. I take her along a couple of detouring hallways to avoid McMullen, go around to my office and we both sit inside. Now I can meet her eyes directly. They're large, dark eyes that don't blink. There are tiny streaks of red across each cornea. It makes me feel the weariness acutely in my own self, and for a second I can almost swear that some kind of sigh passes between us, sounds somewhere close by in the world.

"You know, Babe, I was impressed by the honesty of your letter. I thought it took courage to write that. But I think you were a little rough on yourself. A certain amount of physical potential can stay with you, you know. It can. The rest is all in the mind." This gets no reaction, not even a blink. Only tension and pallor, and a pain that the fixed, nervous smile cannot hide. "Tell me, how have things been for you this year?"

"Lousy."

"That's not surprising. We aren't machines, after all. Sometimes our bodies seem to be—machines, I mean—but because our emotions are inseparable from what we do physically, we can't ever function as predictably as machines."

It's all come out fluidly, perfectly. I tell myself: Coach, you're *good*.

"Everything really has to be in balance for excellent performance. But when we go through something traumatic it can throw the system way off, right? Different emotions cause different levels of hormones to be secreted, and this makes you feel lousy. You try to pull out the good times, the right splits, the extra effort—but it's just not there to give."

The kid breathes, her lips tremble a little. "I don't want to lie about anything. I told you—I told you how bad I am now."

"Well, let's just say that right now I'm more concerned with how you feel about it. How *do* you feel about it?"

She shrugs stiffly. I remember first seeing her at a senior meet, knowing just by looking that she was one of those kids into whom time and money had obviously been poured. Tall, broad-shouldered, clear-skinned and lean. That meet had been filled with them, a cream-of-the-crop high school gathering cut from the same god/goddess mold. Barefoot, dripping, they couldn't help but strut. Like greyhounds, they'd been simultaneously pampered and hard-pressed. They knew a lot about goals and discipline and prodigious physical effort. But they moved in a rarefied atmosphere. Trained to excel, but only at certain things. The rest of life sometimes eluded them—or else maybe they were sheltered from it—and, watching, I knew that when the shit really hit the fan many of them would abandon sport altogether.

She was being touted as the next up-and-coming breaststroker, already an American record holder in one event, heir to some-one-or-other's throne, expected to make the national team that year or the next, go to the Pan Ams, eventually the Olympic Trials. Impressive size, speed, talent. But I remember thinking even then that the girl lacked something. No killer shark instinct. She'd come this far on a gold-platter combo of genetics, practice, obedience. There wasn't any brute in her—no spark of desperate effort, no trace of need or hunger on her face, in her pose. Too perfect. No hate, no fear. *Sans* desire. Anyway, she'd already been successfully recruited by Bart Sager at Southern—which was a place flooded with talent, as many qualitative levels above State's program as the gods in heaven are to folks on earth.

"Um—"

Encouragement is needed, Coach. I nod and smile.

"I don't know what I care about any more." The voice sounds cold and detached, which surprises me. "Like I told you, I feel I could at least give it an honest try. But, you know, I don't think that I'm, like, interested in ranking nationally any more. Or qualifying for the Trials or anything, you know, or the Pan Ams, or like that. I just don't have the ability or the interest."

"What about competing? Are you still interested in that?"

"I think so. Maybe. I'd just, like—I promise I would do my best."

I bend a paper clip out of shape, curl it into a distorted circle and drop it on the desk. Like my insides. Twisted metal. Funny how life follows some blueprint other than your own. The fluid words of Super Coach have deserted me for a moment. I must meet Babe Delgado's tired eyes with mine.

"Listen, Babe, I'll be honest with you too. I'm proud of our program here. I mean *my* program—credit where credit is due." Then I can't help grinning, can't help being pleased when the girl grins back. "When I came here this school was at the bottom of the division. I told them I could rebuild things, create a good solid program and produce a team that would win for a change. That's why any coach is hired in the first place. And that's exactly what I've done. It hasn't been easy, but I'm good at it, and I'm proud of the accomplishment. We've been ranked in the top three of this division for the past four years. Last year we missed out on first place by a few points—and that gives me some administrative maneuverability. I recruit better athletes, for one thing. Put yourself in my shoes a minute. You were ranked nationally. Why wouldn't I want you here, even if you're not at your best this week or this month or this year? It gives my program prestige. Now, the semester starts in two weeks. I can offer you a free ride. No frills"—I wince at the word, which is McMullen's, not mine—"but I think you'll see that the offer is not unreasonable. It certainly won't hurt your pride."

The kid says nothing. This makes me nervous but I don't show it. Then Super Coach kicks in again.

"If you decide to enroll, we'll try to make sure you get into any courses you like. I don't require the women on my team to room together, socialize together, eat together or anything like that. I *do* expect them to make practice—and most of the time that's doubles, a.m. and p.m. unless you're tapering—but again, what you do outside of practice is your business. I won't expect you to win all the time and I won't expect any records. But I'll want you to participate in all aspects of the program, and to encourage everyone else, and to expect no special treatment, even though you're head and shoulders above them. Also, I will build a medley relay around you. That's all." I toss another paper clip and it hits the rim of the mug, bounces in perfectly.

"My own room," she whispers, blushing. But the eyes never blink, stare straight in at mine. "I need my own room. A single. In the best dorm, okay? but not with all the jocks."

I toss another clip. So easy. God. I dare not breathe.

Basket.

"Okay, Babe. Let's take a walk. I'll show you the facilities. Then we can have lunch."

We stand and the tense face seems to shiver for a second, and I see it's covered with sweat.

"Jesus. I can't do them any more, you know. I mean I just cannot deal."

"What," I urge gently. "What can't you do?"

"Flips."

"Well, I guess you'll have to do open turns then."

It sounds right: brisk, matter-of-fact. I motion for her to follow. Another door, loss of the calming, clarifying light. Down many halls, past weight rooms and whirlpool and sauna. Recruiting, you spend time sussing out what each kid wants and figuring how to deliver it up to them on the spot. Some of them want to be entertained, some just to feel at home, some to be ordered around a little and have all the limits set from day one. Some are withholding, push their luck. Few ask for nothing but the contract, though. And because it's so rare, I tend to disbelieve that it's happening now.

Still, I will do what it takes for those extra points between first place and second. Improvise. Steal. This girl's got plenty of problems, but so do I. First place—cold, bright, accessible, final— is the only home I want now. One national-class kid and it's in the bag.

The pool's empty, glinting a clean pastel blue, lanes sharply delineated. We stop to look through unbreakable glass windows on the observation deck. Babe Delgado looms next to me. Taller. Bigger. Something I recognize now in her: a fear of the water. We both glance sideways at the same time and our eyes meet. Then there's this silent question I read in the puffy damp face, honest, searching, not a plea but a query: Are you going to help me?

I let Super Coach speak through my own eyes and say: Yes, sure, you help me and I'll help you. For those few extra points.

I smile calmly. "It used to terrify me."

"What?"

"Competing. Even thinking about my race sometimes. I'd throw up."

She laughs. "Really?"

"Sure. No matter who you are, the pressure is there."

That strikes some chord. She sweeps hair impatiently behind an ear, glances down at the pool again and back at me and then smiles. The pallor lifts a little.

"Okay. I think I can deal, I'll do it."

"Good."

"But I have to lose some weight. I mean *before* I get in the water—"

"I don't want you to worry about that now, Babe. We'll set up something with our nutritionist, okay?"

"Oh. I'm a vegetarian."

"Really? Well, each to her own. You'll be doing some running anyway, and some swim bench and medicine bag—everybody's going to be working pretty hard around here to get rid of a few extra pounds, including me." I pat my abdominals, risk a wink and breathe an internal sigh of relief when the kid smiles again. "September's dry-land month, anyway. Now let me show you around downstairs. Let me show you the Nautilus."

I stay late, clearing up all the paperwork I can. There will be hell to pay later on in the week. Another rickety bridge to cross in a flood. Free rides don't rain down from heaven, and this particular one will have to come out of some other coach's hide.

Toward evening I pass a free-weights room, hear the clink of dumbbells, plates, bars, a female voice I recognize, a young man's I do not:

"Ah, shit, Danny!"

"Get it up, goddammit! Get it up like a dick!"

"Ten!"

"There! There you go—here, I'll take it, Miss Macho Deltoids—"

"Oh shut up."

"Ellie, you did it."

"I don't believe it."

The two of them spill out, towels around their necks, T-shirts damp with sweat. An uncommonly handsome boy in his early twenties, short, muscular, definitely gay. The girl medium-built, with tenacious fists gripping the towel, a pretty Semitic face that looks hurt and swollen now around cheeks and mouth. She sees me and blushes violently. I nod.

"Ms. Marks."

"Hi!"

"Welcome back. We'll talk about it later, but I want you to do the four hundred IM this year. That means the long warm-up."

"*What*? Do I have to?"

"Yes."

"How come?"

"Because, I'm the coach and you're not."

On my way down the hall, I hear gagging sounds. Then foot-steps and the slap of damp towel on skin and cloth.

"Coach? Excuse me." The girl's eyes sparkle, embarrassed but shrewd. "Do you have any time maybe? I mean, can I talk to you?"

I tell her why not, and we head back to my office. There she perches on the edge of the chair Babe Delgado sat in earlier, looking much smaller. She keeps pulling at her sweaty shirt, twisting the towel with nervous hands. Pain pounds out the back of my head. I think lovingly of aspirin.

"What happened to your face, Ellie?"

"Oh, nothing. I mean, I got these two wisdom teeth pulled."

"If there's still some bleeding you should not lift weights."

"I'm okay."

"Well, then. What's up?"

"I have to talk to you." The voice starts out breathy, gets hoarse with nerves, then faster and faster. "Listen, maybe you were being a little too hard on us last year. I mean, it's like, basically everyone really wants to work really hard for you and to just *win*, you know? So I thought that you could sort of give us a break. Not, like, expect any less from us or anything like that. But more encouragement sometimes. I mean—you know what I mean."

The pain becomes an obstacle in my throat, and I clear it. There's a silence you can sink back into, always waiting like the fear, but waiting to hold you up instead and comfort you. I sink into it now, realize how long I've wanted that, just that: to sink back into something. Then I look at Ellie Marks and wait for her eyes to stop darting around and meet my own. When they do she blushes—suddenly, a deep scarlet.

I lean forward and speak softly. "I'll take your advice under consideration."

"You will?"

"Of course. It's possible I was a little out of touch with every-one's needs last year, and that's why we came up short at the end. But this year will be better. I think I can promise that."

Yes, Coach. I bet you can.

She stands mumbling thanks, thanks for listening. Thank *you*, I tell her, calmly, with mastery, thank you for bringing these concerns to my attention. It is part of *your* job, after all.

When she leaves I sink back again, thinking that I like the kid—my team captain and a hard worker, with mediocre but consistent times in the 100 and 200 breaststroke, an honors student most semesters. Comes from a difficult family background, racks up points by being a real team workhorse. Has a scholarship. And a crush on the Coach which, like all such things, the Coach will pointedly ignore.

Later, I change into sweats myself. The place has pretty much cleared out, I've managed to avoid McMullen all day, and one of the weight rooms is empty. I shouldn't, but do—heavy reps of bench press and even a few shoulder dips. The amount of healthy cartilage remaining in my left shoulder is laughable—old war wound, DeKuts would call it—and several specialists have recommended surgery. I keep putting it off. Too much to do. Anyway, I've had enough of hospitals.

I work triceps, lats, pecs, abs, deltoids, until I can hear the gristle rasping against bone in there, and when I raise the left arm to stretch it, tears burn my eyes. There's this rule of mine: to do whatever I make the kids do. Last spring I didn't, got alternately underweight and flabby, remote and mean. Thirty-four years old and I started to see facial lines. Elasticity was leaving me behind. But that stuff is over now, Kay three months dead. And if I cannot do this out of desire any more, I will do it out of habit.

Warm breeze mixed with post-twilight chill washes through the open window driving home. Send head honchos out to rich alumni—real estate bigwigs, investment bankers—and get them to establish a new scholarship. Or siphon free rides away from less successful teams and call the siphoning something else. A plot for McMullen to work out with the boys in Administration.

It is on my head, this recruitment. Their money's buying damaged goods, but damaged goods are sometimes salvageable. Maybe Babe Delgado deserves something. A different kind of chance—for what, I don't quite know. And maybe the kid can be fixed. Enough to pull a few good races out of her, anyway. Then, like Lewison says, she and I can tell them, Hey folks, fuck off, because we have won enough around here.

But I don't know. What I saw in her face today was long-term loneliness, a barely contained revulsion at the world. Can't say I blame her.

To check out the competition, McMullen used to joke whenever we went to these national meets. And both of us knew what a joke it was, because the kids we saw there were the big-time burners, Division I stuff, national-class material, a lot of them world-class. Still, there's no law against looking.

Which meet was it? Indianapolis. Two, three years ago. Bart Sager was there, with bells on, because Southern seemed headed for another national championship—*The Big U,* they called it. A totalitarian-run stable of talent and power. But some of his kids looked unhappy to me, and one of them was Babe Delgado.

Not so for the backstroker Liz Chaney—she was a real live monster, a confident sort, set an American record in the 200 and we saw her do it. She is dead now, along with most of her teammates, buried by the winds and waves of Angelita. But that day in Indianapolis McMullen ignored the electronic timer on the wall and zeroed his own stopwatch. *I want to get these splits. This kid's going to set a record soon, girl.* I asked him was it in the air and he said yes, it's in the air. He was sweating excitement. For a moment I liked him because he was genuine, almost worshipful, without the usual bullshit. *She's a cool cookie, huh? knows no fear.* Every backstroker was in the water ready to start—except for Chaney in lane four, who was wiggling to the rhythm of some dance tune in her head, feet shuffling, arms rocking, hips thrusting. There was a bratty smile on her face. She turned completely around until she was facing Bart Sager. Then stuck out her tongue.

I REPEAT. ALL SWIMMERS IN THE WATER. THIS IS THE WOMEN'S TWO-HUNDRED-METER BACKSTROKE. FOUR LENGTHS OF THE POOL.

Liz Chaney scratched her ribs like a monkey.

SWIMMERS IN THE WATER. A WARNING IS ISSUED TO LANE FOUR.

She took a small hop and jumped in feet first. Shouts echoed to the ceiling mingled with laughter. I glanced at Sager, saw that his face was sweating red, and he was smiling. Then I asked Pete if there was any truth to the rumor.

Which one? he asked. They say Bart Sager's in love, I told him. And he said It looks that way, doesn't it.

TAKE YOUR MARKS.

In lane four, Liz Chaney grabbed the rung of the starting block, back curved perfectly toward the water. A split second wiped the grin from her face. When the beep sounded, eight swimmers arched backwards, hands piercing the crayon-blue surface, went under, pulled, came up, but she was already a length ahead.

I drive into purpling sky, turn off the campus road and left onto Route 3. There were other things in Indianapolis. Sitting there by myself in those stands after the meet, McMullen and his stopwatch gone, noticing how bright ceiling fluorescents successfully eliminated tired old stains from the walls. The only thing new about the place was the pool, gleaming, bright, sparkling a cool welcome. I was waiting for some sound. A drip. Aware—for a second, suddenly, out of nowhere—of this dark all-alone thing in me that could pull me right down into it. It would happen easily, if I let it, would happen when I was alone.

But I wasn't quite alone then. Someone else was there, and I watched her: this big, tall, broad-shouldered girl meandering back and forth behind the starting blocks looking wistful, a little lost, unutterably lonely as she paced, swinging the embossed equipment bag that said SOUTHERN—THE BIG U on one side. Words left me thoughtlessly:

Babe.

I leaned over the bleacher railing to offer a hand.

Babe, I'm Bren Allen. The women's coach at Northern Massachusetts.

We shook hands then. Her face had changed since that high school meet—wasn't, after all, as open as it had been then. It was older, strained, full of a surprising discomfort that seemed to run very deep. Still, the body was lean and perfect, designed for the sport. Great genes. Kay would have said I was being a fucking Nazi—all that crap about genetics. Anyway, I smiled.

So. You had a bad day.

She nodded once, tiredly.

Listen, we all do. Anyone who tells you she doesn't is lying. But I noticed something, I think—I think you can get more out of your walls.

You do? The response was immediate and eager. *That's what I keep saying, but he—I mean—* The kid stopped suddenly, embarrassed, unwilling to speak his name. I was being diplomatic and waved a comforting hand.

Ah, well, never mind. Sometimes it just takes an old breaststroker— then gave a conspiratorial wink. *We're specialists, right? We can see these things very clearly sometimes—sometimes the rest of them just don't know.* A dim light of hope sprayed the face. I could see her grabbing at straws. *You're so good that it's difficult to see your mistakes, Babe. But I think you're a little flat coming off your walls. Not much, just a shade. Still, it's probably worth half a second right there—*

God, you're right.

Anyway, I said, *maybe you can use that in the future.*

The kid thanked me profusely, a lot more profusely than the information was worth, and I wished her all the best of luck. Then watched her leave, gym bag sagging against her legs. A perfect athlete, the likes of whom I would never coach.

The driveway's in rotten condition twisting through trees, past a garden in even worse shape. Kay spent plenty of weekends watering and weeding. It was her thing entirely. Early on she'd asked if I had any interest in learning about roses and I told her, None whatsoever, why? Case closed. But once in a while, when I least expected it, something would send gentle shock waves up my neck and I'd turn to see her holding petals between thumb and forefinger with a teasing look. Saying, Well, Coach, are you still uninterested?

Things spill from briefcase, purse, and gym bag as I head up the steps. I open the door and Boz jumps out panting welcome.

"Hey guy."

He slobbers all over the first draft of some long memo I'm supposed to read, wags so hard his entire rear end shags from side to side while he noses through my sweats.

"Come here, dude." I sit in the middle of everything and he licks my face. I pull his ears, scratch and rub and caress. He's hungry and his whines prick me. Things point accusingly—frantic paws, untended grass and flowers, overgrown trees.

"Let's get you something to eat."

I do, then walk him, then head inside to turn on every light in the place, pull every shade, draw all the curtains. Thinking about Delgado. My original prediction turned out to be right. After that senior meet she'd been absorbed quickly into the fifty-meter expanse of big-time college swimming. It looked for a while like she'd maintain her top-ten ranking in the 100 breast-stroke, but she didn't. Nobody heard that much about her until a few years later. Sager had taken his entire team to San Juan for winter break—a few of his kids were slated for international competition there later that year and he must have wanted to give them practice in the Pan Am pool, which tended to run shallow. They spent two weeks there, doing heavy doubles and getting to a peak. Not Sager's fault—given the resources, I'd probably have done the same thing. But their flight back soared into Angelita.

People talked about it for a while. It made every newspaper, national radio and TV station—one of the worst disasters of the century. No one expected survivors. Unbelievably, there were two. One was Babe Delgado.

I stop halfway to the bedroom. My robe's draped over a bathroom door and I undress in the hallway instead, shower, rummage through the medicine cabinet for aspirin and take three. There is nothing in the refrigerator that I'm hungry enough to eat. Now, just tired, too tired to do much else but sleep.

The horror is that, if I sleep now, I'll be awake for good in an hour or two. But if I wait until the exhaustion passes I will be awake all night. And a couple hours' sleep is better than none.

I give Boz a biscuit and he curls in front of the dark television set, munching. I take a blanket from the linen closet and stretch out on the couch. Listen to his tail thump the rug.

Kay, what now?

A clock ticks. Lights blaze. I'm ashamed of this—return of an old childhood phobia. But lack the energy to fight it tonight. I'm afraid of the dark.

Soon, for an hour or so, I will sleep.

Before I do, she comes to my mind very sweetly.

Aside from the swimming, things always seemed sorry and confused to me. Then there were women, and life got comprehensible, began to seem very real somehow. But even then there was this split between one life and the other: love and a couple of friends here, work and everything else there, and the thought of ever bringing these lives together sent frightened chills of nausea right through me. It still does.

A closet case, Chick always said, *I don't know why I bother with you, Bren.* But aside from that one incident in our college days— which was a mistake, and at least never ruined the friendship— Chick and I went way back deeply, comfortably. And she was the one who introduced me to Kay.

It was at this bar, a few of us were sipping beers together, and after Kay asked me what I did and I'd told her, after I asked what she did and she'd told me, and after we'd both oohed and aahed politely about it, we didn't really have much to say to each other. But once in a while, in the middle of cigarette and liquor and perfume smells, electronic songs and all the talking, our eyes would catch and hold. Some nice music came on the jukebox and, just to pass the time, I asked did she want to dance.

One dance turned into another. In between we talked, I don't remember about what. But it felt good, we bought each other things to drink and after a while danced some more. I turned around once, very late, to see that Chick and the others had left. We laughed about that. Then Kay said, Here we are, a big cold beautiful WASP and a plump warm little Jew, and do you really want this kind of trouble? and if so, what are we going to do about it. I'm not so cold, I told her. She said Yes you are sweet- heart, but everybody's got their reasons. We kept dancing and I held her close, thinking that what she'd said was probably true. Thinking how obviously and immediately different we were: her dark warmth and all the scholarly talk talk talk I would never be privy to, while the career I wanted was stretching gradually, logically ahead the way DeKuts had always said it would, into this collegiate annex that had nothing to do with books—the living, working fear and the need to use that fear for myself and for others, to physically win, that she would never understand either. And I thought how everything was going along just fine as it was—the path straight and clear, the work absolutely sepa- rate now from anything like love—how safe and simple that was, and how this woman I was dancing with could be a real diver- sion, a hammer in the works. How I didn't really want any has- sles, certainly didn't need the thing she called This Kind of Trouble.

Dancing with her, I decided all this. And at the same time felt something in her give before anything in me did. What hap- pened then was that the soft silent force of it pulled me right in, so that the thing I didn't want was also somehow the very thing I needed, and I knew suddenly it was in her that I'd find it, in the dancing together of her and me, and whether I wanted it or not it was the thing I must have and be part of. I held her closer with each passing second, closer and closer without even meaning to. Until the grip was fierce, full of an irrepressible ache. Until I felt myself holding on for dear sweet life itself like someone being saved from drowning, and I couldn't let her go, so I just kept holding on.

The Clock

ㅎ ㅎ ㅎ

(F E L I P E)

It chimes from the hallway—Barbara's father's clock, old polished wood and a brass-rimmed glass case dark with age. I noticed it the first time meeting her parents. Palms soaking into the
knees of my best dress trousers, scotch on the rocks swimming
untouched in the tumbler before me. I was suddenly glad I'd
had no time for the beach that summer and therefore no tan.
It made me more acceptable to them—in other words, more
white.

I focused on the clock then, right across the living room. It
was enclosed in burnished brown, possessed no blue or gray
Anglo-Alsatian eyes to drill the countenances of potential sons-
in-law like ice picks. This comforted me at the time.

Ten, eleven, twelve, it chimes. Midnight. The gentle ringing
fades. I rest in the dark, and listen.

I always listened at night for a sound from my daughters or
my sons. Sometimes, with Barbara still asleep, I'd get out of bed,
walk barefoot down the hallway. I would open the door to each
room and go inside, and stand there looking at each face.

I listen now for other sounds: a car engine, squeal of the
garage. Early this morning she left. I heard the press of her
weight on carpeted stairs, jangle of keys before the front door
creaked open and shut, and I listened to her drive away with a

flame like fear in my throat. But I said, Delgado, calm yourself. Examined shadows on the ceiling. Felt the rise and fall of bed-sheets as Barbara breathed next to me, reached over once to touch the blanketed curve of her body.

I slide out of bed, throw on a robe, walk the hallways of my house feeling like a thief, as if it's something that is not mine at all and will, in the end, be taken away. The carpet's wall-to-wall, very thick. I love to tread it without shoes or socks, gliding across the hard-won luxury. It reminds me of a time—not so long ago—when I knew I was a man who had everything.

Teresa's door is open. From the threshold I watch her sleep, mouth agape, in the dim illumination of the nightlight she insists on. Because, she says, there are things under the bed that crawl out in the dark.

Scaredy-cat, scaredy-cat, Roberto taunted once. She hid her face, soft dark hair falling over it in shame. Jack rescued her that day, saying *Shut up, asshole. There's no law against being scared, you know,* and flicked his thumb against Roberto's ear. A painful snap.

Faint pools of light glow against the base of the stairs. Plastic crackles, the refrigerator door booms shut.

At the kitchen table Jack's piling tuna fish on slabs of bread. Chocolate-chip cookies are heaped in the bowl before him. Standing there, he sways slightly like a bear on scent, sucks mayonnaise from a fork and blinks in surprise.

I wave. "Hungry?"

"Yeah. Want some?"

"No thanks."

My son's face is changing. A serious, handsome face, ridged by black curling hair and thick brows. He's begun to shave sometimes. And at sixteen he's as tall, now, as Babe. But while she's taken after my side of the family and is naturally muscular, solidly built, Jack has taken after Barbara's and is slender, all legs and elbows, big feet planted firmly on the ground.

Hot breeze comes through the screens. He gives me his look of pity, the one that says: *You've been pretty jumpy lately, old man.*

It's true. Up at night a lot, dreamy-eyed and far away from them all at breakfast.

"Any idea where your sister went?"

I try to make this sound casual. Watching the wary expression that lights his eyes, I know I've failed.

"Babe?"

"On second thought, I'll take one of those cookies. You didn't hear her go out this morning, did you?"

"Here." Jack straddles a chair, shoves the bowl across the table. I sit too.

"Did you?"

"Nah." I know he's in on whatever the plot is, covering for her. But he smiles openly, shamelessly. "What's the matter, Dad, couldn't sleep? You want some of this sandwich?"

"Not really."

"Well, you ought to try and turn in. I'll bet she gets back soon."

From where? I ask silently. He acknowledges it silently, too, covers up by munching bread crumbs through his grin. A good boy, Jack, good soldier in the war between generations. We sit and I watch him eat for a while. Then I must admit defeat, cuff him gently on the shoulder and turn to go upstairs, saying You get some sleep too, *señor*.

But the clock doesn't leave me alone. I listen. Soft wooden ticking. Twelve forty-five. Water runs in the bathroom, the sink, toilet, fluorescent shafts stripe the hallway carpet then disappear. At the door to the master bedroom the nerves seize me again, invisible insects crawl around the inner walls of my stomach and no, no, I can't go in there just yet.

They said You must expect some emotional problems, Mr. Delgado. Any survivor of a disaster like this is bound to suffer psychologically. A certain amount of anger is not unusual. Yes, and a great deal of suppressed pain. We call it a post-traumatic disorder. It precedes the period of mourning.

I wanted to ask many question then. How long would it last, this disorder? And what can it possibly mean to mourn when there are no tangible symbols left to speak of your loss—no coffins, no urns of ash, nothing to mark the extent of grief, to ritualize it—no powerful healing words to chant to yourself?

In the hospital room those first few days her eyes were swollen shut, big, like the scarred halves of ruined Ping-Pong balls. I wanted to cry. To pluck out my own eyes and give them to her. I sat in waiting rooms wishing more than anything else that I could trade places with my child. It would have been so much easier.

*   *   *

To sacrifice.

What Tía Corazón said when, as a final act, I brought Babe there. Telling Barbara I was taking her to a highly regarded nutritionist in Florida. Because she would eat nothing at first, starved herself down to skin and bone, and the doctors were threatening to put her back on an IV. We had tried everything. Special food supplements, vitamins in megadoses, various foul liquid protein mashes made in blenders. More internists. A hospital social worker. Until, in desperation, I took her to Miami.

Tía Corazón. Remembering, I can feel myself flush with a kind of shame.

But who is to say that *that*, after all, was not the thing to turn the tide? Isn't it true that she began to eat again shortly afterward? So maybe we have that mad old witch to thank, Tía Corazón with her candles, her powders, her incantations and her spirits—because, yes, my child began to eat again. And lived.

Sacrifice. Felipe, how much do you want her life, and how much the treasure she wins? Pick up this card and look. Crown of the heart or of world kings, *muy señor mio,* you'll have to choose. Sacrifice. Your house disappears like wind. *Bastante.* Excess of the body. She's trying to turn into air now. For sacrifice. Take the egg in your hand, my child, it's enough struggle. Eat. Eat. Drive out the death in your heart, and eat.

She lit candles, eyes rolled up into her head, the feathers spread across my daughter's chest sprayed with warm red droplets. Calling on the Seven Powers.

That mad old witch.

I stared into candle flames and saw them: the hearts for sacrifice, raw, soaked with life. Smoke singed tears from my eyes. They ran down onto my fingers, and when I held the fingers up against flame and shadow the drops were thick crimson, staining my face and hands. Then the thick dark stain turned to gold in front of me, burned pure and clear by the shimmering, flickering light.

It's what I've waited to hear: hum of a car, methodical crunch of a garage door closing. Rubber soles on cement. Then the sure scrape of keys against a doorknob, driveway lights switched off, and I am already down the stairs.

She sits on the living room sofa with a single lamp on. Ankle on knee, arms stretched wide, easily, she looks relaxed and then sees me and starts a little, flashing a tense smile.

"Hi."

"Went for a drive today?"

"I had some things to do." In the lamplight her face looks colorless, bloated.

Beneath this pale puffiness the face is young, big tired eyes and a child's lips. When I sit opposite her the eyes shift anxiously. I wiggle bare toes against my carpet. Look down and for a second find them very ugly, misshapen and unfamiliar, as if they're monstrous digits belonging to someone else. My words sound lame.

"Rough day?"

"I don't know. I drove up to see this coach at State."

Calmate. Not too many questions. They said it at the hospital, *Let her lead the way, do not force anything, express your interest but above all do not pry,* and I wanted to ask how would it be possible to achieve all these attitudes simultaneously? but in the end was embarrassed to say it.

Now I say instead, very cautiously, "I didn't know you were in touch with anyone—I mean, anyone like that."

"I applied late. A little while ago. I had to get some records and stuff—and I had to have some things sent. There was this mess with papers, sort of, because I still have more than two years of eligibility left."

Postage, application fees, letters requesting recommendations and records—I'd have been glad to help her. But she has done it herself without asking anybody else and now, though afraid in some way I expected to be, resentful in another way I did not think I could be, I am also proud.

"You know," I breathe, "you don't have to—"

"Brenna Allen—she's got a pretty good program there. It's Division Two. But she said they'd get some money—"

"You know you don't have to worry about the money. You know it doesn't matter to me—I can take care of it all."

"Yeah, but you don't have to."

I watch her eyes in the dim light, a kind of sorrow grips them until they meet mine, large, dark, hurting.

"I mean that you don't have to compete if you don't want to. Or even swim any more. That's not important to me."

"I know, Dad." She leans forward, natural and calm for a

moment. "Look, let's just see. I don't have any idea how things will be with me, really. I don't even know *what* I want these days, to tell you the truth. But I liked her—the coach up there—I liked her a lot. And if I—I'll probably—well, I mean, let's just see."

Okay, I say. Okay, *señorita*.

We are silent.

The tears I have in me never fall any more, I don't know why. Ever since the visit to Tía Corazón. As if I let them all out there and the conduits are now permanently closed, sealed by unspeakable things. I want to cross the carpet between us and hug her close, stroke her hair the way I do Teresa's and tell her everything will be all right, that I myself will see to it, will watch over her, protect her. But she's pulled back already, settling firmly against the sofa. There is this unhealed part of her gazing out warily. It's always been there in her, anyway—the part that comes from Barbara: a silent, austere pride that makes you careful of handling her casually, or of touching her at all.

And who is to say that this steely untouchable side of my daughter is not, in some way, her greatest asset? Maybe it's that, only that, which pulled her through alive. You, Delgado, you pride yourself on your ability to embrace both these aspects of your family—the love of what is lavish and romantic coupled with the need for discipline, regulation, order—but can you say that in the end it is always love that pulls you through? Maybe survival has nothing to do with love. Maybe, sometimes, it is merely a matter of sheer will, will pitted against even your own desire to stop, to die. Even if your desperate Cuban witchcraft were conclusively proven to work. Mechanisms of ritual, of love. Bah humbug. No. You don't really know her so well, Delgado. You really don't know this daughter of yours.

"Babe, listen. Your mother and I—we want you to be happy. That's all."

Such bullshit, Delgado. What is it now that stops you from saying what in your heart you want to say? *I love you. I am proud of you. I would take the pain away from you, if only I could.*

There. What stops you?

The fact that these expressions of caring would be too much. I'm supposed to go easy on her. No pressure, the doctors all said that. No pressure. Not even the pressure of knowing how much I care. She'll assume it as another burden. Something else to carry, along with the weight of a team of dead souls.

"Don't tell Mom."

I give her a questioning look.

"I mean, I'll tell her myself. Tomorrow. That's what I mean— okay?"

It sounds a little desperate. I nod. Okay, I tell her, whatever you say.

We sit a while, not speaking. My feet worship the carpet— thick Belgian wool. Mahogany-paneled walls. A house where everything has been tastefully done in materials of the highest quality and where, more often than not, cost has not been a consideration. Proof of the times my money purchased fulfillment—for Barbara and myself, yes, but more important for my children. Handing over all those American dollars blithely, easily, for uniforms and fees. The trips Babe has taken: to Texas, Mission Viejo, Toronto, plane fares, club dues. I whistled while signing checks, pulling credit cards from my wallet, proud, fiercely proud, that after the life I had come from I could provide all these things for my children, my beautiful, protected, talented children. Because I remembered how in the end my own father could not—not in the blinding heat of Havana streets, resources dwindling daily while we waited at the tips of bayonets. I promised myself then that when I was a man myself I would have as many children as possible and a big house to put them in. That, somehow, I would seal them there and keep them safe. So they would never suffer the agony of the world. This I promised. Now, running naked soles over the lush carpet, I know I've failed.

"Are you all right, Babe?"

I wish I hadn't said it. But stern pride rushes over her again, protecting us both. *Sure*, she tells me, *I'm okay*. Then my hands slap the chair arms with a cheerful finality I do not feel. Well, I say, time for bed, eh?

"You go ahead, Dad. I think I'll stay up awhile."

"Still thinking things over?"

"Yes, sure. Don't *worry* about me. I'm all right, you know."

I nod apologetically. Yes, I mumble, I know, Babe, I know. As if I am the child and she the parent, and I've been caught after bedtime with the lights on and quietly scolded. As if I've never grown up, after all. I stand to clumsily kiss her forehead. Her skin is cool in spite of the heat, slightly damp. Damp clings to my lips as I head upstairs.

Sacrifice. It begins.

With the house, she said. Wind tears through it, blowing wood from the walls. Look at these patterns. There, your house, land of treasures, honors, the world. Cold as the bones that flesh hangs on. Here, the sacred heart. Burning. Heart of fire, of light. In between, the clock. It keeps you chained to both worlds. Call the Powers—they'll set her free. And you, too. But the price is great. Choose, Felipe. Flesh or the walls?

Now calm your tears. They're here—the Powers. To hurt and to heal you. Look.

One pointed magenta fingernail spanned the sparkling trail of altar powders. In candlelight thick red tears dripped down, clung damply to my lips.

I brush by the clock's ticking. Half past one.

The bed is warm, Barbara long and perfectly outlined under the sheet. Normally I would press against her, put my arm around her and rest my face along the back of her neck while she sleeps. Tonight, though, I stay apart. On my back with my eyes shut. I'm still not tired. Ever since then, sleep has become less and less possible. I'll be beat by morning, will walk through the office corridors like a feverish ghost.

If you want a good troubleshooter or systems analyst, try Phil Delgado, he's our man, recommend him for anything. He'll set you up the right way from the beginning, root out whatever's causing you grief and fix it on the spot. A great guy, Phil is. Terrific professional.

What sort of business are you in? she asked that first time. And I answered, Computers. The wave of the future. Then reached across the restaurant table to take her hand. The fingers were long and slender, nails shone darkly, their gloss reflecting crystal reflecting dark sweet wine by candlelight. She wore silk and her bracelets were from expensive places, heavier than fourteen-carat. I knew that, to have her, the money would count. Success, winning. To be not just good, but the best.

There would be a house, I thought, and children. A very big house. She was everything I wanted, everything I still want, in this land in which I had come to be. Strong eyes, refined clothes, a cream-softened touch that would seek out and discern those with the talent for winning.

Twenty-two years ago. Both of us were so young—yet somehow, even then, exactly what we would become. I liked to see our different complexions in the summer, my skin against hers.

What is he? some friend of hers asked once, when she thought I couldn't hear, *Not Puerto Rican, is he?*

When I saw that all the hair on her body was pale, too, even the hair between her legs, I was shocked, and laughed, and thought about how beautiful our children would be. I worshiped her, worshiped this, her country. Strove with every fiber of my conscious life to be fully American, to obliterate all traces of foreign behavior and appearance. To be pale-skinned, accentless.

To be white. But there are certain genetic predispositions somewhere in here—latencies that, in the summer, dominate. Browned by sun, I always looked like some kind of *mestizo*. Barbara loved this secretly, though she blushed over it in public.

There are other public things she'll never know about. My trip across America with college buddies, years before I met her, in a rusting Ford with chrome on the sides and torn red vinyl seats. From east to west, across the most exquisite farmland I had ever imagined, between two rivers big enough to be arteries of ocean, across the newest mountain range of the earth, jagged desert peaks eclipsing clouds, cutting into your eyes like spears reflecting unforgivable bleak bright sun, skull deserts, salt basins, rocks layered the yellow of autumn leaves and maroon clay. The engine rumbled us along edges of highway. In Los Angeles, I baked brown on the beach and it did not matter. Once in a while, on the sand, a group of Mexicans would wander by and, with a mixture of relief and shame, I heard and recognized the different cadence of their Spanish words, flirted casually with the dark girls, all the while knowing nothing would ever come of it. Because I was meant, I told myself, for finer things. Whiter things.

With my buddies and our rattling car, beer cans and aspirin and a dwindling amount of cash we traveled back a different way, up along creek beds and piney ridges and shadowed black hills. A land so extraordinary that I promised myself to return one day, and show it to my children.

Which I did. A man of my word. Jack was an infant, Babe six. It was the year she started swimming. I had money by then—it was just starting to swell a savings account—and my beautiful fair American wife, and I had a nice car. We drove into state parks, past bubbling springs and bear cubs, herds of elk, rainbow-colored canyons, through windstorms and summer rain. Emerging into hot sunlight again at a place called the Corn Palace in Mitchell, South Dakota—an auditorium boasting glass display cases filled with information about the winning of the West, its exterior a gaudy architectural extravaganza of gold-tinted domes and spires. Nearby were situated many shops selling postcards and sunglasses and trinkets for tourists, along a wood-railed boardwalk constructed to resemble that of a nineteenth-century frontier town.

Barbara and the kids wandered off into some shop. I was tired, and sat on a bench. I leaned back. The sunlight felt good on my closed eyelids. Maybe I dozed briefly, I don't remember. But something made me open my eyes to the shadowless boardwalk, the hot white air, sound of a child giggling, then another. I began to make out shapes of blond white children in the light, fat parents holding their hands, the figure of a small boy pointing at me, giggling: *He looks like Uncle Zeke!* A fatherly voice mumbled something back, a hushed drawl. The tiny white finger kept pointing, though—at me, at something to the right of me. So I turned that way.

What sat beside me on the bench seemed, at first, to be human. The skin was a tawny dark leather, the hair long and swept back from the forehead and broad hawkish nose by a full eagle-feathered headdress. The hands in the lap were lifelike, turned up in a kind of supplication. There was a buckskin jacket, worn tanned buckskin moccasins. On second glance, though, it was a thing with no life in it at all—nothing but a stuffed, man-sized doll. A red-lettered placard hung around its neck, settled against the leathery buckskin chest.

TAKE YOUR PICTURE WITH UNCLE ZEKE.

Somewhere, a camera flashed.

There were more children now, more parents. The sun was bright, my eyes tired. I could hardly make them out. Someone laughed. The laughter swelled in my ears, sun in my eyes, until for a second I thought I was enveloped in an indistinguishable, suffocating white mass of flesh, and sweat, and pointing fingers.

He does, came the boy's voice. *He looks just like him.*

Then I did something I will never understand.

I smiled back at the big indistinguishable mass of white things blinding me, and turned back to Uncle Zeke. His form was clear, his features noble. In that moment, I wished him alive. And put my arm around him. Then kissed his leather cheek.

There was more laughter now, the deep chuckling of adults mingled with the patter of children's voices. More cameras sounded, clicking, flashing miniature popping explosions. I looked back at them without seeing them, lifted a hand to my face and dropped it in surprise. For some reason, I don't know why, there were tears in my eyes.

Then someone took my hand. Small fingers, soft flesh. And out of all the obliterating white shapes I saw the darker form of a very young girl. Serious, big wounded eyes. Thick dark hair. Skin honey-brown—flesh of my flesh, the color of me. My oldest child, Babe. Who held my hand in both of hers, gently, urging me away from this white erasing center of things. Saying, Come on Daddy, let's get out of here. Let's you and me go home.

Señorita de mi corazón, I said.

Girl of my heart.

She lifted me up by the hand and I followed, rose easily for just that moment into a safe unanchored place that was warm and still and dark, and all my own.

I remember, now, how she looked not so long ago: tall, strong, lean and tanned, bubbling competence, winning. What she'd been trained for since childhood. No ordinary-looking girl. A girl meant for special things.

Two weeks after we brought her home from the hospital I happened to step into her room and found her sitting on the floor against the bed, head bent nearly to her knees, face beaten and thin, and she looked up at me with the frightening new hollowness of her eyes and said I'm sorry, Dad, I'm sorry. I am so sorry.

What? I asked desperately, kneeling beside her, what? What are you sorry for? But she wouldn't answer.

Barbara and I argued that day, bitterly. One of our few true knock-down drag-out fights in all the years together.

Leave her alone, Barbara said. *Don't you understand that she wants to be alone?*

Alone? I stormed back. *Alone? Do you think she knows what she wants? Alone in the ocean for fifty-one hours, and you tell me to leave her alone again. What in the name of God is wrong with you?*

The argument did not recur. Still, it left a scar. When I think back I'm hard-pressed to come up with another one as bad—not even concerning her parents. No, she and I have always gotten along magnificently. But I wonder, now: Did the sacrifice begin *then*, with that fight?

Even before the visit to Tía Corazón, did I call the Powers without knowing it?

Because somehow—since Angelita—there has been this feeling in the house of a strange new presence, something damaged, enraged, askew.

What nonsense. Outmoded superstition, Delgado. A lapse into the very forms of irrational thought that have enslaved people's minds for centuries.

It was an out-of-the-ordinary fight, though, not like our little quarrels.

The ones we had about naming each child, for instance—those first two times I lost out, and *Mildred* and *James* were the results. I still don't like their names, really, but reconciled myself when the nicknames caught on. *Babe. Jack.* Friendly-sounding.

With the next two I stood my ground. My second son would be named *Roberto*, and there would be no substitute like *Bob* or *Bobby*. Teresa would be Teresa, without the anglicizing h.

I felt better, then.

Which is odd. Since I really don't mind the subtle corruption of my own name. I even introduce myself to others as Phil. Not Felipe. *Phil Delgado. Hello there, pleased to meet you.*

I gaze up at the ceiling. Blank darkness. Remembering hot sunlight, red-stained streets. There were soldiers stationed outside our home. And I asked my father what they wanted. *Nothing, Felipe,* he said. *Go to bed.*

But I remember the smell of his sweat, full of helplessness and terror, while we waited. Odd that after all that—the fear that was like a rotting acidic substance dripping through all the organs of our bodies until we felt more dead than alive—we survived. Still, such things change you. You become a different sort of person in your soul, a man less capable of spontaneous thought, action, feeling—a person willing to give up certain things called for by the heart in order to shore up security against the future.

Barbara moves drowsily.

"Phil?"

"Hmmm."

But she's sleeping again.

It's okay, I say. Everything's okay. I move closer to her on the bed. Turn away from the ceiling, the darkness, bury my face against her neck and, in sleep, she sighs.

Yes everything is okay. We are all, all safe here in this house I've bought, with plenty of food in the refrigerator and money in the bank. I have a terrific job, a beautiful wife, four children, two sons, two daughters. Nearly perfect family. Perfect life. And it's a free country. Why do I hurt inside?

Things change. Something happens in an instant to alter the course of your own life, or the life of someone you love—a thing beyond your control. So there is nothing you can do.

What Bart Sager said. There was the matter of Babe and the Hedenmeyer boy. Her inexplicable failures.

There was Angelita.

Then the hospital. Nightmares of her. Of that tortured Kenny living inside machines.

The fight with Barbara. Already, it had begun—sacrifice. The Powers were here, I'd called them, and simply failed to know it.

What did she say, that foul old witch? Shame of my family in Havana as well as in Miami.

Your house disappears like wind.

As soon as Babe began to eat again, I sensed it.

One weekday evening when it seemed as if things were returning to a little normalcy. Barbara went out with friends for the first time in weeks. Jack was at cross-country practice, Roberto banging something together with hammers and nails in the garage, burning incense to obscure the odor of the cigarette he was secretly smoking. Teresa was riveted by the television in the den. And I sat on our living room sofa glancing through a newspaper, sensed shafts of light streaking out into the upstairs hallway from behind the half-opened door of Babe's room.

I lifted my head to look up. Something rose along the back of my neck with a buzzing, snapping sound so that I broke out in sweat. Saw my house drifting into wind. The center that had held us a family—happy, successful, winning and beautiful and spectacularly American all these years—about to diffuse like fragments of flesh on skeletal bones. And I saw—suddenly without having words for it, because there are no words in the world for it—that Tía Corazón was right, I had to choose. But before knowing it or being able to stop it I had made my choice—a choice that came before understanding, out of nowhere but a dark place in the primitive past, in my primitive heart—from the wind and the death of Angelita, from the pain of seeing my firstborn child swollen and desiccated in a white hospital bed, her body shriveled to unrecognizable proportions. Something had come to me, offered itself, and without knowing it I'd opened my heart to it, and because of that the unknown thing had planted itself inside my beautiful American family and inside my magnificent, expensive, American showcase house.

I looked up that evening and things became silent for a moment. Then I felt it—I felt it: the ineluctable working of the Powers. Something like insects gnawing the innards of everything I'd lived in and purchased up until now. Silent tremors making almost invisible cracks in the house beams, shingles, concrete.

Sacrifice. For the seven saints.

Look, Felipe. Into the life of your child. Into the heart of the candles. Into your own heart, the sacred heart of flame.

Purple-tinged fingernails trailed the powders. Feathers floated. Kneeling on the floor amid the incense and incantation, something flashed from the corners of my eyes. My daughter's passive chest and neck and the spattered drops of sacrifice, warm tinted water, thick scarlet. Flame of life from the hearts of the candles.

Listen, Felipe, don't be ridiculous. Calm yourself, dry your tears. Make your choice. Bring her back from the air, give the spirits something else instead.

Hold the egg, my child. No more sacrifice. The house will be wind, and you return to flesh. Eat. Eat.

The heart or the world. There is your choice. And time helps you see this. So look to the clock.

But the house, I said. The plans.

Then said nothing.

Candles burned, water from my eyes shimmered on fingertips in the flame and shadow—first a dense red, then the blank, blinding color of light. And I picked my child up in my arms, and took her home.

You may plan security, Delgado, you may strive all your life to attain it for yourself and for those you love. But try as you will, sometimes the world intervenes and strips it away. A lesson your father learned too late in life. He was ruined by fear and by plans. Arrived in Miami a broken man.

A lesson Tía Corazón never had to learn.

"Barbara."

She's sleeping.

Listen, Barbara: There are things in the world that we don't know about. Spirits, demons with primitive names, hovering to invade our fondest fortresses.

Sometimes they live inside us. We call on them when we feel despair. And without even knowing it, accept them. Then feel them work among us. To heal. Or to destroy.

What do you think of that, my love? What do you think?

And you, Delgado. You. What do you think?

Nothing, I whisper. And sleep.

Delgado

🐬 🐬 🐬

(B A B E)

I smell chlorine and panic. Then turn the corner quickly, lope up a flight to stay there on the landing between floors telling myself quiet Delgado quiet, you are alone and safe. But somewhere doors swing open. Damp air blows right through, steps on concrete are coming up, getting closer, I sway against a wall.

"Lost?"

The face stares down, beaming, young. Team letter fitted neatly over the broad chest of the sweatjacket. He has really broad shoulders and thick telltale neck, a breaststroker, reminds me of Kenny so I don't want to look at the face but do. Then it is just some other blond guy, one I've never seen before. My voice from the other end of the hole tumbles out like confession.

"I'm looking for Brenna Allen."

"Third floor. Come on, I'm going up there myself."

I follow, feeling helpless.

Feeble, Delgado, very gutless. Pussycat.

He points the way telling me around that corner and to the left, better go to the receptionist first, she'll let them know you are here. When he turns I watch him, thinking Kenny, watch his strong back. But he pauses to face me again with a puzzled expression. I know it on others, dread it. And the question:

"I've seen you before, right?"

Shake my head weakly.

"I mean a couple of years ago, maybe—I know! Senior Nationals. Industry Hills."

"Not me."

"No? I thought—well, never mind. Forget it." He grins again, mischievously. A spark of scrutiny there and something in me shudders hard, I am sweating everywhere inside these good clothes and will look a mess. But he just shrugs, says, "Anyway, good luck," turns again and walks away, gym bag slung over one shoulder. For a minute I hate him and the kind friendliness of his voice, his strength, his Kenny-ness, hate the smell of the air, most of all hate the flabbiness of my own arms and thighs.

The reception desk is there around a corner at one end of the hallway they've carpeted, very upscale, but nothing like Southern with its big sparkling assumption of wealth. I start to talk and this friendly girly face smiles back saying Yes, may I help you?

I freeze inside the hole of me, pull the lid shut over.

"May I help you?"

Open it, Delgado. Pussycat.

I do and peek out.

"Ms. Delgado."

Babe, I say, call me Babe.

Another face smiles back, not the Kenny boy or the May I Help You girl, but a woman. I remember her face from years ago. It was younger then, smoother. Brown hair, wide forehead. In her mid-thirties but she keeps herself in pretty good shape, must do weights a lot, the skin almost youthful, lined with something sad around the eyes.

I stand.

She is not short yet suddenly I am at least three, four inches taller and feel clumsy, gigantic, very sweaty and fat.

We shake hands. Bren Allen, she says, glad to see you again. Come on into my office, we'll have some time to talk. So we do. The lights there are pleasant, somehow calming. She has trophy cases, bookshelves with old books, new metal filing cabinets, a computer, stacks of paper on the dark wooden desk. I step in like stepping into a cloud. For a second my eyesight goes the way it has done ever since, tunneling into the hole of me so I must shut my eyes and spin, and when I open them there is the face of this woman materializing again out of the cloud of pleasant fancy light, there is the kept-in-shape body attached to the face, and things are beginning to clarify here in the light and the calm.

We talk. The usual things. I don't remember specifics. It isn't too hard until she asks that question: What about the bad times, the rotten splits, and how do I feel about it? Then no more smiles from me, no more nice. I cannot answer, which is very rude but what can I do? Thinking of things you cannot tell about. Those times after the hospital when I stayed awake all night waiting for the morning alarm to buzz, triumphant because I'd lasted the black time through without sleep or nightmares but dreading the hole of the morning. Dragging my butt through another goddamned day, not concentrating. Falling asleep everywhere—on the starting block at the club for Christ's sake, and in class—leaning against a busy hallway wall nodding out until the booksack fell from my hands and people passing by thought I was stoned. Professors trying to get my attention.

I had to drop out. Then bag it completely for a while, no more school, no more workouts either. There was this thing with people's faces, that they seemed so far away all the time, voices too faint to hear even when they were right in your face. Disgust at the way things looked and sounded. Fear at the strangeness of it all. The mindless, motherfucking exhaustion. And whenever I shut my eyes, skin floating away on the water. Jesus, forgive me. The continual taste of blood. Forgetting how to flip turn.

Forgetting? How to flip? Shit, Delgado, you've been doing it since the age of six. Wrists swiping pool lights, deftly turning underwater. But there was the day it eluded me. Getting to the other end of fifty meters and forgetting what to do. See, it was like it fled my reflexes utterly—how to turn—I willed it, I swear I did, but the body I'd been left with would not respond. How do you feel about that, Delgado—huh? Well. How would you feel, lady?

But I answer Lousy—some of the truth, not all. When she says the thing about money and how it will not hurt my pride I want to say Pride? What is that? but say nothing. She needs me to give something here and now. A promise. Tell her I will try for her the way Sager said always, always to try and win no matter what, but this is no longer the Babe of old here, folks, this is the new one a.k.a. The Hole, and I can't promise anything to any would-be coach, not yet.

In fact I'm starting to feel like I did back in high school days, a little coy, a little cagey, when all the big guns would come around personally to make recruitment pitches and have these serious talks with Mom and Dad in the living room, then take us out to dinner. The phone kept ringing so much we unplugged it. But whenever I was face to face with one of those guys and he was giving me some earnest rap about how great the University of Such-and-such was and how I would fit right in with the program and how they would tailor this and that for me, for me alone, I would do my number on them: I would smile the nice innocent jock-girl smile and pretend to not quite understand all of it, to sort of zone out. And all the time I was waiting, waiting for an offer I could not refuse. Waiting to be challenged and seduced. All the time my moron jock-girl smiling silence said to them things they never would have guessed. Like, My mother is whitebread DAR, sir, but my father's name is Felipe Delgado, his skin gets very brown in the summer and so does mine, and he suffered a lot before coming to this country and he struggled very hard to make a go of it here—so how much of what are you planning to fork over for me, pal? because to tell you the truth they can't pay enough to make up for how hard I have to work and how bad I have to hurt in order to do what I do—I mean, what do you think it is? like, just good genes? or the luck of the draw?—so if you believe you will convince me to endure all those stupid laps for bullshit, white boy, you can just get down on your knees right now and kiss my half-Cuban ass good-bye.

And while I thought these things and held out in polite youthful gee-whiz stupidity, each one of them began to look sort of funny to me, a little odd, vaguely ridiculous. Until Sager came along and made me the offer that was better than all the others. With his pure pale white skin that had white-blond hair across the knuckles, wispy eyebrows almost invisible over eyes that were so delicately blue, as cold as dry ice, and saw right into what I was thinking and feeling, knew immediately how bad I hated all the swimming and the water, understood that I wanted something I hadn't even come across yet, and set himself up to keep me from whatever that was. What the pale eyes said under all his praise, his encouragement and nice talk and substantial offer, was that he was not one of these funny guys, he was not in the least bit odd or ridiculous.

Watch out, the eyes said, I can hurt you.

Yes, I told them silently, yes. But I can disappoint you, Kemo Sabe.

From the beginning, then, we were dark and light, tit and tat, underneath the mutual wanting and signed letters of agreement set toe to toe against each other, enemies in some way we didn't even understand yet, but from the first we recognized it.

So I am thinking this sitting in the nice calm office with Brenna Allen. I'm starting to be dumb-jock silent and coy with her, too, when I look at her eyes and see nothing ridiculous there either, only a hard dark thing that is bitterly difficult but will not be my enemy. And it blows the lid right off the hole of me so that, in a moment, I stand and say too much.

"Jesus. I can't do them any more, you know. I mean—I just— I cannot *deal*."

The sweat's running off me like a cold shower. Things start to get weird in my vision again and I hear a voice float along gently, from far away.

"What," says the voice, "what can't you do?"

"Flips."

"Well," it says quickly, coolly, "I guess you'll have to do open turns then."

And with that, she wins my heart.

I follow her like a big clumsy puppy dog, out of the good tranquilizing light, through other doors, down other halls toward the smell of locker rooms, past a faint hiss of steam. My insides tunnel, compress, but I keep breathing. She walks slowly alongside me. Being very polite, I think, managing not to look at the fucking freak-show spectacle I am putting on. But the funny thing is that as we get closer and closer to places of danger the fear begins to ease.

Open turns? Well, of course. Back to basics!

There is to say the least a kind of humiliation in that: Babe Delgado, resorting to open turns. Still, it seems suddenly feasible—a sure way of turning around at the wall and swimming back the way you came, and I want to bless her or something for telling me how, for giving me permission.

Out on the observation deck the sick comes back when I look down. Nice new pool, each lane empty.

How many lanes, Mildred?

Eight.

And how many swimmers?

Eight.

That's right. But how many will win?

Just one.

For a moment it is mammoth, threatening. Shut my eyes and the hole is real again, black desperate horizon, skin bleeding on water. But I lean against a wall and don't faint, open eyes, shake my head so the nausea recedes. It is only a pool down there after all. This is only another building reeking competition and chlorine. And I've spent a lot of time in places like this.

She tells me the stuff about terror and puking. But I think of other things she said before in her office, team rules, her voice echoing in the background like something at the end of a tunnel—what was it? *The women on my team,* she said. Women, not girls, and it sounded very strange.

That's when I let her win the rest of me.

I say: Okay, *Bren.* I will deal.

There is the thing with my dad to get through. Then I go upstairs, check to make sure he's not still lingering anywhere in the hallway, check to see that the door to Jack's room is closed, Roberto's too, so no one can observe. Then I go through to my own room, quickly run a wet hand along the wall, flick on a light.

They're screaming for me again.

Hey, Delgado!

Delgado!

I lean back against the door breathing hard and refuse to open my eyes. But only silence. I open them like slits. Shaded lamplight brightens each corner. A neatly made bed, bookshelves on either side of the bed with texts and paperbacks so neatly aligned. Each shelf top doubles as a night table. Framed posters on the wall, French impressionist art I know nothing about but once thought pretty—or maybe it was my mother who thought they were pretty, I can't remember.

One wall is blank with a large delineated rectangular space paler than the rest of the wall surrounding it, left by the bulletin board I took down finally and stashed somewhere in the closet. No, not just somewhere. I know the exact spot: left-hand side when you face the sliding doors, stuck behind a cardboard carton filled with old meet results and stacks of age-group ribbons in tiny silk-backed cases, the ones there are no room for any more downstairs in the den where they put up those glass showcases for my medals. There, and in the living room, entire shelves are filled with the big and small trophies I've won, have been winning, for how many years? fifteen years. Since the age of six. A long time to be winning.

It was good to stash the board away, to silence all the snapshots and their voices. Putting it out of sight helped. The voices diminished, came from inside instead of from the pictures, now never sound in the day any more, only in the dark when I open my eyes. But there's this price to be paid: my choice of clothes has become, shall we say, definitely limited. See, I'm afraid to open the closet door.

Big brave champ, huh? Monster, animal.

Fucking bunny rabbit, Delgado. You pussycat.

I open my eyes all the way to an orderly girl's room, with nothing in it any more to set it apart from other girls' rooms in similar homes in similar towns in America. Now, though, the silence makes old remnants of ripped-apart stomach bubble up inside, the fronts of my thighs are damp, shudders travel in thin wavering lines from the knees up, then back down. I consider the closet door, how I could rummage wildly through the barrier of hanging clothes, pushing boxes of ribbons and medals aside until I can see their faces again and hear their voices again and feel them surround me the way they used to, barking like seals, holding kickboards to pound the water, the joke we would chant at each other when Kemo Sabe wasn't around, boards splashing in rhythm: *Dog meat! Dog meat! Dog meat!* Then give the war whoop. Our rebel yell.

My hand slips along the wall, shuts off the light. I bend down slightly with one foot forward, one back on the starting block, in perfect position. Always did have to work on my dives. In the dark I open eyes wide. Slide down along the wall to crouch, flabby, out of shape, thighs can't take it any more. In one dark corner I sit.

Dives.

Swing the arms, grab a fatless thigh in each hand and gently shake, try to loosen up the muscles stretched long and taut so close to the surface.

No good. Cold creeps down my spine. Under white lights the pool glitters blue. Over the intercom, this blaring metallic voice announces lane assignments, names, school teams. I try not to listen.

THIS IS THE 100-METER BREASTSTROKE. TWO LENGTHS OF THE POOL.

Yes, sure. Two. Thank you very much. In case I forget?

I lean, roll a little on the balls of my feet, trying too hard and I know it. No good. Screw all this for today, huh? Let's call the whole thing off.

The beep sounds like a mini-cannon. Dives, dives. I get off the block too late and know it. My timing's shot from the word go and I know it. Plus, lately, my walls have begun to just suck. The first and only one's still too far away.

Spectator shouts roar to the high ceiling, an indistinguishable echo. In the bright-lit pool, bodies glide. This is the slowest stroke, the oldest stroke. It may appear to the observer to be a manifestation of perfect ease and grace, but from the inside when you do it all out, as perfectly and as fast as you can, when you do it to win then you look monstrous surging out of the water, a creature from some dark lagoon with foreign bug-goggle eyes. It wrenches every fiber of every muscle and it burns you all up with effort so that when you touch the wall to finish you have forgotten how to breathe, have forgotten everything but the naked agonized rasp in your empty lungs and heart. The 100 demands such complete control, so much raw strength. Yet the entire event will be finished in a little more than a minute. If you think about it, it seems unfair.

That's what I trained for every day since the age of six. Fifteen years. Two workouts a day including holidays, unless I was sick or tapering.

Television cameras pan to a ceiling shot. Announcers' voices pipe in louder than the shouts and echoes. All those experts, media talking heads, pretty faces whose agents have bartered with networks for their few minutes of air time. Their voices and comments will blare out to thousands of homes while I'm swimming—while I'm failing—voices I will hear later, cringing, because someone has thoughtfully recorded it all for me on videotape.

"Uh-oh. It looks like Babe Delgado's off to a slow start, John."

"That's right, Bill. She's a little late off the block with that dive. Now, she is the top-seeded swimmer in the final here of the women's hundred-meter breaststroke—that means she came into this heat as the fastest qualifier. But if you've followed the career of this young lady, you know that she's had some trouble maintaining a high level of performance this year and last—"

"That's right, John. Her performance has been erratic. You're the expert! What accounts for this kind of slump?"

"Well, Bill, it's difficult to say. These kids train so hard for so long, you've almost got to expect it sooner or later. Who knows? Something's got to give. But, believe me—and I went through this myself!—if you're a true champion, you come back stronger than ever."

"Well put, John. Now they're approaching the halfway point of the women's hundred-meter breaststroke final, here in Indianapolis. Oh! You can see that quite a race has developed between Penny Johnson of Stanford—she's in lane three in the middle of your television screen—and Martie Rourke of the University of Florida, in lane one. Martie is from Australia, but she goes to school and trains in the States—and if she can take this final, here in Indianapolis, what a surprise it will be!"

"That's right, Bill. Martie swims with the Australian national team. And it's a testament to the toughness of this competition, to the high quality of the field here in Indianapolis today, that Australia's national champion in this event could qualify no better than second to last. These kids are fast."

"It looks like Babe Delgado is back in the race now, John!"

"Well, Bill, she's playing catch-up right now. She can see Penny Johnson next to her in lane three, and she knows that she has to make up at least that half a length to beat her—see her looking over now! You never do that in the hundred, never! Babe Delgado has got to be a worried young lady at this moment!"

"It looks like she's pulling even with Penny Johnson, though! But she can't really see what's going on over in that first lane there—that's at the top of your television screen—can she, John?"

"No Bill, she can't. And that's going to cost her right now, as she gives it everything she's got. We're coming into the final ten meters of this race. Remember that these kids are dead tired now, Bill. This is the part of the race where nobody has anything

left. This is what separates the men from the boys—excuse me!—
these are girls down there, aren't they? But I can tell you from
my own experience, a champion digs down deep at this point
and comes up with the goods."

"Tell me, John, do you think Babe Delgado will come up with
the goods?"

"Hard to say, Bill."

"There she is in lane four, Babe Delgado of Southern University, which is one of this country's big collegiate swimming powers, John—"

"You can say that again."

"Will she make it? Oh! She's neck and neck with Martie
Rourke, over in lane one at the top of your screen, and she's
passed Penny Johnson!"

"Yes! But Penny is coming back! It's down to the last couple
of meters here, it's going to be one-two-three for these three
talented girls, Bill. And they touch the wall!"

"And here we have the final results, John—what a surprise
this is! In first place is Martie Rourke, the plucky Australian
from the University of Florida, who actually came into this final
with one of the slowest qualifying times!"

"That's right, Bill. And it just goes to show you what sheer
willpower can do. Martie Rourke was just not expected to win
here today. She had the disadvantage of coming into this race
with one of the slowest qualifying times—which meant she was
over against the wall in lane one, and that's a disadvantage to a
swimmer. I know what that's like."

"I'm sure you do, John. Can we see some more results on the
board here—yes, there we go!"

"Right, Bill. As you can see, Babe Delgado, who used to be
the American record holder in this event, hung on to pass Penny
Johnson for second place. But the time is not particularly
impressive."

"No, John, that's right. That's not a fast winning time—in fact,
they were all way off record pace. Now, Martie Rourke, the
winner of the women's hundred-meter breaststroke final here in
Indianapolis, swims at the University of Florida, but she com-
petes internationally for Australia. So that still makes Babe Delgado the top American woman in this event here today."

"Right, Bill. But Babe Delgado cannot be happy with her performance here today, and she cannot be happy with that time! It does look like she's having another bad year. Now the question really is, will she qualify for the Olympic Trials next summer at all? Two years ago she was the American record holder. But it just goes to show you how quickly things change in this sport. If I was Babe Delgado right now, Bill, I'd sit myself down and do some serious thinking."

"And you can see that Bart Sager, the coach at Southern, isn't very pleased."

"No, Bill, you're right about that. Bart Sager expects his swimmers to win. But I'll tell you, if I was heading for the Pan Am Games or the Olympic Trials, I'd want someone like Sager in my corner. I would say that he and Babe Delgado have some talking to do!"

"Well, that concludes our coverage of the women's hundred-meter breaststroke final, here in Indianapolis. As a disappointed Babe Delgado, the former American record holder in this event, gets out of the pool. Coming up we have the final of the men's four-hundred-meter freestyle. But first let's pause for a word from our sponsors."

There's that dangerous squirm of the muscles, numb and electric, moving under the skin like sacks of worms. I can't feel anything yet though and when I stop fighting to breathe I pull myself out somehow, walk dripping across the wet tiles to where he's waiting. No color left on me any more. I feel how pale I've become, almost as pale as him.

"I'm sorry."

"You're sorry?"

"Yes, I'm sorry. I blew the dive—"

"I know you blew the dive."

"But it's my walls—"

"What do you mean, your walls? What's wrong with your walls? There's nothing wrong with your walls!"

He shifts from foot to foot, helplessly furious, ringlets of icicle hair plastered against his forehead. His face is broad and handsome, glaring down.

"I'm sorry."

Why is it like that, my mind stuck on two words like a record with needle grooved into one track, seems everything these days is a constant apology. And I'm sick of it all. Sick of the water.

Of Kemo Sabe, Mister Pale Face here. The whole team. Sick of myself.

"You're sorry. *I'm* sorry. If you want to get to the Trials you're going to have to qualify, you know."

"I know. I know."

"Good. Then we all know. Go on, go relax. Take a shower. We've got relays coming up. You *are* planning on doing the medley relay, aren't you? Well, I want you to hit that dive. I want you to nail it. Go think about it."

"All right."

"Go think about it."

On my way out to go think about it Hedenmeyer grabs me, smiling. I pull away. His forearms are thick, naked and red where he shaved off all the hair.

The row of bathroom stalls is deserted. I head for the farthest one and throw up. But what comes out is just colorless liquid, clear and pure. Later I walk past the recovery room to the far side of the lockers and sit on a bench, wrap myself in a towel, try to stop shivering.

"Yo, Babe."

Her hand gently guides my head, presses it against a Lycra belly. Liz tugs each ear, strokes my hair.

"You going to shave all this off for the Trials?"

"What Trials?"

"Come on, doll, they didn't name you Mildred for nothing, right? Don't worry about it! You crying?"

"No." I glance up at the laughing eyes. "I'm all right."

"Just don't worry, Babe."

"I'll be okay. Really. Really and truly, cross my heart."

"Okay. Okay. I've got the two-hundred coming up, gotta go."

"Well for Christ's sake, *go* then. Don't worry about me."

"Who's *worrying*, Mildred, *God*. It's like, I just want *you* on the fucking *relay* with me next summer, *okay*?"

"*Okay.*"

To please her, I laugh.

"Don't listen to him, Babe. He's a jerk."

"Yeah?"

"Yeah. Kemo Sabe him stupid, lotta smoke, no wampum. He's just jerking off. Everybody *else* knows you. I mean, you can deal, right? Just remember."

"Go on. Go on for the two, then." I squeeze her hand and push her away, half-crying, half-grinning, watch her walk out to do the thing no one beats her at. Call to her, "*Hey*. Good luck. Like, kick butt, part the waters, make them eat dog meat, you monster."

She turns to blow a kiss.

Delgado!

In the dark I rock back and forth, close the eyes and lose them all, spin dizzy without moving, open eyes and hear them again:

Delgado!

Swing the bag in one hand, red, blue, gold trim around embossed letters: SOUTHERN—THE BIG U. It's heavy with wet towels, wrung-out racing suits, soap and shampoo and skin cream.

Delgado!

Look around. The empty stands have a worn, desperate feel. Shift the bag from hand to hand, pace. The pool sparkles, golden-lit, new. But the walls are as tired as the city itself. Ceiling lights bleach them of stains.

Up near the ceiling the electronic timer displays multiple zeroes. Zero. That is you, Delgado. Bunny rabbit. Tonto. The great American hero.

There's a bus waiting, but Sager isn't even in it yet and it will wait a while longer. Close eyes and turn around, move in a slow and leisurely dance. Now, no tension. Now loose and full of grace. All at the wrong time. Off today, boy were you off today, Delgado.

But I pulled out whatever was there for the relay, didn't I? Nailed that dive. Because, like she says, we are special. So we ought to have whatever we want. Anything. Just reach out to touch. Reach out. And take it.

"Babe? *Babe!*"

It sounds through the door. A thin whisper and faint rapping sound, tiny fist against wood.

"Ba-*abe!*"

I freeze. Dark spins. All the bleachers gone, the lights and people and splashing gone, gone the smell of chlorine, of soggy things crushed against the bottom of a bag, echo of sneakers squishing pool decks and bus gears grinding through downtown cities for the airport. Liz and Kenny gone. Kemo Sabe gone. Alone in my room in the dark, sweating terribly, out of shape, sound frozen in my throat while Teresa knocks on the door insistently whispering my name.

"Hey, *Babe!*"

It's like my heart's trying to get out through my chest. I fumble along the wall for the light and flick it again, remember to breathe once, twice, try to still the shaking of hands and legs, run a shirt sleeve over my face. I open the door.

Teresa stands there looking up. Her pajamas are buttoned all wrong—one hole empty at the top, an extra button undone at the bottom. She alone can make me smile. Her hair is soft, caught between hallway shadows and the sure yellow light of the room, half of it is black, half a shimmering gold. She blinks, pouty lips trembling.

"Babe, what's wrong?"

"Wrong? Nothing's wrong."

"Yes it is. I heard you talking."

"Talking?"

"Yes. Like you were talking to somebody—were you? But there's nobody here."

"Me? No. Oh, no." I kneel, run a hand through my hair and steady myself until for a moment things feel almost okay, all right enough, anyway, to touch my little sister's shoulder, touch her cheeks gently. "Listen, Toots, it's nothing. You had a bad dream."

"But I heard—"

"Forget about it, Toots. You see anyone here now?"

The dark eyes run cautiously around the room, uncertain. When they meet mine they're confused—makes me feel incredibly guilty.

"No," she says finally, puzzled. "No, I don't."

"Well then, there *isn't* anyone else, okay? So you don't have to worry. Everything's fine."

Sure, Delgado, it's all just swell. Just as fine and swell as it can be.

I pick Teresa up and stand. Both shoulders ache, pain shoots along the left rib cage, across the groin, jets through both knees.

To what do you owe your longevity, champ?

To drugs. And surgery.

I kick the pain off, kick away memories, hug my sister closely so that her soft little-girl hair crushes against my cheek. It's calming, very gentle and sweet.

"Come on, Toots, let's put you to bed."

"I don't want to go!"

"Shhh! What if they all wake up? Come on, I'll read to you if
you like—"

"How come you get to stay up all the time?"

"Because I'm afraid to sleep."

"That's *bull*shit."

It's not but I give a laugh anyway. Step into the hall carrying
Teresa, nudge the bedroom door closed behind and move slowly
with this burden, soles silent against the thick wall-to-wall carpet,
silent under the ticking grandfather clock that's been in my
mother's family for generations—since the time they were forced
to free their slaves, or something like that.

"You want me to read to you?"

"Yes."

"What do you want me to read?"

"The Cat and the Rat."

On my shoulder the kid's dark hair is messy, floats around her
face like a halo in the dim glow of nightlight, and I tuck her in.

"All right, Toots, I'll read for a while. But then you have to
go to sleep."

"It isn't fair."

"What isn't fair?"

"It just isn't."

The lampshades on her dresser are decorated with happy
clowns and rabbits that have pink noses and these perpetually
cheerful grins. I turn one lamp on and search the floor for
books, find *The Cat and the Rat,* then read quietly for a while until
I give a glance sideways sitting there on the edge of Teresa's bed
and see that she's about to doze off, lips parting, eyelids sagging,
hint of a snore in each breath, one more page will do it.

" 'I say,' said the Rat, 'it's getting almost impossible to live in
this house with that mean old Cat!' "

That's the ticket. Turn the page but she's already asleep,
drooling a little onto the pillow. Her face is smooth and innocent. I turn out the dresser lamp when I leave.

The light in my room is still on. For a moment I'm grateful.
Then I hate the light and the stark flat way it shows my face in
the mirror. Fat, Delgado, you are fat. Big fat paleface, I mean
totally out of shape.

The day washes up through the hole, floods over. Closet beckons once more feebly but the plea is too weak this time, I am too tired to listen. So I do the usual: head for bed and kick off my shoes and snap a bedside lamp on before turning the overhead off, grab a thick novel from the shelf and crack it open, slide under the covers fully dressed. Just get into that empty blank place, Delgado, that place deep inside the hole where there is nothing—no thought, no image, no feeling or memory.

There, yes. You can do it automatically now.

And you can deal, right?

This thick book sits uselessly next to me on the bed. A decoy. In case my dad pokes his head in and sees me, he'll think I fell asleep reading, too tired to turn off the light. How many mornings have I fooled him like that? Kept the eyes closed, pretending? Too many to count.

The day swarms up and out, sick flood in my guts.

What did I promise Brenna Allen? To try? And accepted a free ride?

What I want now is to erase the promises and signatures as if they never were, take everything back and say, See, I can't possibly do any of this, it has all been a terrible mistake, I am sorry. But I sat there over lunch instead, even managed to make some kind of small talk. Sat there in the office with the good calm lights and shelves stocked with books, took a black pen in my hand and signed a letter of intent. All these things I did, for real. Like, it's going to be so easy.

You and me, Kenny. Things ain't what they used to be.

Delgado!

What the air sounded like after a while. I held onto him and the flotation cushion, ripped through the outer cover with my fingers to moor his hands inside it to make a stronghold.

Delgado!

It was the wind, yes. Because neither one of us spoke. We couldn't. I thought that maybe he was dead. Broken body bent against one cushion, circled by another, neck at crazy angles, I couldn't even tell if he was breathing. Things punched down my throat into the hole—water, salt, wind, the sick seesaw motion and ugly fire of thirst, sudden crunching agony when sharp things knocked into me and him, and for some reason I do not even remember I clutched the torn shreds stuffing the flotation cushion and refused to let go. Until everything blew up swollen inside, burning pain of mouth and lips, each soggy breath fought for, resounding like a scream.

Kenny, I said, what about sharks.

The cold. Made me shiver until I could hardly breathe, could barely keep holding on. Then heat. Sunlight glinted off metal on the water, wormed its way through the swollen slits my eyes had become. In the middle of the heat and light I started to shiver again, to shiver so hard I thought my fingers would rattle free of the cushion and leave me to sink, to drown.

Dog meat.

Shoulders and legs not working right. Something broken. I could not swim. Could not see, because of what shone blindingly off the water and surrounded us, making everything shudder and blaze. This light. This light.

And I asked, Kenny, where are we? Asked, in a croak I could not hear: Do you see it?

Then thought I heard someone call my name.

Delgado.

But I don't remember.

Closet door. Photographs. The little notes scrawled. Names on a calendar.

That light.

I've forgotten so much.

"Delgado," I whisper, just to hear someone say it.

My fingers are cold. I run them over the cover of the paperback on the bedspread. Maybe I have read this book, too, and just don't remember. Maybe this is life from now on, fatso, and everything will be like this: You will crawl through all the seconds, all the minutes, managing smiles to protect everyone else from the hole you know is there waiting for you, making promises that cannot be kept, in a world of sick guts and frightened longing, until it will seem that there has never been anything inside of you but the failure. It will seem that you have never been capable of any motion at all except to rip into something and grab and cringe, dig your fingers in and hold fast to the pain, have never carried anything off with sureness, or elegance, or grace.

My big, graceful girl.

Señorita de mi corazón! He'd call me that, too—every night as soon as he got home from work, toss me in the air. He twirled me in circles like an airplane, dangled me upside down, played bucking bronco while I perched astride, digging in imaginary spurs. It was pretty outrageous. I mean, I don't think the other kids got that—not Jack, for sure, not Roberto.

Señorita de mi corazón! He said it, for the last time, when I was six years old. The year I started to swim.

It was my dad who drove me places. To clubs, to different coaches. Because, they said, I had talent, had to be developed. But I'd bug him on those drives, stick a hand out the window until cold wind whipped through my fingers into the car with a moaning sound.

Why do we have to go so far away to swim?

Because. It's too cold at the beach.

No it's not.

It is, Babe. It is. If you got in the water there now, guess what would happen.

What?

You'd turn into a terrible *chica de hielo.* Do you know what that is? A *chica de hielo?*

No.

An *ice girl.* A girl who turns into frozen white forever, and makes everything she touches cold. That's what you'd be—a terrible ice girl.

No *way.*

Yes indeed, *señorita.* Just remember that. Never turn into an ice girl, Babe. Promise me. Don't ever turn into an ice girl.

Okay, I told him. Okay, I promise.

Now we're here together for another long drive. But Jack is with us, stuck between suitcases and things in the backseat like a slob, plugged into his Walkman. Glancing sideways at my dad while he drives, I can't say for sure that I've kept the old promise at all.

"Why do they call it *Indian* summer? Do they mean American Indian or, like, Pakistani?" Jack unplugs himself, rummages in the trunk, hauls out a couple of bags and a box packed thickly with books, drops them on the ground. I give him my disgusted look.

"You shouldn't take it personally, honey," my father bugs me. It's the thing with Mom again—he can't get it off of his mind and I wish he would.

"I don't."

"She thought too many cooks would spoil the broth."

Jack's struggling across the parking lot already. I head him off and fight. He doesn't put up that much resistance—no upper body strength—and I grab the heaviest suitcase. Hear my father locking doors and trunk, coming after us, and I hurry ahead to avoid him.

I couldn't give a damn about the whole mess, really. He and she can slug it out at the country club. On the new patio. In their bedroom. Either way, I'm out of it.

There are carts full of suitcases, opened cartons of notebooks and records and clothes, music ripping from a dozen rooms, kids with parents or with each other hauling things around. The place looks like some airport in time of war. At Southern, things were pretty nice and calm until all the parental units left. Then shit flew from the slingshots to the walls.

Seventh floor, Delgado—your brand-new Division II home, all expenses paid.

Hold the elevator! he yells.

We don't.

He gave me a check this morning.

But I signed the letter, Dad. It's a free ride, I told you.

Take it, he insisted. *Take it, open a bank account somewhere, I just don't want you to worry about anything, honey.*

I'm not worried, I said.

Well, I almost said it. But I saw there were these tears in his eyes. So I just told him thanks and kissed his nose, folded the check in squares and stuck it in the pocket of my jeans.

Maybe he feels helpless—for which I would not blame him.

"You got your own room?" Jack raps knuckles against the wall of the elevator. CRACK KILLS, reads the graffiti, ACID DOESN'T.

I nod. He gives me the thumbs-up.

"Way to go. That's what I want out of this cross-country gig, I'm telling you. A free ride, and my own fucking room. None of that roommate shit. You taking any good courses?"

Vague titles come to mind, nothing stays. Think, Delgado. What exactly did you tell them you wanted to study?

"I don't know. Some literature class, I think. And a couple of other things—"

"Do you have to take math?"

"No." The light blinks on, off, elevator screeches to a stop between floors. I give him a smile—sometimes he's so earnest. "No, I don't have to take math any more."

"Awesome. When does practice start?"

I freeze again, shrug. This frightens him into silence. We're inching up now agonizingly, fourth floor, fifth. Sixth. The elevator boxes us in, filled with the day's heat, with a smell of musty books and tightly wrapped packages, sweating clothes, human bodies. Like locker rooms, but without the water or the flesh.

Seventh floor, and we have to step over things in the hall. Other doors open along the way. Music blares from one—some tape, a potpourri of Sex Pistols and Plasmatics and The Clash— and the girl inside dangles a cigarette from her mouth while she rearranges books on a shelf, ass to the hallway in a pair of tight jeans. Jack stops to admire.

"Come on, jerk," I mutter.

He does, grinning.

Number 710. The door opens easily.

Boxes slide from my brother's arms. "At least you got the right key." Yes. I walk in. It's empty.

Best room on the hall, though. Clean, spacious, with bathroom and study annex—more a suite than a single.

Good for you, Miss Coach. Chalk one up for the new Kemo Sabe.

I lean out an open window and look down at the courtyard, opposite side from the parking lot. Hear footsteps coming: my father. Shitty music howling from down the hall. But somehow, in this free-ride room, I can be above the noise now. No *señorita* of anyone's heart any more, but a big dark ice girl, hovering over all the hot afternoon in a thick still cloak of silence.

Wisdom Teeth

ﭏ ﭏ ﭏ

(E L L I E)

Danny and I have always had this pact: You come with me to my dentist, I'll go with you to yours. The pact remained in effect through childhood and adolescence—even when we went to different schools. When we both wound up at Northern Massachusetts—which was the only institution giving scholarships to East Coast mediocrities that spring—we celebrated together, and the dental pact was reconsolidated. So he was with me the last time, two days before we left for senior year. Wisdom teeth are basically the worst.

It's too weird. What they do is, before they rip them out, they give you pills and Novocain and this gas and you just soar through the ozone. Later I had blood-soaked cotton wadded into both sides of my mouth. Danny got scrips for painkillers and antibiotics, then held my arm all the way down in the elevator.

I watched him hail a cab. We were both wearing wraparound sunglasses with mirrored lenses. Flying on Novocain and Valium, I felt like some kind of branded calf, numb from the chin up, wobbly from the neck down. A Checker stopped and, inside, we propped our feet on the fold-out stools. I could sense without feeling that blood was dribbling between my lips. He dabbed my face with a tissue then—the kindest, softest gesture in the world—and that's when he said it for the first time. Out of nowhere.

"Ellie," he said, "you have got to tell them."

No way, dude.

I didn't even try to respond, though, just waved the foolhardy notion off and bounced miserably when our cab hit potholes. I wanted pain to break through and start for real, because it would drown out the torture in my head.

"You've got to. Because I personally cannot go on any more being, like, the surrogate boyfriend at weddings. I am too committed to Gary. You've got them all thinking that the worst-case scenario is you marrying me, old faithful, their favorite *shiksa*—"

"*Shegetz*," I said, spitting blood.

"Whatever. I can see all the raised eyebrows now." He sucked in his cheeks, rolled his eyes the way he always does when imitating his parents or mine. Usually it makes me laugh but that day it made me hate him, so much that I had to close my own eyes a minute in case he saw it—the hatred, I mean—jetting out of me like laser beams. He didn't, though. "*Nu*, Zischa? What's with the Alonzo boy? Any good news? So he's a *goy*, so what? like they say, if it works don't fix it! Tell the two of them to maybe take a shit or get off the pot, if you know what I mean!"

I knew. But couldn't help resenting him, even more than usual. If I hadn't felt like chucking up my very guts I would have said something, too, when we turned onto 14th Street— told him he wasn't funny any more, and to leave me alone about it. Told him that ever since he started seeing Gary—the Great Gary Hesse, grad student extraordinaire, in truth a straw-haired bespectacled nobody who I keep calling Rudolf or Hermann by mistake—he has been a real goading pain in the posterior about my lack of a love life. And I wanted to tell him, too, to keep his Wop-Spic hands off my people. Because I was in this very foul, very racist mood.

It occurred to me that Danny was always telling me what to do. How much weight to lift. What girls were my type, and who he thought I would look *aesthetically pleasing* alongside of. What clothes to wear. What classes to take.

Like this stupid lit course on Hawthorne and Melville you have to be a junior or senior to get into, he said that I *had* to take it, absolutely *had* to. So I waited for it until now, senior year, like I was waiting for the Messiah, and I dropped Journalism 458 because it meets at the same time, and all the while he was telling me how I wouldn't regret it, how the professor, Kay Goldstein, was this fabulous woman who knew everything about everything and how he thought she was kind of riveting and sexy in a plump lipsticky sort of smart Jewish way, in addition to which he thought maybe she was gay—at least he had heard rumors to that effect—but it didn't matter anyway because she was just the best teacher in the world, she had made him, on several occasions, want to put his head in his hands and get down on his knees and just weep with insight and compassion.

I listened to all this as if it was the word of God, not just of Danny Alonzo. I signed up for the course. And then it turns out that over the summer this once-in-a-lifetime Dr. Kay Goldstein has dropped dead, and some nobody is going to teach it instead.

We went past the Projects, sun glinting like a spider's web of light through the cracked windshield. He reached over and brushed my forehead with his knuckles. For a moment, I wanted to cry.

"It'll be all right, Ellie. You'll see."

I kept the sunglasses on but gave a squinty look.

"When you tell them, it's like walking on the moon without a spacesuit. You sweat. Your heart goes crazy. You can't breathe. But you do it, and so do they, and before you know it the moon walk is over and you're coming back alive."

Then what? I thought, hoping maybe he'd shut up for a change. He didn't.

"Not that they jump for joy, or anything. I mean, who wants to hear that the seed of their loins has gone queer? But they get over it. They do. And you know what?"

What, jerk?

"You feel freer in a way. You feel, like: Okay, now I am liberated. I am free to finally love someone."

I cried, keeping my mouth shut tight and the blood in it. Tears gathered under the bottom rim of my sunglasses, spilled down both cheeks. He took another tissue and silently wiped them off.

I knew, all of a sudden, what the tears were for. They were for wanting love, and for dreading loss—loss of everything I'd ever had: Zischa. Lottie. My people. My home. Wanting love so much I was willing to pay the price and give all that up eventually, if I had to—even my present, and my past.

See, I wanted it so badly—to love, and to be free—but I wasn't quite ready for it. And because of all that, I was crying.

Danny paid the fare, helped steer me off the sidewalk into the stuffy old hallway, barely lit with this ancient sort of imitation-rococo lighting they keep threatening to renovate but never do. The elevator was busted again. Definitely bad news: I would need him, now, to aid my crawl up five flights.

It would be a triumph for Lottie, though, who never takes elevators if she can help it. Carrying bags of groceries up five flights after work, week in, week out. Cradling abandoned dogs, garbage-slathered kittens, in her arms, up five flights to bathe them and bandage them, down five flights to the street and the veterinarian's office near Houston where she made sure they had their shots, bought medicine for their injuries and diseases with money we did not have, posted adoption notices on the bulletin board and brought them back home, up five flights to wait. Never kept an animal more than two months. But never failed to see one adopted. *All in good homes!* she'd boast. She'd cross-examine prospective pet owners like some social service demon, each question geared to root out hidden cruelties and passions. Scuttling past elevators with a visible shudder.

Railroad cars, she says, *prison cells. They box you in—and then, who knows?*

Whenever she says something like that I get an image in my head: This old daguerreotype of her, Lottie as a young woman, with hair piled high on top of her head and these very, almost, art-deco frills around her neck, and Oskar, her baby boy—*My Oskar!* she would say, *seven months! a joy!*—swaddled in lace and blankets, proudly cuddled on her lap.

Also I get this other image: baby teeth, taffeta discolored with dried blood. Smoke blows over it in the Polish wind, German wind. You can smell human hair in the wind.

For plenty of years, growing up, I went to sleep with bedtime stories like that. I went to sleep with puppy tails slapping my pillow, cuddling balls of living fur I'd never be allowed to keep, wedged between the beat of cats' hearts and Woolworth's clocks—calico, electric, gray tabby, windup. Smell of vaccinations. Dreams of tattoos. Until I stopped begging *Please Lottie, please may I keep them?* and she and Zischa had a fight, and then—for a long time—she would not bring them home at all.

* * *

Those were the years I'd punch kids out in the playground for teasing Danny. Soon, though, he discovered free weights and biceps and he was punching them out himself. And I was in another school, beating other girls at the forty-yard freestyle—all our swimming done in a crumbling twenty-yard city pool we'd take a bus to for practice four nights a week, with once-weekly meets on Saturdays. Coaching courtesy of Mr. Marachietti, a boys' gym teacher who had volunteered for the job—and who, unlike others I have had the displeasure to swim for since, at least never did any harm. He was a big, balding guy who used to get red in the face and jump around on the wet pool tiles when you did a fast set, almost falling on his butt every time, and he called all the girls Miss. Actually, Mizz.

Mizz Marks! he'd yell—pronouncing it *MAWKS*—Mizz Mawks, keep it up! Just keep working hard. You could maybe get a scholarship somewhere, you know—pay for your education, finish a college degree. You'd get a good job then. Or get married, have a couple kids. But keep doing stuff like this, keep working hard, and you'll stay healthy the rest of your life.

I'd say: *Okay, Mr. Marachietti.* And do an extra forty as fast as I could. Just to see his big belly flop. Just to see him jump up and down flushed with excitement. Telling me good bright comforting things about my future with a humble, kindly voice.

"Come on, Ellie. It's the five-flight freestyle."

"Yaaah."

But at the bottom of the first flight I stopped, a little dizzy. Wondering about being boxed in, and the smoke, for the first time in years.

Lottie's teeth are false. So are Zischa's. The old ones rotted away from hunger long ago—the roots so frail, they told me, you could reach in and twist a molar out. There wasn't even any blood. And the roots were dark coils, like tiny worms. Odorous. Dying.

After Marachietti there were other coaches. Public school guys. YMCA teams. City league. The kids came from good schools and bad. Some of us qualified individually for the statewides in high school one year. I went up to Albany alone, and came in last in the consolation final of the 100 breaststroke. At the end of it my lungs and arms felt like they were filled with thumbtacks. But qualifying, I told myself, that was the main thing.

Afterwards I went into the locker room and sat on a bench. Just plunked. The floor was solid wet gray. Every other locker was painted orange, alternate ones yellow, and for some reason only the yellow ones were rusting around the edges so they looked like old egg yolks streaked brown. The rasping pains pinched away from my shoulders and thighs and ankles one by one, like insects departing on poisoned feet. The long aching burn in my chest eased. On my skin, drops of water turned to sweat. Tactility, disappointment, reality and the capacity to hurt in a beaten, throbbing way—all that returned to my neck and arms, fingertips, the backs of my hands. My eyes were a little puffy from the goggles. I'd had this leak in the left one and some chlorine had gotten in, blurred my vision, temporarily obscured things inside a rainbow-tinted halo.

I felt racing-suit Lycra soak into the worn-down wooden bench between my legs, leaned back against concrete and thought about how I'd done it, done the main thing. How I ought to feel more pride. And I watched some girl at the mirror, all showered and dressed, her hair dry, putting on makeup. A subtle powder-puff swipe upwards at the cheekbones. Definite cherry-red heart shape of the lips.

The door opened, air blew in and out. For a moment, with the waft of hot damp, I could smell her: baby powder and a tonic-like perfume over flesh. There was something else, too—a darker smell—something deep in a way, like a permanent musk. It was almost bitter, I guess. Sour. It made me want to taste it.

Not that you can taste a smell, really. Or give it a color. But I breathed it in as deep as I could. Then leaned my dripping head back against the concrete wall and shut my eyes, and for the first time since very early childhood no images came to me of railroad boxcars or molars or tattoos. I did not see little Oskar eyeless on the ground. No stained, ruined lace, no skeletal limbs bulldozed into mud.

What I saw instead was this thing, sort of, that was like a combination of color and smell and taste put together, and I didn't fear it but wanted it. It was deep, sour, musk red, floating outside of me but also down inside, in a place that had not been touched, and it was surrounded by a brightness. By this color-tinted light.

The door opened again, different air blew through. The cherry-red lipstick girl picked up her bags and left. But my new image remained. And I understood. In that moment, many things about my life made sense.

Consolation finals are sweet sometimes, too. Even when you come in last.

Later, when I met Coach Allen, she looked at my distinctly unimpressive, definitely supporting-cast-quality record and laughed. But she said, very seriously: Will you work this hard for me? Will you maintain this consistency? If you do doubles, if you always make practice, I think we can improve your times. I think you will add something to our program. *My* program—credit where credit is due. You will get your college degree, too, and maybe an education. But stick to the pro-gram, okay? Work hard. A few years down the line, believe me, your time will come.

Can you work that hard?

Yes, I promised, yes. I would work that hard.

Thinking, all the time, that the reason I would was because I'd seen something about her face, about the way she walked and talked, that reminded me of consolation finals. Maybe some time long ago she had rolled a dripping head back along con-crete, in a rusty old locker room after a race, after finishing last, and the deep, sour, red musk thing had come to her, too—and maybe, in that moment, it had given her wisdom, and peace.

On the second-floor landing I wobbled. Danny grabbed my arm. Saying Easy girl, easy. Seventeen steps just four more times. Take them one by one. And by the way, *amiga*, you should tell them pretty soon. They're not, like, spring chickens any more, you know. Sixty-five years old—whatever—don't you think that at their age, after everything they've been through, they can stand a little truth?

"Move it, will you?"

"I'm trying."

"Come on, Nan, burn. I thought you lawyer types were stur-dier." But on the downside of the trunk, which is definitely mov-ing too slowly up a clattering staircase, I weigh pros and cons and reconsider everything. Like, this upstairs room will exile me from life on the ground. Downstairs, Nan and Jean have access to the kitchen at all hours. Which is unfair, because they already have each other, whereas I have no one.

On the other hand, I will no longer be directly below a bedroom active with nightly passion, tossing and turning in frustrated loneliness—curious, impatient, full of aching envy—while two lovers proclaim their mutual ecstasy upstairs. Because that's what the hurt is for: a lover. Someone worthy. Although, at this point, anyone may apply.

"Ellie, cut it out!"

"Come on, Nan. Otherwise I stay *downstairs* this year and make tape recordings of you two going at it."

I push harder until the front of my T-shirt's drenched. Nan staggers to the second-floor landing, the chest crashes there, and she plops heavily on her end shoving glasses back up her nose with one perspiring hand, saying Thank God. I remind her she's an atheist, has never believed in God. That's not it, she tells me, she just always thought that God didn't believe in her. But if she gets through this year with passing grades, she says, she is prepared to change her opinion.

I pull the T-shirt out and flap it to wash air over my breasts. They feel clumsy, untouched. My voice sounds sullen.

"To think that you used to be such a raving radical."

"Well what about you, young'un? Miss Lady Regimented Swim Team Co-Captain Drill Sergeant of the Year."

"Oh, shut up."

"Coach's pet."

"I wish."

I do wish.

Even though Coach is such a pain in the ass. Uptight. God, is she ever. But very, very hot in this cool kind of thirtyish Puritan jock bitch way. Basically I guess just a closet case. Must be all that suppressed passion. Maybe that's why she went psycho on us last year. By midseason everyone hated her guts. At the same time, we all felt basically willing to die for her. You'd hear it in the locker room after some practice where she'd really tightened the thumbscrews—everyone would bitch about her, someone would imitate her, and someone else would chime in from the shower steam: *Aye-aye, Captain.* Underneath the jokes, they meant it. And as far as I know they're all straight chicks, too, so go figure.

My new bedroom's small and narrow. Standing in the middle with arms spread I can almost touch the opposite walls. When I tug at the jammed-shut window it opens with a shriek, chips of ancient paint falling everywhere. Hot sunlight burnishes the tops of trees and you can hear insects buzzing, a bicycle squeaking by on the sidewalk, a stereo blasting from blocks away, car wheels churning, but no air blows in to cool the sweat.

The term starts in a week and a half. Pretty much everyone who hasn't moved in already is doing it now.

Nan squeezes my arm, gently. "Don't worry, rookie. It'll happen, you know."

"What will?"

"Love."

Sure.

But this familiar shadow sweeps right through me—of yearning, of solitude. So that I want to blurt: *It's easy for you to say, you're older, you've got Jean, and you know what you're doing.* I keep it to myself.

The shadow feels bigger now, my parents in it. I want to take time back for them, before the piles of leather shoes, jewelry cases, perfume bottles, golden teeth, tattooed numbers on flesh spiraling into puffs of smoke in the sky, long before my birth. Before the act of love, or need, that produced me thoughtlessly—someone, anyone. But, like cowboys in some movie falling to their knees at a desert oasis, what they didn't see was the sign with skull and crossbones. End of the line. Seed of their loins gone queer.

Still, here I am wanting my own acts of love. Or need. Like my body and heart would emerge scot-free. Like any of me could ever detoxify.

I remember, when I pat Nan on the back, to do it lightly. The weights have made a difference—I'm definitely stronger, faster. Miss Lady Regimented Swim Team Co-Captain Drill Sergeant of the Year. And okay, yes, I have this minor thing for Brenna Allen. Minor.

"Love, huh?"

The words sound so bleak.

"Yes," Nan says firmly. "Come on, kiddo, let's grab some lunch. Jean's coming back soon and we're going to have to get to the library."

"Already?"

"Already."

"Is that what it's like?"

"What *what* is like?"

"Love. You bump in the library with your books."

"Sure," she teases, "exactly." Then tells me maybe I ought to just take it easy for a while, it looks like my face is still kind of swollen and shouldn't she get me a washcloth. I say no, it's my badge of honor. Even though the cheeks feel bad, and those holes in my gum hurt like jagged metal at the lightest tongue touch.

Dirt sifts off the window ledge to grass and cement below. Some guy from crew runs by, panting heavily in the still afternoon, strides long and muscular. It reminds me of weight-room sessions at the Y with Danny, him being so proud of his thighs getting bigger, and all the rest I can't ever think of giving up, but somehow must.

Another Indian summer, early September, with things about to start but not really moving yet. Like my love life, maybe. Or lack thereof.

He's right. I've got to tell them.

Lottie. Zischa. Listen—

But I can't. I just can't hurt them.

Sooner or later, got to.

They will feel so bad.

The high point of the week would definitely have been my evening *tête-à-tête* with Coach Allen. For which all of those long-suffering team ingrates are, without knowing it, in my debt.

Would have been, but wasn't. Because now—when I have worked all summer to get my sprint times down, and am poised for vast improvement in the one and two—now, my last year with this team, the year she promised all along would be mine—she is changing everything around. Saying: Sprints, the fifty, the hundred—they're really for nerve-racked perfectionists, Ellie, talented neurotics whose systems are geared for one perfect blast of effort. Form. Intensity. But longer events require more—what's the word? Equanimity? Inner stability. Maturity. Mental technique. You have these qualities, I think. That's why I want you to try IM. And maybe, when it crops up, some distance free—

Distance? Free? That was news to me. I started to resent her then, but said nothing.

"We'll change your workouts," she said, "and see which way to go. And another thing."

What now?

I cringed a little, sitting there.

"Karen Potalia was nearly put on academic probation last year. I've talked with her about it, and she's getting it all together a little better, I think. But we both agreed that being co-captain is too much of a responsibility for her right now. I am not replacing her, though. That leaves you. It will mean more work. Can you handle it?"

"Yes," I said numbly.

For you.

"I want you to keep a hand on the pulse of this team. Let me know what you feel there."

Sure, Coach. Just pile it on.

But the week's real low point is buying books. Especially for this regrettable lit course I have got myself into—as luck would have it, its many, many assigned readings stacked high.

The temperature is an even hundred degrees outside. The bookstore a swirl of insanity-provoking, falsely lit activity. Day-Glo highlighters and the flaming-pink 350-page notebook with optional binder are apparently their hottest-selling items. Meanwhile all the zit-faced freshmen flashing parentally bestowed credit cards are shoving me aside.

Part way through my book-buying spree, which I cannot afford if our phone bill is also to be paid, the air-conditioning blows out. And I realize that I'm fighting with this tall, very hefty girl for the last remaining copy of some 800-page tome. She actually got to it before me—by a mere second—but here we are, sweat trickling, paper rustling, her holding one end of the book and me the other.

I look up. Thick shoulders, puffy face. Big dark eyes set in olive-gray sockets—it's the kind of flesh you have after you've been totally, totally sick for a long time. And the face seems strange being so pale. Odd somehow. The lips are slightly African-looking, and the nose—like she ought to be brown instead. She just lets go.

"Um—sorry."

"No," I say, "go ahead, my pleasure, I mean, take it, it's yours. The bitch is dead, anyway."

"Huh?"

I drop it into her basket. Which sets off a chain reaction, causing everything else in there—pens, highlighters, notebooks, paper clips, Scotch tape, and what seems like several dozen thousand-page novels by these nineteenth-century bores who simply could not shut up—to spill over the sides, hitting the rim of my own basket, creating a regional disaster between us. Heat gets under my skin, makes my gums hurt more. For a moment I want to jump up and down and stomp on things. Then I just want to cry.

"I'm sorry!" she blurts.

"Well, *chill*," I hiss, "it's not *your* fault."

I remain relatively calm, though. It's that childhood training. *Not a peep,* Lottie would tell me, *good girl. Not a sound.* And I'd sit, very still, trying not to breathe. Waiting for her to come back from the vet with some small salvaged creature. So quiet you could hear flies land on the fire escape.

I kneel in the aisle and sort things out. My basket. Hers. Everything's together in a heap. I start separating books. Hold up the ill-fated paperback, its cover this incredibly rotten picture of some blond sailor, with a boat and a fish in the background, and reach up to hand it to her.

But she's gone.

There are only other people in the aisle, buying texts for Journalism 458. Japanese 202. Advanced Javanese.

Her books, markers, pens and tape are stacked next to mine now. It strikes me that in some way the ashen face looked familiar. But I can't really place it. For a moment this weird thought occurs to me: to wait, kneeling there, until she comes back. Small and still in the sweaty afternoon.

Not a peep, *schatze.* Not a sound.

But I stand instead, put my stuff in my own basket and then, seeing that she has been so kind as to leave it, take the last copy of the book that started everything and tuck it under my arm. The front cover's bent backwards from the spill, a bunch of page corners twisted down. Maybe they'll give me a discount.

*　　*　　*

Karen Potalia whispers that she has something to tell me. I rub her back gently and say I already know. There are tears in her eyes. I like Karen—another hard worker, from a big family down in Boston—she does a pretty decent 200 breaststroke and fly. Always puts on perfect makeup before and after a meet. Last year she got engaged to this guy who goes to school in Rhode Island and wants to be a teacher.

Our locker room has been steamed, scraped, repainted. Every locker a fresh-coated shining white. Even the showers are dripless, the walls sharp and dry, the only smells clean gusts of chlorine and pH factor, pine disinfectant, Windex.

"You may ask yourselves, What's in it for me?"

Brenna Allen is stalking. Each year, a different theme. Back and forth in front of the benches. Eyeballing every face to make sure we are all riveted, simply riveted.

"What's in it for me if I help my team win—if I help even one other person win—at a cost to myself? What if I do so many relays there's nothing left in me for my own *individual* race? Or I work, and I work, and I cheer on everybody else, maybe I get thrown into a new distance, a new event, and I just don't seem to improve? Now, where is *that* at?"

I gaze at her, wide-eyed, as serious as possible, kissing my last chance for a reprieve good-bye because I know exactly who this particular speech is aimed at. Then when her eyes fix on the next tensely eager face I zone out a little, let my glance wander sideways.

She is here. That girl from the bookstore. Looking taller than ever, ill at ease. Drops of sweat on her chin. Extremely familiar. But the name slips away—disturbing, almost there—and I try to catch her eyes without even wanting to, still embarrassed about the bookstore scene.

She doesn't look my way, doesn't seem to know I exist at all. And even though she's sitting on a bench with other girls, it seems as if the others are not even there, that she's all alone, big and uncomfortable in this clean white place. The place itself seems much too small for her.

"—Or you might ask yourselves: Who cares if I miss a couple of workouts? It isn't exactly a sin, is it? Certainly, *God* doesn't care—"

No, Coach, you're right about that. God doesn't.

"—about me—little me all alone in the water here—" This gets a big laugh "—trying to make good time, trying to win, trying to make the next repeat—"

Despite myself, I feel my face crack. Then the thing I hate worst begins—a violet blush, what Danny calls my scarlet letter. From the tits up, until my forehead pops out in a bright red sweat. *Next repeat.* She said that for me. I always do make it. Sometimes with half a second to spare—my trademark. *Hammerhead Marks, Make It Or Drown Trying,* some of them wrote once, in indelible ink, on the T-shirt I used for drag-weight. And we all had a chuckle. But I never wore it again.

"—Or maybe just trying to get out of bed in the morning when your alarm rings. But what I want you to begin thinking about is this: The caring, the will, has to come—not from the outside, not even from supernatural forces, no—it has to come from you. From some place deep inside you—from a place inside every one of you." She's in good form this year. I watch her move. Strong. Graceful. Her torso is looking great now—must be the weights. "How do we get to this place? For one thing, we *train.* See, when the chips are down, you must learn to preserve yourselves. To stabilize. To concentrate on what you know—on your form, and on your strength. We maintain self-integrity by maintaining the integrity of our mental and physical effort. We learn how to do this by training—training hard. That means practice. Because, eventually, you will find that no matter what it is you're going through, as long as you are alive in this world the truth of any experience is expressed in the body—and the body tells no lies."

Now she does that thing she does each September when she's giving the first speech: swivels around with her shoulders, head and eyes following—suddenly, dramatically, focusing in on one person at random to make sure they're listening. Because what she truly, truly despises is when you don't even *look* like you are. She shoots daggers around—but everyone is.

Aye-aye, Captain.

Still, she's a little tired or something. When her eyes flicker over my face briefly, then on to the next one again, they look bloodshot and weary.

"You will find your balance, you will learn how to maintain your mental and physical integrity, and sooner or later you will find that you're not necessarily alone. Someone else is there in the water with you, struggling towards the same goal. You're part of something much bigger than yourself. We just don't generally see all the ties that bind us, because they're invisible, they're more or less psychological. But, believe me: On this team, in this program—in *my* program! on *our* team!—they exist, just as surely as *this* exists." She picks up a towel from the stack. Laundered, folded, red lettering across it, waiting. "And sooner or later, when you're holding on to something for dear life—a dream, a hope, a goal—you will discover that others are there at the opposite end of whatever you're holding on to. You will find that training, learning the proper techniques for your own self-preservation, understanding the elements that make up your integrity of body and mind, automatically leads you to give your best effort *consistently*. But not just for yourself. It leads you to do your very best *for everyone else on this team*. Let up, or stop caring, and you let someone else down. Let up, or stop caring, and it's not just yourself you watch go under—it's others, too. So when you work for yourself—in *this* program—on *our* team— you must automatically work for everyone else. That means co-operation. Encouragement. That means team effort. That means we hold on to each other mentally, during a meet, when things get tough, and we just do not let go."

Okay, I say, silently. Enough already.

"Now. We have a lot of work ahead of us. There's a big, big prize that I want you to keep in sight—"

Zone-out time again. I look at the faces. Especially at the one that refuses to know I am here. Recognizing, now, the essential form of her: shoulders, thighs, flexible ankles, arms for days— strip the blubber away and she's some kind of swimmer. The kind I used to dream of being, but never ever would be. Because I had no talent. No breeding.

So, Big Weird Girl. Who the hell are you, anyway?

Because, for sure, you are someone.

Someone, anyone, Zischa used to tell me. It had to be someone. It could have been anyone. I lost two daughters and a wife, your mother, a son and husband. We met, we had a task to accomplish. Unite in defiance. Procreate. But we did not expect to succeed.

Unite? I wanted to ask. *Against what, Zischa?* But never did.

He'd go on then, talking the way he always does, about *them*— fascists, overseers, bureaucrats. Those people, he'd say, the *gray*

people, who would turn this whole world the color of birdshit—
if you let them.

Then: *Ellie, my child. You must not let them.*

Brenna Allen introduces me as team captain. I stand, take a
bow. Around me, they're all laughing and applauding. Then she
introduces some freshman, a new scholarship kid, does a really
good 200 freestyle and butterfly. And another girl, a walk-on. I
should listen for their names, but don't. We can get around to
all the Welcome Wagon stuff later.

"—someone who we're very glad and very fortunate to have
swimming with us this year—"

Someone, my child. *Anyone.*

"—Delgado."

And then I know.

Record holder, 100 and 200 breaststroke. National team.
World-class kind I fantasized about being myself, until reality
set in. Like, Mission Viejo, Foxcatcher type. Stanford, Michigan,
Indiana. UCLA. Southern. Pan Am Games. The Olympic Trials.
A perfect contender. Then that thing happened—the whole
team. It was, like, totally grotesque. All those champions, the big
big boys and big big girls. All the U.S. Olympic hopefuls, practically, down the tube at once. Didn't even wait for the East Ger-
mans to decimate them.

You are waving faintly, Big Girl. Waving feebly from your seat
on the bench. Not standing to take a bow. As if you are, for
some reason, ashamed. Avoiding everyone's eyes. But you can't
banish remnants of recognizability from that face—the years of
color photos beaming artificially back from the pages of swimming magazines—once, I think, even *Sports Illustrated*—at all of
us high school and college nobodies.

But what is she doing in this division?

"Christ," Potalia mutters next to me. "Guess I'm dead meat
now. The game sure has changed around here."

But our Coach is judging everyone, eyes daring us. For a moment, the eyes have settled on me. Captain Hammerhead Marks.
I am expected to do something—something appropriate.

I stand, grinning. Daring her back somehow. Most of all, daring Babe Delgado to look up, and look at me, and recognize my
face, too—I want this very badly, although I don't know why.
But I put my hands together and clap, vigorously.

"All *right*," I say, with enthusiasm. "Watch *out!*"

I do my job: Stand and lead them all, applauding.

But Babe Delgado remains sitting as if she is more or less frozen there, big hands laced nervously together in her lap, pale face turned down, eyes fixed on the concrete ground.

In the hallway there's an almost continual scuffing of feet, basketballs echoing against hidden surfaces, barbells slamming on rubberized mats. I lean against the wall near a water fountain.

Babe Delgado takes some time getting her things together. In fact, she's the last one out of the locker room, and when she steps into the hallway I'm waiting. Then we're face to face. I think I can see something aside from glazed tiredness in her expression: something shrewd, almost friendly, flashing back at me momentarily from the big dark eyes webbed with red. I feel myself grin nervously.

"Hey."

"Ah-hah."

There's a wry tone to her voice.

But at least she has noticed me. Whether she remembers the bookstore, though, remains to be seen. In an embarrassing, needy way that is new to me, I want her to.

People jostle around us in the hallway. The doors at one end open and heat blows through, touched with a smell of something—the beginning of crushed leaves, maybe, and a faint odor of sweat. It seems like she might want to talk. I see her mouth form words once or twice, then the lips purse in a kind of exasperation. She looks frightened. I blurt out something to save her.

"Which way are you going?"

She shrugs. But when I head down the hall she walks alongside me, a good five inches taller, and for a moment I feel like I'm much, much younger.

And I'm trying now—very hard—to think of things to say. A passing sleeve snags the spiral binding of my notebook. She bumps into me and mumbles an apology. Then words are tumbling out of her quickly, as if they're very important.

"You're on the swim team, you're the captain."

"Yes, I'm on the swim team. But not exactly in the same *league* as you."

"What," she says faintly, blushing.

"My name is Ellie. Ellie Marks." I maneuver a hand from bookbag straps and offer it. She stops to shake it, her grip very firm—this surprises me.

"Babe Delgado."

"I know. I know that's who you are."

The hallway has ended, glass doors swinging in towards us. Babe Delgado's blush fades, leaving in its wake a sheet of sweat across a forehead that still looks all wrong being so pale. Nervously, she wipes it off. Something warns me to continue with the innocuous chat.

"Coming on the team retreat this weekend?"

"I guess so. She requires it, doesn't she."

It's not a question.

"Tell me something—did everyone always call you Babe? Or does it cover up some deep dark secret?"

This, however, goes over about as well as toxic shock. She starts to look strained. So, even though there is something repugnant and frightening about it, I grab her arm for a moment in a kind of pity, and squeeze it gently before releasing. Thick forearms. My fingers don't circle all the way around.

"Hey!" I say, "just kidding! Listen, do you have a class or anything now? We could go get some coffee—there's this cheap little place I'll show you where everybody hangs out."

"Um—some other time."

"Come on," I urge. Not because I particularly *want* to spend any more time with her if I can help it—especially at the present ratio of work to social results—but because I am suddenly flooded with the urge to be nice, to fulfill my designated role. "Come on, I'll even tell you *my* nickname. Now that's a horror story, for sure."

"I'm sorry," she says, "I can't."

Then she's down the hall before I can respond, walking very, very quickly, amazing for all that bulk. I ought to be pissed off but a warm, quiet pain fills me instead. Something in her has evoked it. So that, for a moment, I want to race down the hall, press her arm again and hold it and say: *Hey, hey, slow down, Big Girl, it is going to be all right.* But I don't.

The Team Retreat. Brenna Allen believes in it, says it is good for the individual mind and collective head-set, so we do it at the beginning of every season: a weekend away at this place upstate that has cheap cabins, smooth hills, woods and lake. We'll run together, do push-ups and sit-ups together, eat together, listen to her yammer on about goals and discipline and glory. Coach's intensive seminar in teamhood.

On the other hand, aside from workouts, there won't be much more regimentation for the rest of the year. I guess her theory is that it's better to start out with a lethal dose. Catch us during dry-land month and we're baptized, immersed before we even hit the water.

On the bus I want to sit back and plug into a Walkman, wear my wraparounds, shut out the world. My exalted team position doesn't allow for this, though. The freshmen have questions. Everyone else, complaints.

As we head farther north, you can see leaves just beginning to tinge gold, sense a hint of cold in the air. Our Coach sits in a front seat, right next to Babe Delgado. Neither of them appears to be saying much. Delgado stares out the window.

After lunch there, and cabin assignments—I'm stuck with the freshmen, one of whom spends a great deal of time bemoaning the lack of a suitable electrical outlet for her blow-dryer—there's the usual: talk, medicine ball, more talk, calisthenics, visualization. At one point we're all lying flat on our backs on a breeze-rippled grassy hillside, eyes closed, arms and legs outstretched, creating mental images of our race. I try, getting through each lap in detail up to 200 yards. I can push the details on to 250, then 300. After that, though, it blurs. People in the stands yelling *Pull! Pull! Pull!* turn into people laughing. I breathe in water, snort and choke, cling to a wall and then turn badly. It rushes by me—chlorinated foam and wake against plastic lane dividers, the hollow swoosh of an arm, gasp of breath, skin and limbs glowing in the bright pale blue like ghostly elements, breathe, stroke, pull, stroke, pull, up, around, breathe, twisting my mouth sideways over the waterline to suck in air. After a while I can feel it, a little—the rhythm. But I still catch myself cheating on each turn, cutting almost, dangerously, too close or flipping too soon, barely brushing toes against tiled cement, gasping lung pain, losing treasured seconds. Smashing pool gutters with outstretched legs. Scream of the ambulance as I am rushed to a hospital, shattered left ankle wrapped in ice, and multiple murmurings in the background: *See, Coach, you should have let her stick with the one and two. Never should have made her do distance. Oh, why? Why?*

Enough already.

I open my eyes to blindingly sunny sky, puffs of clouds, Brenna Allen gazing down at me with a hard, dark irony in her face.

"Are you all right, Ms. Marks? You look like you're in pain."

"Last hundred!" I shriek. "Oh no! It's the wall!" And everyone around me laughs, their female tones light, giggling, sharp music in the bright, bright air. I grin up at her mirthlessly and don't laugh at all. And I can tell by the glint of understanding in her eyes that she knows, how for just that moment, I hate her.

Her lookout post, we call it—the porch to Coach's cabin, scattered with broken-down old lawn chairs that she's folded and stacked neatly in a corner. Except the one that she sits in herself every night after dinner, facing out to the lawn and lake and mossy-smelling woods, watching.

That first evening I'm heading past the lookout post on my way to shower. She's sitting there, legs crossed and feet propped on a porch rail while the sky purples, mixed gray and red around the edges of trees. She's entirely in shadow. I can feel her watching, though, and I wave.

"Ellie. Come on up for a minute."

I creak on five ramshackle steps.

"A nice sundown, wasn't it?"

"Yes. Awesome."

"Have a seat."

I perch near the stair railing, holding my towel and bottle of shampoo, ease away from a rough spot threatening splinters. Her face is hard to see. Once in a while, there's the flash of glistening eyes, white teeth. Sometimes a hand gestures, and the flesh seems to shine against all the sawdusty wooden dark.

"Well, how is everything going so far?"

"Okay," I say, without quite meaning it. Knowing, anyway, that it's not quite what she wanted to ask either. She smiles briefly.

"Keep your hand on the pulse, Ellie. What does it tell you?"

"Listen, Potalia's afraid of being cut. Come to think of it, so am I."

"Nonsense."

"Maybe you should tell *us* that."

I blush and am glad the darkness hides it. My voice sounded harsh just now, very clumsy, surprisingly bitter. Not my own at all.

Brenna Allen's chair tilts backward. I can't see her expression, but the even keel of her own voice doesn't change.

"I certainly will. I will tell her that. And I'm telling you now."

"Good."

"Now, there's something I'd like you to do."

The last time she said that signaled the end of all my modest expectations. I steel myself. More bad news for Miss Captain Drill Sergeant Team Workhorse. But this is the reason I was called up onto the porch and invited to have a seat. So I listen.

"I'd like you to keep an extra-careful eye out for the new team members this year. Especially Babe Delgado. Please try to be her friend, if you can. Show her the ropes."

I laugh. "Ropes? You think she needs *me* to show her the ropes?"

"You might be surprised."

I kiss even my dreams of relaxation good-bye. Last year. Last chance. It occurs to me that I was probably always destined to be just this—Hammerhead Marks, Coach's hand on the pulse, good for a giggle—nothing more. Destined always to strive, never to improve. Bus rides to meets will be me doing the mother hen, team nanny number again.

But in the dark, now, something's changed for me. I look in her direction without adoration or fear. Words leave me, as thoughtlessly as the day I was conceived by naked survivors— two beaten people rolling on top of each other—that was all it took.

"Can I ask you a question, Coach?"

"Of course."

"Why did you do it? I mean, make me change events? I've been working so hard! And it's my last year."

"I just think it's the right thing to do."

"Why? Because you're the coach, and I'm not?"

She nods. And we both know it—but don't say it: Some day soon, the answer won't be good enough any more, and I will want to hear something real. The truth, for instance. Babe Delgado.

"I don't like it," I mutter.

"That doesn't matter."

"No? You promised me! Stick to the program, Ellie, you'll have your chance. But now it's, like, you take away that hope, you basically just take away my faith—and you think it doesn't matter?"

"Not as much as *you* think. See, from my point of view, perseverance is really much, much more powerful than faith. Or hope. You'll find, as you get older, that you really don't always need hope in order to go on. You only need an ability to see things through. An active will—with or without hope—that's much stronger than any instinct for happiness."

"You're wrong! Completely wrong."

"Well," she says, "we'll see."

"What—I mean, what, exactly, do you think we'll *see?*"

"What you're made of," she says quietly. "We'll see what, exactly, you, and all of us, are made of. Things are shaking up and shaping up a little differently this year, we're in unknown territory, so it's a good opportunity—right? It's a good opportunity to see what we all are made of."

"I can tell you *that,* Coach. Personally, I am made of this— here"—I hold out an arm, pinch the flesh—"See? Skin, muscle, et cetera." I tug my hair. "This too. You can cut it, shave it, kick it—burn it—you can even kill it. And that's all there is."

"No—that's not all there is."

"What do you mean? You're always saying it yourself—all that stuff about the body, how truth is in the body—"

"No, Ellie. You haven't listened. I said that truth is *in* the body—I did not say that it *was* the body."

"Fine, great. Well, that's just a little too heavy for me!" And now I'm scared. Because I've never talked to her this way: challenging, mocking and nasty. "So where does all this leave me?"

"With at least two hundred new yards to learn about. Or maybe several thousand. But whichever way you take it, the rest of your life." The chair thuds upright. She leans forward. "I'm not playing games, Ellie—I'm serious, you know. You must set an example. If you can't do that by immediate accomplishment, you need to do it by your attitude. Pull people in, help them when they ask—even if they don't ask out loud. Sometimes the things you need to do to win hurt much, much more than you'd ever believe. That's probably why losing is normal, in the end—most people *don't* win."

"Why?"

"Because normal people cannot stand the abnormal pain of it."

I twist my towel, feel myself give in a little. For a second something in me opens up, like a tiny slit or crack through which you can glimpse things. I want to love her again. But the slit closes, leaves me lonely. I can feel how all alone I am inside: lightless, talentless, tiny and desolate, without a win to my name.

It comes to me as a little voice. When I listen, it's a plea. But when I say it out loud it is merely bitter.

"Why me?"

"Because it's what you *can* do."

"Thanks," I spit, "thanks a lot."

She chuckles—gently. The softness stuns and disarms me. "Ellie, don't be so hard on yourself. Or on me."

"What do you mean?"

"You know the old saying, my favorite one? Talent gets you fifty yards, the rest is all just guts and work."

"Sure. And then there's Babe Delgado."

"Ah," she says, "but it's true for her, too."

Closest she has ever come to being motherly. For a second I stop hating her.

"Listen, Ellie, just give it a try. What you simply cannot do, believe me, your body will not do. But at least unexplored territory is always interesting, isn't it?"

"Not necessarily." I stand. Feeling very angry, totally ripped off. Otherwise, I'd never speak to her like this. "And I'll still do it for you—I'll do whatever, anything you want. But I want *you* to know something, too: I intend to tell you from now on, *Coach*, when I think you're right. And also when I think you're wrong."

"Then do it," she sighs, tiredly. "Just do it."

I wait at the top of the steps facing her, as if there's something more to be said. Maybe I'm waiting to be dismissed. Or put at ease. She doesn't do or say anything, though, just sits tilting the chair gently, back and forth, in the night. After a while I turn and leave her behind on her lookout. The creak of the chair mingles with the breeze, with the faint leafy rustle of trees.

*   *   *

More talk the next day. More push-ups, sit-ups. More grassy outdoor visualization exercises, during which I take a nap.

Afterwards, she divvies us up into pairs. Running buddies, she calls it, and everybody groans. I am paired with Babe Delgado. Then she maps out a few cross-country courses to take—over a couple of hills, into and out of woods. The trails are marked, the other edge of the woods not far, and everything borders civilization. Unfortunately, there is no hope of getting lost.

"Half an hour," she says. "Run. Don't cheat."

Delgado, for all her heft, can really move. I find myself chasing her down, stumbling over field rocks and mole holes. Speculating on the general unfairness of it all—here I am, in what is basically the best shape of my life—and here she is, in what is probably the worst shape of hers—and she's cutting me to ribbons. Reminding me again that she has national-class heart and lungs, whereas I most assuredly do not. When we get into the woods, leave the others to take their own paths, I am nearly brained by swinging branches and have to face facts: I can't keep up.

"Hey," I gasp, "will you just *chill,* goddammit!"

She doesn't hear. Too far ahead, bouncing through the trees. There's a flash of flopping T-shirt, straining flesh.

"Babe!" I yell. "Slow down!" Then silence. I wait several minutes. Until I hear her big feet brush mud and moss, the rhythmic crunch of leaves louder. She's breathing hard now, standing right in front of me with a pleased look on her face that makes me feel mean.

"We're supposed to stick together, you know. This isn't a race."

"I'm sorry, Ellie." She says it gently. "Are you all right?"

"Nothing surgery won't fix."

She starts to laugh but stops herself. Then slaps my shoulder tentatively, says to come on, there's a place up ahead, we're not supposed to cheat but we can check it out, anyway, and take a rest.

We head off the trail at a jog, step through mud and bushes. Shielded by trees, we hear the sound of other voices—girls running now just past us along the same path.

What she's found is some old messed-up cabin, deserted a long time ago.

She moves the broken door off with one arm, quickly, easily, just shrugs it aside. Insects stop whirring, birds go into a chattering panic punctuated by sudden moments of silence. We step in on the rotting wood floor. Slats have been nailed across the windows, but some are ripped half off, and wherever the holes are light streaks in, zigzagging the floor in zebra stripes, making delicate, dust-laden cobwebs in every corner shimmer like tarnished silver.

When she walks across the room I notice how her legs bend backwards like bows, feet press out a little penguinish. All those years of breaststroke—it's a trademark—almost deforming, surely distinctive. She wipes her face on a T-shirt shoulder.

"Running. God."

"Well, at least the sweat's physical, not mental."

She heads for one window that still has shutters locked tight across it, wrenches the lock from the wood to open them. More sunlight floods in, and country air. I get the sense that she's trying to joke a little, but her face shares no expression. She turns, swallowing nervously, at a definite social loss.

"How are you, anyway?" I ask.

She seems startled and blinks. "What do you mean?"

"I mean, what's it like for you—you know, being here. Is it, like, totally freaky? Do you feel sort of weird, or just, I don't know, just happy to be alive?"

"Oh. I don't think about it much."

"Really?"

She leans on the windowsill, backlit by green shade, sun-lined shadow.

"Well, no, that's not true. I mean, I think about it a lot, but it's hard to explain. Some days are good. Some days are bad."

Then—I don't know why—because the silence makes me uncomfortable, or because it seems that there's an unspoken invitation in her own silence, or because I promised I would, I blurt:

"What was it like?"

"Pretty bizarre, I guess. Pretty wet and salty."

I laugh a little. She doesn't.

"I don't remember that much about it, to tell you the truth. I lost, you know, I lost some people, my boyfriend, and my best friend. So it's, um, sort of heavy."

I nod. She measures out the words like evenly rounded tablespoons.

"It's like, one day you're a certain person, then something happens and you're changed. You can't help it, you just are." She avoids my eyes. "Sometimes, things remind me. I don't really go around thinking that they're dead, or anything like that. There are times I feel they aren't at all—dead, I mean—and it's like I'm going to see them again, anyway, in a few hours. Or I notice something about somebody else, you know? And I remember one of them." She cocks her head. Her tone changes, until it is almost-defiant, shaky but insistent. "You, for instance. Liz Chaney—she was my best friend. Sometimes you get this expression on your face, or you joke around a certain way. And you remind me of Liz."

I walk to the window opposite her, look out and peel a rotting slat off to see more clearly. The sun fills my face, something like sorrow nags my chest, so for a moment I'm choking on this very strange regret, on a heartache throbbing behind some heavy weight that's been there all my life. I look out at the trees, hear her breathe across the room. Feel that, for the first time ever, she is focused completely on me—caring, now, and waiting.

I think of all the things I'm a replacement for. Co-captains. Lottie's Oskar, Zischa's little girls. Piles of hope gone up in smoke. But still, somehow, there's this part of me that never was touched by that. Or by lost races, tufts of kitten fur, empty pillows, infant ghosts that would come in the night. Another few thousand yards or meters? Let our Coach make a fool of me, then, what else is new? One thing I'm used to is losing. But no one ever could make me stop working to win. And if I don't know all that I am, or can be, I basically do know a few things I am not. Like, I am not Oskar. Or Zischa's girls. Or a world-class swimmer drowned and buried in the sea.

I turn to Babe Delgado. She seems expectant, almost smiling.

"Well," I say, gently, firmly, "I am not Liz Chaney."

She nods, a little embarrassed.

Suddenly I visualize like crazy.

A perfect mental image comes to me of this race. Burning pain in the water, pale gasping, blue foam. At the end of the eighth lap the wall disappears. The pool stretches on and on, shimmering, limitless. There is no other end. And I say, *Okay, come on then.* Say: *You fucker, I dare you. Just come on and be what you are. And do what you do.* One more stroke, pull, reach. Then the water disappears too, and there's nothing ahead at all. Nothing to move through. No air to breathe. In my mind I'm afraid, but reach out anyway.

Sunday

ऊ ऊ ऊ

(C H I C K)

Bren called on a Sunday.

Sunday. Bloody Sunday.

Saturday Night. But Sunday Morning.

It's the day all my depressive clients tailspin. They come in crazy on Monday, which inevitably unfolds as a litany of angst and lamentation. I always supply two extra boxes of tissues then: one near the armchair opposite mine, one near the couch.

On the phone, she sounded controlled but raw.

Or was it raw, but controlled?

I found myself wondering—not for the first time, either—whether her raw, ragged pain was a response to the control, or whether her control was a response to the raw, ragged pain. I suspected the latter. But, with Bren, you never can be sure.

Could she come down to Boston for a visit the following weekend? she wondered. There was some three-day holiday, Catholic, Jewish, national combined, coming up. Dry-land month almost at an end, her kids would hit the water soon. Then things would get really hectic. But for this upcoming long weekend the place would clear out. She wanted to see me.

Sure, I told her, I want to see you too.

Good, then. And there was this other thing—a special request—heck of a time to ask, she knew, but would I consider taking care of Boz for a while? She meant for several months. The dog missed Kay and was out of control, tearing up furniture, urinating on the rugs. She was gone too much of the time to deal with it, was getting to the end of her rope, she needed help. And I'd always liked Boz, always talked of getting a dog myself. Anyway, would I think about it? She had a lot of sorting out to do. Something concerning Kay's ashes.

Yes, I would think about it. But I wouldn't promise anything. Better bring the dog down over the weekend and see how things worked out, I told her. And I asked her to consider this, too: What would she be getting rid of by giving me the dog? What would she be losing herself?

"Don't torment yourself, Bren. Just keep these issues in mind, okay?"

"Okay," she said. Obviously relieved that the discussion had contained a minimum of what she called "your jargon."

As I hung up the phone, it struck me that there was more to this business than just getting rid of a troublesome dog. Not quite the same as some infant handing its mother a used diaper—although there were elements of that in it, to be sure. But I felt entrusted with something precious instead. As if she was giving me a piece of Kay—and of herself along with it—to have and hold for a while.

There's this pain inside me, a client told me once, *that I can't get at to cure.*

He said it a little shamefacedly, sitting there in my office. A terribly proper, well-dressed young man with a face that looked like the face of the ruddy-cheeked, blue-eyed Jesus I'd seen gazing back at me in a clear suffering glow from the pages of my childhood catechism. He'd been coming to weekly sessions for six years at the time, sitting on the edge of my office's big deep velveteen couch every Friday afternoon at five-thirty sharp, and never leaning back. Part of the pain was for love, lack of intimacy. He had a terror, not of sex, but of relationship.

We'd made some headway, but the going was excruciatingly slow. I wasn't really sure I cared for him that much. I'd suggested more than once that he consider consultation with another therapist. But he insisted on staying with me.

Can you tell me about the pain? I'd ask.

He would only shake his head and murmur that it was a throbbing, deep inside, elusive yet undeniable. And when I asked how long it had been there, he said he wasn't sure—possibly since birth. At any rate, for many years now. He was dying then, although I didn't know it yet.

Our sessions continued—he was never late. In the winter, the windows were framed against a snow-brightened darkness by the time he arrived, and in warmer weather sunlight came rippling through with the sound of traffic from across the river. That year some of these sessions suddenly became very active, very talkative. Others were embarrassingly quiet, as if I was sitting in the presence of a blushing stone.

As his condition became obvious I watched the deterioration. He lost weight, so that his expensive three-piece suits hung on him. Next to go was the ruddy, beautiful color of his skin, which turned to a strange tone that wasn't white but a mixture of pale green and gray.

Week to week the changes were often dramatic. Before one session, I found myself anticipating his arrival by wondering what new physical calamity had befallen him during the last seven days. It was as if I'd given the illness primacy in my own mind, personified it—so that whenever he walked through the door it wasn't him but his disease wearing a good three-piece suit, nodding slightly, saying hello and sitting neatly on the edge of my deep, soft velveteen couch.

I caught myself doing this, and had to cut it out. But it was a good lesson in the frailty of even a supposedly well-trained mind: how easily we let the agony of an experience blot out its essential lessons—especially those of the frightening liminal stages of existence, like dying—while conveniently ignoring the human being who is enduring the transformation.

Of course, this disease deformed him terribly. Gone were the good looks of a South End Jesus. His neck and throat swelled, so that at times he could barely talk. His eyes were forced almost shut too, and his vision became minimal. He began to lose his hair.

During this phase of illness, he started sometimes to lean back against the sofa. And to talk more openly—not about the present, which he rarely mentioned at all, but about the past: his childhood, parents, school years. His first love.

Then, one Friday evening, he showed up in casual dress: blue jeans and a flannel shirt. Sitting on the sofa, he kicked off loafers, crossed his legs. The socks were mismatched—one blue, one gray. He began to speak, very gently, about things he'd done in his life that he regretted. How he had run from offerings of love at the first sign of difficulty. Had responded to the experience of tenderness in lovemaking with a kind of rage. How dare anyone come so close? How dare they try, really try, to touch him? To pierce the armor of his control? He had lashed out so often, then. Had caused considerable pain. Now, he wished he had not. And we talked about the futility of regret.

Another week went by. He came back, on time as usual, wearing a baseball cap, crossed his legs on the couch and sat there looking very dignified.

Lately, he said quietly, he'd been thinking a lot about his health.

Sometimes it was hard for him to believe that he was only one man any more. The illness had taken on a personality, often seemed to be lying next to him in bed, like a Siamese twin. He spoke to it, pleaded with it, cursed it. Wished it death—knowing that when it died, so would he. There were even times, he said, when he'd come close to giving it a name.

What name would you give it? I asked.

My own, he said. And wept.

Some invisible weight seemed to fall on him so that he swayed sideways, collapsed on the couch, pulled the baseball cap from his bald, swollen head and held it between his face and the cushions while he cried. I crossed the floor to sit there and hold his hand.

But the following Friday he showed up in an ebullient mood.

It was his twenty-eighth birthday, he told me, and I ought to congratulate him.

"Congratulations," I said.

He handed me a thick paperback, with an illustration of a snow-capped mountain shrouded in multicolored mist on the cover, and declared that he had a favor to ask. He'd like the remainder of our sessions together to be more lighthearted. It was a bit of an imposition, he knew, not at all what I was generally paid for—but he was having trouble reading these days, and wondered if I'd mind spending our time together, each Friday, reading various portions of this book to him?

With some hesitation, and a few professional misgivings, I agreed.

So during our next few sessions I read out loud.

Once, I looked up and realized I was no longer in control of my own office. My power had fled, something else had taken its place. It wasn't him, really—although, at first, it seemed that way—it was some other force, an almost tangible one, that was very present in the room, that entered and left with him. And it wasn't the disease, either. But it was a strong thing, hovering, waiting. At times it seemed dangerous. At other times benign. Welcoming. Almost loving.

I turned back to the book then, in which a doctor was reprimanding a patient. I read, and felt tears swell, spill, peppering the thin page with blister-like water marks as I understood that to serve doesn't necessarily mean to cure, or even to alleviate.

The following Friday he didn't bring the book along. Colorless clothes hung from his frame as he settled quietly on the couch and said nothing. The two of us sat in a strangely comfortable silence.

I realized something else had taken place in him over the past week, another change that wasn't entirely physical. His body was emaciated, bent, fragile now, inconsequential—a ruined stick around which cloth wafted like a scarecrow's suit. But his head seemed enormous. Swollen, barely recognizable, it was omnipresent. As if all the weight of his body had gone straight up there. His tortured cheeks glowed, making the face almost luminous.

There was a difference about him, too—as if something new shone through even the luminosity—an unspeakable, nameless substance that was terrible, but also extraordinary. He was running a high fever. Even across the room, I could feel heat radiate.

Finally, he turned his head sideways to see me better out of the slits of eyes. Then he said something very strange. At first I thought it was just feverish delirium. Or maybe there were lesions on the brain now. Then I understood.

"I felt very frail this morning. Very light. Like I could fly. And you have to stop holding me down."

I reached to turn off my clock—set to go off in another two minutes, signaling the session's end. What I did next was sheer instinct, it certainly didn't come out of clinical psychology texts. I crossed over to sit beside him on the couch, and we faced each other. And I told him, very slowly, that I knew. That I thought we'd done a lot of work together over the past seven years. That, as far as I was concerned, he'd grown tremendously, and that I had been a fortunate witness to his maturation process. So—with his consent, of course—I now felt entirely comfortable with the thought of terminating his therapy. We could do so now, or the following week. Or we could take longer, if that was what he wanted. Anyway, I would always be available to him if he needed help. He could always call me.

"You, too," he said. "You can always call on me. If you're ever in trouble, or have need. You can call on me any time."

We stood and shook hands, hugged each other. I could feel the bones of his shoulders and ribs knobbing out against the flesh. He left then, and died on Sunday.

Kay and I were friends, but it was always a difficult friendship. We competed for the same things—including Bren. Kay won. I didn't fight it. Bren was too crazy about her.

And I loved Kay, too—for her savvy, for her mind.

But she and I clashed sometimes. Our styles were different. It was a cultural thing, I think: her with the Jewish guilt, me with the Catholic. Or, as she said once, the spikes *she* nailed into her own hands and feet were, at least, purely *metaphorical,* whereas she wasn't sure about mine. Then she grabbed my hands, palms up, searching ostentatiously for stigmata. Very controlling. Mildly insulting. I told her, later, that it had made me want to slug her.

Still, she was good for Bren in so many ways.

And I respected her when she said she didn't want to see me any more. It was too depressing, she said, she hoped my feelings weren't hurt.

So I stopped going up there and just called on the phone a lot. At that point, I was more concerned for Bren than for Kay. Because, in some way—in the way she always knew how to be— Kay was all right. She understood herself. And resented dying horribly. Like most of us, she loved as much as she could. Often, not enough. But she tried, up to the end, to get better at it.

For all those reasons I could say good-bye to her when she chose. I could cry, and let her go.

* * *

Bren is, always has been, so different. A stoic. Borderline noncommunicative.

The thing she calls "the incident," for instance, was a full-fledged kiss that surprised us both. It had force and sincerity, and a kind of tenderness. But at the time we were much too young to make anything of it.

Things would be made for me of other kisses, with other women. But the truth is that while my brothers and their wives, my friends and their lovers, built relationships that seemed suited to the long run—I have so far failed at lasting intimacy. Every day of the week, I tell myself, I work through the gamut of human woes with an emotionally suffering clientele. But who am I in my own life, really, to act the expert?

In the middle of berating myself, mercy will kick in. I'll examine, reexamine. Conclude that I simply haven't come across a real matching of needs, or of tolerance, in any woman I've loved. That love alone certainly isn't the whole story—and isn't always enough, anyway, to make a union stand or endure. Some women marry men, some women other women. And some of us live alone. The last two options are mine. Heads or tails, I say, I'll have to keep feeling it all anyway—in my life, in my work. I will have to make the best of it.

Sometimes, after all this internal babbling, mercy kicks in in the form of an order. Spoken only once to me out loud—by Bren, actually, long ago: *Shut up, Chick. You talk too much.*

And the damnedest thing about my relationship with Bren is that, without having much in common except for the fact that we both fall in love with women, we've been friends for so long. Over the years, I found that when she was out of my life I didn't miss her. Although I'd think about her often.

"Hiya, Chick!" She waves.

You can always spot her in a crowd: that stiff-shouldered, almost martial gait, fine features and thick dark hair—a more than handsome woman—and, from halfway down the block, Boz pulling her along with his leash, my first impression is of how great she looks. I wave back, she sees, but closer up I realize she's actually thinner and seems tired, the high color of her cheeks a little feverish.

She drops her overnight bag. The dog's jumping up and down

in friendly panic. I don't know which one of them requires the most immediate attention, so for a moment it all feels like triage. I sort things out: quick belly pound and ear rub for Boz, Bren in my arms.

"It's so good to see you, sweetie."

"You too." She lets her head rest on my shoulder a minute. Then pulls back.

"Long trip?"

"Mmmm, bad traffic. I'll make a deal with you—you take him, I'll take the bag. My shoulders are killing me."

That's when I tell her the first unguarded thing of the day: *There are no deals here, Bren. Just ask and receive. Or ask and don't receive—but at least find out why not.*

I grab the leash, nearly get dragged half a block with my other arm flailing in a distinctly undignified manner—Boz is crazed, and strong. But I collect myself, sweep hair back off my collar with one diva-like motion that makes her laugh, then pick up the bag too. She moves to fight me for it and I say, very deadpan: No you don't, Brenna Allen. Don't you butch me around.

I'm a pushover for animals, especially dogs—they're so needy, and, unlike people, their needs are relatively easy to fulfill. Open can of food. Fill water bowl. Take for walk. Reap endless adoration. Become instant center of another being's universe.

I write down "narcissism" as a diagnosis so often during the week.

But, practically speaking, that's self-love that excludes others. Not a yearning to *be loved* by others.

Although, in my book—off the books—any neurosis is just that: a distorted longing to be loved.

And then, of course, to love.

Bren admires the walls' wood finish, and a new area rug, imitation Oriental.

"The place looks great, Chick."

I tell her I'm profiting as people get sicker and sicker.

She knows where the guest room is. She and Kay slept there several times. But I take her into it anyway. Fresh towels are laid out on a chair. Everything's neat, clean, open drapes letting in sunlight. I want her to feel welcome. To feel ultimately safe. Boz wags along and jumps on the bed.

It occurs to me that I don't feel quite safe myself; this weekend has been worrying me. I realize I'm afraid I won't be nurtured at all, will spend the time being a caretaker and a mother—again—the way I do all week. But on weekdays, at least, I get paid.

I tell myself: Lady, you are a selfish pig. Your friend's lover has recently died, for Christ's sake. You ought to have more compassion.

So I head into the kitchen with Boz slobbering frantically after me, set up a water dish for him. Pull out some fruit and cheese for us.

Very compassionate. Very motherly.

I promise myself to be a good mother now, not a bad one. Because mothers are first and last in the heart.

And Bren, in particular, is the stoic she is partly because of her parents—both of whom were about as warm as an icehouse in winter—but especially because of her mother, who gave her a cold model of love to act out. To rebel against. She was a handsome, cold-eyed, hard-working woman, Bren's mother. She kept a neat and dustless home, seemed to easily maintain a considerable but equal emotional distance from both spouse and children, and punished, not with rage, but with silence. Her expectations were high; her disappointments, many. I can still remember visiting once, during college days, sipping perfected coffee out of matching cups and saucers, feeling the chill settle deep, deep down as she and Bren chatted, saying little, listening less. Every once in a while her eyes would slide sideways, and evaluate me. I felt like a hawk's prey being sized up for the kill. But the kill never came—I realized, later, that she had been frightened, too. And once, in the pale northern eyes, I thought I saw tears glimmer. But I wasn't sure. Years later I would share these thoughts with Bren. Suggesting that her own manner of coping with pain was—like mother, like daughter—not to reach for help, but to bear the pain in silence.

Oh, Bren said, dismissively, *that's just a lot of your jargon, Chick. I was never really close to her, anyway.*

Yes, Bren. That is the point.

My own mother was my hero.

Her name was Mary. Mary Logan Clifford.

Unlike her holier namesake, nothing was easy for her, certainly not giving birth. Five brothers surrounded me. Each labor had been long and painful. But she took on difficult things, family, and work, and love, and grappled with them as if they were the unwilling strands of a dry mop—wringing them apart one by one, making them fit in her hands, soaking and twisting and feeling them, thoroughly, in an attempt to know more, to serve better. Staring at her only daughter, eventually, with large loving eyes clouded by panic.

I saw that movie about the homosexuals, the one they showed on TV. Is that your life? Because the way I felt, watching—like what it must be to have a heart attack.

I had to assure her, then, that I did not engage in certain types of sexual activities involving whips and chains and stirrups.

She was relieved. Otherwise, she said, she would have worried about me suffering in this life as well as in the afterlife.

"Those people, your patients. They're homosexual too?"

"Well, Mom, not all. But most of them."

"They know you're that way?"

"Yes," I said, "of course. They tell me a lot of their very personal stories—I have to tell them a little about who I am, you know? It's only fair."

She liked that, the part about fairness.

But don't tell your father, she begged. *He'll have another stroke.*

Later, though, she began to cut things out of the paper and save them for me. Articles about homosexuality. Same-sex couples. Gay rights. Especially when women were mentioned.

Her death was quick and unanticipated. A day of hemorrhage, a week in the hospital. It wasn't pretty. Left no time for goodbyes. But she died in unconsciousness, eyes fully closed. And there was still enough body left to lay down in velvet, dress in a dress she had made herself, place her stiff waxy hands over the space between her breasts, put good makeup on. The sharp stab of grief—and then, grief's softening—she'd left to us completely.

"Here, Bren. Eat."

She does, setting cheese rind aside on a plate. I watch her chew a Macintosh apple seriously, thoroughly, the bites larger as her appetite seems to grow. When it's finished she sags visibly at the kitchen table. Autumn sun streaks her face a moment, splits it into flesh and ghost-white. Boz settles down near the water dish, against a sink cabinet. I sit across the table from Bren. Thinking how strange it is to see her here in my kitchen alone. Strange and unlikely, strange and painful. But not necessarily bad.

"Tired?"

She nods.

"Hassled?"

Tears shimmer in the eyes and dry without spilling. I have a sudden urge to feel her forehead, take her temperature, but wisdom rears its ugly head and I stay where I am.

From across the table I can watch her control at work. Quelling all that grief. Hunting it down, lassoing it. Tying it hands and feet, burying it skin-deep. There it is: the last pat of deadening shovel on fresh earth, open wounds. She looks up and manages a grin.

"Work's been crazy."

"Ah."

"You sweat for years to build a team that wins. I've got one kid—I recruited a national-class swimmer for the first time, Chick. This girl—"

She pauses, struggling.

"What, sweetie. What about her?"

"Nothing. Just funny that it's happening now, I guess."

"That what is happening now?"

"Success," she says. "Winning."

I ask if they're the same thing.

I used to think so, she tells me. But these days, I am not sure.

We take a walk by the river. Boz gets tired of straining and gasping and, after a while, calms to a steady trot interrupted by occasional sniffs or pit stops at the bases of trees. I can feel them both relax more. This reassures me, too—that everything is safe after all, that I'm doing things right.

There's a wind, a heavyweight eight crew out training in the waves, taste of fall in the air. Whenever a young woman jogs past Bren winces a little, turns her face away. I ask if she's afraid. This evokes a look of suspicious perplexity.

"Afraid that you'll run into one of your girls?" I tease. "Your *crème de la crème*?"

"Oh, hush."

I tell her, the way I always do: Bren, you are a closet case. Then squeeze her arm briefly to soften the goad. But she really is afraid, and pulls away completely.

"Actually, something sort of humiliating happened this week."

"At work?"

"Well, yes. I had a visit from a new English professor, Ralph Brown. It turns out Kay left a lot of files and paperwork in her office—you know, lecture notes, things like that. This guy is teaching one of her old courses. Anyway, he found some letters."

"Letters?"

"That I'd sent her."

She blushes. Wind whips the red face and I want to cool it with a washcloth. Boz shuffles through a hedge. The leash weaves around branches. We spend some time untangling ourselves.

"So. Did he read them?"

"I don't know. They weren't in envelopes."

"Personal stuff?"

"Some of it."

"Sweetie, I'm so sorry."

We sit on a rise, look across dirty, wind-boiled water to the city. She appears, for the first time, to want very much to speak. So I listen.

"He seemed like a nice guy. Skinny. Black. Thick glasses. He had a nervous tic—his cheek kept rippling. Very soft-spoken, perfect clipped English, I even thought he was gay at first, but then I couldn't tell. It seemed like he was trying to be discreet, you know—he just explained who he was, said that he'd found these with some of Kay's notes and thought I would want them back. And he kept apologizing for taking my time. It was strange, Chick. Really strange."

"It sounds traumatic. But also like he was just being decent."

"Mmmm. I thanked him and shook his hand. Then I went into a state of shock."

"Did you talk with him about it?"

"Yes."

"Well? How was that?"

"I honestly don't remember. I don't remember a word. And I can't even guess how he knew where to find me."

"Maybe someone told him."

"Who'd know?"

"Bren. Sweet lady. You'd be surprised at how many of our supposedly deep dark secrets are common knowledge. In the public domain, so to speak."

She stands quickly, firing off a nasty look. Boz growls and stalks away with her.

All of which is to say: Shut up, Chick.

I do. And follow them both, brushing leaves from my rear end.

"DeKuts says fear is innate," she told me once, about fifteen years ago—prelude to the first time I ever received that same nasty look. We were shuffling through dried leaves around a campus quadrangle. Avoiding some upcoming class. Surreptitiously catching the eyes of women strolling by. She'd come from a swim team workout and fatigue dented deep lines around her cheeks and forehead. At the same time, there was a healthy flush to her face, and a kind of rangy willingness, a suppleness, to her body. Unbending stiffness of shoulders and knees lay in the future. Youth has rubber-band resiliency—part of its grace a pure lack of consciousness about pain's fierce potential to limit motion, to make once-big things small.

"What does he mean, 'innate'?" I goaded. "Innate in relation to the body? Or innate in relation to the mind?"

"Oh come on, Chick. To the *body*, of course. Same thing, anyway. It's all one organism."

"Sure, but so's an octopus. Or an ant colony, for that matter. You have a lot of separate parts that make up the whole."

"So what? What are you really trying to say?"

What I really was trying to say was that DeKuts—whose influence over her I found distasteful, whom I hated sight unseen—sounded to me like a sadistic, misogynistic bastard, and made me, in some way I couldn't define, terribly jealous. But I wouldn't tell her that. At least, not then. So I lied a little instead, blurting out the first half-comprehended thing that popped into my head.

"That the body and mind are *separate*, Bren. When your mind's gone, your body may still be technically alive, but it's worthless. So nothing—certainly nothing like fear—is innate to the body. Fear is all in the mind. And personally, I think it's your wonderful Mr. DeKuts who's putting it there."

That's when she gave me the foul look, blushing slightly in resentment, her lips compressed. And said it, for the first and only time out loud: "Shut up, Chick. You talk too much."

I told her she was rude, a stuck-up jock. Typically, a combination of superficial pride and genuine core-deep decency kept her from responding.

It caused a rift between us, for a while.

The present rift heals quickly, without further discussion. We walk until the dog's tired, then head back to my place, where we feed him, watch him settle in a corner, twitching with dog dreams, and we think about feeding ourselves.

"Let me take you to dinner, Chick."

"Why? You feel like stepping out?"

She shakes her head, a little embarrassed. I understand and avoid saying anything; it would only lead us back to the old argument again:

But Bren, if *they* are there dancing in a gay bar, too, it doesn't matter if you know them from somewhere else, does it?

Yes, she'd say, yes, you don't understand. You don't have my job. You don't know all the risks.

Risks? What risks?

Suppose some rich parent on an alumni committee catches wind of the fact that his eighteen-year-old daughter, his pride and joy, is spending hours a day in a wet racing suit under the watchful eyes of her lesbian coach? Do you honestly think the reaction would be favorable? They'd be howling for my blood.

Why? You don't mess with those kids, do you?

Of course not! You know me better than that, Chick. I like mature *women*, not girls. And even if—I would never! I think that's immoral.

So?

So? *So?* You don't know straight people the way I do. You don't have to work with them day in and day out—and maybe you're lucky—well, good for you. But I know the way they think, and when it comes to *us*, believe me, their minds are full of sleaze. They think we want to jump someone's bones twenty-four hours a day. Perpetual sex on the brain. Especially in sport—anything to do with human bodies. Like we've got nothing else to worry about.

Then I'd sigh, and say something like: For God's sake, Bren. Maybe they don't *all* think that way.

But it's another argument I'd fail to win. So I keep my mouth shut, and make us dinner. I tell myself: Listen, lady, who do you think you are anyway? Marching around in the gay-pride band. Thirty-five years old, two years out of another rotten relationship and you're still going on casual dates with friends of friends, having occasional mediocre sex, no new love on the horizon, certainly no threat of intimacy to speak of. But you've got no problem preaching the therapeutic party line to others. No qualms about telling them how to live their own gay lives. Exactly where has your oh-so-open existence landed *you?*

Then it comes to me, like a blessing: I ought to be more charitable. More merciful. To Bren. To myself.

I realize that this saving grace of mercy flows, not from my own nature, but from my mother's. I thank her for it now, silently.

The sky's dark outside. Chill blows in the window. I move through a few minutes of blessing and peace while vegetables steam, rice boils, sea trout bakes. Sensing, behind my back, the thump of a dog tail on finished floor. My friend hunched over the table, now, in inexpressible grief. I move all the stove knobs to off and turn to her, reach for her. Her shoulders are shaking. Her face hides in her hands. But she isn't crying at all—no sound comes out, not a single tear. I offer arms, shirt, breasts. She lets herself fall against all of them, and I hold her while she tries to weep. Painful, I think, terrible. Monstrous aching inside. No cure for this loss, my arms around her a pathetic bandage.

And still, despite that, they feel right.

Dinner stays half-cooked. We talk about a lot of things.

Kay, the house, Boz. Her job. This new kid on the team, who will help them win big meets—some girl with a Spanish-sounding name I won't remember. She asks about me, too: Do I still love my work? Have I been seeing anyone since Marianne? I tell her, Yes. And: No one important.

Mostly, though, it's good to feel comfortable in her presence again. Even though she's a wreck, and I feel the dim jangling danger of unexplored emotions sloshing around in the bucket of myself, at least we're both finally, fully here—at a kitchen table, on a living room sofa, holding hands like friends, reaching to touch a cheek or shoulder.

Boz whines to go out and we walk him together, bundled in sweaters against the breeze from river and bay. Ambling between streetlights, fire hydrants. The dog seems happier, jumps against my thighs in some sort of supplication and gives a canine version of a smile, I think. I rub his chest. Taking a shine to the idea of him, of keeping him, despite myself. Watching us, Bren laughs. A full laugh, prematurely ended—she's cut it off intentionally like an unwanted digit. Walking back against the wind, she takes my arm. Whistles some tune. The good mood begins to make me nervous. It's like being on the edge of something— her grief the true reality to take into account, the more permanent underlying condition she is likely to relapse into at any second—and, instinct tells me, I ought to maintain a certain detachment. But I let her take my arm; because we're friends, because she has done it so many times before. I let her press the arm with her fingers; because, I tell myself, sixteen years means something, and it's okay to trust.

Keys in the door. A burst of comfort and warmth. Boz off the leash, light dimmers turned, sweaters off. We broil dinner, throwing everything together: too-dry fish, stale rice, fatigued vegetables. Bren eats with surprising appetite. Watching, I feel good. And I eat too. The danger signals fade away. Between bites she is matter-of-fact.

"Ever cremate anyone?"

"No. When my mom died they had a wake—the whole traditional thing. Billy got drunk again, it made Dad furious. They went into the basement and yelled at each other. Marianne showed up late, she and I had our last big blowout fight, in front of everyone. Pat's kids started crying. So did his wife. The whole thing was a mess. Still—it was good in a way. It was a time and a place to get it all out, you know? All the grief, all the mess."

"Well, when you cremate someone—"

"What, sweetie?"

"—They make you pick out an urn. I chose one—just any old one—it didn't seem to matter. Later, though, I had second thoughts, that maybe Kay would have wanted something special. Like a vase in the shape of an old whaling ship."

She laughs. So do I. She scrapes her plate clean, drops fork and knife across it with a sudden clatter.

"Anyway, they give you the remains in a plastic bag. It looks like dusty chips of gravel—not ashes at all, really. The bag is sealed. And you put it in the urn, you take it away." She glances up at me, her face uncertain. "I've been fighting with the bunch of them long-distance, the whole Goldstein clan. They told me the cremation was some sort of defilement, they wanted a regular burial—a coffin, gravestone, all of that. And some rabbi to bless her. As if it would wipe out everything about her life that they didn't care to see. Me, for instance. But she hated that stuff, you know. 'Keep me out of the ground, Bren!' she said. 'Keep me out of the ground, and away from those men in their little black hats!' "

It sounds just like Kay. I can feel myself smile.

We clean the table, wash dishes, wrap food up and stash it in the fridge. Bren dries utensils, places them neatly in rows in the cupboard drawers. She hums softly, seems happy again.

Now it's late. Boz is sacked out on the pseudo-Oriental rug. I scratch his ears for good-night, give Bren a forehead kiss and tell her to sleep well, ask one last time if she needs another blanket. No, she says, not a blanket.

In the bathroom I wash up, brush teeth, glare at the mirror and mentally slap myself around. I am putting on a little weight. Short-featured Irish face hovering at the borderline of early middle age, wrinkles etched around eyes and mouth. Always too serious to be cute; now, too old as well.

Instinct blinks some danger signal again, warning me to think a while, figure out what is going on. Bren. Food. The dog. The ashes.

Phrases well up in me—from prayers, I think, from long ago. Our light, our sweetness, and our hope. Banished children of Eve.

And I tell myself: Stop it, Caroline. Give yourself a break. These dynamics are exhausting. Grief's dynamics always are. But the day is over, and so is the pain. Just go to bed. Just go to sleep.

My bedroom light's on. In the hallway, she stops me.

"Chick. Come here."

I am here, I say. Then my face is between her hands and she's kissing me.

"Bren, no. Just wait."

I don't want to, she says. But there's a kind of terror on her lips, in her voice. I pull back, see the struggle—between the terror and her mastery of it. Part of the mastery, though, is a masking that doesn't work. The failure makes her sullen.

"Bren, listen to me. We need to talk this one through."

"Oh no. Talk, talk, talk."

"It feels like a land mine."

The mask falls into place and grins. "Don't worry, okay? I'll make it feel better."

"For God's sake, Bren—that is hardly the issue."

Then she says it, out loud, for the second time in sixteen years: Shut up, Chick. You talk too much.

She says it softly, though, and for a second the mask falls away, the tears refusing to spill are real, raw need mingling with fear on her fingertips touching me. Please, she says, please. And I know it's wrong, but what I know offers no alternative. Something else seizes power. Tosses me up in the rift between body and mind. Mercy. Desire. With nothing to betray but a vase full of ashes. She rocks against me, I rock back, and I just can't help it. I love her so.

A rule—one of Bren's, in fact: When set in motion, physical acts appear graceful if unimpeded, allowed to find their natural rhythm and inevitable cessation. Stopped midway, however, they appear clumsy, full of error.

Another rule—one of mine: When error begins, analysis follows. This is the distinguishing quality of human nature.

So it is graceful, almost perfect, to move into a room with one hazy light on, pushing clothes slightly aside, and feel this swaying together, this swell that comes with the electric pulse of mouth on flesh. To hear breath, only breath, not know if it pours in and out of my own chest, or hers, motion of her hands against a thigh, then this fluttering wave of wet dissolution, crumbling of knees, curling up of toes, and the force spreads through each nipple, arches the back of my neck. I let my tongue trail the perimeter of her ear, can sense her making short, short sounds that seem lost, and urgent. But in the middle of this trembling half-blindness I feel wisdom rear its ugly head again. And I begin to see. That her eyes are shut tight against something monstrous. Her face remembering pain. She is pulling clothes off left and right, very quickly—mine, her own—in a terrible hurry. As if anxious to get this thing over with.

That's when grace begins to elude me.

"Bren, wait."

"No."

"Can we just—"

She waves it away.

I sit on the bed's edge, half-dressed, half in and half out of a deep, enveloping want. Light blurs the walls. She has opened her eyes now but doesn't look up, concentrates on removing each sock, letting down a zipper, undoing buttons, until she is naked and, watching, I feel something push up inside me and cry to get out, examine the shape and breadth of shadows darkening her body, quick surge of pain in my own throat at this sudden rush of recognition: how much I adore that body, the skin taut over bone and muscle here, but a little flabby now with the onset of age there, altogether strong yet wildly imperfect—a body to be adored, and also forgiven. I ask myself if I can take the punishment of self-denial. Tell myself: Of course you can, lady, you're not some saint in a frayed-rope shirt, and this is no demon and no angel but your friend here of sixteen years. You are both just women, nothing more, nothing less. In the twentieth century, thankfully, and not the fourteenth. Where there are no heavenly rewards, you say, and no hellish punishments—only life to be lived. So just do the right thing.

That's when I decide not to fight the tide. Realize that I must not be the one who rejects, not tonight. Maybe she is making the right moves with the wrong person. Or else maybe the wrong moves with the right person. But only the future can show which is true.

For now, grace and perfection have fled utterly, clumsiness reigns. I offer a leg and she pulls a sock off with one strong motion that lacks even a touch of romance, tosses it emphatically to the floor, as if to say, It's a dirty job, but someone's got to do it. I offer the other leg. Same thing. Then stand, feeling cold and dry, peel down everything else I'm wearing, dump it all without ceremony, and sit completely naked on the bed. Dog-gedly, she sits beside me. I see it bubbling up just below the surface of her eyes and twitching lips, a barely suppressed panic. She is functioning, now, on stubborn automatic. Places a hand on each side of my neck, closes her eyes, pulls me forward to kiss. I press against her arms and feel them shaking. Run fingers over her breasts, where the nipples are soft and flat and the sweat is of fear, not arousal.

She hauls me down sideways on the bed.

That's when I halt all the motion.

When I reach—simply, surely, as if I've done it a million times—hold her face calmly in my hands, thumbs stroking her eyelids, gently, until she opens them, and looks, and sees.

"Bren. I've known you so long."

She hears, lets it sink in. For a moment, it seems she might cry. We watch each other's eyes. Until she rips my hands away like scabs, clamps her own hands over my eyes and pushes with force so that I roll far away on the bed, blindfolded.

"Don't," she says fiercely. "Don't look. Don't you dare."

Girls used to say it, say it all the time. At sleepover parties. In bathrooms. Locker rooms. *I'm getting undressed. Don't look. Don't look.*

Most didn't.

Some were like me, and—once in a while—would steal a peek.

I do that after a while. Peek across the bed, where Bren is stretched on her back over the peeled-down blankets, one arm covering her face. Her body's tense, the muscles fixed, and she seems frozen in the soft light of the bedside lamp. After a while I move closer. I dare to pass a hand over shoulders, breasts, belly, then back up to neck and chin, run a hand over the arm she's thrown across both eyes.

"Sweet lady. It's all right."

But I take my hand away. It's all this touching in the first place that caused everything, anyway, caused such tension and terror.

I tell myself I should have known. Then accept the fact that I knew all along, just ignored it.

The radio alarm's digital face glows bright green. Seconds shift rapidly. Minutes. Not touching seems to work. Soon her arm slides away to reveal the entire face, stiff with humiliation, apology. Her eyes meet mine. Silently say they are sorry, so sorry.

"Bren, it's okay."

"No."

"It is. Don't hurt over this. I think it was a mistake, you know? Maybe you're just not ready to be touched."

She blushes. Even in the dull light, I can see it, and am suddenly amused. Knowing so well how very properly mannered, controlled, terribly formal this woman can be. A stickler for propriety and discipline, stiff spinal pole, regular pain in the ass. And despite that, so sweet sometimes. So gentle, really. I've seen it, in the way she would touch Kay.

She clears her throat. "Do you mind if I turn out the light?"

"Go ahead."

In the dark, her struggle is palpable. I sense it. And stay well on the other side of the bed this time, avert my eyes to watch the glow of Cambridge streetlamps filtering through blinds, listen to an occasional car pass by.

"Bren."

I wait for a response that doesn't come.

"Bren, look—do you need to be alone? You can tell me, you know."

But she reaches for my hand, presses it lightly in hers. Then our hands rest together on the bed. Our fingers interweave. And I feel, suddenly, very tired. Capable of this, and no more: one hand, lightly holding. It makes me know, suddenly, certainly, that she was not the only one flayed by fear tonight; and this one action, this holding of hands, has taken all our strength.

She pressures my fingers. Her own are shivering.

"Chick—"

"What is it, sweetie?"

"The last few days with Kay, I saw something weird. It was once, when we tried—never mind." She tells me fractured, half-comprehensible things then, in between long dead pauses. Something about objects washed with light, and burning. I encourage but she can't continue. I wait. Finally feel her effort crumble on the other side of the bed.

I am praying silently now, thoughtlessly. Praying to any saint who might exist, and listen. To my own mother, dust in a dark, dark coffin, deep scar in my memory. Asking for assistance. Patience. For mercy and courage.

Holy Mary. Mother of God. Our light, our sweetness, and our hope. To you we something or other. Something. Or other. I've forgotten the words. To you we lift up our voices? To you? We cry. Maybe. Banished children of Eve. No. Yes. Banished children of Eden. Of Eden? Of paradise. Your different children, the ones locked out of paradise. Instruments. Of thy peace. So let me finally know it. You. The act of it. The art of you. Teach me the true act of love.

After a while I can feel her sleep. I ease our fingers apart, pull a sheet and blanket up to her chest. Then I leave space between us on the bed, huddle under blankets myself. Until I sleep, too.

She isn't there in the morning. Actually, it's Boz who does a perfect job of waking me up—licking my face all over, pressing into my belly with leathery tough paws. I pet, pat, pull at him. He grunts happily. Then flops down with his massive head against my breasts, gives me adoring glances.

Am I your new Kay? I ask him.

It doesn't seem to matter.

The room is mine. Entirely familiar. Yet there's a strange sensation, waking up in it now: as if the night is not over, is somehow still waiting to happen. I smell fresh coffee, hear water running. So I get up, naked and chilly, toss on a robe. I'm a sucker for fresh coffee. And, maybe, for other things.

Bren is rattling around the kitchen. She's fully dressed, looks showered, spry, avoids my eyes.

"I walked him already."

"Ah."

"Coffee?"

"Sure. Black."

I sit, feeling sleep's crust on eyelids and lips. Things seem mildly surreal somehow, and I must look a mess. She's whistling again—whatever monotonous tune she was whistling last night, just before we became graceful and then clumsy—and pours coffee into a mug, blows steam from her face as she hands it to me. The mug rattles out of her hands and scalding black spills over napkins, the tabletop, my lap, the chair. I jump, flapping drenched folds of robe.

"It's okay!"

She's thudded into her own chair and is pressing her cheeks with both fists, lips tightening. Boz slinks out of a corner and circles around us. I kneel beside her.

"Bren. Sweetheart. It's okay."

"I am such an idiot."

"If you're referring to last night, that was my mistake too. But talk to me. Please talk to me. Maybe it will help."

She shakes her head.

"You can't know unless you try."

She breathes, a painful sigh. "I don't—"

"That's it, come on."

"I just don't remember how."

"How?"

"I've forgotten." She blushes. "How to make love, I think. The fear of it—it's disgusting. I've forgotten that I ever was a lover."

"When you're ready, you'll remember."

"And here you are. My friend. But what do I do? I use you. I abuse you."

"Listen, Bren, that takes two."

I say this, knowing it's a fruitless panacea, poor salve for profound wounds.

"No. You don't understand." She stifles herself, ashamed. "Kay and I—"

Then, I remember her struggle last night, and think I know what it is she can't say.

I can imagine it, can attempt empathy, but in the end she is right—I wasn't the one there—exposed minute by minute to the physical devastation of a lover, seeing someone whose form had once been beautiful and arousing become unrecognizable, distorted. Mopping up every conceivable type of bodily secretion. Trying, in the midst of all this, to cling to the memory of desire.

To watch friends die—even a parent—that's different. Terrible, and all those things. But, in the end, less intimate. Not the same as watching the co-protector of your most tender vulnerabilities die, watching your own desire die with them. And if the love is there, you will fight it, fight against that extinguishing of desire, in any way you can.

"You don't have to," I say gently, "but if you want, you can talk about it."

"It's too—in *here*"—she massages her stomach. "But we would. Sometimes, even when she was really sick, we would. She didn't feel—attractive. I mean, it wasn't exactly the first thing on her mind. I think she just did it for me."

"Made love?"

"Sure," she says, wryly, "in a way. Something like that."

I reach to touch her knee, her arm, tell myself to back off. And wonder if I can ease any of this pain for her, after all; wonder do I even have the right to try. Because the pain is hers alone, in the end. Bren is the one who'll drive back north this afternoon to face life for one in a house built for two. The bedroom she shared is half empty. The garden Kay nurtured on weekends will be dry now, shrubbery and grass unattended, and there is furniture accumulated over the course of a decade. Kay's clothes are still hanging in the closet. Her insensitive relatives will continue to ask insensitive questions. Bren's own family will, as usual, be more or less absent. There is no one there to share it with, because all these burdens are carried in secrecy—self-imposed secrecy, I say—a secrecy, she will claim, imposed by the world. Still, no one else can step inside the pain of that with her. Not even a best friend. Not even a best friend who loves her.

I can't dent a piece of that armor, can't pierce an ounce of isolation. Here I am: this imperfect servant of suffering humanity. And I cannot fix a goddamned thing.

"Listen to me, Bren. I'm your friend. I am here for you, I'm not going anywhere. I love you, sweetie—don't you know? We can be pals who just hold hands if you want—"

"No!" It comes out a sob.

Then the tears—so many, I didn't know there'd be so many. They flow in nauseous waves with each sob, shake her whole body, go on and on for many minutes, until her hands drop to the coffee-stained tabletop and her eyes, dripping, haunted, meet mine.

"I can't, Chick. God, I can't! I can't see you any more."

"Why, sweetie? Why not?"

"You knew me with Kay. You knew us together. And when I see you, God! it reminds me of everything. I can't take it—you don't know. I miss her so much, Chick. In some ways, you're just like her. And I can't see you—because it reminds me, and I just can't stand my feelings right now, they make me want to rip off my skin."

That's when I do the last unguarded thing of the weekend: I grab her reluctant hands, stare sternly up into a naked face that I would like to soothe, shelter, heal, and smack—a face that makes me angry. Because it's so obstinately willing, even in this extremity of grief, to shut me out completely now, call a halt to sixteen years of friendship.

"Listen, Bren. You can live however you want. You can go home, you can crawl straight back into the closet you've built, you can lock it from the inside and throw away the key. But don't expect that that's going to make all the pain disappear. Just because you stay isolated—just because no one around you knows you loved another woman—doesn't mean that any of it, that any of the truth, is going to disappear. And don't think you can shut *me* out! I think I'm the best damned friend you've got, and that's true whether or not we ever make love, you know? I knew you with Kay—well, so what? I also knew you *before*. I've seen you being terrific and I've seen you make an ass of yourself. And I never stopped being your friend, and you'd better not forget that!"

Something streaks by the window then. A starling, dark dash across the sun-bright autumn day.

Sunday. It is Sunday.

This shuts me up. Deadliest of days for the lonely, the sick. Dead end of the week, when you imagine everyone else and their lovers huddling in front of fireplaces far, far from your own cold cellar of misery, holding hands, touching intimately, passionately, reading newspapers and literary supplements and sports sections, reaching for glasses of warm beverage and taking walks along quiet tree-lined avenues, going to brunch, making love.

Sunday, when your own isolation drips down in front of you like the dying tip of an icicle. Take a jog, a dip in some pool, a long solitary trudge through drifting leaves; nothing cuts the thick dull edge of it. If you aren't sheltered by mate or family, aren't happy inside your own life, it's a day of unavoidable despair. She faces all that now—and she knows it, for sure—another day of mourning alone. I squeeze her hands harshly. Kay was never mine to lose. But there are some things I've known firsthand in my life, and—without regret for it, or even sentimentality—loneliness is one of them.

"You need some time alone, well, that's fine. Just don't tell me to stay permanently out of your life. I sure don't want you permanently out of mine." It comes to me, like a sigh: fifteen years ago, our kiss. In a hallway, on stairs between landings, at a party. It jumped naturally out of nothing but the two of us and was sudden, wonderful. Then over in surprise and fear. Last night bathes me with a kind of nostalgia—the graceful part, anyway—until I remember the rest of it. "Personally, Bren, I don't think your closet ever *was* big enough for two. I don't even think it's big enough for *you* any more. And I'm willing to bet that it's not nearly big enough to mourn in."

She cries again, more softly now.

I resolve to say good-bye for a while, if that's what she wants and needs. Tell myself that in a little while Bren will go, I'll stay, and Kay's dog will stay with me. Boz won't mind when I give him the party line about how crazy it is for people to be ashamed of loving who they love.

Then I wonder if Kay somehow engineered this—this temporary bestowal of the dog on me. A last request? Postmortem control? She might have.

But I'm here to hold her lover while she cries, and, for a while, Kay lets me.

Holding Bren, I remember, and think I understand, what she tried to describe last night. The weird thing she saw, those last few days in the hospital. After something Kay told her. They had held each other, tried to touch however they could. A hot, bright thing, like fever, only it wasn't that. From Kay, but not really. And not from Bren either. But from everything. No. It was *in* everything. Everything around them. Always had been there, she thought—only, that day, she had seen it for the first and only time. Like taking the lampshade from the bulb.

She pushes me down with arms, weight, tears, so we're lying on my floor with the dog skittering around us, and I hold her against me and stroke her hair. Until I cry, too.

Is there something of Kay in me now? Crying because I will miss her? Holding on to say good-bye?

Loving the fact that I love her?

Big West

🐬 🐬 🐬

(B R E N)

First Friday in October, and after morning workout Bob Lewison passes by with a casual *Hey Bren, gearing up for Big West yet?*, reminding me of many things I'd rather not think about. Weekend conferences coming up. Right as the kids are hitting the water. Although, thankfully, our trainer, who doubles as my assistant, can run the workouts I've prepared while I'm away. Also, I don't have to present any papers this time around—just moderate a panel—the prospect holds an ugly, banal immensity for me. It means reading. Thinking. Tying seemingly unrelated things together, in public, in front of an audience, in a neat verbal way that must seem relaxed, casually knowledgeable, off the cuff. In addition to which, this unsought invitation to be panel moderator has upset the apple cart around here, in more ways than one. Grinning, looking hassled and older than he did in August, Bob stops to lean across the threshold.

"Pete's nose still out of joint?"

"Probably," I sigh. "What about yours?"

"No complaints. But sit with me on the plane down there, huh? I'll be editing up to the last minute."

He hurries away looking insane. I resign myself to mopping up another of his stitched-together presentations—which are never as lame or preverbal as McMullen's, but are nevertheless marked by impatience and a frustrating lack of clarity. Somewhat manic, Kay would say. Sophomoric attempts to philosophize.

I would have wanted to tell her, then, that there was nothing wrong with attempting to make the sport you loved a metaphor for the rest of your life; that whether the metaphor held up to the test of time, and truth, and life itself, was probably less important than the fact that some struggling human being somewhere found such comparison useful. But she would most likely have responded that I was just too prosaic. And, in a way, she'd have been absolutely right.

"Ho! There's our lady superstar. Coach of the Year, Bren—you're bucking for it, aren't you? Makes us look good. So stay the course."

Pete tosses a memo in the form of an airplane through my office door. It settles on some pencils and I unfold it: a warning against wasting department-issued stationery.

"Pete—" I begin, but he's already down the hall. Too embarrassed, too pissed off really, to face me yet. My chairing of this panel—at a professionally weighty conference for which he has not even been asked to submit a paper or presentation proposal—has been a blow to his ego, intended or not, a definitely perceived slight. He may now see me as some kind of open danger. Rival. It's probably for this reason that the level of competitive stress has risen significantly on the men's team; he must have them win, to prove his own worth. For this reason, too, he has ripped Mike Canelli off the redshirt list too early.

I consider chasing him down the hall to make an appointment for inevitable confrontation. But the phone light blinks and buzzes. I sit on the edge of the desk, pick up, hear the very young, girlish secretarial voice:

"Someone named Phil Delgado for you, on line one."

Ah, of course. Delgado, I've been expecting you. Though I did not know which one it would be—you, or the mother, or maybe even a sibling, an uncle, a grandparent.

I move slowly, slight smile on my face, as if through an often-rehearsed dream. A major pain-in-the-ass element of coaching—the athlete's family.

So it begins, I think; with the father. You must always expect it, but at the same time you never really know who will make first contact, or what they'll all have up their collective sleeve in the end.

I press the blinking button. Brenna Allen speaking, I say. Careful to sound calm and friendly. Then I listen to the pause, and the smooth husky vaguely accented rush of baritone words that follows as he introduces himself, says how glad, how very glad he is, to finally get the chance to speak with me. Genial voice. Inviting. Warm, practical, carefully measured words that you immediately yearn to trust.

Used to being a player, I think. Sophisticated. Convincing. Aims for class, competent operations, for respect. Generates money. Proud of his success. Good businessman.

"So. How is our girl doing?"

Conversational. Very good disguise. Unless you listened for it specifically, you would not catch the nervous undertone.

"I think she's doing very well, Phil. Physically, as I know you know, it has been and will continue to be a long hard road for her—"

"Well of course! Of course."

"—But, from my point of view, she's doing even better than expected. And I can't say enough about the quality she brings to the program—I'm not just talking about athletic ability, now, I'm talking about character as well."

"Mmmm. She's feeling okay? Emotionally, I mean."

Warning sirens go off in my head, just as I knew they would sooner or later. I remember to stay somewhat amused. To choose good, calm, neutral words carefully.

"Well, Phil, I can tell you that she's doing well in school. She appears to have made some friends and to be in good health. Never misses practice."

"Good. Good." There is a pause, during which I sense the impending pop of exposure, or explosion. I get ready. Usually, it begins with the third question. He breathes deeply and I hear it over the line: painful, sighing. "Listen, there's something else I need to speak to you about. It's about this matter of—well, she mentioned something to me during a recent phone call about a diet she'd gone on—"

"Yes."

"Do you know about this?"

"As a matter of fact, Phil, I do." I grin, try to sound entirely casual, hope that he will somehow sense it over the phone, and that it will disguise the fishing expedition I must now begin myself. "Do you speak with her often?"

"Um—well, yes. No. What I mean is that I call her a few times each week, but she usually isn't there, or doesn't answer. I guess we actually speak once every week or two. But I try to keep in touch."

"That's nice. That's nice that you do. Your family must be very close."

"I don't know, Coach Allen—"

"Bren. You can call me Bren."

"—Okay, Bren. How do you tell if your family is close? All I know these days is that I worry about my child. Because she's had problems with—around these things, you know, in the past."

"What things? Keeping in touch with you? Being close?"

"No! No. I mean with *dieting*. Starving herself."

"Well, I think you can stop worrying about that. This particular diet is something she decided on, in consultation with a professional nutritionist who works with us here. It's been specifically, individually, scientifically designed for Babe. Basically, it involves a reduction of sugar and low-quality fat intake, and eating enough calories of high-quality proteins and complex carbohydrates, and taking vitamin and mineral supplements every day, to ensure that she'll stay nutritionally sound during training and competing—"

"But she's not losing too *much* weight, is she? I mean, I just hope that she's not starving herself."

"Well, obviously I don't sit down with her at every meal to see what her eating habits are. But, from what I do see of her, she looks extremely hearty and strong. This diet—let's not call it a *diet*, okay? let's just call it a nutritional regimen—is designed for optimal physical health and strength more than for any particular kind of weight loss. As far as Babe is concerned, though, there's been some fat loss, some muscle gain. All the good things that come with training."

"Ah. Just so it's not too—too extreme."

"I want you to know, Phil, that extremity is not the name of the game around here."

For a while, he does not speak. Then, "Oh," he says wryly, "well, that sounds refreshing."

Both of us laugh.

I begin to like, but not to trust.

"Tell me, Bren. Do you think she'll make a complete recovery? I mean, come back all the way?"

"Hard to tell. Probably not."

"I mean, emotionally."

Emotionally. Second time he has said that word.

All this talk of feelings, of psychological well-being. And from a successful father, too; interesting. Usually, in my experience, it is the mother who worries about inner life. Either way, though, there is often this split: one parent puts his or her ego and energy into caring about athletic success; the other, into caring about the mind and heart and soul. If both care only about the athletic success, you may have on your hands a powerful and insensitive athlete whose life will one day smack her full in the face with surprises—all the demands of love and grief, for which she will not have the heart; or for which she must, on the spot, immediately begin to develop one. If both parents emphasize the nonphysical, though, you may have an underachiever on your hands, a self-castigator, who falls short of genuine potential; one who will experience a sense of physical regret and competitive frustration for the rest of her life.

When I respond, I do so with utmost care. I will hang up liking but not trusting him—which is okay; but it will not be okay if he hangs up without both liking and trusting *me*.

"Listen, Phil, I want to be completely honest with you." Which is not really true, but I want him to think it is. "Your daughter is a very talented and mature individual. I think you know that."

He mumbles assent. Over the wires, I think maybe I hear his strain. Choking of vocal cords. But I'm not really sure.

"And you also know that she's been through a lot. Enough, some people would say, to have killed an ordinary person. But here she is with us, alive."

"*A Dios*," he whispers. "Thanks to God."

"So when we talk about her, let's be very clear about the fact that we are speaking of an adult here. Whatever her assets or deficits, she's a grown woman. Sure, I'm her coach—and sure, she talks to me sometimes. But, out of respect for her, and for our working relationship, I think that whatever she says to me, whether it's of a personal nature or not, ought to stay confidential."

"Ah," he mutters. "I see."

"Although, certainly, if you feel you need to discuss something with her, I encourage you to do so. Directly." I am careful, now, to sound anything but hostile. Openly friendly and admiring;

full of praise; above all, kind. "Parents who really care about their children's happiness as openly as you do—well, that's pretty rare. And let me tell you, I think it's great."

"Well, thank you."

He sounds subdued. Relieved. I am, too.

We chat about weather, and other things. He is calling long distance, he tells me; he's on a business trip. In Miami. Yes, he misses the family, misses being back home. Although he has a few relatives there and, once upon a time, knew the city like he knew his own heart. The place has changed so much over the years. Still, some things never change. The heat, for instance. Ninety-eight in the shade, but air-conditioned hotel rooms. Glad he has finally had the chance to speak with me, one on one. Babe thinks highly of me. Now he knows why. She's been through so much pain, too. He's proud that she has the courage to live again, even compete again. He hopes she knows how much he loves her. How it is not *him* trying to force her to attain some standard of national-class or world-class excellence—no, not now, not ever. Because he loves her for what she is. Yes, he thinks he can say that with a clear conscience. Unlike other people he could mention. Other people, and their kids. The things he has seen. Well, no need to tell *me* about it. But Babe is so fortunate to be swimming for me now. Just speaking with me, he can tell. Strong, honest. Respectful of the kids—yes, he likes that. And this conversation has been a great relief. He's glad Babe's okay. He's glad everything is on the up and up.

And I think: *the up and up.* Inaccurate use of the term. Sounds odd, too, coming from him. Kind of an Anglo, Protestant American, upper-class euphemism. What Kay would have called WASP Vocabulary. Country Club Phraseology.

Absolutely amazing. How, with one simple phrase, Bren, your people can make everyone else feel like dirt.

Fine, Kay. What would you like me to do about that? Study Yiddish? Convert in my spare time?

God, no! My people have their own shit to work through—

Shit? Or schtick?

Shit, *darling. But good for you.*

"Listen, Phil, it's been great to talk with you, too. There are some really fine individuals in this program, and it's always a pleasure to get to know their families. I want you to feel free to call me at any time. Okay? If you have any further questions or concerns, or whatever."

This part is a memorized speech; I could recite it in my sleep. I wonder if he has heard many like it before. Chances are that he has. Were they convincing? All those other coaches? The famous ones at expensive clubs—what kind of raps did they have to dole out to parents? Speeches better than mine?

It's time for a break. McMullen and I usually have lunch once a week, on this particular day. But he's obviously avoiding me; his office door is locked, and no one in. I curse him on the one hand, wish him balm for his bruised ego on the other, am secretly glad that he won't be at this conference to hassle me, secretly on edge at the suddenly new possibility here of departmental warfare—which would automatically put me, the younger party, the more recent addition occupying a more junior position on paper, and a woman—in jeopardy, regardless of my comparative value.

But I'm not hungry anyway, and skip lunch for a brief session in the nearest weight room. It's pretty empty during lunch hour, with just a couple of heavyweight crew members pumping away on the squat machines, and I'm glad for the relative solitude. There, though—somewhere between bench press and lat pulldown—whatever healing my shoulders have managed to do during the past couple of days comes completely undone. I sit on an empty hydra-press machine in defeat, shoulders, neck, and upper arms throbbing. I'd like to whimper, but won't allow it.

Sometimes I am my own Coach, too.

Shower, and sauna. Wooden heat box blessedly empty. On the upper bench I stretch out, soak in warmth, long for Kay. But there's a strange twist to this longing: it makes my mind ache, then crushes any arousal of the body as soon as it begins. So that, lying there, I feel oddly, physically dead, unattracted and unattractive to the world. Sweat rolls readily down my cheeks. Tears do, too; but they blend right in.

Half an hour before afternoon workout and I'm examining individual training programs, comparing actual results with predicted results, cheering myself and the kid on whenever things jibe or exceed expectations, figuring out where to start troubleshooting when results fall short of a reasonable goal. So far, so good; there are more pluses than minuses on my side. Always, in my head, I keep count.

DeKuts used to have a belt hanging on the wall in his office—worn, cracked brown leather, tarnished buckles—that he'd actually notch with the long blade of a camping knife whenever something he could claim as a victory transpired. He also kept a well-used flyswatter around. Sometimes you'd walk in and he'd point to the wall the belt hung on, raise his wiry dark eyebrows quietly, but with a kind of menace. See that? he'd say, Which do *you* want to be, little lady? A notch on my belt or a fly on my wall. You'd look to the right or the left of the hanging belt, then, and see what he meant: a crushed fly, black body shattered to a single bloody streak, fractured wings translucent, almost invisible.

I eschew such methods. It's a point of pride.

Still, there is this lust for keeping tabs. Omniscience of the win/loss tally, the imperative for tangible triumph. It's as much a part of me as of anyone. But I wonder sometimes—like this afternoon, pausing over a log book, watching the last pale cold streak of sunlight fade west across my desk—how much of triumph ever is truly tangible; and how, in the end, is it measured? By being really exceptional? or simply by being a little faster, fading a little more slowly, than anyone else around you in a certain event, on a given day?

Or none of the above.

And if you cannot measure it absolutely—genuine victory, I mean, in sport, in war, in any kind of endeavor—then how do you account for your life, in the end?

Just *accept*, Super Coach. Accept the whole deceptively chaotic, troublesome patterned mess of what was, what is. Accept this. Even this. And live.

No, I tell her, softly. It's not what I can do.

Oh? And what *can* you do?

Win, Kay. I can win.

But what if you do *not* win?

I want to call her now, bury myself in her voice the way I'd cover my face with her arms, her breasts. Like an ostrich, feeling as if, that way, I could hide myself from the world.

I almost pick up the phone, dial her extension. Then I remember that I can't, really can't. She will not be there today; will never be there again, on any day. If I call her office, Ralph Brown will answer. He has cleaned out all her files. Maybe read some of the letters I sent her as a young lover, long ago. She liked to keep them with her in a secret place at work, she said; to remind her, on bad days, of what in her life was real.

Kay's little office, with room and phone numbers that I knew as well as I know our home address, is gone to me now, just as surely as she is gone. For a moment, my throat closes, and what washes over me is a wave of panic and grief in which, abandoned, I am lost.

No, I tell myself, don't. Workout is in less than half an hour. You cannot fall apart.

Somehow, this stern command works. I stop the tears. My throat begins to clear.

I realize that there are certain tricks to be pulled out of the bag here. For instance: If I acknowledge that she is gone forever, that I will never, ever see her again for at least the rest of my life, the tears swell and throat aches again, and I cannot stand it. But if I tell myself that she is not here on this particular day; that, for right now, for today, I will not see her, the weight feels smaller somehow, and easier to bear.

The telephone buzzer sounds, flashing bright red.

"Yes?"

"There's a Barbara Delgado for you, line three."

"Kathy, could you tell her I'll be with her in just a minute?"

I use the minute to purge throat and sinuses and damp eyeballs with tissue, toss the ruined wads perfectly into a wastebasket, make peace with the fact that this is undoubtedly the worst possible time for me to have to deal cogently with anybody's mother. But necessity beckons, regardless. Win or lose, I accept its dare.

Some things, after all, are working in my favor. Better, far better that I will have this chance to be a calm, authoritative, disembodied voice to her than a wretchedly tired, grief-smeared face.

I press the third button, and am pleased to hear my voice come out as rehearsed—friendly, firm, knowing: Hello. This is Brenna Allen.

"Coach Allen, we haven't met. I am Mildred Delgado's mother."

The voice is refined. Words perfectly formed. High alto, maybe, second soprano. Dancing classes. Finishing school.

Bren, I tell her, call me Bren.

"Bren. Brenna. Wonderful name. I went to school—oh, about a million years ago—with a girl named Brenna. Her family was German, I think. Possibly Danish."

Well, I say, We are scattered all over.

Uncomfortably, both of us laugh.

"I suppose I called just to more or less sort of touch base, Bren. My daughter tells us absolutely wonderful things about you!"

Maybe. But, I know, that is not the reason for this call.

"Thank you. We've developed a good program here. Babe's participation will enhance it even more."

There is a pause.

"Well, since you bring it up, I suppose I ought to tell you that that is partly why I called. You see, I have some concerns, some very serious concerns, about my daughter."

Silently, I wait. My nose drips, remnants of the would-be tears; I would like to blow it, but don't.

"Now listen, Bren. May I speak frankly? On the up and up?"

"Of course."

"My daughter is in—has been in—a very bad state. Part of it is due to the accident, of course, and the trauma of that, you know, all the injuries and shock. But the rest of it. Well, quite frankly. There were some really very serious problems even before that—I mean during the time she swam for Bart Sager, training for the Pan Ams, I could tell, I knew, that she was really not herself. Please don't misunderstand; she was always *difficult;* but this was different."

Different? I echo. Calmly. Openly. Willing her to speak, and at the same time wishing she had not called.

Yes, she tells me, different. Because it was then—oh, about halfway into her second semester at Southern, that this truly intolerable behavior around food began. It was apparent during a brief spring-break visit, from the physically overweight, bloated way she looked, the neurotic way she had begun to behave—well, for goodness' sake, it was apparent to the *world* from the deterioration of her times in every event—that something was not quite right. During meals with the family it became obvious what that was: Her eating habits were now disgusting and strange. She would gorge herself at dinnertime on red meat—always center cuts, always rare; barely touching her bread or vegetables; eating until she looked ill, then asking to be excused. And breakfast—that was worse, in a way. Because of what she did with the eggs. Eggs, eggs—it was always eggs; eggs hard-boiled, or sunny-side up. The hard-boiled eggs she'd take apart as if dissecting something in a laboratory—peeling back crumbled pieces of shell, prodding the white apart in pieces, rolling the yolk whole in the palm of her hand, or staring at it, as it lay on her plate, in a kind of fascination. Sunny-side up her fascination with yolks continued; she'd poke them with a knife, watching as mystified and intent as a child, jerking backward in a kind of fear when the warm yellow gel-like globes burst.

"What," I say quietly, "what did you feel the reason was for all of this—behavior?"

"I don't know! *She* claimed that Bart Sager had put his sprinters on a high-protein diet. But it seemed obvious to me, after a while, that this was in fact something she'd taken on her*self.* Because—wouldn't you know it—by the end of that semester she told us she'd decided to become a vegetarian. Why? I—we—wanted to know. Oh, she said, because the very sight of meat made her sick. She would never eat it again. And what did Bart think of all this, I asked her. Oh, she said, she didn't even care what he thought. Didn't even *care*! It was her own business, she said; *he* would think whatever *he* wanted; but there was no way *he* would ever change her mind. Well, for goodness' sake! What on earth were we supposed to make of all that?"

I don't respond, but don't have to. She continues without pause:

"And the next time she came home she was impossible. Really. Just impossible."

"In what way, Barbara?"

Now there is a silence; she is somewhat taken aback by my use of her first name, and, without really fully understanding why, both of us know it. Still, I'm glad. It has, somehow, given me an upper hand—which I need—because this, for all its careful disguise, is combat.

And for a moment I am this young, young woman, barely past adolescence, standing in shadows at the top of some stairs, about to do battle with my own enraged mother.

But that, too, is a way of connecting.

"Well, Bren, *you* know how it is—we take care of these children as if they're pure gold—flying all over the country with them, or for that matter the world, and rushing them off long-distance to the best internists or orthopedists every time they suffer a sniffle or an ache or pain. Then there are coaches and teams to cope with. And the other parents. And special diets. And separations. Sometimes, to be honest, you find yourself wondering if you're doing them a favor or a disservice—you wonder if it is all really worth it in the end. You worry: Are you neglecting the others? Being fair to everyone else, and true to your child's talents and desires, and to your *own* desires and values, at the same time? And then one day they look at you with resentment. Because, for all your efforts, encouragement, support, you have failed to do everything *perfectly*."

There is anger in the voice. Disappointment. And a terrible suffering I cannot pinpoint.

I ask her, very quietly, if she thinks that children expect perfection from us, after all? If, given the choice, they might not choose love instead? It occurs to me, as I say this, that Chick would surely approve.

Oh, of course, she replies. But there is so much more they need to learn, to succeed in life! So much more than love.

It occurs to me that maybe she's right.

There is success, there is winning.

And if I want Babe Delgado to win for me, insofar as I am able I must keep these people—these privileged people who gave birth to her, raised her, fed her, coddled her, drove her, loved her, punished her, supported her, came closest to her—completely off her long, thick back.

"Keep an eye on her, Bren. You will, won't you?"

"From the point of view of her swimming? Of course. And her health? Well, as much as I possibly can. Sufficient rest, nutrition, healthy habits—these are all things we like to emphasize here—"

"Yes, good, but I mean her weight. Her weight. It is imperative, absolutely imperative, that she face up to reality and start to lose that weight. *You* know, and *I* know, that unless she gets her body under control again her swimming will never be the same."

"Barbara," I say, "what if it never *is* the same?"

"Her body?"

"Yes. Or her swimming. Is that something *you* can live with?"

Oh but it's not me, she says, It's her, don't you see? It is all just for her, in the end.

This is a stalemate, and we both know it.

Still, I tell myself, stalemate is better than defeat. For all I know, Barbara Delgado is telling herself the very same thing. That, like me, she will live to fight again.

We chat about this and that. Weather. Massachusetts neighborhoods. She is being a *bachelorette* this week, she says. Bachelorette. The word sounds odd somehow, as if it ought not to really exist. Yes. Taking care of the kids. Going out with the girls. Her husband is away on business. In Los Angeles. Unfair, don't I think? that husbands get to go away like that, develop splendid tans on some beach near the Santa Monica Pier, and do a little business in their spare time? But what about us ladies?

L.A., I think. But he said Miami.

Oh, I say drily, I suppose we all survive.

"Tell me, Bren. Are you married? Children of your own?"

"No."

Ah, she says, I see.

And I think: Touché.

Okay, lady, send out your first range-finder. See what damage it does. But pick on someone your own size; send it out at me, not at your daughter—she's been through enough, don't you think? Even though, for all we know, Babe is tougher than us both. Even though, for all we know, you may love her more than your own sweet life.

There's an extraordinary clarity, sometimes, to the sky along the Pacific coast. You can see the perfect outlines of cotton clouds, puffs as defined as human muscle, shift and keep pace with the wind. The graying of the sky will blur color, but not form, turning Bay waters slate gray, too; a monotony of tone broken only by the white-bubbling extremities of waves, or shadowless triangle of a human figure wind-surfing. And, not so far off, you hear the ships. Especially after twilight—when the pinks and beiges and pastel shutter colors of homes dotting each hill are gentled to slate tones, like the water and the land—you hear foghorns, too, cutting through the bright mutter of feet scuffing sidewalks and Golden Gate grass, traffic, voices.

I was here twice before with Kay. Once for a conference she had to be at, from which I kept my distance and just roamed. We flew back east a few days later, my mind filled with vague images of magnificent flowers, petals the color of salmon blooming in green oceanside parks, eucalyptus trees, salty air mixing with the smell of cedar chips on dirt trails, waves exploding against sharp cliffs, superb food, women.

It was for the women that I brought her back with me again, two years later. The city she'd seen dimly sifted through the pages of an academic conference—spiced by a single opera excursion, and dinner at some Chinese place—was different from the one I'd found in my meanderings. Once, that first time, I'd paused in twilight in a twisting nexus of hilly streets, watched women walking by arm in arm and hand in hand, casually, naturally, openly lovers, as if they walked like this every day. Which, I realized—with a kind of shock that traveled through me, leaving some dull deep ache of longing behind—was probably true. Smells came to me: wet salt, oil and metal and leather, something sweet. Men walked by, too, some obviously together, some alone and boldly evaluating the others. Handsome men. Muscular men. Sometimes a bare knee or glimpse of buttock poked through torn denim. Aftershave perfumed the air, key chains clinked. But it was the women I watched, not paying much attention to how they dressed, really, but intently scanning each face; and I noticed that some of them watched me, too, with grinning eyes that met mine, teased, invited, winked, before passing by. *Hey honey!* someone called from a rooftop café, *Come on up and party!* I glanced up to see two of them leaning over a railing, staring down, faces in the shadow too dark to tell whether or not they smiled, but I knew without seeing that they did. *Hey, my friend likes you! Come join us! Enjoy yourself.*

For a moment I wanted to, but thought of Kay, and didn't.

Later that night, though, we had a fight.

I don't like the way you're ignoring me here, I told her. There's this whole terrific city out there and we could be seeing it together and you're missing it, Kay, you're missing it.

She turned her hands palms up, in that Jewish Mediterranean gesture that means, Well, so? Saying, What would you like me to do, love? Skip this conference? Not give the paper?

No, Kay. But we need more time together.

Oh, God. She rolled her eyes, crossed arms over her breasts and took this stance, like she was guarding some fragile trail between here and something terrifying, at the risk of her life; and no one—even I—was going to pass. Despite this, this inexplicable fear I sensed in her, she smiled. The way she smiled was with the fear, sure; but also with a kind of triumph.

Look who's talking! Super Coach! Miss I'm-Too-Busy-Right-Now, Kay!

She was right.

Well, partly.

It shut me up, anyway, and I spent the evening sulking while she did some last-minute revisions of the paper she had to present the next day. Both of us went to sleep early, grumbling good-night. But I woke up in the dark to feel her running a hand along me, rolling naked hips into mine.

Don't leave me, she said. And pulled me to her, flicked her tongue into my mouth. Then without thought of who we were in the world, or to each other, without remembering anything about gentleness or tenderness, or even love, I followed the natural course of the motion and rolled over on top of her and rocked full against her, pressing her down into the soft part of the bed, feeling her arch up again and again and push me along, like I was some rhythmically flexing bridge spanning her and myself, and we kept moving that way roughly, hot damp elastic friction, breathing very hard and panting sounds of pleading and of power to each other, until I felt her thighs and toes stiffen under mine, then pause, groan, then break open. I wouldn't stop but kept sort of riding her, then, until I heard both of us half-laugh, half-cry, and felt her burst all over and through me, and then I surrendered control, gave myself up to her and to the motion, shook and dissolved into wet shattered pieces.

We fell asleep like that, without a word. In the morning she had her wake-up call early and hauled me into the shower with her, shampooed our heads and the hair between our legs, made me scrub her back thoroughly, leaned against a tiled wall in the full spray of water and steam, facing me, placed a hand along the backside of each thigh to urge me closer. We kissed until the water began to run cold, dripping into our eyes, spouting up our noses, so that we laughed, and almost drowned.

We stayed naked and opened a window wide. Sea breeze blew

in. The weather was cool, shifting between sun and fog. We dried each other off with towels and the breeze, dressed for room service, drank a lot of coffee, ate muffins with jam.

Come here with me next year? I asked. But *not* for a conference.

All right, she said, In the summer.

Later she went off to give her paper. I kicked around the city feeling lazy, sated, drowsy, like a well-fed animal. It was there—near that hilly nexus of streets in the Castro, as I wandered in and out of shops smiling at people, at women and at men who were all naturally, casually, unquestionably gay—where I felt there was this dark cold thread inside me that might be broken, that could be changed to something resembling the nature of light. If only I could stay there somehow, in that city—with Kay, with my very own love—and wake up every morning to know how intrinsically, undeniably mine the city was, how at the core of it stood this still-unfulfilled offering of ecstasy and freedom, a self-contained world in which straight people mattered not at all. I could feel the bright sure power of that. Beyond the power, very close, lurked dignity; and beyond that, I knew, there was peace.

I thought all these things. But my life as I had made it was elsewhere, and we caught a plane out that afternoon. Kay's presentation had gone well; on the way back home, she slept.

We had tentative plans to return next year, in the summer. But things piled up for her and for me—there were papers to write, reviews to edit, last-minute recruiting and funding and scholarship hassles—and, between one thing and another, it was nearly a full two years before we went back; this time into a dry California August out of which only the Bay area seemed to emerge unscathed: cool, calming, flourishing.

Walking up and down those streets again, jet-lagged, slightly numb, I couldn't shake the feeling that I'd died and gone to heaven. That evening we went out together, into the part of town where you could live your whole life and never see a straight person. Kay looked dark and elegant, moving beside me, taking things in; you could hear the click of brain and heart wheels spinning, absorbing, theorizing but also enjoying; and I held her hand. Usually we did not walk hand in hand anywhere but through our own backyard—which was so carefully tree-shrouded—and to do it in public made me self-conscious at first. But after a while I relaxed, and I could feel her relaxing, too, sinking into the natural sweet solidity of it all: two lovers, together several years by now, out for a stroll in the evening. We ate Japanese food in a too-modern bright-lit industrial-looking place, where delicate wall prints softened the decor and everyone was gay—waiters, chefs, clientele—and women couples, in leather, or denim, or frilled skirts, or tailored executive dress, or combinations thereof, abounded. It was obviously nothing new for any of them. They were out on dates, or talking business. They did this frequently; it was no special treat, but a part of their everyday lives. And because of that, I imagined, they did not talk much about being gay, but about their natural human problems and joys instead. Later, we browsed through a bookstore. Kay bought things. She touched my cheek once, gently, leaning against the cashier's counter, told me how nice this felt and how good it was that we had come here.

We got back to our hotel before midnight, stripped and showered, started to watch cable TV but soon turned it off and made love for the first time in weeks—loudly, enthusiastically. It was so tender and surprising, so well synchronized between the two of us, so pleasing and good and so much fun. Her coming always unhinged me in some way I never expected, catapulted me into this bright high-voltage place from which I emerged quivering, sweating, then sedated. Lying there, afterwards, I wondered why we did not do it every night—or every week—or, at least, more often.

Marry me, I mumbled to her. Jet lag had overpowered nearly every conscious sense, orgasm every other. Sleep was roping me in quickly, binding me first at the ankles, and my leg muscles twitched. Kay stroked my hair, fit my head perfectly between her breasts. Mumbled back that she already considered us married, and I ought to, too.

Fine then, I told her, Let's move here.

She was silent awhile. I thought maybe she'd fallen gently asleep. Then:

I'll watch for openings, she said—calmly, quickly, taking me by surprise, so that I woke up a little—If that is what you want. But are there opportunities for you around here, Coach?

Probably not, I thought, Since every club coach in the world wants to be here or in L.A. or in Texas or Florida, and I could feel the dream die quietly in my chest, and didn't reply.

I slept and had strange dreams—which, in the morning, I would not remember. Although, Kay told me, I'd had a busy night: rolling away with all the covers, twisting and kicking and babbling up quite an incomprehensible fuss. So that, some time in the predawn hours, she had woken up very groggily again to hear me speak—and, she said, I had told her great and interesting things about us, about life—but, half-dreaming herself, she'd forgotten.

Now, I am jet-lagged again, gazing out my hotel room at a San Francisco afternoon again, and things seem unchanged but also changed utterly. This conference stifles me. Which I resent. Still, in a way, it's a relief. I cannot be myself here—here, where I've always felt most myself—but maybe that's good. Restrictive. Safe.

The apparent sameness of the material things I'm looking out at—buildings, street signs, layers of paint—seems mystifying somehow. Like a pool you return to, after being badly injured. All the things that once seemed effortless have become, for the time, impossible, each movement a frightening attempt acted out with caution and with pain; the other wall you once reached in seconds now unattainable, except in the make-believe of the mind—and when did the mind ever really suffice to satisfy physical need, or passion?

But no. This is really much worse than all that.

The creeping steely rose-tinged sky over pastel buildings—it's empty. These buildings, too, are empty. And the streets, ghost streets; the shop lights, phantom lights. To be here, this fall, is no longer like dying and going to heaven. Now the feeling is merely of death—not Kay's, either, but my own.

I would like to cry, only the tears don't come. They're blocked, frozen inside this obstacle of chest and throat. I touch my face expecting to feel a familiar grimace and don't. The face, too, is straight, blank, unmoving, numb. Standing, I shift from foot to foot, and feel nothing. Will myself to speak, to whisper. Nothing.

What must I look like? Stiff. Agitated. Blank and sullen and weird. An automaton. I stay where I am, avoid mirrors.

And, for the first time, understand Babe Delgado.

*   *   *

Bob Lewison knocks later, looking remade in a nice navy blue high-neck sweater and pale sports jacket, definitely off-duty, smelling of aftershave.

"Have dinner with me, Bren. You're the only one I love."

The *only* one? I tease. Well, he says, around these parts, anyway. I tell him that's a dangerous stance to take, pledging his troth to one, and one only—here, at least, in the city of love. He laughs. Saying, Tell me about it. Or better yet tell my bouncing alimony checks.

We sneak along hotel carpets past colleagues' rooms, carefully skirting the concierge desk—where a lot of them are clustered, pestering the polite, efficient, handsome gay man in deep scarlet uniform for ideas on where to eat—and take a cab into Chinatown.

The air's chilly, clear; the sidewalks less tourist-crowded than they'd be in summer, curbs punctuated here and there by the soundless blinking-on of streetlamps. We choose a place that's neither crowded nor empty, settle into an obscure table and examine vast menus, surrounded by the subtle babble of English, Mandarin, Tagalog. Order drinks first and sit back sipping them, plucking frilly straw decorations from the rim of each glass.

"How's Delgado doing, Bren?"

"Oh, all right. This isn't the year to tell, really—she's just getting back into it. Lots of hard work, diet, swim bench and free weights, lots of taping up to do—she's got *extremely* damaged knees and a bad ankle or two, and the shoulders aren't exactly in great shape, either—you know how it is. You play Coach Fix-It, you try not to hurt them—well, anyway, you fix what you can."

He leans across the table, elbows crinkling paper mats. Looks around before speaking, and when he does he speaks in a near-whisper, as if describing conspiracy.

"Fine. So tell me, the truth now, Bren—I mean, a Lamborghini can be fixed, right? you fix it all the time—is this kid really spectacular, or what?"

"Was."

"Can she still pull out a great race or two?"

"Yes," I admit. "She can."

He grins, raises his glass. "To your winning then, Coach."

"And to hers."

"Amen," he says, "drink hearty now."

We do.

He tells me the indoor track season is shaping up okay. No chances for a top-three finish this year—too many injuries, too many seasoned runners graduated—but a couple of guys are looking good, and strong, and for all any of us know one of them might make All-American. Skinny, stringbean distance kid. Senior this year. Does the five and the ten. Appearance very deceptive: your typical runner's greyhound physique, you know, ninety-pound weakling look; but this guy can just about bench-press his weight.

Impressive, I say.

We order food, more drinks, and keep talking sports. Partway through the second drink and the egg-drop soup, something tugs at my insides, a sense of discontent. I wonder why. Tell myself that, Once upon a time, Brenna Allen, you could talk shop nonstop, into the wee hours; once upon a time, living and breathing and talking and thinking these things, these athletic things, made you happier than anything else in the world. Yet now, when all the work is beginning to pay off in a big, big way—now when, let's face it, it is really all that you have—it seems banal. Unnecessary. Boring. Or obscuring, somehow, as if it blankets something else altogether; but what, or how, you cannot or will not see.

The main course arrives. I realize that dinner has gotten pretty sloshy. We're chugging down the drinks like folks on death row facing an execution date. Maybe the consumption of booze hides something else, too, for both of us. But it occurs to me that I really don't give a damn. I have gotten drunk only twice before in my life: once in college, after which I was terribly sick; once on Kay's birthday, after which she and I kissed and fell pleasantly, nakedly asleep. And if this is the third time, so be it. I've been disciplined enough, for long enough. Even if it kills me, tonight I don't care.

We muddle through the food and beverage, babbling away. The restaurant lights become dim. Although maybe, I think, it is an illusion; your eyes are glazed, Super Coach, averted from the real light, seeing only its dull, dull shadow.

Mounds of rice soaking up soy sauce. Fortune cookies. *You will be successful in love,* mine reads, and I laugh. We pay the check, leave a tip larger than either of us can afford.

Outside it's colder. I huddle chin-down in the long, sleek folds of a lightweight autumn thing Kay made me buy, wait in a slowly spinning sidewalk crowd while Bob goes away somewhere, then returns in a cab.

The Wharf, someone says. I don't know who.

Soon, though, we are moving arm in arm through a bright-lit crowd near ships and the Bay, sniffing chilled salty air and hot dogs, candy, cloth, frying things.

Out on the oily black water, moonlight shines. It cuts right into the middle of the Bay, a harsh reflection that is sheer bright silver, glistens like a wound, blinds in its intensity. For a moment I'm frightened, and look away.

"Bob. Can you see it?"

"What?"

I shake my head; it's gone. "I don't know. Never mind. The sky."

"Sure." He moves ahead and turns to face me, scuffing his good shoes on the wharf, tries to dance a jig. "The sky's up there, right? And everything else, present company included, is here—"

Both feet stomp. The gesture is intended to be firm but, standing there, he weaves slightly back and forth, and both of us laugh. Wandering remnants of crowd, sweatshirted tourists, bump against him. I manage to inch forward, arms open, as if to rescue him. We hold hands then and stumble somewhere else.

Ugly, piercing pallor. Ceiling fans. Costumes circa 1900. Sitting at a fake marble tabletop, we examine some boat-sized chocolate fudge sundae, buried beneath cherries, sprinkles, whirling fists of whipped cream. He dabbles at it with a long-stemmed spoon. Once in a while he faces me, serious expression, very earnestly. And I listen—although, later, I will not remember any of it—while he tells me the story of his life.

You? he says. We're moving again, walking through the windy, crowded dark. Time has passed—a lot of it, I think—so it must be late. I think. But I am not sure. I can feel myself giggle. It sounds odd, phony, girlish.

"Oh, you know me, Bob. My life's a closed book."

"No, Bren!" He faces me again with exaggerated urgency,

grabs both my shoulders, while everything else twists around us both. "That's just it! I *don't*—*I do not*—*know* you. And I *want* to—"

"You *want* to?"

"I want to! Know you! That's right! From the heart and from the soul, woman! Very, very much!"

"Well, *caveat emptor*, my friend. Buyer beware."

Huh? he says, but I never reply.

It is later that things slow, and die. Later, on rolled-down sheets, in a hotel room, after all these strange foul-tasting kisses we have numbly bestowed on each other. I am feelingless and naked, and he is merely naked. I can feel his fingers somewhere along my thighs. Doing something—I don't care what. I'm sitting over his body, straddling him, thinking that he's in good shape for his age, very lean but muscular, only moderately hairy, nice abdominal muscles, strong, strong legs, decent chest—but there are no breasts there; though, out of habit, I reach for them.

Now he is struggling, and I am, too. To help him, I think. But maybe it is to hinder something else altogether; both of us fumble, between his legs and mine. The part of him I hold is a little hard, mostly soft. We are both trying very seriously to insert it inside me. It seems important. I don't know why. For a moment it fits, stiffens and he pushes up and forward, and I feel something I barely remember—it has been so long, so many, many years—a foreign protrusion, half ticklish, half bruising inside me, and I wonder what to do about it all.

Then it dies like the evening. His movement slows. He falls out of me, limp and tired; tiredly throws an arm across his eyes.

"Christ."

"Forget it, Coach. My mistake."

"Christ," he says, "who's Kay?"

"Nothing. No one. The love of my life. She died."

"You're kidding."

"No, Bob. I am not kidding."

The spin of things seems to calm. More becomes visible: blankets under feet, drawn curtains, terrible art on the walls. The objects of this room. I lie beside him, numbly, a rumpled fold of sheet between us. Realize, for the first time all night, an actual, strictly physical sensation: my mouth is dry and sore, the tongue so dry it feels cracked. He looks at me sideways, eyes widening when they lose focus, narrowing when they regain it. Then he yawns, and closes them, hides them under his hands.

"Excuse me for not jumping up and ordering flowers, Bren. This is all a little rough on my dick."

"I don't give a shit about your dick, Bob. I don't give a shit about anything. All I want to do is sleep."

"Yah." He rubs his forehead, glares at the ceiling. "Well me too, sister." Then he props himself on an elbow, with difficulty, eyelids falling closed, barely opening, manages to keep his lips from slurring. The eyes stare at me accusingly. I watch them, and blink.

"So? What's up, Bob?"

"So. That's really the truth? You are some kind of dyke or something?"

"Yah, Coach," I mock. Carelessly. Tiredly. "But skip the Or Something."

"Well," he says. And falls asleep.

I do, too.

The next day is a headache, during which I lie low—skipping all the conference panel discussions and presentations I'd planned to attend, dodging every phone call, checking to make sure the DO NOT DISTURB sign still swings firmly from the outside door-knob before double-locking the door again and staggering into the bathroom to vomit. Luckily, I have no actual assigned duties until tomorrow afternoon. Sometimes, Coach, I tell myself, luck is really with you.

Towards evening the nausea fades, the headache dulls. I begin to feel very sorry for myself, and consider placing a long-distance phone call to Chick—on the pretext of seeing how Boz is doing; in truth, to whine about my life—but don't. I watch as much TV as my bloodshot eyes can handle, sleep off and on until dawn, wake up feeling drained, and empty, but no longer in desperate shape. I order a high-protein room-service breakfast, drink plenty of orange juice with aspirin, shower and do sit-ups and push-ups, shoulders complaining all the way, and put on lots of makeup, a terrific dress, jewelry, nylons, heels.

I spend half the day mingling with coaches and exercise physi-ologists and Ph.D. candidates in sports pedagogy. All the coaches have heard about Delgado, and want to know too much. The panel I moderate goes well. I manage to blurt out appropriately sophisticated introductions, and to tie all the seemingly unrelated strands together in the end—although, later, I will not remember exactly how. I do more mingling until dinnertime, take phone numbers and trade calling cards, eat sparingly at a bland hotel restaurant with two colleagues, wincing at the sight of mixed drinks. One is a female basketball coach—who lives and works down South, has a wedding ring, talks a lot about a husband— but our eyes meet often, and I wonder; the other an affable enough swimming coach from some school in Wisconsin, a little too young and too confident. But interesting things sometimes pop out of too-big mouths, and he went to school with Bart Sager, he says, long ago, so I listen.

A real tough-love kind of guy, Bart was. Nut case, really. Stuck on monster sets. Drilled them to the bone. Callusing, he called it. Though his eye for technique probably left something to be desired. But he loved them—he loved those kids so much, he would actually cry about them sometimes. Liz Chaney, now; that girl was, to him, the meaning of life. Rituals, he always said, make them stick to the rituals. Eat together. Shave down together. Draw blood together. Build up champions.

Draw blood? I ask.

Oh, he smiles, Bart probably meant it metaphorically. Still, you couldn't be sure. There was always this edge to Bart—a hard, borderline crazy edge. He remembered things in biology labs, for instance, though they had not been partners; stuff Sager did with animals.

"Animals?"

"Yeah. Mice, rats, guinea pigs—you know, experimental fodder."

"What, exactly, did he do?"

"Oh." He sweats, gulps beer too fast, and avoids my eyes. "Just things I heard, really—I mean, nothing I can say for sure. So it wouldn't do to go spreading the word, right? The guy was successful, he was going to be a great coach, there were always plenty of people jealous of him even then. So some other guy accuses him of being nuts, right? So what."

"Nuts—how?"

He shrugs, shimmying out of it all with a distinct lack of grace. I don't know, he mutters, suddenly abashed, suddenly very low-key. I heard he was into some sort of crazy shit. Like, some theory of sport as growing out of primitive ritual shit, sacrifice, all that sort of crap. Blood sacrifice, in which every athlete had to watch, and participate. But don't believe everything you hear.

He excuses himself for the men's room, and is gone a long time. In the meanwhile, our check comes. The basketball coach and I pay.

Bob Lewison passes by, head down, and keeps his distance.

Later, he is camped outside my hotel room, sitting on the hallway carpet with his back against the door, like some kid waiting for a busy professor's office hours. His face and hands look older, tired and gray; I can see the way I feel reflected in them—and, probably, the way I look. But he stands when he sees me, rubs his own sore neck with a wry expression, as if anticipating something unpleasant, yet necessary.

"Bren. Can we talk?"

After a little hesitation I tell him sure, why not. My chest thuds with anxiety; but the feeling is, luckily, muted by my own exhaustion and omnipresent headache. I let us both in. Settle onto the edge of a newly made bed, while he moves luggage aside to slump in an armchair. Suddenly, although I've never smoked, I wish I had a cigarette.

"Shoot, Bob."

"It all really happened, didn't it? Last night, I mean. And everything that I thought got said, got said—"

"Right."

"Well, look. I'll never tell—if you won't."

"What's that supposed to be, Bob? Some kind of blackmail?"

He opens the tired hands in supplication. "Christ, no. To tell you the truth, lady, it's more of a plea. I am embarrassed as hell."

Staring at his face, I realize that he's not a bad-looking man; nor particularly insensitive, really. He is just a man, and has committed no crime. But, on the other hand, neither have I.

I want to tell him how tired I am, how much I hurt inside. Something stops me, though, so I'm silent. Sitting there, I'm aware of rocking slightly back and forth. The dull room lamp illuminates us in tones more gentle than fleshy reality. Against a wall, our bodies move as shadows.

He shrugs. A big shadow bobs up, and down.

"I had a couple of guys on the team once—good, solid middle-distance runners, both of them; I know they were messing around with each other. I mean, it happens sometimes. But these kids were a couple of gentlemen. Genuinely seemed to care about the sport, and the team. Nothing ostentatious—looking at either one of them, at first, you'd never have a clue."

"Oh Jesus, Bob." I can feel my face crack wryly. "Forgive me for laughing—I know you're just trying to be cool and understanding, at least I think you are. But my—I mean Kay, our relationship—it was a lot more than messing around, love; it has nothing to do with kids in a locker room. What it has to do with is adult, it's for real, between grown women. I mean, you are talking about my life."

I don't believe I just said it all out loud like that. Panic takes hold. I can feel my forehead perspire. Stunned, vulnerable, I look away.

After a while, he grunts. In assent, or disgust, I can't tell. Then he makes a fist of one hand, and mimes smacking his own face with it. He grins lopsided. Now his voice is quiet, somehow calming.

"When Janice and I broke up—"

"Yes."

"I didn't want to live. For a while, I mean. You know, I got addicted to that Sominex crap, scrips for insomnia and anxiety—you name it, for a while there I'd pop it. I didn't know what to do, exactly, with the rest of my fucking life. A few nights I went out looking for hookers. Not that I could get it up too well, mind you, I felt pretty shot up inside, but I guess the point was to just sort of escape from myself, for however long, if I possibly could. Then one day—I don't know why—I woke up, and threw out most of the meds, all the over-the-counter shit at least, and then I put away the pictures of her and me and the kids. And everything I'd taken with me from the house—bedspreads, towels, even a bunch of dishes—I tore apart, or broke against the wall, not in anger, you know, but very calmly and deliberately, and then I threw it all out. I cleaned up my place. I went out later and bought new things, cheap, lousy things. But they were what I could afford. And for whatever reason, Bren, that was the end of me wanting to die."

I nod, dully. Yes, it means, I understand. But the truth is that

I don't understand—at least, not yet. There is still too much grief; I cannot feel that kind of anger; maybe, I think, I never will.

"So I know a little about what you're going through," he says. "And, thank God, Janice and the kids—even though, to tell you the truth, there are times when I hate their guts—at least they're all alive. I don't think I could take it, losing them completely. "

"Oh," I whisper, "it's interesting."

"Yeah. Look, Bren—why the hell didn't you tell me all this before? I thought we were friends."

"Not really. I didn't trust you."

"Why the hell not? I'm a pretty nice guy!"

Despite myself, I laugh, gently, and he does too.

"You *are* a nice guy, Bob. You deserve some nice woman's passion and love."

"Just not yours, I guess."

"Right."

"No room for doubt?"

"Doubt? Oh no, Bob. Really, no."

He sighs. "Kay, huh? Kay who?"

"I don't want to talk about her, Bob. At least not now. She suffered a lot. I loved her. I'd like to just let her rest."

We're quiet for a while, and still. Finally he leans over toward me and reaches for my hand, and I pull his square, firm fingers one by one with my own, playfully, like a child. He tells me he is tired, very tired, and it's time to get some rest. But he would like it if, in time, we became closer. He has always admired me. He hopes there is something about him that I find admirable enough to respect, too. Sometimes at work he feels so alienated and so lonely he could cry. He and I, we have been professional allies in a way, haven't we? Complementary administrative talents; similar approaches to coaching and to sport. He hopes that, eventually, we'll be friends.

The Rock, and Roll

ᵔ ᵔ ᵔ

(B A B E)

Breaststroke:
Kick sweeps the water in, arms sweep it out, catch and down, shoulders and head up and forward, breathe, lips dripping, arms circle in, down and out, and in, and up, hands together like a prayer, kick sweeps out, circles down, and in, and arms sweep out, catch and down, and you just don't stop, and you must not look. If you look, you lose.

There is no glide. No ease, or rest.

But there's this: the rock and roll.

From crown of head to lips, to hands, to hips, and down. Like a dolphin, like a wave.

It's in the timing. In the hips. You want to flex them, but not too much. Enough to generate propulsion, yet without intruding. Enough for motion, and optimal power. For the reach. The pull. The thrust.

October 1st, I step into the locker room shivering. Goose bumps on my arms, lips puckered, fingers shake so bad I can't get the combination right, finally have to ask Ellie and she does it for me. Glancing up once, rolling her eyes when she sees the kind of shape I'm in, she mutters Oh just *chill*, Delgado, just get *over* your big bad self why don't you? Then she makes a face, I laugh, the locker swings open. Quarter to six.

"Fifteen minutes!" she shrieks. "Fifteen minutes to mayhem and destruction!"

Someone groans, someone else giggles.

Then: "No! No! No! I con*fess*, Coach."

They are all watching her, faces washed pale in the pinkish fluorescent light. She twirls a pair of goggles like some bolo whip, stands on a bench and stomps her feet, gasping.

"I con*fess*—I am guilty—"

"Of what?" someone yells.

"Guilty of fear! Guilty of mediocrity! And you know what? It doesn't matter! I'm gonna do it anyway! Because truth is in the body! And *this* body—on *this* team—tells no lies! So step aside!"

Her Coach imitation isn't bad. By now, they're all laughing.

"Step a*side*!"

"Aye *aye*, Captain!"

She jumps down, goes storming through the place turning on showers, flushing toilets, running sink faucets, alternating between her Southern belle and her madman imitation until everyone starts yelling back—at her, at each other—and the noise echoes, bounces off the walls and the water. When she passes by me foaming at the mouth, eyes rolling, I understand for just a second that part of it is serious. She's afraid somewhere; somewhere deep down she's hurting, and angry. And this—this weirdo team captain stuff—is how she gets herself through it.

I look around to see if any of them know. They don't. Too busy howling at each other, stripping, getting suits on, showering, laughing.

I pull the sweater over my head, unbutton my blouse and when my legs start shaking too much again sit on the bench, untie my laces. I look up in time to catch her eyes. She's naked, pulling on her suit. Flash of muscle, curling hair, skin and belly button, and she turns away once, then around again to look back, jut her chin at me, jam the locker shut with a caveman "Huh!" so that, without meaning to, without really knowing I'm doing it, the sound comes out of me in immediate response: "Huh!"

"Huh!" she grunts, triumphant. "Time to see what we all are *made* of, right?" And pulls the suit up hiding her breasts, smooths thin straps over each shoulder before heading for the showers.

It comes to me, then, this rhyme from some club locker room, long ago:

Made of lace, fall on your face.

Made of oak, sure gonna smoke.

Terror rushes back like worms in the pit of my stomach. I put my head between my knees. Okay, Delgado, get over your big bad self why don't you. For a moment I do, and can sit up again, can start to get undressed. Five of six. I'll be late, but can't help it—have to wait until they are all gone, so that by the time I'm naked I'll be alone. Because what *I* am made of is scars and flab—and even before the hospital there were the bad knees, sore ankles, aching shoulders, all the overused tendons and frayed cartilage held together with Ace bandages, or sometimes drugs. Now, despite dry-land month and the diet, there is all that, plus a still-noticeable amount of excess fat through which new muscle is just barely beginning to show.

It's fear of what might happen in the lanes and the pool, yes. But also this motherfucking shame. See, I've lost it, don't even remember it—the feel of the reach, and pull, and thrust. Flesh, muscle, moving in water. My breaststroke. The rock, and roll. And I am so ashamed of my body.

Before, at my worst, I was good. Smooth-moving, strong. Competent in the water. There was this thing about it, the key to it. What I said I'd never be without because no one and nothing could take it away from you once you had it—not Sager, not losing a race you ought to have won: A feel for the water and the stroke, that's born in you.

Until Angelita took it away. And I had to fight, really fight, to find my way back—to even a dim flicker, a dull little chipped-off piece of it.

Weeks it takes. Days of hell. I won't remember them much.

Just the shocked wet shattered first-day feel. By night, my shoulders won't move.

The unspeakable second day. I can hear joints grinding. Hear metal pins clicking against bone. Think the left ankle will collapse again, but it doesn't. Feel that I will not survive.

I won't remember the third day at all. Or the fourth, fifth, sixth.

But by the end of the first week, the sensation of physical crisis and alarm has passed somehow and only pain is left, ravaged muscles in an unfit body.

It seems I will never get it back.

Two more weeks pass in an aching blur.

Then—for a moment, a glimmer—the second workout of the day, on the third Friday, I do it, and I feel it: power of the sweep and pull, undulation, power of the kicking thrust, undulation, the breath, the prayer, the dolphin animal surfing waves, thrust on by the force of its motion so that it does not stop—and for that moment, that glimmer, I have it back again, and I know it. I make the interval, start the final repeat. Everything hurts, burns me breathless, I am stunned with pain but it doesn't matter, nail the wall, pull kick surface, keep the pressure on, twenty to go and the undulating agony of it shoots through me with a savage undeniable surge, catch and down, flex at the hips, kick thrust, over and into water, and I let it do what it does and just ride it, move along the searing curving electric wire of it, don't look, don't stop. The rounded gold wall light looms ahead like a beacon, a promise, foggy in my steamed vision now, blurred by the effort of the pull thrust, and I stretch, reach, kick it to touch it.

Stop. Cling. Try hard to breathe.

The goggles leak, I think, that's why they fogged. But when I pull them off they are warm and dry inside, hot where they touched my face. Under the wet my face is hot, too, and my whole body, almost sweating. Something throbs like a drum, makes my left breast move forward, recede, forward again, into the wall and the light—my heart, beating. I look up to see Brenna Allen nod, her voice calling out my time, echoing numbly, incomprehensibly away. She crouches over the lane and smiles.

"Good, Babe. *There's* your pull. Good for you."

"Can deal," I blurt. I don't know why.

"Sure you can," she says, "be proud of yourself. Two hundred swim down, take it *very* easy, and you're out of here."

Then I see I'm the only one in the water. The bunch of them are out of the pool standing around, dripping, watching. Just staring intently, like they've never seen anyone swim before.

"Ouch." Someone whistles. "Whoa, girl, whoa."

Then, all at once, they applaud.

It clatters, rises, swells for minutes before Bren breaks through it with a sharp demanding clap of her own.

What do you think you're doing? she says. This isn't exactly individual time trial day yet, people, and if you think you're ready for that you are sadly mistaken. In fact, I would say that by the looks of it you all have quite a way to go, quite a long and painful way to go. And, believe me, you certainly won't get there by standing around watching. Ms. Marks, you're not even through with your main set yet. Your fun is just starting. It's going to be a long afternoon—I'll put that in writing—and that goes for the rest of you too. Everybody back. Back. Back in the water.

But I realize that she doesn't look angry. And she let them applaud for quite a while.

I push off to swim down, feel the catch of fingers on pale water, pressure against a palm, wrist, forearm. Bubbling effortlessly past toes. Freestyle toss, reach. Slide through the Jell-o. Pull like a snake. Easy, Delgado. Take it easy. For a moment, a glimmer, the first one in many, many years, I love it again, and I want it.

Unpredictably, in erratic bursts, nonsequential pieces, it comes back to me the following week. And with it, also in fits and starts, like disjointed parts of a puzzle long scattered, the effort of the 100. Hardly bearable undulating wire of hot bright sensation that's too refined to be pain, really, and goes deeper than skin, deeper than muscle—grabs you and racks you at the level of the nerves. Fucks with your reflexes, with the electric impulses that make you move, and live, and breathe. Something shattering waits at its other side.

Bitching bust-up, Kenny joked once. Then, seriously: *What do you think it is?*

I don't know, I told him, *but it's there.*

Well come on, Babe. Let's go for it.

I'd shake my head a little, weave back and forth.

Afraid? he'd whisper.

Mmmm. A little. But more—um, just—respectful?

There's this difference, Sager used to say, between sprint and distance events, so listen up, animals: Distance can make you hurt, it can make you afraid. But the sprint can shut you down, just like that, because what it really is, is a war between your own power and your ability to control it—to unleash it, yet at the same time to contain it perfectly for the fifty or the one hundred meters—for long enough, my animals, so that you win before it shuts you down completely. Not your run-of-the-mill discomfort. Not the kind you take on every day. No. For special people, special agony.

See, it doesn't make you afraid. Not exactly. It makes you sort of shy.

Like a pussycat. Here, pussy pussy pussy.

And remember, pussycats don't swim.

Breaststrokers! Who's sprinting today? Lane three for my animals. Two for the pussycats. Delgado, which will it be? Have you decided yet? Or is all this wasting your precious time?

Two, I said. Lane two, Kemo. Meow.

And all of them grinned nervously, except Sager and me.

"Babe, relax."

"Huh?"

"Relax. It's the end of the repeat, not the end of the world." Bren keeps an eye on the clock. I'll go at the top—fifteen seconds ahead of the rest of them. Quarter of a minute less to catch some breath. The big red moving hand hits fifty-three, fifty-four. Heads ominously, inevitably, for the sixty.

"Sweet dreams," she says, and a whistle blows.

The fourth week. Thursday. Morning workout. When I feel it coming more frequently now, can almost reach out to grab it— the pull, hip flex, kick, the timing, the harsh bright scream of it.

Afterwards in the locker room I strip and shower thoughtlessly. For a moment I actually forget to cover my torso with hands and arms, to twist and bend this way and that, turn halfway to the wall in some futile attempt to hide all the scars, the misshapen imperfections and excess baggage.

But the past two and a half weeks have begun to strip me down for real, and when I dare to look at mirrors I see something almost emerging now: a big, definable thing that will be firm but not hard, made for the motion, shaped like a woman.

I dress. Still early, there's time to kill. No class for two hours, and the distance freestylers are just finishing their swim-down. I head upstairs. The steamy chlorinated atmosphere recedes, air freshens, cooling my skin.

The hallway leading to the lobby is long, lined with shatterproof trophy cases and old framed photographs of various teams. I wait there for Ellie. Thinking, all of a sudden, that maybe something good is happening now. Something inexpressible, inside me. That my skin feels alive. I am beginning to sense my real parameters, where I reach to, where I leave off—and, somehow, I need to let her know. People brush by, minutes. I stare at polished trophies. At dull-edged black-and-whites.

She stumbles off the landing looking tired. The tips of her hair are still wet.

"What's the matter, Delgado? Turning into a gym rat?"

"I thought we could go for breakfast."

"Lead on."

"Are you sure? You look really beat."

"How perceptive of you. I *am* really beat. In fact, it's my middle name these days: Eleanor 'Beat' Marks. But you—you are beautiful, Delgado." It occurs to me that she means it. Her voice is humble, matter-of-fact. "You are totally, totally awesome."

We walk quietly past trophy cases. She's acting strange, not yakking away like she usually does. I touch her shoulder, ask if she's really all right and she mumbles Yes, sure, nothing heroin won't fix.

I can feel my skin tingle in the air, muscles aching but healthy, hips moving more freely inside looser clothes now. Sometimes, lying flat, I can reach down and feel bones. And there have been other times during these past few days, moments that actually stretch longer now into minutes, when I've felt good, really good. So simple, so small. But I never thought I would have that again. Sometimes, during those moments, she has been there too.

I want to let her know. Like maybe she'd give a damn, or it would make her feel better.

The words go through me again so that I really hear them: *Beautiful, Delgado. Awesome.*

They make me want to cry—I don't know why. Because of something sad and sweet, floating on the tip of my mind, like a memory. I sigh and think I have it. Then, in a blink, it's gone.

She stops, leans against the side of a trophy case. "Listen, I think I'll skip breakfast."

"Oh. Well, what about dinner?"

"Yes, what *about* dinner?" he says, popping up out of nowhere. The big guy from the second-floor landing, a month ago. Small bright dark eyes, fair hair with a dyed-in streak of black down the middle. Tall, about Kenny's height. He has shaved so closely there are tiny rivulets of pink on both cheeks, a small chunk of red where he cut himself. "What's the matter, Ellie—forget your manners? Introduce me."

She shrugs and plucks his sleeve, plucks my sleeve, then puts our hands together. Weird listlessness in the way she moves. I try, but can't catch her eye.

"Okay, Mike, this is Babe Delgado. Babe, meet Mike Canelli. Coach McMullen's wayward star."

He presses my fingers, presses my palm. His hand is big and cool. He keeps holding on, and the skin gets damp—with his sweat, with mine.

Then he lets go, babbles about how he was exploring caves out West this summer and broke both his arms, so he was going to redshirt this year, but not any more, the strength is coming back. He and Ellie get into some banter, which sounds half serious. Winstrol. HGH. Testosterone pills. This makes me nervous. But I tell myself to chill, it is all just talk.

Finally she sighs tiredly, pokes his shirted belly and suggests that he get cracking with some weights, some treadmill, some LifeCycle machine. She tells me to come over after workout tonight, if I want, and we'll have dinner.

Okay, I say. But she's already gone.

I press a hand against the trophy case. Glass glitters. My thumbprint stays there, cloudy and wet.

He traces it with his, cocks his head to meet my eyes. His own are glittering. There's play in them, and something more serious—I can't tell if it's good or bad. "Dinner. You could have it with me some time."

There's a clean chalky smell to his clothes and chest.

Wind blows from the lobby. I head that way. He stays alongside, speeding up and then slowing down to match me, making sure that our shoes hit the floor in perfect rhythm. The cold breezes in more forcefully, swinging doors rush people through, waft the edges of paper tacked to bulletin boards.

"I knew who you were the first time, Babe."

Right, I say, good for you.

Senior nationals, he tells me, Industry Hills, I was there, did the one and two but had a bad day, the worst. So here I am. And here you are, too. That's lucky for me.

*　　*　　*

Kenny was eager, sloppy sometimes, and open. You could see it in the opened-up breadth of his chest. Shaved down, peaked, ripped, the skin was pink over muscles and looked stretched somehow, smelled of water and powder and nothing else, like a naked clean-washed newborn's. He liked girls, women, really, really liked them—happily, fearlessly, without having to know them, in a way that most men don't. Then, too, he had this thing for me, this adoration that was open-book earnest—like there was a hole in him I could fill. Even though he was strong. He was looking for, he was needing, completion. But the searching was honest, unashamed. And I loved him for it. For that.

Liz was different. Never sloppy. Except when she meant to be—which isn't the same thing. And never open. I mean, not really. She was more sort of—incisive? Sure. She'd figure out what she wanted, reach for it and take it, just *it*, and leave the rest. Very exciting. Very *noblesse oblige*. On the inside, anyway. The outside was all for show.

They were my friends. My loves.

Strong, and noble.

Mike Canelli is neither. I can tell just by walking next to him, not listening. Even though there's also something about him that feels both sloppy *and* incisive. Maybe it's this weird combination—added to the fact that he is definitely not noble, or even strong—that makes him seem, I don't know, inevitable.

We walk out of the hallways, across diagonal open blocks of cement between buildings and greenhouses and parking lots. There's a hint of winter in the air, cold wind gusting, and everywhere students, bright coats, booksacks, dry, blowing leaves. Into a cafeteria. Nasty fluorescent lights. He's talking the whole time. I don't listen, really, just pretend to, nod once in a while like I understand, like I care. Thinking about what his chest would look like shaved down. Under the sweatshirt, under the lettered jacket. Kenny had this bright, stiff, thick curling blond hair that spread from the bottom of his neck across both nipples, and trailed down his abdomen, then ended. To swim peaked and clean, he'd take a razor to it. Electric, then hand-held, for a close, close shearing. Something Liz and I never had to do. But I'd watch him, and her, sometimes, in fascination. Their chests so different: One expansive, self-contained, male, nipples like two little buttons closed to the world; the other so soft looking, asking for lips and hands somehow, nipples larger, more versatile, a way in instead. But mostly, in both of them, I kept seeing these parts of myself.

Not physical parts, really.

Screw it—I can't explain. Watching their skin come away baby-fine and raw made me shudder. I could feel the way my own skin would be, after shave-down: naked, open, sliding unfettered through the world.

There's coffee. Toast. Sick purple jelly in little sealed plastic containers, dimmer lights of some student café where Mike Canelli is making a big deal out of paying for us both—and I'm still not listening to him, really, but I force myself to wonder, wonder hard, if he looks any good shaved down, and there are other, different things I want to keep thinking about, and other, different bodies, but I stop myself and concentrate on him.

Like that shrink said at the hospital. A nice guy, young and not yet jaded, horn-rims, Jewish I think—my mother loved *that*, you can bet—seemed unflappable, unjudging. Just a suggestion, he said. Suitable stuff for fantasy: Male figure, substitute *him* toward the end. Behavioral technique. To get you out of what we call this post-traumatic fixation, back to normal life, the everyday world. Try it, see how it works for you.

Only this nice Jewish guy, with all his best intentions, never asked what was normal, or everyday, about all the things that happened in the world that had drowned.

Me, Liz, Kenny—the three of us knew. It was like our little secret. But the way it ended felt like punishment. All alone, it wasn't normal any more but something to keep inside because there was no one left to share it with; I couldn't sustain it on my own, and I gave up trying.

Not that Liz and Kenny turned out to be perfect sharing partners.

See: everybody fucked everybody over eventually. Puerto Rico. Hot. Hair. Palm trees. Melting pavement. Smelled of shampoo. Sweating. Blue pool, gray ocean water, and the light.

Nice, my animals. When you see it, you know you're doing righteously: white light, light of pain and of power. My animals. My warriors. So swim right into it. Into and through the light.

Strip down to quivering muscle. Blood and bone. See what you're made of. And then dig deeper.

Animal power.

He is nuts, Lizzy.

Sure, she smiled. But a great coach.

Oh, God. He knows about us.

So what? Don't freak out on me, Babe. You like it, don't you? I mean, we can do what we want—right? America's finest. Future Olympic heroes. And no one, I mean *no one*, is going to risk that precious gold. Least of all Mr. Asshole. So stop being so uptight. *We* are in control here. *We* are the fucking gods.

But it was the gods who betrayed me in the end.

And I betrayed them, too. By surviving.

"Here, have some more coffee." Mike Canelli pours it, black and lukewarm, into the stained, chipped cup. "Tell me, how's the great comeback?"

"Comeback?"

"Yeah. I mean, it's pretty fucked up, isn't it? At sixteen, they said, I was making my comeback."

Weight of it crushed him, too, maybe, somewhere along the line. I hear myself laugh. Not out of amusement but out of recognition, sympathy, pity. He laughs with me and his face crinkles near the eyes, nose turns up a little.

"You know what *I* said? Fuck *you*, I said. I mean, my daddy's rich, and my momma's good-looking, and I am both. So I *refuse* to suffer! Let the bozos do *this* shit—personally, I'm going to have a life: count the money, blow some dope, get laid."

I laugh again, but it's not real this time. Stop listening to what he's saying, and concentrate on keeping him in my mind's eye: suitable material, for the normal kind of fantasy. There's the smell of him, mix of showered-clean sour and sweet—not unpleasant, really. Does nothing inside me, but with patience, who knows? Heavy neck, arms, shoulders. Broad chest. If I saw him naked, without the sweatshirt and jacket? Would it work for me then? With practice? Some great new mystery be revealed? Anyway, there's nothing wrong with trying. I mean, get back into this much-praised normality that I never was part of in the first place. Nothing special about you now, and nothing particularly godlike, Delgado, so at least *try* to fit in.

"Well, you're pretty quiet. What are you—the deep, dark, silent type?"

I don't know, I tell him, How many types are there?

"A few." He grins, almost defiantly.

"So what type are you?"

"Try me."

And there's nothing inside me, not much, anyway—or maybe just the faintest dying little trail of a thing—that makes me want to try at all. What about it? he's saying. What about dinner? And I think: No way, forget it.

"Fine," I tell him.

"Seven. Okay? Where do you live?"

"Around."

"Weird address."

"Um, look. I'll meet you somewhere."

"Um, okay," he mocks. And smiles, tells me where we can meet. And I don't like him much, but on the other hand I sort of do; he's all right, bright and funny in this cruddy kind of way, his body's big, well-formed—an okay swimmer probably; face strong, calculating, handsome; and aside from that, there is something he might show me.

Watch, Liz. You're not the only one who can be—what did you call it?—*versatile*.

I know then that I'll do it: Dark rooms and beds, foreign tongue, a hard chest against mine.

Step into it, Delgado, step into the room, take off your shoes like you are stepping into something sacred. Step into it and try it and go through with it this time—and figure out, finally, what all the hoopla is about.

The thing with lots of guys—it was true sometimes with Kenny, too—is that they can keep talking about themselves for hours, never let you get a word in edgewise, never ask you a single question about yourself, and end the evening thinking that they've just participated in a great conversation. As Liz used to say, the difference between dialogue and monologue sort of eludes them.

What's good about this is that you yourself are basically absolved of all responsibility. You can adjust to the fact that there's a voice droning away in your face, make yourself nod or smile once in a while like you are interested, or understand, and set your own mind on automatic pilot. Think about all the things you really *want* to think about. Do a little introspection.

It's relaxing, really. Like meditating in the middle of a hard day's work.

You can't drift off completely, though. If there's a pause in the monologue, you have to fill it up with a short, giggly laugh. Even if what he just said wasn't comical.

Then, if he looks perplexed, and leans across the table and says something like, "Hey, what's so funny?" you give a sort of goofy, little-girl grin, and reply:

"I don't know! I mean, you're just so—in*tense!*"

Anyway, I do all these things over dinner with Mike Canelli at the Donut Hole. Which, Ellie says, is where all the kids on scholarship or work-study go because they can afford it, and all the rich kids go because they think it's cool to hang out with the poor—or, as she insists on calling them, "the working class," which is what she calls herself, because her parents are retired and basically don't have any money, and her father, who back in Europe was this very educated guy, had to come to this country and make his living driving a cab. I do all these surefire things, both of us eating the Donut Hole's special of the day— some kind of pasta—and I imagine him naked and it feels sort of unreal, unconnected, but I think: Okay. Why not?

He pays. Cash. Though he makes a big deal of flashing all his plastic-covered credit cards. I am not impressed. My dad got me a whole slew of those before I went to college; obviously, Mike Canelli's dad did too. And back when I was sixteen, some company that makes competitive swimwear sent me a Gold Card.

"Look," he says, "I'll walk you home."

I try to come up with some reason for him not to. Even though I'm curious. I mean, what would really happen? But this anxious chill goes through me, I remember Ellie, and dinner at her place, and I'm already late.

I tell him no, but thanks, some other time, right now I've got to see a friend off campus.

"Ellie Marks?" He rolls his eyes. "Watch out for *that* one."

"Why?"

"Never mind." He grins. "Only, just don't get *too* buddy-buddy with her—okay? She might develop the wrong impression."

"What do you mean?"

"I mean, rumor has it that she's one of those girls who, like, doesn't date boys. If you know what I mean. And if you want

my opinion, your lady coach falls right into the same category—
so watch it."

Like it is some shocking piece of news. Some phenomenon I
have never even heard of before. Like he expects me to puke, or
faint, or turn to him sweetly and earnestly and say, Gee Mike,
you're kidding! Thanks for the warning! I never would have
guessed!

What I think of saying is: Oh, *gag* me. I mean, grow *up*. I
didn't exactly fall off some cabbage truck into the world of sport,
you know. All the pools, showers, saunas, weight rooms, Jacuzzis,
massage tables—all the damp nakedness, the hints and whispers,
the sight and the feel of bodies touching, by mistake, or on
purpose. Get on the clue train, pal. Physical people may inevitably do a wide variety of physical things. It's how they express
themselves—in winning, in losing, in love.

What I say instead is: "Don't worry, okay? I mean, I don't
exactly feel en*dan*gered."

"Yeah? Well, I've seen some things in locker rooms. That guys
do, I mean. Makes me want to barf." Standing there, helping
me on with my coat, he wrinkles his nose, fakes vomiting sounds.

"Gee, Mike. That's pretty small-town of you."

"I'm a small-town kind of guy, Babe. Basic values. Narrow
mind, big heart." He hands over my bookbag. "And a thing for
big strong dark beautiful females. But maybe you can enlighten
me. Tell me all about the major leagues and the world's great
cities. Make me more sophisticated."

I blush, I can feel it. He grins, more or less triumphantly. It
pisses me off a little. But at the same time there's something
pleasant about all of his unpleasantness. Something genuinely
hopeful and affectionate in his face, his eyes. So what can I say?

"Friday night, Babe. There's this concert in town. The Deadly
Meatheads."

"Who are The Deadly Meatheads?"

"Local band. But they're pretty good, and they've got this great
drummer. A bunch of us are going. I'll call you."

Okay, I tell him. Then I'm immediately disgusted with myself.
But part of me feels glad.

This part of me hopes that he does call, will hurt if he does
not. Thinks he is conceited, even nasty, intolerant, intolerable;
but also, somehow, adorable.

*   *   *

I'm later showing up at Ellie's than I thought I would be. It's one of those old run-down sagging student slum houses that are all over the place near campus. But walking up the porch steps, seeing some old couch there covered with a tarpaulin for winter, and a rusty watering can; ringing the doorbell, hearing feet on wooden floors, the creak of a shutter, something inside me starts to feel like I wish the place was mine, like I've been homesick for it, or for something like it.

Then the door starts opening, I can feel light flood my face and the sweat start on me even though it's cold. I stare at her, beyond her to the old messy comfortable unfamiliar yellow-lit place, torn furniture, books and clothes thrown everywhere, smoke billowing from the kitchen. And something about stepping out like this, alone, at night, to actually visit someone, seems overwhelming. Too much to deal with. My throat chokes, and I'm afraid.

Then, too, there is all this unspoken emotional *stuff* to get through. I don't know how to even describe it. She seems sad, like she did after morning practice—heavily, wearily sad, but unwilling to explain it. I don't want her to be this way; I want her to be sunny and joking like always, goading me in fun.

Otherwise this so-called dinner will turn into a major bummer.

But I feel like such an inept jerk. There's the familiar sensation, that returns to me as if it never left: of being a big, fat, sweaty freak, sticking out of my surroundings like a sore, sore thumb.

Ellie tries to pretend she's cool, doesn't care. But it's all a sham: she's embarrassed about things not being right, food burned, dessert ruined, the place a mess. I want her to know it's no big deal that the fish caught on fire and the ice cream melted—I mean, I don't eat fish, and won't eat dessert. I want her to look me in the eyes—which lately she has been avoiding—and mock me, and smile, and tell me to chill, seriously chill Delgado, everything will be all right.

But there's been something lost between this morning and now. Neither one of us is saying anything about it. I wish I knew what it was; it's in the air, almost, between her and me—like we just suddenly stopped being friends, and neither of us wanted that, but neither of us could do anything about it.

"I'm queer," she blurts.

I have only known this all along.

Out of consideration for her, though, I do my slightly-bewildered-but-well-intentioned fumbling jock routine.

I swallow hard, try to muster a look of surprise-but-not-horror. "You're kidding."

"No, Delgado, I am distinctly *not* kidding."

She's freaked, I can tell—whenever she's freaked, she gets this oh-so-tough tone to her voice. I rush in with some stupid words, like I'm trying to comfort her. "Oh, um, look, I mean, it's okay with me, Ellie. You know. Whatever. I myself have—I have known plenty of gay people. I mean, people generally don't think about it, but there are *plenty* of gays and, like, lesbians, in sport—right? I mean—um, well, it's really okay with me."

"*Gee whiz* Babe, *gosh*, um, thanks." She crosses her eyes in jest, but sounds bitter. "I mean, God forbid that it should *not* be *okay* with *you*."

Blank-faced, I blink like a moron and let that one slide.

"Listen," she says, "just forget it, okay? Please? Just forget I said anything. And *don't* tell anyone else. Especially anyone on the team."

Just then the smoke alarm sounds off and she races into the kitchen. I follow, find her twisting around there like a maniac, smashing at the high-pitched-drilling little wall box with the stick end of a broom. When she's exhausted herself, dripping sweat, and the alarm's still ringing, I cross over and reach up and pull it off the wall.

The outside door slams.

"Oh, *God*. Ellie, is that you trying to cook again?"

The roommates poke their heads in. I'm surprised; the way Ellie's always talked about them before it's like they're old enough to be her parents, but here they are just a year or so older than me, I think, and neither one looks much like I expected her to. I would have figured that Ellie, being such a dedicated jock, would be living with a couple of power lifters or discus throwers or something—and these two are anything but. Nan, the one with glasses, is a skinny little scholar type, kind mouth, serious wrinkled forehead. Jean's heftier, a little chubby even, wears her hair long and dresses like some old hippie from before I was born; she has freckles, full lips, stern eyes.

Both stare at me a second, give each other glances, raise their eyebrows. Ellie blushes. Then she blurts out:

"Nan, Jean, this is Babe Delgado."

"Whoa. Nice to finally meet you! We've been hearing so much about you!"

I shake Nan's hand, hear Ellie cough off to one side like she wants to puke or sink into the floor or something, and then Nan says This is my lover Jean, so I shake Jean's hand, and can't really think of much to say. I mean, what am I supposed to say? Something like: Well, hi there, I guess you're both lesbians too?

They spend some time then cleaning up, clucking over the kitchen. Ellie and I head out to the living room, such as it is, to blab about the team, and the lit. class, which I am currently flunking.

Later, when I leave, I turn around at the door pushing it open, letting cold almost-wintry gusts in, look at Ellie fully for a moment, want to tell her things. But I wouldn't know how, or even where to begin. She seems frail tonight. Not just frazzled but really, really tired, with a flush on her face like fever, and this angry defiant kind of hurt in her eyes. She smiles, briefly.

"Good luck with Mike."

"Who?"

"Knock-knock! anybody home? Mike *Canelli*. The person we've just spent all night *talking* about."

Tears come into my eyes, suddenly, irrationally, for absolutely no reason, and I step out on the porch, into the cold encircling all the deep protective warm folds of my coat, and blink them away, glad no one can see. It used to happen all the time when I first got out of the hospital. Unpredictably. I was at the mercy of these tears, in a way—never knew when they'd show, rivulet down my face unaccountably, put a fog and ache in my throat.

God, I mumble at the bottom of the porch steps, inanely, to no one in particular. *Please, please, just love me.*

"Huh?" Ellie calls from the doorway, arms guarding her chest from the cold. She coughs. "Sorry, I didn't hear you."

My eyes are dry again. I glance up at her. "Nothing."

"Well, look, I'll see you tomorrow."

"Right."

"And next time, *you* cook."

Usually we'd both laugh on a line like this. But, tonight, neither of us do.

I want to ask her if it's going to be okay. Will this stuff in between us come apart soon, so she'll be Ellie to me again, the Ellie I depend on? I want things to be the way they were, less than a day ago. Before Mike Canelli. Before she said that stupid word, *queer*—a piss-poor way of describing how you feel love.

"Ellie?"

"Yeah."

"I won't tell anyone. I promise."

"Oh. Thanks." She waves, steps back into the dim yellow light of the place, the piles of books and old clothes, wafting remnants of smoke from our ruined dinner. Against the backdrop of light I can't see her face or eyes. The door begins to shut by increments, so there's less and less of her. Wait, I want to say for a minute, wait, don't go, let me back in. Let me back into this warm yellow old house with you, a house my parents and everyone on the team at Southern would despise, and let me stay in it with you, and live.

I have been so homesick.

The door keeps closing. Wind slaps my ears. The last things I see, in silhouette against the inside light, are her wiggling, waving fingers; then a fist, and one solid, firmly held thumbs-up gesture, before the light disappears and the door clicks shut.

I stand and watch maybe a minute or two. There's a lamp on behind ratty old window curtains, shadows moving across it.

Then the wind starts to freeze my earrings and I pull the rim of the wool hat down over them, over my eyebrows, hoist the bookbag onto my back and head for campus. The ankle's starting to act up again, aching fire near tendon and bone, and both knees hurt too, and neck, and shoulders. Bren told me she understood; once she herself had been pretty addicted to aspirin, she said, and to this painkiller they inject right into a joint or muscle that numbs it, but she had to cut all that out. So from one old breaststroker to another she was advising me seriously to stop taking Tylenol 3. And I did, but go tell that to the pain. It won't be impressed. It will dance around like a mockingbird, right in your face, and bubble up, and thrive. You'd think that you would finally get used to it. Only you don't. Pain doesn't get easier to take with time—it gets harder.

And I have been around that, too, for most of my life.

*   *   *

Days start to swing by in this blur, all of a sudden, I don't know why. There's morning workout, afternoon workout, weights three times a week. I make every workout—always a little late, as usual, but always there—and somewhere around then I hear that Ellie is sick, really sick, pneumonia, might be out the rest of the semester but no one really knows. A bunch of them call her from the phone in Brenna Allen's office. I figure I'll do it in private—from my own room, thank you. But a couple of days go by, everything's normal for me, workouts and class as usual, I miss her, but I feel okay, and I don't.

Then a couple more days. I know something's tugging at me, making me want to call her and also *not* want to call her. There's this war in my guts, like some big old jellyfish is getting wrenched apart in there. In between, in the jelly of the jellyfish, is me—and the struggle terrifies me, paralyzes me. I do not call. Sometimes, when the phone rings, I don't pick up.

Whenever I do, it is Mike Canelli. Gossiping about stuff happening on the men's team. Cracking jokes. Putting Coach McMullen down. Asking about my classes. Pestering me to stay on the phone longer, meet him for coffee at such and such a place, for a beer on such and such an evening, go out to this movie, or that bar, to see such and such a band. I don't like him, but I sort of do.

"There's this great steakhouse in town, Babe. Prime cut. Sirloin. Have Amex, will travel. I'll take you."

"Don't," I say, "I'm vegetarian."

"You're kidding. For how long?"

"I don't know. More than a year or two, I guess."

"Very cool, Babe. Very Thoreau of you. What on earth made you do *that*?"

The fog sets in again, inside me, around me. Oh, I tell him, never mind.

"Well, what about Italian? You know, pasta, carbohydrates, yummy yum yum."

Sometimes if a day goes by and he doesn't call, I start to feel kind of relieved but also very bad, like I'm losing something, like I'm being rejected. Then, too, I'll start thinking, *Screw Mike, what about giving Ellie a call, Delgado? I mean, what in the world is wrong with you?*

I'll think about my hand reaching for the phone, dialing her number, and I'll just freeze up inside.

*   *   *

We go to the Italian place on Saturday evening: Mike and I, and his roommate Jeff Brader, a backstroker who does the 100 and the 200 and the 4 x 100 medley relay, and Jeff's girlfriend, Emma, who is slender and blond and wears some nice fourteen-carat jewelry dangling from her ears and neck and wrists, and has these really fantastic clothes and these great leather shoes she says her mother bought for her in Los Angeles. The three of them pick me up on campus, and we head toward town in Mike's car. Jeff bullshits with me a little about team stuff, gets rowdy with Mike, doesn't seem to have much to say to Emma. She, likewise, doesn't seem to have much to say for herself—to him, or to anybody. I look at the good makeup, the expensive jewelry and terrific silks and cottons and leathers of her getup, feel a little ashamed somehow—although not of myself, really— just somehow embarrassed in a way, for *her,* and full of a strange kind of pity. I ask a couple of questions, just to try and be polite. Like, what is she studying? and she says she doesn't know, a little bit of everything. I can tell by the questions she asks Jeff that she's not an athlete herself.

Mike parks crookedly in the restaurant parking lot. It's cold outside, air full of a nasty wind, sky gray and heavy-looking, like it might snow later. There are blank parking spaces on black lined tar surface, opening our way to the restaurant.

The only problem getting there is with Emma. She doesn't want to mess her shoes up. But the air's freezing, the ground icy, and she does quite a sidewalk dance around all the unlit iced-over puddles, the mounds of crusted mud and dead leaves, that could catch on a heel, ruin leather, scuff toes.

"Jeff!" she yells, almost slipping. "Je-EFF!"

He waits for her in the entryway with Mike, cracking up.

She almost falls on her rear end again and I reach out to give her a hand, propel her rapidly across a slick patch with one palm pressed against the small of her back, the other gripping a coat shoulder. No muscle tone. She seems all upset and nervous. Still, she's giggling. I basically shove her toward the entryway while those two idiots stand there making faces, and I feel sorry for her—but also, in some way, I really despise her.

Thanks, she mutters.

"Great," says Jeff. "Nice ice dancing."

Mike laughs. "Pairs competition."

It's a nice place: candles set in glass, dim lighting, plenty of space between tables. The tabletops are covered with actual linen, the napkins cloth, not paper, and each chair bottom and back is lined with a soft tasteful plush. I wonder if my mother would approve.

We are all dressed totally to the max. Everyone here comes from a family with some money. I am almost down to fighting weight these days, and clothes I haven't worn because they were too small on me are beginning to fit, and look good, and my father's been bugging me to go out and charge a bunch of new clothes to those credit cards he gave me.

I am wearing perfume, too, and real gems in each ear, and expensive nylons that don't rip easily but feel like sheer silk, and this dress my mother told me to get once because it is slenderizing—which it is. Maybe Emma's clothes are more L.A. But it's not that at all that makes me dislike her. I think maybe it's not even *her* I dislike so much as it is the guys themselves; Jeff treats her like she's some kind of bimbo, and Mike just sort of goads him on—and whether she really *is* or is *not* a bimbo seems beside the point. I mean I don't care, but it doesn't seem fair.

I wonder why my first reaction is to hate her, though, instead of getting pissed off at them. It's like I want to be on their side, somehow, by ganging up against her in my mind.

I notice that they're talking to me differently from the way they talk to Emma: With her, they joke and tease and flirt; with me, they joke and tease a little but more respectfully somehow, as if they might even consider talking to me seriously—like I'm one of the boys. Must be the athletics they assume we have in common.

Which may or may not be true. Personally, I think that their approach to the sport is pathetic. I think they're full of bullshit; typical devil-may-care big-tough-muscular-guy bravado nonsense from whiners who are basically afraid to really let it *all* hang out and give up on their *image* and just hurt.

Liz had a term for guys like them: Dogmeat.

But I do feel a kind of relief that, for whatever fucked up reason, they seem to genuinely differentiate between me and Emma. I wouldn't know what to do if they spoke to me like they do to her. Although, to be honest, she doesn't really seem to mind. The parking lot incident just sort of rolled off her back.

Every little deprecation and verbal cattle prod seems to be something she expects.

I have to admit, too, that she's obviously had a lot of practice with their crap, handles it well. Which is something I know I would not be able to do; I'd probably freak out, and leave, or cry, or yell, or smack them both. For some reason, knowing that she is better at taking this shit than I could ever be makes me feel inferior to her. I mean, as a girl, in a way, a normal girl. As a woman.

Because I realize—and I've known it before, but never really *felt* it until now—that all those years I spent training my guts out, girls like Emma spent training themselves for other things. For the rest of what their lives would be. Lives with makeup, and clothes, and boyfriends, and men. It seems weird and ridiculous to me, as if she is one of a bunch of Martians who just landed on my planet; but I realize, too, that *I* am the real Martian here—I am the abnormal one, in the eyes of the world. Emma never would have dreamed of qualifying for the Olympic Trials, of attaining that level of skill. But, while I was busy attaining that level of skill, I missed out on normalcy.

Not being normal—for the first time, I feel it, really feel the pain and the anguish of it deep, deep down inside—it sticks in your craw like stones. And part of the pain, I know now, is being so alone.

On the other hand, I think, so what?

I *don't* fit into their world anyway. Maybe, swimming or not, I *never would have* fit in.

We get our menus and the background erupts again into this constant chatter of goading and teasing between Emma and Jeff, Jeff and Mike. Repartee time. It's not particularly clever, but there is enough of it, constantly enough, so that I feel a little on edge, sort of intimidated.

Mike's eyes light with mischief. "What are our lovely ladies eating tonight?"

"Me!" Jeff howls.

Emma wrinkles her nose. "Je-EFF. That is really *gross*."

"I don't know, Ems. You never seem to mind."

Mike slugs his shoulder. "Okay man, shut up. We happen to be in a decent place, you know. Plus, Babe isn't used to scumbags like you."

"Is that true, Babe?" Jeff pulls an innocent wide-eyed stare, swallows loudly. I look at him and can't think of anything to say, so I don't. This seems to make him uncomfortable. After a minute he shrugs, shoots me a look that is half apologetic, half resentful. "Well, I promise to change my ways, then. If just for tonight." He leers at Emma. "But not for *all* of it."

The waiter comes by, asks do we want anything to drink. Mike says a double Johnnie Walker on the rocks please. Jeff orders a beer. Emma says she will have a white wine spritzer. I ask for a Manhattan. I've never had one, and don't even know what the hell is in it, but I heard my dad order one once and always wanted to myself—I just really like the sound of the name.

Mike winks at me. "Ah. A girl after my own heart."

What? I say.

"Hard-drinking, good-loving."

That's a lot of horse manure. He has maybe seen me have a beer once. And as far as good-loving goes, who knows? *He* certainly doesn't. I mean, I don't even know if *I* do. We have gone places together a few times in the last couple of weeks, have never had more than a hug and a kiss on the cheek. And the last time I did anything, really anything, with anyone, feels like it was so long ago that it might as well have been in another lifetime. But Jeff laughs, and Mike has a moment of glory. Which, for whatever reason, I don't want to destroy.

The drinks arrive. I watch my Manhattan swirl golden-brown around ice cubes and a cherry so red it glows. Emma immediately sips at her white wine spritzer, which is bubbly and colorless.

The waiter asks are we ready to order.

"Ladies first." Jeff smiles at me, at Emma. He sounds almost bitter.

Emma tells me to go ahead if I'm ready, but I'm not. She says she isn't really either, but if she waits any longer she'll get into this bizarre state where she just can't order at all, and it drives everybody crazy, so she guesses she'll just have the linguine with white clam sauce.

The waiter looks at me expectantly. He's a young guy, slender and clean-faced, smells of tomatoey spices, and grease, and aftershave. I can feel myself start to sweat. What do you say? But I save myself by waving one hand a little as if I just don't care, and manage to blurt: "Um, I'm not quite ready, why don't you guys go ahead and I'll order last."

Jeff orders chicken cacciatore, garlic bread, and a cold antipasto. Canelli says he'll have minestrone and a hot antipasto to start out with, then some pasta carbonara, and a small plate of Italian sausage on the side.

"I mean—" he looks at me "—if it doesn't bother you or anything."

"Oh, it won't."

"What do you mean, *bother* her?" says Jeff.

Mike glances his way arrogantly. "Babe is a vegetarian." He says it so seriously and so proudly that, for a moment, I like him. But, now, it is my turn. The terror swells up inside. He turns to me, a sweetly protective look on his face. "Have you figured out what you want, honey?"

Honey. That is a new one.

Thinking about it—the "honey," I mean—I can feel my fear diminish a little so that I almost give a nervous laugh. But I keep cool, and don't.

I ask the waiter if there is something he can suggest from the menu that is good but doesn't have meat in it. He thinks a minute. Then says to try the spaghetti with garlic and butter sauce.

"Okay, fine." I want to wipe my forehead. Instead I lean my elbow on the table for a moment and put my head against my hand, and manage to scrape a little sweat off that way.

"Is that all you're having?" asks Jeff.

"I guess so."

The waiter chimes in: "The portions are really pretty big. It's plenty." He's saved me somehow, and I bless him.

"Wow," says Emma, "how long have you been a vegetarian? I mean, do you sort of just-say-no to all meat, including fish? And chicken? Or do you eat it once in a while?"

Jeff sneers. "If she ate meat once in a while she wouldn't be a real vegetarian, Ems."

"Right. But, I mean, what made you become one?"

Well, I tell her, it's a long story.

"No, I mean, did you have some kind of dream about a bunch of innocent cows being slaughtered, or little piglets squealing, with, like, lots of blood and guts—"

"Christ," Jeff mutters, "shut *up*."

Emma blinks. For a moment, a frightened pain comes into her eyes, but then it's gone. Still, I see it, and it surprises me. She rubs traces of lipstick from her mouth corners. I wonder how she knows it was there. Must be instinct. Like anything, becomes natural with practice.

"I mean," she says gently, with this fearful quaver in her voice, "I mean, like, I really don't mean to be rude or anything. It's like, I just think that when someone makes, you know, a decision like that, like to become a vegetarian, in this society—"

Jeff and Mike guffaw. *In this society,* Jeff sneers, *All right, professor.*

It stops her for a moment, then she just ignores them and continues.

"—It's like, maybe it means something happened once that sort of changed you. In order to make such a decision, I mean. So I guess I'm sort of asking, I mean, in all sincerity, really and truly—"

"In all *sincerity,*" Jeff mimics.

"—Did you see something once, like a bunch of animals, actually being slaughtered? And did it fill you with—"

"*Fill* you with," says Jeff.

Emma takes a deep breath, keeps staring at me with wide eyes, so that I feel for a second maybe she is fighting away tears. When she talks, the voice is a whisper.

"—pity?"

Something cold rushes through me. Something dull rolls down my face, across the makeup of my cheek. Sweat, or crying, I don't know. There is this blockage in my throat that hurts. But my eyes seem dry. Still, I can't feel much but the big solid cold rushing through—can't tell if I am sweating a lot or crying emotionlessly, and for a second I feel as if everyone at the table and everyone in the restaurant has gone completely silent, and is staring at me, Babe Delgado, former champion, former animal, now a meatless freak. I force some words out.

Sure, I tell her, something like that. But it's, like, too weird to explain.

"Sounds kinky," says Jeff.

Mike gulps his drink. When he talks he is angry and disgusted. In the dim light his face is flushed, and he looks Jeff directly in the eyes. For a moment, I like him again—really like him.

"Man, what is wrong with you?"

"Nothing, last time I checked down there. When was the last time *you* checked, Canelli?"

"Suck my dick, asshole."

Jeff slams his empty beer mug on the tablecloth. Emma waves a hand calmly between the two of them.

"Okay, you guys, that's enough."

Jeff glowers at Mike, then at her, ignoring me. When he talks it is to Emma, and he sounds a little grumpy and crestfallen, like a kid complaining to his mother. "Did you hear what he said?"

"Come on, Jeff," she says gently, "just *chill*."

"Stupid faggot," he mutters.

Mike glares. "Oh shut up, dickless. Get a life."

Emma gulps some of her wine spritzer. "Look, can we just have a nice dinner and forget about all this? I swear, you two are such babies sometimes."

I stare at the Manhattan. Ice melting. I reach with numbed fingers and grab the sweating glass, will all my taste buds into numbness too and swallow as much of it as my mouth will hold. It burns, makes me want to gasp and spit it out, hits deep inside near the tip of my stomach and almost makes me puke. I shudder. Sensation returns to my face and hands. Now I, too, am looking at Emma as if she alone has some kind of wisdom that will save me, save us all.

She waves again mildly, to everyone, fingers fluttering—a very feeble kind of gesture, but we are all fixed on her as if she had just jumped onto the table brandishing a sawed-off shotgun. She smiles at Jeff and Mike. Quietly. Assuredly.

"Now, why don't you two patch things up? *We* are going to the little girls' room." She stands, beckons me. "Come on, Babe."

I take the napkin from my lap and fold it neatly on the table, next to my empty plate and half-finished Manhattan. When I stand my head buzzes a little, weak and hot. But I follow her almost blindly as she picks her way among tables and booths, with a sort of senseless faith, like I'm following some trusted military leader into combat.

The door to the ladies' room swings open and closes behind us. Too-bright lighting. Pink sinks. Empty beige stalls. This smell rushes over me, a very thick, heavy, musky smell: women's flesh, perfume, blood. There is something terrible and revolting about it. Also, though, and at the same time, something wonderful—

it is warm, and real, makes me feel my heart pound hard, makes me feel terribly edgy and nervous but also quite at home. So that I want to run away. And also to stay, to stay forever.

No, I say to myself, silently. Then: Help.

"Whew! Touch-up time."

Emma sets her purse on the pink sink ledge, pulls out a makeup bag. She presses hands to her hair. Examines her face from different angles in the wall-length mirror. Grabs a tube of mascara and unscrews it and starts to reapply it. I do the same.

"God. Those guys are such a pain sometimes."

"Mmmm," I say.

"But Mike really likes you a *lot*."

I believe her. Somehow, though, it seems unfair; why should he suddenly decide to like *me* so much, without knowing me, really, without me even being sure that I like him at all?

I see that some liner has smudged around one of my eyelids, spend time fixing it. Maybe I was crying before after all and didn't even know it.

Sharp, Delgado. Very sharp indeed.

Emma puts on fresh lipstick. I do the same. I glance at both faces in the mirror, under the ugly lights. She looks a lot younger than I, though I know she is not. Much smaller-framed, very slender, hair longer and permed and naturally blond. Her lipstick is a glossy cherry color. Mine is darker. She smudges her lips together, smiles.

"Wow, that's a really nice red."

"Thanks."

"What do they call it? Wine red or burgundy or something?"

"Yeah. I think."

She drops hers into the compact case, pulls out a hairbrush that looks like some kind of torture instrument—spikes all around the tip, black-handled, metal-capped.

"So. Do *you* like Mike?"

It takes me by surprise. Something shoots danger signals along the back of my neck. Reminding me that I am at a loss here, don't know how to handle myself, what to say or do. I try to cover the alarm up by rummaging through my purse, pretending I am looking for something.

Finally I say, "He's a nice guy."

"He's a *great* guy. I mean, I've known Mike for a really long time, he and Jeff have been friends for years, practically. But Jeff's acting like a creep tonight."

"Why do you go out with him?"

It blurts from me before I can stop it.

She just shrugs. "I don't know. There's nothing much better out there, really. You know what I mean?"

I don't, but nod anyway.

"I mean"—she continues, carefully patting strands of wavy yellow hair behind an ear—"who wants to keep looking forever? He's okay most of the time, he's got a great body, he doesn't forget to call when he says he will, he opens doors for me, and when we go out together, he always pays. Sure, he's a jerk sometimes. But you can't ask for everything."

The words are hard, matter-of-fact. She seems completely different now from the meek and gentle person taking shit and making peace out at the restaurant table; still, that person seemed completely real, too—just like this one—and I wonder if, in her heart, Emma is either one of them, or neither, or both.

"Come on, Babe. Back to the war."

I would rather be back in my little dorm room. Or bathing my knees in the locker room whirlpool. Or, for that matter, falling on my ass in a deep, dark cave.

Or hanging out with Ellie in that poor tired warm old yellow place she lives in.

But I can't. Ellie's really sick, no one will see her for a good long while, and I haven't even called her.

The Manhattan spins through my stomach, lurching and burning. Really sick. And I haven't called. It's fear spinning through me again, not booze. Fear of the sickness, and vomit, and the water. Animal flesh. Blood. The way animals shriek when you kill them.

You are animals, my geniuses, animals, because only animals survive in the wilderness. This water here, see, this is the wilderness. And you, my geniuses, must be not geniuses but animals. Eat, eat. *Bon appétit!* Guts of our ancestors. Age-old ritual—works every time. Living meat beats dead meat, believe me.

And everybody laughed.

I follow Emma out into the restaurant. Understanding that, in this particular wilderness, I am sadly lost. She alone knows the rules of survival, and—if I do as she does—I will learn them too, and get along, and probably wash on in with the tide. I don't even like her. But I certainly don't pity her any more. And, somehow, I trust her.

Mike and Jeff are sitting at the table, heads slightly bowed, not really talking. They've ordered another round of drinks for us all, and are chowing down on antipasto. Jeff looks up.

"Well, Ems. Did you ladies gossip away?"

"Sure." She winks at me, sits. "All about you guys. But I will never tell."

"Right," I say. And I sit, too.

Jeff chuckles warmly, puts an arm around Emma's chair and glances her way with real affection.

Mike looks across the table at me with a kind of delight, and relief; like he wasn't quite sure of what to do about me before, but suddenly recognizes something familiar in me, and—now that I am familiar—he can invite me into his club.

Our dinners arrive. We drink, and laugh.

After dinner all four of us pile into Mike's car, and he drives along dark wintry streets, hugging the contours, making the wheels screech sometimes, running one red light and a stop sign. Dead leaves blow against the windshield. In the headlights they look like enormous winged night bugs, flying right toward us.

Jeff and Emma are quiet, cuddled together in the back seat. They seem really relaxed now, at peace, her head resting on his chest. Mike drops them off at his place, which he shares with Jeff and another guy on the team, and some other guy who used to throw discus but is now in business school. I watch them walk, arm in arm, to the front door, their dark-coated backs to us. For a minute, I want them to turn around and come back and stay awhile—not because I want *them* to be with me, but I don't want to be alone—or, at any rate, alone with Mike, which feels like kind of the same thing. But he turns to me, looking a little shy, trying to cover it up with a sure, harsh tone of voice, shrugs and says, Well, where to now?

Oh, I tell him, take me home.

Thinking that, if we're going to do it tonight, at least the sheets are clean. And I will definitely make him wear a rubber.

I more or less hope we don't.

At the same time, though, I'm curious.

He parks in a side street near central campus, right around the corner from the dorm. I turn to him, wave a hand the way Emma did. Thanks, I tell him, I had a good time.

Me too, he says. Then he says he'll walk me to my room, it's pretty late and girls have been raped on campus walking alone at night; there are a lot of creeps in the world.

In the elevator he takes off one of his gloves and one of my gloves, too, and holds my hand. I don't really mind. He presses my palm with his thumb, lightly caressing. Then, in the cracked dim light as we squeak past floors, he turns my hand palm up and examines it.

"Weird."

"What?"

"Your life-line. It's really strong. But short. I mean, there's this break in it—here—a definite break—and then it's like it continues again. Very firm. Very long. Sort of like you died, you know? then came back to life."

"Where'd you learn to read palms?"

"This great-aunt on my father's side. She was sort of a witch—you know, from the old country, believed in spirits."

"What old country?"

"Italy. My dad's grandparents were from northern Italy."

I tell him my dad is from Cuba, and I have this aunt who is into the spirits, too, though she does not read palms.

The elevator stops and he keeps holding my hand on our way down the hall. Somewhere, a door slams. There's the far-off sound of a toilet flushing, stereos and CD's roaring behind walls, beer cans opening, someone giggling. There is the pseudo-revolutionary mural on one of the walls. He stops to gaze at it. Saying, What is this, some kind of Commie shit?

Yeah, I tell him, probably.

I don't tell him the rest of what I know, which is basically stuff that Ellie told me: how Communism was once this really honorable thing to be in America, back in the thirties; how her own dad was a Communist or Socialist or something in Poland, and believed in the rights of the working class, and of all people, to a decent life; and how it was just as much for being a political radical or liberal or whatever, as it was for being a Jew, that the Nazis wanted him dead.

Mike hasn't let go of my hand, and I pause at the door. His

fingers lace with mine. It feels okay. Not particularly thrilling, but not bad either. This makes me hopeful. He smiles, and then for a moment seems anxious. Finally he blurts: "Look, Babe, can I come in?"

"Yeah," I say, "okay."

I unlock the door, switch on a light. Bed made. Drawers shut. Posters intact on walls. The small refrigerator hums softly. Tiny red CD light glows on a shelf, between speakers.

This is great, he says, like a whole little suite. I mean, you've got a bathroom and kitchen space and everything. Free ride?

I nod.

Well sure, he says, what else would it be.

We take off our coats and lay them on a chair. He looks nice, sort of—polished shoes, good brown sweater over his dress shirt, nice pants. The handsome face, strong chin and blunt nose, big forehead; golden eyebrows and hair cut very, very close, with the dyed-ebony little pigtail in back—it's good, it's nice. When he gets over himself he'll be a manly man. Succeed in business. Father children. Fool around on his wife, but in between bad times make her happy. They will have a nice house. On some winter nights he'll make his kids sit around him near the fire and he'll show them all his age grouper trophies from the glass case on the wall. U.S. Swimming, he'll boom proudly. Qualified for Senior Nationals in high school, went down to Industry Hills to fight it out with the best but I blew it big-time—too lazy to practice, that was my problem. Wound up in Division II. Sure had a blast, though. Had a car, had some credit cards, spent some time drinking and chasing pus—chasing girls. Me and my good pal Brader. Yeah, I was best man at his first wedding, when he married Emma. And after she left him for that fucking Cuban restaurant owner—greasy nigger spic bastard—I was best man at his second, third, fourth, and fifth weddings, too. Poor slob. The alimony and child support's killing him. Who'd have thought we would turn out this way? There's a lesson in this, kids: If you want to succeed in life, you've got to make the right goddamned choices *early*.

Ho-NEY, his wife will say, don't SWEAR in front of the KIDS.

The kids will look up at him and he'll wink, sharing a private joke, silently making a pact with them to continue swearing but not when she's within earshot. They giggle, happily. Loving him.

Not knowing that he's a double-dealing handsome bastard who steps out on her—and on them—all the time. Knowing only that he is their funny, playful, powerful father. And the mother is not funny, or playful, or powerful at all. So they stare up, adoring.

There are four of them. Two girls, two boys. They all have his hair, his eyes. His name.

"Do you want something like—I don't know, tea or something?"

"Nah. Come here. I didn't finish your palm."

I sit next to him on the couch with about a cushion's space between us, extend my hand and he turns it palm up again, presses various lines and curves with his fingertips.

"Well, after that weirdness, that break, you're probably going to live to be about a hundred. No kidding. I see a little confusion early on, some messing around, you know? But then one relationship. I mean, you mate for life. No children, though. Wait. There's one. Just one."

He explains what all the lines mean, points out where they are. Then offers his own hand, palm up.

"Go ahead. You can read mine, if you want."

"No thanks, Mike. I already know your future."

"Oh yeah? What are you, some kind of prophet or something? Tell me."

Oh, I say, Why spoil things? I'll just let you live it.

"Well then. Why don't you just tell me what the near future holds in store—"

"Near?"

"Yeah. Like the next hour or so."

He's grinning, half mischievous, half serious, a little nervous. Trying to cover up the nervousness with the right mix of eager humor and bravado. I don't know how I know this, but I do. Then I feel bad for him, and for me. And these other dark things well up inside: self-revulsion, worthlessness.

"Whatever," I say. "I don't really care."

He leans back, confused. "You don't?"

Oh, I want to say, sure I do, but it's really not worth going into, let's just do it and get it over with, okay?

Instead, though, I start to cry.

"Hey, Babe. What'd I do?"

"Nothing," I blurt. "It's got nothing to do with you."

He scoots across the cushion between us, puts his arms around me kind of clumsily. I cry against the front of his good brown sweater, smearing it with mascara and rouge. Pressing my palm, his hands were graceful and knowing; now, patting my back and hair, they feel openly fumbling, young, insecure.

Hey, he keeps saying, hey, hey.

"You know," I sob, "I've got scars all over."

"Yeah? Like, where?"

"Like everywhere." Thinking about them makes me want to throw up. Another sob gushes out, my nose running against his chest. "It's really gross."

"Well, look." He clears his throat. "Everybody's got problems, you know?"

"I know."

"No, I mean—like, do you really? I mean, last summer I was really fucked up, I couldn't even wipe my own ass."

"What did you do?"

"Asked the nurses. Christ, it was fucking embarrassing! Sometimes my dad, or my brother. And sometimes"—he blushes a horrible red when I glance up at him with mascara and eyeliner dripping around my cheeks, making me look like a raccoon—"I'd be so fucking embarrassed that I wouldn't ask anyone. I'd just walk around"—he laughs—"with my ass full of shit—"

Suddenly, we are both laughing. Loudly. With laughter that isn't full of comedy, really, but of relief.

"Well," I gasp, "that's kind of where I'm at, I guess. Too fucking embarrassed, and my ass—"

"Yeah," he grins, his eyes wet with tears. "Oh, God!" Then he laughs even harder, until his face starts to crack, and I hug him.

Which is sort of how it happens. His face against my chest, half-laughing, half-crying, both of us in this giddy emotional state—which feels confusing but also like release—and he presses me over onto my side on the couch, and lies there squashed up next to me, and we start to kiss.

It's nice at first. He has soft lips; I like the firm, square feel of his neck and shoulders, and there is something endearing about his not-quite-gone pot belly, ballooning into mine. Fine, okay, I think. So far so good. There's this moment when I think he really sees me, too, and wants to know me somehow. His eyes are shining and open, friendly, honest, wanting. But then they shut, and something harder settles over the face, something urgent, and I look inside myself for the same urgent thing but find only a warm-tinged, fuzzy-edged emptiness. Then, too, this borderline-mean determination: I will not let him see the scars, not any of them; we can do it if he wants, as long as he has a rubber, but it will be in the dark, with at least a few clothes on. Maybe, if I feel safely unseen like that, or if I can at least shut my eyes and pretend, I will even enjoy it this time.

I did, sometimes, with Kenny.

A week goes by like this. I fall farther behind in my classes. I concentrate hard during practice. First meet of the year is coming up—a home meet, thank God—and I'll need every last ounce of guts just to show my face. Mike Canelli says he will, too. Coach McMullen convinced him not to redshirt. Which, if you ask me, is a dumb mistake—he's still overweight, and his arms and shoulders can't really take it yet; but nobody's asking me—and, on the other hand, look who's talking. Mike calls a lot, pestering. It's not his fault. I mean, I like him. He's just a guy, doing what guys do, trying to get laid; plus I think he probably likes spending time with me. But I can't tell. Maybe he would be just as eager to spend time deep-sea diving, or parachuting. Something new and different. Delgado, she's a challenge. Plane crash survivor. Swims okay. Even talks back sometimes. Never takes off all her clothes.

We do it a couple more times, actually, during the next few days. Always in my room, on the couch, in the dark. Afterwards I feel the warm, fuzzy, tender sensations inside. I like the feel of his hair and his flesh. I like all his muscles; I even think his flab is kind of cute. But the stuff he does to me feels so empty—and it's not his fault, but mine; it just really does not move me, even though I try, shut my eyes and try, imagine, pretend. By the end of the week I am walking around tired and guilty. I mean, here I am, using him as a kind of experiment, and he doesn't even know it.

Friday night I go over to his place after dinner. It's one of those split-level apartment complexes filled with students. Their place is a mess. Not like Ellie's place, though—this is more of an expensive mess, the kind of mess I am used to: VCR's, CD's, color TV, high-tech cameras, good clothes in unwashed piles, dirty Teflon pans and an encrusted Cuisinart cluttering up the kitchen, empty bottles of imported beer on tables, rugs, chairs.

Mike takes my coat.

Emma and Jeff are stretched out on the sofa looking stoned, watching MTV. They both turn, grin, wave. There's some guy dancing around on the screen to this tune that is a cross between rap and heavy metal.

Are you black enough!

Are you black enough!

Are you black enough for me!

"Hey Babe," yells Jeff. "Are *you* black enough?"

Emma smacks his arm gently.

"Shut up, asshole," Mike mutters.

I decide to ignore them all. Which is difficult, with Mike complaining about his shoulders—and it's serious, but predictable, really, because he should have redshirted until his arms and back had at least come all the way back to strength—but I still feel like snapping at him: Oh, be quiet you whining little white boy, everybody's shoulders always hurt in this game so just shut up and deal; I could tell you some things about pain.

"Something special tonight," he winks, "for dessert." He goes to the refrigerator and pulls out a little jar, uncaps it, shakes things into his palm. "Here, Babe. Take one."

"One what?"

"One little piece of bliss. A few hours of sex and fearlessness, guaranteed. The thinking man's drug of choice."

A few hours. I figure he's got practice in the morning, too, and wouldn't sabotage himself; and it's not exactly the first pill I've popped, so I shrug and swallow it with water.

He takes one too, then shuffles over to Jeff and Emma and hands a couple out. Emma oohs and aahs about it, saying how much she loves this stuff and how rare it is to get any these days, and wherever did he find it?

Under a rock, Ems, snorts Jeff. And she slaps his arm again, saying Je-EFF, shut UP.

Mike tells me half an hour, max, you'll know when it hits, then we'll have some fun. I toss some empties and cassettes aside, and settle into a recliner. I can hear, but don't listen to, him and Jeff and Emma chattering away against the busy, flashing background of MTV.

After a while they get quieter.

I watch dull reflections of television images on the ceiling, dancing. Then my eyes travel down along the wall, catch the direct glow of a lamp, and something buzzes through me like shock. When I open my eyes again, everything is brighter—shot through and tinged with a quivering halo of light.

Someone giggles.

I ask may I make a phone call. Sure, Mike says, go ahead. There's a hush to the bright air—lights and colors enhanced, sound muted. Quietly, quietly, I move into the kitchen. Then I dial a number and break out in nauseous sweat, and fear slams me right flat down on the floor, phone cord wrapped around me, words frozen inside.

"Hello," says a voice.

"Hi," I hear, "can I speak to Ellie."

"Ellie's sleeping. But I'll take a message."

"Oh," I whisper. "Never mind."

Someone leans over, casting a shadow. I hand the phone away and he hangs it up, then stretches out right next to me on the kitchen floor.

"Oh, no."

"No what, Babe?"

"I'm afraid."

It is oozing out of me, through every pore. As if the fear became a solid tangible poisonous thing inside, and then something pierced it, melted it, so that now it's gushing out in wave after wave from my skin.

"Hey," he says gently. "Just chill."

"It's Angelita."

"Who?"

"No one," I tell him, "never mind."

Then the nausea fades. I can feel the sweat on me chill, and dry—just like that; and, just like that, open my eyes wider to see the light still there, lifting and surrounding everything, but glowing now, less sharply, without the hot bright edge of fear. Mike sits up. His hand crushes kitchen floor crumbs, and they're beautiful, just beautiful. I gaze up into his face. A youthful, common, friendly face, smoothed and informed by the light.

"Mike, you're an angel."

"Wow." He chuckles, happy.

"You know, you're full of love. And so is Angelita."

"What's that, Babe?"

"Wind," I say. "A storm."

"Ah. You know, Babe, I could make you happy."

"Um. I don't think so."

"I could hold you in my arms. It'd be nice, naked."

I reach for his hand and he gives it openly. Open Hand Boy, I think. Remembering. But it took pills for him to be this way; he isn't really Kenny.

He caresses my thumb, my palm. Gently, full of love. "We could be tight, Babe—we could, you know, be lovers—"

"No, Mike, that's not what I want. It isn't your fault, okay? I just don't want to be with you. I mean, we can't fuck any more."

"Why not?"

"Because, I really don't like it."

"Oh, wow," he says. His face is open, hurt. "I'm sorry."

"Don't be. You are, like, my angel. I can't explain. But I want to thank you. You've been really good to me."

"I have?"

"Sure. And also—look, don't take this the wrong way—"

"Yeah?"

"You need and deserve new friends."

In the living room, someone snorts. MTV flashes on, off. In between the lyrics, which are rushing by my ears now and make no sense at all, I hear kissing sounds and giggles.

I move to a vertical position, tread lightly, very lightly, through the gentle glow that is soft and almost soundless. My coat and boots and bag are stashed away under a bunch of other things; I search the mound to find them, feeling how special, how fully textured and pleasurable, each object is within my hand. I fade down, and up. Sitting. Standing.

"Hey," says Emma, "don't go. It's cold out there."

Jeff laughs. "Babe's darker than you, Em, don't worry. Night is night. She will fade right in."

I squish my feet around in socks and boots. Pleasure. Warm, sweatless glow. Push an arm into my coat. Another. Muted sound of buttons. I clench a fist. Fit on gloves. Swing my strong arms. Loving. Strong. Fearless. And, for a moment, feel awash with pity. I'd really like to help them.

"Jeff."

He glances over the back of the couch.

"See a doctor, Jeff. You're in desperate need of help. I am not kidding. Seek immediate medical attention for your hatred and your fear."

He chuckles in a way that is surprised, but also somehow unperturbed. "Screw you, Babe."

"No, no, I don't think so. Even that wouldn't cure you."

"Yeah." Emma grinds her teeth. Smiles. "She's right, you know."

I step out into the hall, down some stairs, floating. There is snow on the ground. Halfway home, I roll in it. Not too hot, not too cold.

Angelita, I say, who are you. Teach me things.

But the light is all outside me and, after a while, starts to recede. I sing softly as it goes, try to hurry back before I feel it leave completely, get into my room and turn on a lamp just in time. Then I make myself some tea. I feel a headache rise, and pound.

The next morning, my limbs are like rusted metal wedges in the water. Really, my heart is in it. But the rest of me malfunctions.

No one says anything. At least, not at first. For that, I am grateful.

After practice, I crawl out of the pool last and limp past Etta and Brenna Allen with a kickboard, hoping for more mercy.

"Uh-uh," says Etta. "Where you going, white girl?"

"Shut up," I snap. "Just cut it out with that white girl shit, okay?"

She frowns. "Someone's going to spank you, kid, sooner or later. But I don't have the time."

At the locker room door I am confronted by lady Coach. She crosses her arms, looking exhausted and deadly serious, blocking the way. When she speaks, her voice is firm and quiet.

"Whatever it is, cut it out."

I refuse to meet her eyes.

"Whatever you took. However you got it."

"Yeah." I nod, feeling fried. "Okay, Bren, I will. I mean, I already have."

Back in my room I get the first big engulfing wave of panic:

the meet is next weekend, I am fucking up school big-time, and Ellie's nowhere around. I stare at the phone and tell it, Fuck you. Fuck you, I won't call. I will get through it all myself, understand? I am strong enough now. I am well enough. I can get through some homework and a lousy swimming meet on my own, thanks; I can do fine, just fine, without you.

Broken Down

🐬 🐬 🐬

(E L L I E)

It seems that our Coach has decided to teach me my new events the hard way. I basically just hate her now, more than anything or anyone.

The distance workouts are murderous. Half the time I walk around feeling like I'm crippled. The rest of the time I am convinced that I ought to check into a hospital emergency room and get them to x-ray my shoulders.

My insides are in rotten shape, too, from cranial to cardiac region. I'm kept pretty busy attempting to hide the truth about Captain Hammerhead's pathetic psychological and emotional state from my pigheaded team mates. So that I'm learning, with every miserable minute of workout, locker room, and the rest of life—if you can call it a life—all there is to learn about pain.

Pain hurts. But that's the good news.

The bad news consists of everything else.

"Hmmm." Jean dumps a grocery bag into my arms. "Sounds like love to me."

Who asked you? I say.

She tells me I am awfully touchy these days. Moody. And rude. I take things inside, spill them on the kitchen counter without apologizing.

"Ellie, let's talk."

I ignore her, head upstairs. And run into Nan, who looks

steamed-fresh perky, wet-haired, towel-wrapped, whistling on her way down from the shower. She flicks sliding wire-rims back up her nose and winks.

"Hey. I like your new girlfriend."

"Oh, shut up."

"What? What did you say?"

I lose it. Totally. Standing on the stairs screaming like a maniac about how much I hate everything—their false and insensitive assumptions, and this stingy, mediocre place, and Brenna Allen, and swimming, and love, and fear, and life itself.

Wow! Jean yells from the kitchen. *Better call an ambulance!*

I push past Nan, get to my room and smash the door shut behind. Then I let it happen—what I've been wanting and dreading all along: the crumple, the fall. But the mattress is comforting somehow, between me and the floor, and I feel my cheeks sink into pillows that will absorb every tear. Because here, all alone, I can cry.

Dinner was the last straw. Perfect punctuation to what has so far been a perfectly miserable autumn.

But the truth is that it started before then, started when I recognized the sway of things.

That's what I began to call it, anyway—silently, almost without knowing it: this feeling I get toward the end of my main set each morning workout—usually during the third to the last repeat, so no matter how bad it is I know there's plenty more to go. When I start to believe that things just cannot continue like this—my arms turn to lead in the water, shoulders protest that they are all used up, and the right side of my neck feels as if someone's been banging on it with a nightstick. When I'm wrapped inside this pitiless wet blanket of sorrow, and hurting, and rage, I can't fight the slowing down any more, I know my splits have deteriorated and my stroke is falling entirely apart. But at the same time the pain changes, reveals a different piece of itself. Becomes buoyant somehow, and rhythmic. So that I just keep moving—slowly, futilely, but forward. And that, that is the sway.

Later, after the last repeat, after swimming down, after shower and hair-dryer and powdered skin and dry clothes, there's the walk upstairs, during which I notice that I am still in its grip. Moving in the rhythm of the rhythmic part of pain. And there's this blurry halo over everything: eyesight a little hazy, sounds ringing as if they're too far off, sense of touch gone slightly numb. But somehow the organism still works, moving me forward, a kind of coordination in the motion of each bludgeoned muscle.

It's like being encapsulated in something. Insular. Remote. Inside a stream of aching, and sadness, and loss, that no one else can really touch or understand. But you're traveling ahead despite yourself—you don't even know why. Everything visible and invisible just more or less conspires to make you proceed. Like what it must be when you're dying.

I recognized it, this sway of things, some time toward the end of our third week in the water. That's when Brenna Allen pulled me aside and said to bear with it, for a while I was just going to have to do these punishing sets of nothing but distance, distance, but it would make me strong in the end. I smiled and said fine. But I said it like a robot, and could tell that she knew what I really felt inside. *A little whirlpool now,* she said gently. *Next week we'll get you a massage. Good work, Ellie.* She was looking pretty beat herself, a lot older, kind of tired and thin. Not that I gave a damn.

That's when Babe started waiting around for me after morning workouts, too. She was looking better and better all the time—starting to take on the shape of a real bona fide national-class act now: slimmer, ruddy-skinned, bright-eyed, muscular—while I kept getting weaker, paler, less significant. Like something you'd find squirming under a rock.

You're pretty buddy-buddy with Delgado these days, Karen Potalia said in the free weights room that week. *Why don't you ask her if it's true?*

If what is true? I grunted.

We finished one set of push-ups and took a long rest, cheating.

"That she died on her way to the hospital and, you know, came back to life. It's what *I* heard, anyway. They gave her one of those electric shocks or something—you know? Like the bride of Frankenstein. I mean, God, have you seen all those scars? *Barf.*"

"Fuck you, Karen. Why don't you just ask her yourself, if you're oh-so curious?"

"Wow, Ellie. Didn't know it was such a touchy subject. I *apol*ogize."

But a nasty flicker remained in her eyes. It's a part of her that flares up occasionally and makes me uneasy, and I saw it flare higher when the whole giggling mess of them poured in from swim bench and Nautilus, Babe tagging along silently, bigger and taller than the rest.

Karen did more push-ups, huffed, puffed and stopped, then sat cross-legged on the mat wiping sweat from her cheek. I watched her with a sudden sick feeling in my throat. Watched Babe, across the room, fitting plates on a barbell.

"Yo, Babe."

She was fiddling with clinch pins and, when she heard her name, looked over.

"Ellie and I were just doing our push-ups here. And I was wondering."

Karen's tone teased. But the sharpness underneath it, if you noticed, would shut you up and make you watchful. For some reason, everyone had noticed. The noise level was considerably reduced. And they were watching.

"Do you mind if I ask you a question?"

Babe shook her head. I hung mine in dread.

"Have you ever had an after-death experience?"

Somewhere a bolt dropped, rolled against metal.

"No," Babe said quietly.

"Not ever?"

"Not ever."

No one moved. The attention seemed to feed Potalia in a way. Her voice got stronger, she smiled.

"Well, maybe you'll tell me if all that *Sports Illustrated* stuff was true. I mean, can you really do three hundred push-ups nonstop, every day?"

"Oh, that."

"And bench two hundred pounds?"

"No," said Babe, "not any more."

"But you could? I mean, once upon a time?"

"Yes."

"So there's sort of, like, a before and after—right?"

The air was silent, sweaty. I could feel my face change from bitter icy pale to the scarlet letter and I glared at Potalia, furious, telling myself I should have stopped this at the beginning and had at least better do something about it now, even though it was too late. But when I looked across the room I saw that Babe was still crouched there calmly, cradling a five-pound plate in her hands. She didn't seem upset. When she spoke, her voice was even.

"Right. Maybe there's sort of a before and after in lots of people's lives, Karen. Maybe you'll have that in your life, too."

"Hear, hear," I said. "But not soon enough."

Potalia blushed, stared at me with real dislike, then shame, and looked away. I became team captain again. Stood and clapped my hands, trying to get things back to normal.

"Okay, role models. America's *finest* physical specimens. It's caveman time. *Huh!* Pay no attention to that child behind the mirror! The Wizard of Oz has spoken."

They started moving then, giggling a little with relief. Iron scraped aluminum. Palms smeared mats, left damply outlined fingerprints behind, and metal plates rattled up, slammed down.

I knelt next to Babe.

"You okay?"

"Sure," she said. She adjusted one last pin, stood to snatch the bar expertly until it rested beneath her chin, then heaved it up and around to press along the back of her neck, so emphatically that you could hear something like metal creaking in her joints— and maybe that's what it was, because she'd been totally bashed up, after all—but she made it look easy. I thought, for a moment, that there was pain in her eyes. Not hurt feelings, or anger, but a real deep physical pain; and because I was so consumed by it myself these days I recognized it, saw it give her pause, and stop her very briefly. Then she shut her eyes so I couldn't see. Saying Shoulders, Ellie, shoulders. Spot me, all right?

I did.

That was the week I fell, once and for all—right down into the sway of things. The week Potalia stopped talking to me. Not that I cared. And Brenna Allen pulled me aside, to make more promises.

And Babe started waiting for me after morning workouts.

Something weird was happening. I'd try, but couldn't any more—I could not meet her eyes. When I tried, I'd break out in a sweat. I didn't know why. Until that one morning, walking next to her down the hall. Feeling the quiet, tired glow of pain that had trapped me every minute of the past three weeks, and this growing sensation of being touched, thoroughly touched, by a sadness I could not explain. Words came up from inside, out of nothing, swelled naturally to the tip of my tongue, so that I almost said them out loud but then recognized what they were with a shock, and trapped and silenced them just in time:

I think that I love you.

She, of course, strode right along in the invisible sway, many inches taller, much much stronger, miles above me, awesome, emergent. Not even knowing about the sadness. Or that maybe she herself was a reason for it; which was why I could not look her in the eye any more.

But how would she have known? I'd just sensed it myself.

"Are you okay, Ellie? You seem really tired."

"Oh I'm great. There's nothing wrong with me that a variety of addictive drugs won't fix in a jiffy. Whereas you, on the other hand, are looking really awesome in the water, Delgado. Really strong and beautiful. I mean, totally."

She didn't respond, and I wished I hadn't said it. We walked along smothered by one of her deadly silences.

Then I was saved by the bell. Or, in this case, by the dumbbell.

"Wait up, girls."

Canelli bumped his way between us, slapped an arm around my shoulders and squeezed until it hurt.

"Two gorgeous ladies. God, can't stand it. Makes me want to jump right in."

His hair was buzzed close on the sides. He'd dyed a mohawk streak of black right through the gold, from forehead to his wisp of a pigtail.

"Hiya, Ellie. How's our new distance queen?"

"Funny you should show up, Mike. I was just talking about drugs."

"Shame, for shame. Drugs are illegal. What about introducing me to your friend here—"

"Babe, this is Mike Canelli, Coach McMullen's current hardship case, rumor has it a good breaststroker when his arms aren't broken. Mike, this is Babe Delgado."

We stopped in the middle of the hall, they said hi and shook hands, and he leaned over to kiss her knuckles.

"My hero."

She pulled back a little, blushing. He hung on to her hand until his arm stretched, then dropped it with a reluctance that was almost all for show—almost—but, for a second, the thick blond eyebrows rose with something like acknowledgment, or admiration. He was tall, taller than her, much taller than me. Inside the baggy school sweatshirt his shoulders, chest, neck were a lot smaller than they'd been last year, and he was dragging around the remains of a sizable pot belly. But he is a big enough guy to carry all the defects without looking too bad. He tugged my hair, which he always does, and for some reason I let him. Maybe because I was feeling utterly underneath the heel of everyone and everything, and figured it was all that I deserved. Or maybe because Mike is one of those creatures who is always right in someone's face, anyway, so by the time he lands in yours you don't even notice. It's a kind of gift, actually: when other people let you have your absolute way around them, without beating the emotional or physical crap out of you. A gift that I often have dreamed of possessing. And never will. But Mike Canelli does.

He glanced at Babe, who was watching quietly. For the first time in memory, I saw Mike Canelli turn red—a quick burst of embarrassment that whipped his features scarlet and passed immediately away. Strange misery seized my innards. And the morning loomed ahead like some devastating gauntlet: full of torment, impossible.

"Babe, I can't do breakfast."

She gave me a questioning look.

"But *I* can," he said.

"Listen, Ellie, what about dinner?"

"Yes," Mike echoed, "what *about* dinner?"

I ignored him and told her that would be fine, she could come over to my place after workout.

Then I left as quickly as possible. The sway let me do it—just walk forward, down the hall, past people and glass cases and lobby bulletin boards without looking back to see any of them. It carried me through swinging doors, out into browned trees and fresh cold air. I breathed with relief. But there were tears in my eyes, I don't know why.

Dinner. It was the worst.

I got home from last class of the day in time to see what

there was in the refrigerator—which was basically nothing—and grabbed some stuff to throw in my bag for afternoon workout. Then it was back to campus, kicking through piles of carefully raked leaves just because I felt mean. Babe was coming over. I'd have to get creative fast. That's when I really started to feel it: all the force of being broken down with distance, distance. How I was getting smaller every day somehow. And something inside me—some deep-down important shameful and naked thing that had always been protected with jokes and weights and attitude—was getting revealed on the surface. Everyone could probably see: Ellie Marks, slug in disguise. My face turning to exhausted slime. Shivering like both parts of a worm somebody'd cut in half. Like some creature you'd find underneath a rock, or rotten log, or down below in an ugly underwater cave.

In the locker room, she seemed distracted.

"Are we still on for dinner?" I asked. Sure she said, sure. But with a faraway look on her face, like she wished she'd never mentioned it. Hey, I was about to tell her, don't do me any favors.

Maybe I should have. But I let it slide.

Instead I said, What about seven? And she gave me that jock moron look she gives when she's trying to pretend she doesn't understand something, and said could we make it eight instead? she had some work to do. That was my real chance to call it off. I blew that one, too. The whole thing was causing me quite a lot of misery already. I didn't know why—it just was—and I probably could have spared myself, but didn't. Fine, I said, eight it is. I gave her the address, told her how to get there, wondered while she listened with a blank stare if she was hearing any of it at all. I realized she'd never been over before. Well, Big Girl, I thought, Time to get social. There was a nasty intentional cruelty in the thought. It made me want to go bang my head against a metal locker, made me glad I'd kept my mouth shut for once and hadn't said it out loud. On the way home, slashing through all the leaves I'd scattered before, watching the sky go gray and dark blue, remnants of sun fade with the last hints of color from the horizon, I had to ask myself: Okay, Marks, what the hell is wrong with *you?*

And I knew, but wouldn't admit it.

I stopped off in a store and spent the last nine bucks of the week buying things I couldn't afford. Fish. Fancy ice cream. Miss Captain Gourmet. And all the time this thing like doom kept pounding in my chest. It was my heart, beating faster than normal, and in a hard, unhealthy way.

Halfway up the porch steps I realized I wanted to cry, but I couldn't. And that—the wanting, and the not being able to—that was what caused all the pain.

I was the only one home, and made a mess in the kitchen. Some of it I did on purpose, because Jean is such a stickler for keeping things neat, so it was liberating in a way to just sort of splash egg yolks and bread crumbs around and slop oil on the counter, finally shoving things into the oven and gazing in a sort of vengeful self-satisfaction at the general disaster of slimy bowls, crusted breadboards.

It was seven o'clock.

I noticed that my chest felt funny. Like the lungs were a little raspy and my throat a little itchy. My nose was stuffed with chlorine, mouth dry, skin chilly.

I went into the living room and stretched out on the couch, and fell asleep.

The porch wind chimes woke me up, clanging loudly. Before the doorbell buzzed I guessed it was her; she was tall, and would have brushed them with her head. I stared at my wristwatch, the cloth band still slightly damp from workout. Eight-thirty. I felt chilly, the lights in the living room seemed too bright. A smell like a cloud filled the air, along with a sizzling sound. Both came from the kitchen. I sat up then, and for a second couldn't figure out what to do.

So I ran to the door first, knocking over a pile of books. She was there in the dark, looking uncomfortable.

"Babe!"

"Sorry I'm late," she said. "Where's the fire?"

When I got to the kitchen sooty smoke was beginning to dribble from the oven. I burned my hand opening the oven door to a pan of encrusted black substance that stank totally, and saw through the gray cloud billowing out that there was a very expensive pint of ice cream melting on the countertop.

I heard Babe at the kitchen threshold.

"Can I help with anything?"

"No," I said.

Then the smoke alarm went off.

I ran to the broom closet, grabbed a mop. Then I ran across the room and started smashing the alarm case with the mop handle. It wouldn't stop.

"Ellie, let me."

A hand pressed my shoulder aside. Another hand plucked the mop from me like it was plucking some straw out of a glass. Babe reached up calmly, twisted the case off, pulled a battery from between metal pincers. There was a sudden, smoky silence. I could hear myself breathing, sweaty and frantic.

"Towering inferno," I said. Thinking, instead: nine bucks of fish. "Well, there's your dinner."

She blushed. "It's okay. I already ate."

I started to ask why, and with who. But then I just knew; and the knowing stopped me. I waved smoke around with a dish-towel, opened a couple of windows so cold air blew through. It smoothed my face, chilled the sweat on my forehead.

"Never mind. Want some melted dessert?"

She shook her head.

"Well," I said, "I do." And grabbed the pint—Fancy French Cream it was called, or something like that—pressing the card-board sides with my fingers. They gave easily, as if they contained only liquid; which, in fact, happened to be the case. But I had my spinning little mind set on that Fancy French Cream. I pulled open drawers and grabbed a soup spoon. Then Babe and I headed out to the living room, shoved some books and newspapers off the sofa, sat down there on opposite sides while I slopped liquid ice cream into my mouth.

"Wow." She grinned. "I'd like to see you do a barbecue."

Out of politeness, I laughed. I figured all her attempts at humor ought to be rewarded.

That's when the Hour of Misery began. Because from eight forty-five to nine forty-five p.m. I was the fly on the wall, the third wheel on a ten-speed, *persona strictum unnecessarium*. During which time she grilled me, as if she was in training to be an FBI interrogator, about all the details of that unpleasant blowhard Mike Canelli's life. I kept spooning sugary glop between my lips, stopping once in a while to answer, feeling nauseated sometimes and unable to speak—at which times she would just stare at me intently, as if the fate of the world rested on my reply, and I'd start to feel like I was in some torture chamber with electric probes attached to my private parts.

How old was he? How good a swimmer? Did he date a lot of girls? Did he really take steroids? Was he a really good spelunker? So I gulped out the answers, feeling weakly feverish: twenty-two or twenty-three; good enough once to be national-class, but he never worked hard, never made it; I didn't know whether he dated a lot but he obviously thought of himself as some kind of ladies' man; I'd heard that he took steroids last year in training, but wasn't sure, he didn't look like it now; for all I knew, he was the world champion spelunker—but then, spending time underground in smelly old caves had never exactly been my cup of tea.

The place was starting to air out. Back in the kitchen I chucked ice cream away and scraped the blackened pan of charred fish off into the garbage, set it in the sink to soak. She watched from the threshold. Even though I had never been at at loss for words with her before, I was now. I'd start to say something, then panic.

Finally I asked had she done the reading for lit. class. Partly, she said. Well, I asked, had she brought her book along, did she want to do some of it now? Because study time was study time, after all. Midterms weren't exactly too far in the future.

Fine, she said. Then: "Did you ever date him?"

"Who?" I heard myself echo bleakly, knowing full well.

"Mike. Mike Canelli."

"No," I blurted, "I'm gay."

There it was. Unintentional. Clumsy truth. Sitting on the floor between us like some big unmovable clot. I felt this buzz travel up my spine, drain all the red from my face, a tingly sensation pepper my skin like miniature pinpricks as I realized that I had said it without thinking. I wished that I had not. Then thought maybe it was okay to have said it after all, and for a second the whole smoky ceiling-lit room seemed to spin around and around. I turned to see her still there in the doorway, unblinking, with some expression on her face I couldn't read.

"Oh," she said.

"Oh?"

"Um, yes." She blushed. "That explains it."

"It? What's *it*? That explains why I never dated Mike Canelli?

Well, of course. Only a queer would refuse a date with Mike Canelli, right? I mean, who else could resist?"

"No, Ellie." She smiled a little. It was a gentle smile somehow, which surprised me. "I mean—oh, never mind. Look, I don't care. I've known some gay people before. They were good people, good athletes. They were fine. I mean, it's okay with me."

Great, I muttered. God forbid it should *not* be okay with you, Delgado.

"What?"

"Nothing, Babe." And I wanted desperately for it to be ten minutes ago, a day ago, a month ago. "Listen, can we just forget I said anything? I mean, can we erase this dinner from the blackboard of life? Fling it into the cosmic abyss? Feed it to Moby Dick? What do you say, Miss Superstar? I mean, let's just *chill*."

"Do you have a—lover? Is that what you call it?"

Yes, I said bitterly, that is what you call it. And, no, I do not. I do not have anyone. At all.

That's when the door blew open and Nan and Jean walked in. You could hear them before you saw them, one heading across the sad worn old living room throw rug, one starting to stomp upstairs, then stopping. Nose snorts.

I hate torts!

Me too! Yucch! What burned down *here*?

The floor creaked loudly as they ran for the kitchen, squeezing in around Babe. They noticed her, noticed me standing there like a maniac with a mop handle to one side, burnt pan and oil splotches and smoke-alarm on the counter. You could see Jean's eyes go gray with surprise and alarm, Nan's barely visible behind the suddenly clouded spectacle lenses. She took them off, wiped them vigorously on a shirt sleeve.

"Trying to cook again, Ellie?"

"Yeah. You know about Jews and ovens." Then I froze inside, and wanted to puke all over. It had popped out of me without any thought, like a little exploding kernel of hate—at them, at myself, at Lottie and Zischa. I wanted to take words back for the second time that night, and couldn't figure out which set of words I wanted to take back more. So I said to myself: Shut up, stupid, will you?

Will you just, finally, shut up?

Jean frowned in disapproval, Babe seemed not to react at all.

Nan set each spectacle stem securely behind each ear. "Whew. First prize in the annals of bad taste."

Give me a break, I muttered.

All right, she told me, since you ask so politely. She turned to Babe and looked up. Saying, Introductions all around! What about it? And in a way that saved me, so I did introduce everyone, watching Jean's face the whole time out of the corner of my eye. She'd taken in the kitchen mess with motherly disapproval, taken Babe in with nosy interest. I realized that I'd always been more in awe of her than of Nan somehow—even though Nan bossed me around a lot more, kidded me, and her verbal critiques landed a lot harder—in the same way that I'd always been more afraid of Lottie than of Zischa. It made me hate her, and myself, even more.

Nan offered her hand. "Ah. We finally meet. Babe Delgado, of swim team fame."

Babe shook it, self-consciously.

"This is Jean McCallen, my lover, and co-sufferer in first-year law—"

"Oh," said Babe. "Hi." She shook Jean's hand too. Then we all stood there while I felt red horror flush my face, silence sitting in the air heavier than the breeze-thinned smoke. Babe gulped like some embarrassed teenaged boy, finally blurting: "You're both in law school?"

"Yeah."

"Oh. Wow."

"Sorry if we're barging in on anything," Jean murmured. I felt the red horror leave my face, and a ghastly deathlike pall replace it.

I managed to stammer that the only thing they were barging in on was a bunch of bad cooking. And that I hated to put a stop to all the sparkling conversation, but the fact of the matter was that, like the man said, time crept on in its petty pace, and we all probably had a lot of work to do, right?

"Right," said Babe. "Was that Shakespeare?"

"Partly, yes. But the rest was Marks."

"Karl Marx?"

Oh, I told her, never mind.

I promised Nan and Jean I'd clean up later. Then everyone muttered good-byes and nice to meet yous; they headed into their bedroom with armfuls of books—to study, they said, but you could tell from the look flashing across Babe's face that she thought they were going off to bump like crazed weasels.

I helped her find her coat from the bottom of the pile near the door. She put it on and grabbed her bookbag and stood there, for a second, like there was something more to say but she didn't quite know how to go about saying it. Personally, I wanted the whole evening to be over in a very big way. I was feeling lousy: raspy throat, hint of a cough beginning. If I could have erased history, I would have.

Well, so long, she said, and started to leave. Then turned to face me.

"Is it sort of a secret, Ellie?"

"Is what?"

"That you're gay."

"Yes. No. I mean, I don't know. It's like, I guess I just don't have a lot of experience *talking* about it."

"I won't tell anyone."

"Okay," I said, miserably, "that's fine."

I opened the door. It was cold, a starless and moonless night. Only the streetlamps lit sidewalks and roads. You could hear cars pass sometimes. Sometimes kids in luminescent vests clacked by on bicycles, white helmets glowing, backpacks like dark humps between their shoulders. She stepped out, looking a little dazed.

Get lost, I wanted to say. And then: Come back. Come back and love me.

"Hey," I whispered instead, "good luck with Mike."

She stepped off the porch and down a couple of steps, so that when she turned again we were about the same height. I thought for a second that some kind of perplexity twisted her mouth around. It was open, full-lipped, white teeth flashing in a background of the almost-white skin.

Not almost-white, really—better-than-white. To me.

But in the dark, it was just dark.

"He reminds me of someone," she said. "Physically, I mean." Then she shrugged. "So do you." And waved briefly, stepped down into the street and the night. "Guess I'll see you."

During morning workout I felt worse, blew the entire main set of 15 × 200—with crazy, senseless splits that were slow, strained, erratic—and that got Brenna Allen on my back. Hanging onto the pool gutter, gasping in between sets instead of doing the swim-down, I saw the shadow that was her leaning over, through cloudy goggles.

"Out of the water, Ellie."

I hauled myself onto the deck tiles with effort, sat there cross-legged, muscles twitching, while wet dripped off me until I was sitting in a puddle. She signaled them for the next set, lane by lane, then crouched down beside me. I pulled off the goggles, thought maybe I'd see her angry. But she looked worried instead—for a moment, almost kind.

"What's up?"

"Nothing."

"Somehow I find that hard to believe."

Maybe you're right, I thought. But, believe me, Coach, *you* are the last human being on earth I'd tell my woes to.

The humid, disinfected, chlorinated air was kept unreasonably hot all autumn and winter. Still, it chilled me. She called out times, whistled them off for another repeat.

She offered me a hand and I took it, stood unsteadily. "Take a hot shower and go to Health Service."

"I have class."

"Well then, go during afternoon workout."

I vowed to myself that I wouldn't. But I didn't have the energy to fight her openly today. I grabbed my stuff and headed for the locker room instead, looking the perfect team captain, coach's pet, superb little model of obedience. Wondering, as I sloshed along the tiles, if she'd meant to make me this way, after all. Docile. I didn't really know, and a part of me didn't care any more. Because if I couldn't fight her openly, I would fight some other way.

Before leaving the pool deck I turned to watch the breaststrokers. All doing a set of repeat 50's. Babe was lengths ahead of the rest, in her own lane, going on a separate and faster interval.

I took a cold shower. Then, shivering, poked my head into the first-aid room on the way to my locker, watched Etta rolling Ace bandages. She saw me and smiled.

"Rubdown, Ellie Marks? Coach says massage for you this week."

"Nah. I'm tough."

"Tough like iron, or tough like steel? Think carefully now. Remember, iron bends. Steel breaks. You gotta bend sometimes, to make it in this world."

"Right," I said, "tell that to Coach."

She laughed.

I toweled down, and was sweating. But at the same time I was so cold that I actually considered pulling the foul, long-overdue-for-the-laundry sweatshirt that I used to lift weights in out of the locker, and on over my clean shirt and sweater. I didn't want to stink, though.

Climbing the stairs, I could hear Brenna Allen's whistle echo from the pool. I could hear the splat-splat-splashing of a kicking set, ankles flexing in the crayon water, toes pointing, thighs pumping. It all sounded very far away. Like some faint echo from another universe, breaking through a wall to reach me, not nearly strong enough to keep my attention. At the top of the stairs I realized that I hadn't felt it once all workout—the sway of things—and I didn't care.

The rest of them were obviously still swimming. So Babe was not there at the top of the stairs to meet me. Although I had the feeling that, even if I'd lasted the entire workout, she wouldn't have stuck around then, either. Something about those days was over, kaput. Scared away by truth, and by Mike Canelli.

I must have listened to the lecture in Modern European History, because I took plenty of notes. Same with Abnormal Psych. Some time that afternoon I started to cough again, but it went away. I felt better, calmer, like things would work out no matter what, senior year would not be a total disaster, the swimming would get better, I'd work harder than ever if I had to and simply tough myself into a blithering long-distance dynamo, two-beat kick and all, tower of aerobic power, nail my fabulous turn at each of the 64 walls. These thoughts—the first positive ones I'd had in many a week, actually—made me anxious for second workout. I skipped lunch, went to the gym to stretch out, was suited up in the locker room early, and out on the deck before anyone else.

Did you go to Health Service? Brenna Allen asked, examining my face—for something, I don't know, some sign of weakness probably.

No, I told her, I feel okay now. You know, Coach, twenty-four-hour flu. New strains come over here from China every year—they think they originate and mutate on pig farms. Lucky for us the human immune system is a spectacular interlocking mechanism.

And then, when just the flicker of a smile touched her mouth corners, I grinned fully at her and said: From the annals of Biology 103. Which convinced me that med school was not, after all, my destiny.

"No," she said, "nor mine." And grinned back. So that, for a minute, I adored her again.

Then the rest of them spilled from the locker room. I caught a sideways glimpse of Babe, walking slowly out, last as always. I let myself think about her briefly—all the scars that Karen Potalia had made barf noises over, the excess baggage she'd been so hung up about since September—and understood suddenly why she was always last, always so slow to dress and to undress: because she did not want anyone to see her naked, or stare at her body. Because maybe she had some kind of hatred for it herself.

Not that I was any stranger to self-hate.

Not that I was planning to let myself spend perfectly good practice time obsessing about Babe Delgado.

I tried to catch her eye and failed. Something cold clicked shut inside me then, and I decided to ignore her. Succeeded, too. Piling kickboards and pull buoys and hand paddles under the starting blocks. Making sure, very sure, that I did not look her way while heading past for the distance lanes.

I warmed up slowly, slowly. Trying to find something I thought maybe I'd felt once, and lost. Sometimes I nearly had it—throw, reach and there, spear the water and snake pull and there, all the way back elbow up thumb down and there—a feel for the way the water really was, while I moved through it like a respectful and gentle invader—I thought I had it sometimes, then it would leave. But toward the end of the thousand I started to feel the walls, too, and stopped worrying about them. Things got easy. Stroke down, head and neck, over, a little pike. Toes on concrete. Perfectly placed each time. It was light, push off, stroke, stroke, stroke, breathe.

The whistle screamed.

"Okay, ladies. It's Double-Your-Pleasure day."

Everybody groaned. Except for me. And Babe Delgado. I hung there off the stainless steel bar undercasing of the starting block feeling light, invigorated, like I could float, like nothing would be too difficult today. Gazing over a couple of lanes through the slightly fogged goggles, I saw her hanging too, and wondered if she felt that kind of strong, resilient lightness now—and did she feel it every time? and was it part of the work? or did it just happen, randomly, once in a while—to her, to any of us. Then I caught myself wondering and the cold hard thing clicked shut inside. It felt safe, clicking shut like that; as if I could swim encased in this lightweight remote-control armor invisible to everyone else, an armor which shut me off from things, and was vaguely dangerous somehow, but at the same time comforting, entirely protective. So that I felt I was enough, sufficient—even me alone, solitary, faults and all. Not mediocre any more, really, but in some indefinable way excellent, just excellent.

"Distance people, listen up. Three sets of five times one hundred on the one-twenty. That's to warm you all up. We build from there."

The groans sounded all around again. Somewhere, someone barked and whimpered.

"I want to see you *move*. But I also want even splits. Shake it now, don't break it!"

She stalked back and forth. I watched her thigh muscles. Then caught myself watching and the safe, lightweight armor shut me off to her, too, so that I was capable and confident again.

"What's the point here? To know the maximum quality of your own *output* in the long run. Time goes on, and the things that were easy at the beginning get harder at the end. Your first hundred feels a lot easier than your last. I want you to achieve the same *result*, regardless. Nice and fast. But something you can settle into. Anyone swimming the sixteen-fifty for us next month"—and I thought, for a moment, that she swiveled my way, whistle flapping against her chest—"ought to take this one *very* seriously, and I do mean *seriously*, because the alternative is that when it comes down to competition you will be one hurting puppy. In competition—or under any kind of stress, for that matter—we do *only what we have practiced*. Only what we are *trained* to do. Nobody wins by bagging it. You know my favorite saying, ladies: Talent gets you fifty meters. The rest of it is nothing but work."

She swung the whistle around on its cord. It flashed, silver, past a spot of sweat between her breasts.

Okay, I thought, suddenly not resentful at all. Okay. Let's do it.

The whistle spun, reflected lights shining off the water. Then it made its way between her lips, everyone shut up completely, and I took a few good breaths.

It sounded and I knew from the first stab of thumb and forefinger into the water that today was my day, the practice I hadn't even dared to hope for. It was the day my back propelled my shoulders and the arms felt free and easy, painless, slight pressure on forearm and palm with each pull. Like I had accepted the medium completely, and now could dominate it a little—or maybe just dominate myself while I was moving through it, breath, pull, pull, roll, going as fast or as slow as I wanted, nailing each wall at will. I understood, for the first time, that the power of this was not just from the muscles but from the breath. The two were connected, sure. But the basis of it all was the power of breath. Strength could help endurance—or, appearance-wise, cover up a lack of it—but, in and of itself, it was no substitute. Brenna Allen had been right about certain things, anyway. I'd had to sacrifice some strength for endurance, get a little smaller and maybe even a little weaker, somehow—get exhausted, broken down to the right size, in order to build back up again in a different way. And today, today was the payoff.

I aced the first set, even-split everything, maintained the interval. Finished breathing lightly, pushed off to swim down, started to feel glad about things, almost proud of myself. It was a different feeling, really—different from the effort of the sprint. And I didn't even know if I liked it. But, for sure, I could do it.

Water spilled from my ears. The sturdy voice of our Coach echoed above.

"Nice work, Ellie. But a little frightening!" Those who could breathe laughed, and I laughed with them. "Save something for racing."

I wanted to tell her not to worry, there'd be plenty left. But I never had the chance, because the whistle blew and the next set began—this one working harder, deeper, making my flesh red with sweat in the calm blue water, skin heat fogging the plastic transparency of goggle lenses, of the waterproof wristwatch face.

Nice, they told me later, in the locker room, jokes flying back and forth through the steamy shower air. Couldn't catch *you* today, Captain. Is it drugs, or love?

No, I shot back, it's deprivation, and hate.

Well whatever it is, can you get me some?

Sure, raving beauty. Take a number.

I passed Babe on the way to the whirlpool. She was stepping out of it, froth bubbling around the surgical scars on her ankle, quickly wrapping a towel around herself and heading for a massage and knee tape-up the way she did every afternoon, stooping slightly, eyes on the dripping tiles, like she was entirely far away and preoccupied. She didn't notice me; or if she did, she didn't let on.

I tried to catch her eyes for a second but the big, tall, towel-draped body was limping off with back turned. I stepped down, eased into the hot sweet turbulence, immersed both shoulders and popped up. Thinking: Well fuck you too, Delgado.

And thanks for being part of a wonderful dinner.

When I burst out into the hallway after taking the stairs two at a time, she wasn't around. Although I did see the back of her jacket—one of those expensive lightweight things, lined with polypro, fluorescent trimming on the edges, another commodity which, no doubt, her father had purchased for her—rounding a corner near the exit. And another, broader-backed jacket stalking alongside her, little wisp of dyed ponytail straggling out of his collar behind. I glimpsed the side of his face, turning to her once, lips moving quickly, talking, talking. Something stabbed through my insides, left an ache to replace the remnants of the workout glow. I hung around pretending to read notices on some bulletin board. Then headed slowly, cautiously, down the hall, feeling sort of furtive, as if someone would catch me—although what they'd catch me doing, I didn't know. But she and Canelli were nowhere in sight. I hitched my bookbag over a shoulder, headed outside into a cold gray wind. A fit of coughing stung my throat and chest. I shivered but shrugged it off, figured it wouldn't snow today but would one day soon. You could feel it.

Improving athletic skill is a nice ego-booster. But it does not necessarily mean that the rest of your life will improve. Although you may walk out of practice thinking that, at the time.

Wow, I am a regular King Kong here, a real Godzilla in the water, and now all of my problems will miraculously disappear.

Poof.

In reality, though, you step out onto dry land and things are just as fucked up as ever. You still don't have money. Or a lover. Or any idea of what to do with your life. And no one's around to applaud your little athletic prowess, either—at least, not off the pool deck. You realize how little it means in the big, bad scheme of things. I mean, we're not talking world records, or Olympic Trials, or Pan Am Games, or national teams. We're not even talking Division I. The minuscule progress of Ellie Marks, mascot/workhorse of the women's swimming team at Northern Massachusetts State, is not exactly going to set the world on fire. Nor is it likely to set anyone else's heart aflutter.

Which is why, when Nan makes the crack about my "new girlfriend"—like there was ever even an old one—I wind up bursting into rages, racing upstairs, sobbing into my mattress. The crying does no good. Just kicks off another of the coughing spells which have become more frequent over the last couple of days—and this time, at the height of misery, tears smearing my face and stuffing my nose, I cough out a totally, totally grotesque clot of green stuff from deep inside my throat and chest, and it scares me.

I wait until the coughing fit dies. Then have to face it: there are these grotesque little green clot things probably rattling around inside me, and they're not going away. I am not getting better, but worse. Brenna Allen was right the first time: I should skip practice, go to Health Service. Still, if I skip practice, I will not peak correctly. The 1650 and the 400 IM and the first meet of the year are coming up next month.

I would like to make Coach proud of me.

I would like to make my*self* proud.

Because, after all, swimming is the only thing I have left in the world.

This thought makes me cry again.

I dry my face on a sheet, stagger to the phone and dial.

"Howdy, stranger."

"Danny, it's me."

"Ellie!" Somehow he seems disappointed. "Listen, kid, can I call you right back? I'm expecting this sort of long-distance thing—"

"Oh, sure," I say. Then: "No. I mean, help."

I start crying again, telling him I am sick, and in love, and if he really has stopped being my friend then there is no hope left in the world for me.

Wait, he says, I will be right over.

One thing Lottie never would do is lie down on a doctor's examining table. She said too many people had disappeared that way in the camps. *You got sick, you went to the infirmary. Then you vanished. Poof. A doctor's not Jewish, don't trust him.*

This thought crossed my mind, I confess, when they scheduled me at Health Service to see some guy named Dr. Heilbronner, and between coughing fits I decided that if he turned out to be the monocle-sporting blue-eyed balding Kraut I assumed he was, with a shit-squeezing Bavarian accent and fat sadistic hands and anti-Semitism oozing out of every pore, I could refuse to submit to any treatment, I would get up and leave. Sitting there in the fluorescent-lit clinic waiting room, with Danny on one side and this skinny kid filling out a VD questionnaire on the other, I started to panic. But I was damned if I'd let anyone know.

Genital warts? I saw, out of the corner of an eye. *Unusual discharge?* Then: *Sexually active with more than one partner?* No, Mister Doctor Sir. No such luck.

"Ellie Marks? Hi, I'm Dave Heilbronner. Come right this way."

Young, sturdy. Thick dark hair. A kind, acne-scarred face. New resident—I could tell; he seemed so proud of the stethoscope, so concerned about making me comfortable, meeting my eyes. Obviously in the currently popular revisionist tradition of compassionate medicine for New Age people.

So he wasn't the aging Nazi I'd expected.

Just a new young doctor who listened to my chest, took a throat culture, took my temperature. Asked about my activities. Admired the swim team. Admired my scholarship. Shuttled me down the hall for X rays. Examined the results. Expressed concern. Diagnosed pneumonia. A bad break, he said. I was lucky it had not progressed further. But, in any case, it had to be treated immediately. He prescribed antibiotics, and a narcotic cough suppressant, and at least two or three weeks of complete rest followed by a month of no more than moderate activity.

"I can't," I told him.

He smiled. "You can't do anything else."

I sat there on the examining table staring at a life-sized chart of the human body—all organs, bones, musculature, stripped of the covering skin. All we were in the end, I thought: the flesh. Violable. Combustible. Stronger was better, but not invulnerable. A small piece of metal, or microscopic virus or bacteria, could tear it to pieces. And when the flesh failed, so did the person.

"I want you to take five hundred milligrams every four hours, Ellie. And the cough syrup should help you sleep."

I saw into the distance of the bleak and immediate future. Visualizing. Watched the short-course season fade away.

"Are you German?" I asked.

"Somebody's great-great grandfather probably was. My dad's family is from Texas, though. My mom's from West Virginia."

"Oh."

"What about you?"

"German and Polish."

"Got family over there?"

No, I told him, not any more.

Walking down an ugly off-white corridor to the Health Service pharmacy, bumping into kids coughing and sniffling and sucking throat lozenges, or sporting crutches or bandage-wrapped wrists, I felt much worse. But also in a way resigned, like I'd accepted illness, believed the diagnosis; whereas, before, when I had ignored it, it had almost seemed okay, something I could get over on my own, without any help at all—certainly not from some German doctor.

Standing in line, I felt tears drip. But the rest of me was numb.

You okay? Someone asked.

Sure, I said. Nothing Thorazine can't handle.

"Did you tell her?" Danny asked later. "Your Babe, I mean." He spooned cough syrup into my mouth, made me sip tea through a straw. We sat on the sofa with the usual distorted, static-buzzing black-and-white TV picture flickering in the background, and in my weakened state I realized that he had always been a perfect mother to me.

"Tell her what? That I'm gay?"

"That you're in love with her."

"How do *you* know who I'm in love with?"

"Well, let's just say that you don't have to be, like, a *genius* to figure *that* one out, Ellie."

"It's that obvious?"

He nodded.

I covered my feverish face with a pillow and groaned. Told him about her waiting around for me after practice all the time. Long walks across the library quad. Push-ups face to face in the free-weights room. Whirlpool sessions together. I told him the story of dinner, and smoky catastrophe. Swimming. The shriek of the whistle. Brenna Allen. Mike Canelli.

"So now she's going out with the biggest, creepiest jerk in the world—"

Danny snorted. "How do you know that's what's really going on?"

I let the pillow drop, made a face. "Female intuition, okay?"

He stirred my tea, got up to smash the top of the TV set with his palm and, for a while, the picture cleared. When he sat back down next to me he crossed his arms over his chest, and I could see the biceps swelling out the upper sleeves of his sweater so that for a moment I cursed Brenna Allen and mourned my comparative lack of muscular definition, wondered with a high-pitched feverish buzzing sound in the center of my skull just what, in fact, all the work had been for anyway. Danny sighed.

"I don't know, kiddo. It seems to me like you're giving up before you even start trying."

There are two kinds of giving up, I explained, weakly and feverishly but sarcastically: the first of which is quitting because you are afraid; the second of which is quitting because you understand the waste and futility of continuing an endeavor. I myself was not and had never been a quitter in the face of fear alone. And if he really was my friend, it would be to his benefit to remember that.

Thanks, he told me, after a while. Thanks for the lesson in courage. And friendship.

He stood, grabbed his coat.

"Leaving so soon? Why, our little party's just beginning." And I gave the Wicked Witch laugh. But Danny wasn't smiling. "Uh-oh," I said then. "You look really pissed."

"Well, maybe I *am*."

"At little *moi*?" I meant it to be humorous, but it came out sounding feeble, petulant. I wanted to take everything back, including my own birth, but the hot-cold sweating feeling inside my head took hold again, and I forgot how.

Danny shoved his arms into coat sleeves. "Yes, I'm mad at you, Ellie. It's time for you to grow up around this stuff, you know. I mean, I'm sick and tired of being your official guide to gay life. If you love someone, you have to let them know how you feel. It's the biggest, most important thing in the world. It is the greatest gift we ever give." He jammed fingers into each glove perfectly, deliberately. His voice was almost quiet, very controlled. But I could tell how mad he was, and I hated him for it, and I was surprised that his thick callused fingertips didn't come ripping through the gloves. "Tell her! Find out where she's coming from herself! And if she freaks out, then the hell with her—you don't want to know her, anyway. Life's too short." He pulled his scarf out of a pocket, swung it around his neck once, twice, deftly. A nice tartan wool. It looked like a present. "I mean, I never thought that *I* would be standing here, you know, saying this—but since I met Gary things feel really different to me. And I am *not* going to be on call to sit and hold hands with you on a Saturday night while you mope around feeling oh-so-sorry for yourself that you're queer. Because *I* don't think it's, like, any kind of a tragedy! I think it's great! And you ought to at *least* have enough self-respect to think so, too."

There was this weighty, muted stillness between us. The fever rattled in my head, white noise blurred the TV screen. We stared at each other. We were both pretty shocked, I think. He was all bundled up, ready to leave, but somehow didn't look as if he wanted to. So he just stood there, like he was some kind of delivery boy waiting for a tip, and then all the words I didn't even know I'd wanted to say exploded out loud.

"I'm really tired of you telling me how I ought to be, Danny. You think that just because you're getting laid you suddenly understand the secrets of the universe or something. And that you, like, have some kind of right to give me this great sermon on love. Well, maybe I'm not quite the same as you—okay? Maybe I have a life and feelings that are really different from yours. Even if we're both gay; maybe that's where the similarity starts and maybe that's where it ends. Because, quite frankly, I don't think we have that much in common with each other. You don't know my dreams! You don't know how I want to touch someone—how I want to kiss a woman, and everything that it will be for me—I mean, because you just cannot *relate*. And to tell you the truth, I can't relate to the way *you* love, either. And

since you met Gary you haven't really been much of a friend.
So if you want me to show some self-respect, I can start right
now. Go away and leave me alone, okay? And don't come back
until you're ready to understand me instead of just bossing me
around. I'm sick of it, Danny! In more ways than one!"

We stared at each other, he all muffled in his coat with his
face pale, only the angry dark eyes shining out; me in my T-
shirt and sweats, my skin bright red with fever. For the millionth
time that day, I started to cry. But stopped myself. I turned to
grab a tissue and blow my nose and by the time I turned back
the door had slammed, and he'd gone.

To make a lengthy tale of misery short, the next two weeks
were a haze of illness and medicine. I had the foresight to call
my teachers and tell them, and reschedule midterms. But the
first meet of the year could not be rescheduled.

Not that it was some kind of disaster without me. We won
by a handy cluster of points. I heard that Babe wiped out her
competition in the 100, and the 200, and that her breaststroke
leg of the medley relay put us so far ahead that, in the end, the
anchor almost coasted in. Coach took the kid to task for coasting.
Unacceptable attitude during competition, she said. But she
must have been pretty pleased with the win.

Actually, she'd been kind over the phone. Told me not to
worry, just get better. Said there was plenty of season left. But
inside, I think, she knew what I knew: it was over for me, kaput,
my mediocre swimming career had squeaked me through a mediocre college education by the skin of its very thin teeth, and
would end with a whimper. The sooner the better, as far as I
was concerned.

Potalia dropped by one afternoon. It was the first snow. I'd
spent a lot of time just sleeping, groggy with cough medicine,
feeling sick to my stomach from the antibiotics. The cough was
taking a long time to go away, I thought, and so was the fever.
I was surprised to see her. She brought a box wrapped in sparkling gold-colored paper, and a card signed by all the members
of the team—one of those funny Get Well Soon things—and
inside the box was a custom-made velveteen jacket, with fancy
script lettering across the front left breast that read *Captain
Marks,* done in the school colors. There was a bottle of expensive

Vitamin C with rose hips in there, too. I wondered, dully, for the umpteenth time, what rose hips really were.

Potalia chattered away, acting pretty friendly. I would have felt a little wary or something if I'd been up to experiencing subtleties at all, but she didn't seem to hate me any more, seemed anxious to be on good terms again. She said she'd gone through attitude changes lately. Babe Delgado, who turned out to be an okay person after all, was giving her some breaststroke pointers. Things were looking better academically. And, yes, she was still engaged to be married.

I confess that, after she left, I peered closely at every name on the card, and even started to get this sick feeling inside that had nothing to do with pneumonia, until I found Babe's signature scrawled sloppily under some banal words like Hope You Feel Better Soon.

Most of the team phoned at least once or twice—to talk, try to make me laugh, tell me they missed me, ask how I was feeling—the usual stuff. Brenna Allen called, too—a couple of times a week. Once she called and I was asleep. Jean took the message, came upstairs snickering later on. So stern, she laughed, and yet so competent-sounding. Does your coach strap on a six-gun and walk down dark alleys, Ellie? I mean, talk about *commanding!*— be still, my heart.

I threw a cough-drop wrapper at her, feebly.

Several times, a few of them dropped by to bring cookies, which I couldn't eat, and more Get Well cards, which I pretended to laugh at. Nan and Jean played the nesting, nurturing game in between their endless rounds of studying, making me pots of tea, calling upstairs like a couple of screeching mother hawks to see how I was doing. Aside from that, I was pretty much alone. Danny didn't call or come by. Neither did Babe.

The time spent alone got me thinking differently, I guess, and feeling differently, about myself.

One reason was the fever dream. I was lying there in bed, had put *Billy Budd* down across my chest because the words were dissolving and reappearing, wavering crazily on the page, and it was making me nauseated. I spaced out for a while, awake but not exactly conscious. Shut my eyes and saw little SS stormtroopers dancing along the rim of my nose, calling me, thrusting

knives up toward my pupils. I tried to scream, but no sound
came out.

Hi, said one, My name's Dave Heilbronner.

Hello, said another, My name's Brenna Allen

Then I saw Lottie and Zischa sitting on my nose, looking grief-
stricken, panting as if they'd run a long way, staring at me like
I was some kind of stranger. I'm Ellie, I whispered. Your daughter. Remember? But they just kept staring up at me in their
stunted, miniature, panicked little forms, unable to move, or
speak, or recognize.

I smelled hot cereal, and red Passover wine, and chlorine.
Then the smell of something burning—something strange, that
I didn't exactly recognize but thought maybe I ought to—and I
bit into my lip and tasted blood. Brenna Allen wavered in the
air above me, floating on a rose hip, holding a cat-o'-nine-tails,
and my blood was dripping from it. The strangest thing was that
she didn't look mean or cruel, staring down at me; she seemed
sorrowful instead, her eyes full of grief and pity, her lips full
and soft and kind.

Please, I begged her. I'm too young for this. And your Babe
is much too hurt to help.

Or maybe I said: Your *baby's* much too hurt to help.

Later, remembering, I wouldn't be sure.

But I'd always remember what she said to me, next—or rather,
what the hallucination said:

You're alone, Ellie, all alone. And so am I.

I came to in the living room, Nan pressing a cold wet towel
to my cheeks and forehead. I looked up at her, suddenly glad,
relieved, like I'd been reprieved from death itself, to see her in
normal size, the dim flickering light behind her, static buzz of
the TV set familiar in the background. Jean's voice drifted in
from the kitchen.

"I called Emergency. They said aspirin and an alcohol bath."

"I'm okay now," I croaked. And started to cry.

The next morning, fever broken, I dragged myself upright
and turned on lights and leaned against a steamy bathroom sink
to look in the mirror.

The face I saw was changed. Not just so that it looked like
shit warmed over—which it did; it was pallid, thinner, with deep

sleep creases across the forehead and splotchy gray shadows under each socket—but so that it looked older. The eyes were a little softer somehow. They seemed sadder, but calmer. Who knows why. Dark hair curled around the thin, bony cheeks like rat tails.

My knees felt wobbly. I pulled off my foul robe, which smelled like a few weeks' worth of sweat, got in the shower, turned it to warm, and had to sit immediately ass-down while the water rained over me. I lurched across the tub for soap and shampoo. Cleaned myself sitting on smudged porcelain enamel, trying weakly to pretend that I was out enjoying a tropical thunder-shower.

I brushed my teeth. The paste felt thick and unfamiliar, an acidic glue. My lips were cracked and I smeared them with Vaseline. I couldn't see my own face in the mirror any more—too much steam—which was just as well.

Later, I put on a clean sweatshirt and pair of pants. The waistband sagged around my hips. It occurred to me, for the first time, that I'd lost a lot of weight. I felt my upper arms, and shoulders, and reached in past the loose waistband to feel my thighs. They shivered, barely supporting me. Flesh and bone. Not a muscle to my name.

I went downstairs, taking each step one at a time and pausing to breathe, sweaty palm sliding along the banister, holding me up. There were a bunch of gift-wrapped, ribboned boxes and packages on top of the armchair. I shoved them off and sat, sinking in very little. The force of my body felt extraordinarily different than it ever had before. So much lighter. Insubstantial. Like there was only a thin feathery mass holding me down to earth. The effort of dressing, of walking down those stairs, lowering myself into the chair, had taken everything out of me. I wiped a shining lather of perspiration from my forehead. I shut my eyes until the dizziness passed. And when I opened them, noticed the packages I'd knocked to the floor. Happy Birthday wrapping paper. There were envelopes taped to each, addressed to me. Birthday greetings showing through one envelope's onion skin.

That's when it hit me: my birthday. First week of November. How long ago? I didn't know—didn't yet know what date it was. But I'd missed it, missed my own birthday. I had turned twenty-

one years old, finished the first twenty-one years of my life without realization, coughing through a bout of pneumonia. And I'd
woken up later, changed. Was the world going to pull a Rip Van
Winkle on me, too?

I reached for a crimson-wrapped box but the movement was
sickening and I forgot about it, leaned back, felt my head rest
in cushions and my eyes gently close. *You are alone, all alone,* I
remembered. *And so am I.*

"So I am," I said.

I'd said it out loud. It echoed faintly in the room, the sound
a kind of shock.

Then, quietly and suddenly, it was true but no longer
terrifying.

I was basically about half the size I once had been. Pale, gaunt
as a homeless dog, sweaty and faint and weak. But sitting there
in the worn old armchair I felt like I was also, quietly and suddenly, my very own self; in some way that I had never been
before, just me. Not part of Lottie and Zischa's reconstructed
family. Not Brenna Allen's team captain. Not even a swimmer,
necessarily. Nor even just a queer. But something more. And
also, in a way, something less.

The me that I was, I realized, was much smaller than the me
I'd wanted to be a few weeks ago. Much frailer. Required much
less of herself, and of others, and of the world. Could not do all
the strong and funny things she had been able to do before.

Somehow, though, she was sufficient.

Alive and, even in her weakened state, enough.

Start back slow, Nan advised. Choose one thing to accomplish
each day. Add a little more activity each week. Get plenty of rest.
Drink pure spring water.

The last piece of advice, I figured, I'd do without. But the
other stuff made sense.

You'd have thought I would rush off to see Coach first, or sit
on the sidelines at swim team practice. Maybe, before being sick,
that's what I would have thought I'd do. But in fact, on my first
day back into the cruel rotten light of the so-called healthy world,
I chose to go to lit. class. I don't know why. Later, though, I was
glad—it was a good choice, eased me back into things.

They were all chattering away about some sort of comparative themes in *Moby Dick* and *Billy Budd,* I could barely keep up with the ideas. But Brown was pretty decent. He made a big deal about me being back, said to come see him during office hours that week and we'd figure something out about the work and exam and papers I'd missed, and he seemed really glad to see me.

I listened to what was going on that day, drifting mentally in and out. Sometimes, too, I'd stop listening and just focus on his forehead, or his earlobe, or chin. His skin was so dark, so soft-looking, and warm. It had this quality of being burnished, mature—ripe in a way that white skin rarely was. I wondered what it was like to be black. Then wondered what it was like to be him, the person, surrounded by all these little white faces. But I gave up wondering. Realized I'd never know; there were these gaps between people, all people, that were basically pretty wide, that you never really spanned. Or, if you spanned them, it happened out of sheer luck, or incredibly hard work, or both. But the way it was to be in somebody else's body, with all its happiness and sufferings and history, scars, aches, memories, colors—that, you never really knew. What you endured alone, in your body, you were always alone with. In a place and a way no one else could touch.

What I cared about, I confess, was losing my scholarship. There were plenty of reasons for them to take it away, if they'd wanted to; team captain or not, I was becoming pretty unnecessary. Especially when you compared me to Babe Delgado—not that there was even any comparison; I mean, compared to most of us she could just about wrap the pool under one arm and take it with her, if she wanted to. She could lap me in the 200, practically break me in half for the 100. Her 200 IM had, in the first meet of the year, set a division record; if worst came to worst, she could do a terrific 400 IM, for sure; and the medley relay was built around her breaststroke. Potalia, who had always been slower than me in the sprints, was at least healthy and certainly in much better shape than I. Anything I might have handled, she probably could too. So I approached my meeting with Brenna Allen with more than a little dread.

But she was cool—totally cool.

She said to be gentle with myself. Ease back into things. Sit out practice for a while, then start slow in the water, stop when I got tired, basically chill, just chill. Then, when I felt better, we would see about competing. In the meantime there was no rush. But my presence was important. People had missed me. She had, too. It would be good for me to come to every practice, whether or not I swam; it would set a good example.

I walked out in a glow. Almost loving her again.

I saw Babe that afternoon, after my talk with Coach. I was sitting there in the Donut Hole, sipping a cup of tea and blowing my nose and flipping through a few massive tomes I'd missed out on completely during the weeks of fever. Once in a while it occurred to me that the world had started to look different to me—at least during the past couple of days. I was noticing things like colors and sounds more. And this thought kept blowing through my mind: that the colors and sounds weren't really *real.* I mean, they were *there,* for sure—and so was I—but the way I appeared day to day wasn't the way I really *was,* it was just an appearance—and likewise for everything and for everybody else.

I watched lemon-scented steam rise from the Styrofoam rim of the teacup. It was there, sure—for a while; and it was real, sure—in a way; but then, like that, it was gone.

Where did it go?

And what was it, really? A thing that would exist in the same form, anywhere in space? Or something different—something that arose out of something else, changed from second to second, and, after a while, seemed absent? but wasn't really? or had been absent, from the beginning?

And what in hell was its *beginning,* anyway?

"Hi."

I glanced up. She'd lost more weight and gained more muscle and looked great—very fit, very tall and strong, almost slender. Everyone else was walking around with winter pallor. Not her. She had that burnished quality to her face. Or maybe it was just a ruddy exercise flush—I don't know.

"Hi," I said.

"How *are* you?"

"Okay."

There was a definite pause between us, while all around the Donut Hole people put on coats or shook off scarves, trays clattered against tabletops, highlighters squeaked over textbook pages, and the smell of food frying and the color of slightly dim ceiling lights seemed like they existed somewhere else, outside this weird protective cone of silence that had suddenly come down around the two of us.

"Well, hey, look." She shifted her bookbag awkwardly from shoulder to shoulder. "Can I join you?"

"Sure," I said, "why not?"

She did, sitting on the other side of the booth, shrugging her down jacket off, folding scarf and gloves over it.

There was more deathlike silence then. Only it didn't bother me the way it probably would have before. I felt it like a shield—felt calm and at home inside of it. She was fidgeting, edgy and ill at ease; but all that—all of her, and her concerns—seemed to take place out there, somewhere far away, in the world that could not touch me.

"So. How are you feeling?"

"About what?"

"I mean physically," she said, looking confused.

Better, I told her, better than dead.

I'd meant it as a joke, but it didn't come out that way and it wasn't very funny. Neither of us laughed.

I noticed that the veins were full, clearly defined along the backs of her hands, twisting over the wrist, up the forearm. A steady diet of weight lifting. The long, strong fingers knit together. I saw her throat move, swallowing. Nervous marks of strain creased her forehead, settled around her eyes.

"I missed you, Ellie. Everybody did."

I changed the subject then, complimented her on putting our first meet of the year in the bag for us. "I heard you blew them all away."

"Nah." But she grinned, seemed relieved. "I mean, I was *slow*—it was pretty pathetic. My timing's still way off. But I guess it went okay. Anyway, the knees don't hurt too bad."

Good, I said, that's good.

"And my shoulders are holding up pretty well. I think the tendons must be getting stronger. Even the old right ankle— tape it up after workout and *voilà!* no more hurt."

I picked lemon rind out of the saucer, twisted it, dropped it into lukewarm tea. There was another nervous-making silence between us, and this time I wasn't going to break it for her, or me. Finally a pained expression wrinkled her face. The fingers locked together harder; even the knuckles whitened with effort. She stared down at the table, spoke very quietly, almost humbly, without looking up.

"Um. Listen, Ellie, is there, like—anything wrong?"

"Wrong?" My eyes rolled before I could stop them. "*Wrong?* How could anything be *wrong,* Babe? I mean, what's a little pneumonia—nothing, right? Or four midterms missed, and three papers, and about seven books—I mean, a mere drop in the bucket of the world's misery, right? And the whole season shot! and for all I know, if it wasn't for Coach's charity and pity, my scholarship with it. Well, how selfish of me to even care, I mean, it's like, how fucking *bourgeois,* right? Right?"

She glanced at me shyly. I thought, for a moment, that she smiled. Only it wasn't a smile of pleasure, but a release of fear and tension that rippled across her face, then vanished.

"Wow. You sound really pissed off."

"I *am* pissed off. Maybe I'm angry with the breaks. And I'm angry at you, Babe."

"Me?"

"Yes. Because you hurt me. I mean, I have been pretty sick, you know. You could have come by—other people did!—or called once in a while to see how I was doing. I mean, I know that I have been there for you when you were feeling bad, or freaked out, or upset. And to tell you the truth, I could have used a friend over the past few weeks. It would have made a difference. Okay? I mean, I thought we were friends."

She stared at me suddenly, looking desperate. "We were! We *are!*"

"Oh really? If that's what you call being a friend, Babe, you can just go do it somewhere else. It's not what I want any more."

"Now just a minute!" Her palm slapped the table hard, making salt and pepper shakers rattle. "Maybe I've been going through some things too. The last few weeks haven't exactly been easy for me, either, you know. I've got plenty of hurt inside—"

"You *always* have plenty of hurt inside, Babe. You've got so much hurt, how can anyone possibly compete?"

There was no more heat wafting out of the tea. I stood, feeling far away from myself—like I was really on the wall somewhere, invisible, looking over at all this happening, more or less outside of my conscious control, and I'd figure out what to make of it later. I pulled on my coat, jammed a wool hat on.

"Goddammit, Ellie!" She stood suddenly, leaned across the table so that our faces were close. Only she was so much taller, she was looking down at me. "Has it occurred to you that I was a little freaked out by all this stuff?"

"What stuff?" I yelled, noticing that all around us the scrape and clatter of dishes had quieted, and people were watching. "Like me being queer, for instance?"

Great, I thought miserably. Great way to fling myself out of the closet. Well, gather around, everyone. If it was any kind of secret before, it certainly isn't now.

"No! Like you being sick! I mean, maybe I didn't *know* what to do! Maybe I was just scared!"

"And maybe you're just a spoiled brat!" I wrapped my scarf on, so tight it felt like a choker. "You know what, Babe? When you grow up, ask your dad for a quarter. He can spare it—he's a lot richer than mine. Then stick it in a phone and call me. But not until you grow *up*."

Her eyes met mine, dark and fierce. "Go to *hell*!"

"Thanks, but I've already been there."

"No you haven't, Ellie," she said quietly. "You haven't ever been there."

I was walking away, though, heading out of our cone of silence for the door. Passing tables of morons who stared, who giggled, who ignored me.

"And furthermore," she called, "you don't even know the first thing about it!"

I just kept moving. My feet didn't exactly take me faster than the speed of sound. It still hurt a little to breathe. The door creaked open and I fell right back into the world—which was very real again, and ugly, and cold.

Our war lasts almost until Christmas break. Which we get a lot less of than everyone else, because of practice; we wind up staying later than most of the rest of them, then having to come back earlier. I scrape through final exams and makeup papers by the skin of my teeth. Definitely B-grade stuff, but even though I'm feeling better every day I am still all worn out, and what I do is what I can manage. Most of the professors take pity on me.

The week just before Christmas consists of nothing more but tests and double practice. Babe doesn't show up much at afternoon workouts; she is really slacking off, just when she needs to be gearing up. When she does show up she puts in half effort, evoking Brenna Allen's quiet wrath, but she doesn't really seem to care. I catch her glancing over at me sometimes, in the locker room, with hurt and anger in her eyes. I stare back once in a while, at other times try to ignore it.

Then, on December 23rd, I spot her in the Donut Hole. She's sitting there alone, among the mostly empty tables, stirring a cup of coffee, looking big and healthy and beautiful and dejected. I am sitting across the room in a booth alone, stirring a cup of tea, probably looking small and sick and ugly and dejected. I don't know why, but it occurs to me that I have something of hers, and I should just go over and give it back.

She doesn't look surprised when the worn copy of the bookstore paperback, with a bad illustration of a ship and sailor on the cover, falls into a salt shaker next to her coffee. She just glances up. A tear winds out of my eye.

"I'm sorry, Babe."

"It's all right."

"No, no, it's not. I hurt you and I didn't even want to. I mean, maybe I *thought* I wanted to, because *I* was hurting too, but I didn't *really* want to."

My hand rests on one of her big shoulders. She reaches for it, massages it suddenly, gracefully. "God. I thought you were just going to stay away forever."

"No way." I smile. Another tear drips down my nose. "You couldn't get rid of me that easily. One thing I have, is staying power."

"You forgive me?"

"Yeah."

"You'll be my friend?"

It's gray and cold outside, but a benevolent light washes the world. Looks like snow: silver-tinged sky, leafless trees glowing dark against it. To the west, piney hills are dusted white like half-frosted cakes. We drift from the Donut Hole side by side, with our deep coats and bulging booksacks. Occasionally, our arms brush.

"What bus are you taking, Ellie?"

"The six o'clock." I puff out a white cloud of breath. "That should get me into Boston around nine-thirty. I figure if I get the last train for New York, I'll miss dinner—that's one less pig-out—plus, I'll show up incredibly late and they'll be too tired to ask a whole bunch of questions." We laugh. "What about you? Do your folks bug you, too?"

She shrugs. "Not really. Um. Well, my mom, sometimes. But I think—a lot of times I get the feeling they're scared."

"Scared of what?"

"I don't know."

We pause, halfway across the quadrangle on this sleet-frozen path. Our eyes meet—for the first time, really, since before I got sick—clumsily, shyly. She shifts her booksack from shoulder to shoulder, then reaches to touch my cheek with gloved fingertips. It feels soft and a little odd, vaguely uncoordinated, like some other movement might be made, some other thing said. But she drops her hand and smiles. "Listen, you have a good time."

"I will. You do too."

"Okay."

"Promise?"

"Sure."

"See you." I head past the History Building, for home and suitcase. Then stop, turn. She is loping after me.

"Hey!" She waves. "Hey, can I call you? Over break, I mean."

"You want to?"

"Definitely."

We take off gloves, take out pens and paper scraps, trade parents' phone numbers. Now she is the one who walks away first; and I stand there feeling the pleasurable damp chill against my cheeks, the subtle shivering of my legs, that used to be strong. I stand there watching Babe until she's disappeared around a building corner. Feeling entirely good, and a little mystified by how good I feel. Until I realize: In this moment, I am happy. Happy. When was the last time you were happy, Mizz Mawks? A month ago? Longer? It's a good thing, now, like an unexpected gift. Even if it lasts just moments.

Christmas Dinner

🐬 🐬 🐬

(J A C K)

Mom and Dad.
Lucy and Ricky.
Ricardo. Delgado.
A couple of fighting machines.

One day, though, they'll bust a fucking gasket. It'll be like some scene in a movie, only you won't be able to figure out whether it's a horror or a comedy: she'll be bitching at him, he'll be sniping back at her, and all the time they'll be driving this car, a gray BMW, and they'll get so pissed off they start screaming and forget to steer and before you know it they're over a cliff, boom, screeching down into a gully in the California countryside. Or Massachusetts. Wherever.

Anyway, it'll definitely be pancake time. For them, and for the car—scrape the whole mess up with a spatula.

"Jack! Jack!"

I don't answer.

"Jack! Where are you?"

I wonder how long I can hold out.

"James Delgado! Please come downstairs this instant!"

Around here, you always prepare for a hasty getaway. I shove my wallet in a back pocket, grab keys and a CD and shades, and thunder down each step like I'm squashing something evil. Supershades on, reflective mirrors hiding my eyes, hard to see anything but who cares? Now all I need is, like, a fucking sawed-off shotgun. Like the film where Arnold Schwarzenegger plays a cop and he parks in front of some joint and flattens a couple of scumbags with one open-handed blow. Then he pulls out this twelve-gauge automatic number and turns around to see all the *compadres* of these flattened scumbags, who are sitting on his car being worthless—and he's wearing his own mirrored supershades, too—and he waves the twelve-gauge at them and says something like, By the way, my name is John Kimble, and I love my car. Then he busts into the place and starts blowing everything apart.

Everybody go home, he says, the party's over.

Who are you? someone asks.

He looks at them from behind the supershades; he doesn't change expression. And he says: I'm the party pooper.

I saw that one with Cindy. We spent some time in the back row in the dark making out, she let me touch her tits under the bra and they were soft, gushy almost, a little wet with sweat, the skin felt satiny. We were kissing with our tongues and I thought I'd lose it, I thought I'd bust right through my zipper. There was this high, hot and cold, rushing feeling in my stomach and chest that almost hurt, brought tears to my eyes, made me say the words—not to her, thank God, but to myself, in my head: Cindy, I love you.

Maybe she heard them anyway, in her own head, and freaked. Maybe that's why she pushed my fingers gently out from under her bra and her shirt, and whispered, Ja-ack! Let's watch the movie!

I was glad in a way, too. Because I didn't miss the line about the party pooper.

But this is one party I will not poop out of, with or without my supershades—Christmas dinner, the two of them going at it like rabid dogs, the way they have basically been doing since Babe went away to school again. And just in case things aren't dicey enough, our grandparents are coming in the afternoon—not the Delgados, but the Johnson Fennelsworths—so the old man is uptight and the old lady's a fucking maniac.

Teresa's playing with toys near the tree. Roberto isn't in sight, probably jerking off somewhere. There's the smell of cooking pineapple and ham, fresh yeasty bread; the glint of silver and

gold Christmas angels bouncing off my one-way supershade mirrors, and I cross from stairway to fireplace, hitch my jeans, give
a thumbs-up to Toots, head for the dining room and kitchen.

Table's set already. Perfectly white lace cloth. Linen napkins.
The good china out of storage—and the crystalware, and silver—
like it is every year. White and green candles sit steadfast, complete, tall and tapered in polished silver holders, waiting to be
lit.

"Jack Delgado!"

"Yo."

She turns from the oven, her face red and aggravated. Makes
her eyes look extra blue. "What is that you're wearing?"

"What?"

"Those—sunglasses."

"Oh. They're—sunglasses."

"Well, I hope you're not planning to keep them on all day.
And please change into a decent pair of pants before your
grandmother and grandfather get here."

"Gotcha, Mom." I dangle car keys. "Babe said she wanted me
to pick her up."

"Oh, okay. Take the Volvo."

"Can't I take the BMW?"

"No, you may not."

"Why not?"

She twists a dishtowel into frustrated cords, smooths her hair
back down. "Jack, take those things off when you talk to me."

I do. The kitchen looks larger then, brighter, less steamy, just
as menacing. She glares.

"Jack, are you going to give me a hard time today?"

"No'm."

"I'm serious. You know the way your grandparents are. God
knows where your father is. Teresa's too young to understand,
and Roberto is in never-never land. Not to mention Babe. I am
quite literally handling all of this myself. You can act like a brat
and make it more difficult for me; or you can act like an adult,
and make it easier. Which is it going to be?"

"Christ, Mom, don't get so pissed. I'll be cool."

"Fine," she sighs. "Well, go get your big sister." She turns back
to the oven, tests sweet potatoes. "And take the Volvo, Jack. The
Volvo."

I grab my black leather bomber on the way out, turn the heavy fur lapels straight up around my neck. It's gray out, a little drizzly and cold, mounds of snow turning to sleet, washing mud all over the sidewalks. The supershades will get worn, anyway; they are glued to the bridge of my nose. I'm feeling cruel and free.

I will take the BMW. By the time she finds out, it'll be too late—I'll be pulling up against the curb near the train station with a wicked screech of rubber, wishing for big biceps and one of those twelve-gauge automatic numbers to take a few scumbags out, on my way to meet Babe.

By the way, my name is Jack Delgado. And I love my car.

Not that I'm the bodybuilding type.

In fact, the bunch of us on track and cross-country, the runners, can look pretty pathetic at first in the weight room. Long lean limbs. Scrawny torsos. Babe can fucking bench-press more than me. But she couldn't ever run as fast. And I don't mind— it lets us be friends, in a way. Plus, our team is winning all the distance shit this year, indoors and out, and the whole school knows it, and nobody would dare call any one of us a fag. Cindy says I am handsome, that my legs are hard and strong as diamonds, and personally she likes me this way.

Suck eggs, Mr. Universe.

"Where you going?"

"To get Babe."

"Huh." Roberto ditches his cigarette, kicks the butt into a dirty mound of snow. He exhales, long and hard, with a very serious scowl on his face, shivers inside the sleeveless denim jacket he insists on wearing all the time—until it stinks, and practically stands up by itself. "Bringing in the heavy artillery, huh?"

He's a little shorter than me but, at fourteen, already a lot heavier. He'll be the muscular type, like Dad, like Babe. I feel that I ought to assert myself now, for as long as I can—at least until the moron figures out that he's stronger and could probably beat the living shit out of me—so I smack his shoulder roughly. He raises a fist.

"Cut it out, you fucking faggot."

"Shut up," I say. "Are you going to be an asshole today, or what?"

"I'll be whatever the fuck I want to be."

Oh good. What a thrill.

The guy has basically been a creep since his voice started changing, and he almost flunked Geometry and English Comp. When he was a little kid, I remember, he was an age-grouper, like Babe, and he did okay. But he never showed the promise, never had the discipline; after a while he just sort of rebelled against it, and started really bagging it, a couple of coaches got discouraged, and Mom and Dad stopped investing.

"Where's Dad?"

"He went to get Alka-Seltzer."

"Alka-Seltzer? What the fuck for?"

"I don't know, asshole." He plucks out another Marlboro, sticks it in his mouth without lighting it, shrugs. When he talks, it bobs up and down between his lips—like he's some bad movie actor, trying to look tough—but he just looks pimply and pathetic instead. "He said his stomach's fucked up. That's all. So there's some pharmacy open, he said he'd be back."

Poor Roberto. Stupid slob. For a moment, I feel pretty sorry for him.

Then, too, the football coach at junior high said he was a good thrower and sprinter and wanted him on the team. So he went to the tryouts, did really well, but when he made it—and he was going to be first string, for Christ's sake—he just never bothered showing up for practice, and coach kicked him off. Dad was pretty pissed about that one. Plus, there is this girl he likes, Marianne, who apparently is the junior high heartthrob, and she doesn't know he exists. Go for it, Robo! I told him. Ask her out! Make your move! Because, I figure, you have to go for broke in these matters of sport or love. But he never did anything about it, never even asked her to dance at the ninth-grade dance, just hung out and looked at her all night and went outside to sneak cigarettes; and now, of course, she is going out with some shithead from the football team and, rumor has it, they're already fucking.

So on all these levels, he's basically kind of a loser, and the fact of the matter is that he's never been a winner. All of which makes for a great relationship between Roberto and the rest of the world—especially between him and Babe, and him and me. Still, for all that fucked-up shit, when we first saw Babe in the hospital he was the only one who cried.

"You want to come, Robo?"

"Which car are you taking?"

Drizzle spatters my supershades. I twirl the keys triumphantly. "Between you and me, the BMW."

"Shit." He kicks a wet sneaker tip into mud and snow. The hint of a smile twists his mouth corners, then fades. He shrugs. "Nah."

"Okay, see you later. But you'd better guzzle some Listerine, man. Old Lucy's on the warpath in there, and if she catches you smoking she'll tear your ass in half."

The BMW glistens, dry and shining in the golden-gray garage door lights; the door hardly makes a sound when you open it; and the insides, plush and leather, still smell new. I slide in, press a remote switch for the garage-door opener, listen to the door squeak heavily up like a big flapping wing, and, far off, the cold sound of rain. Ignition. Gas. It starts like a good dream: quiet hum, pickup and engine throb almost unnoticeable, beeping seat-belt signal ceases. I turn on dims and the dashboard lights up. CD buttons illuminated. Numbers glowing green.

Party pooper. And I love my car.

Okay, power tool. We are ready for action.

It's weird, meeting her at the train station. I'm used to airports. She'd come back from these weekend swimming meets, usually with Dad. Later, though, she'd go with some coach, or some team, or alone. And I remember, when I was really young, how big she seemed. Coming down escalators, suitcase in hand. Looked like she was taller and broader-shouldered than everybody else. Which couldn't have been, really; but that's how I remember it.

Now, though, I am as tall as her. And almost miss her—because, I realize, I'm looking for someone dark-skinned, dark-tanned, and much, much taller. Until there she is, practically in my face.

"Hey, Jack."

"Yo."

"You look great!"

"Thanks!"

"Actually, you look like a Nazi."

"Oh, shut up," I say. Then lean forward, a little stiffly, and we do this thing we have always done—we bump the tips of our noses together—and, suddenly, we're hugging.

I tell her she looks great, too; which is almost true. I mean, she is too pale, almost white, looks kind of strained, and is still lugging around a little extra weight; but you can tell she's been working out a lot, too. She has more muscle than fat, is beginning to look pretty tough around the thighs and chest and shoulders. Plus she's wearing makeup, for the first time in recent memory, and the color of lipstick looks pretty good, the mascara makes her eyes seem bigger, and her hair's been trimmed. I wonder if she's done it for herself or for Mom. Wonder how to break all the good news to her: that the white-gloved grandparents are coming, Roberto's practically flunking school, and Mom and Dad have gone apeshit.

"Come on. You won't believe the new car." I pick up her suitcase. Gallant Jack Delgado. But it's heavy, and after staggering a few steps with it I nearly fall on my ass, and my supershades pop right off.

She rescues them. Wipes them with a tissue. Tries them on.

"Wow."

"What?"

"Dulls the brilliance of your smile, Jacko. How the hell can you *see*?"

I tell her it's not important what you see when you're wearing them, or even how much you *can* see; what matters is how other people see *you*. She hands them back, half-smiling.

"Good for you, dude. Spoken like a true Delgado."

"What's that supposed to mean?"

"I don't know. It's just that we're supposed to be a certain *way* in our family, you know? Not the way you really want to be inside—but the way they want to think of you. Mom and Dad, I mean."

Outside, the drizzle has turned to rain. Suburban train station—nothing dangerous around here, really—but I make a complete circuit of the BMW anyway, checking for dents, chips. Which, if they existed, would fry my ass but good. There aren't any; Jack Delgado's butt is saved for another day. I open the trunk while she's staring at the car and toss her luggage in, almost dislocating my shoulder. Then make a big deal of opening the door on the passenger side, holding it for her like the gentleman caller should have done for the crippled chick, Blue Roses, in that southern play we had to read last year in Sophomore English. She gets in slowly, like she's moving in a dream, this creepy blank look on her face, and I think: Oh no, Babe, don't go nutsy on me!

She doesn't though. Instead, when I get in, feel the rain-spattered back of my black bomber slide along the seat, adjust my supershades so they're sitting perfectly, just so, on my nose, she smiles at me. It's a big, genuine smile, the kind I haven't seen from her in years. Then she crosses her eyes, puffs up her cheeks, pouts until she looks like some insane wild duck. It's the way she always used to make me laugh when we were kids. And it still works; despite myself, I can't stop my face from cracking and I can feel my shoulders shake, belly rumble, laughing so hard and so suddenly that, for a second, I feel I might melt.

We open windows even though it's cold, blast the CD, burn rubber through puddles, both of us sucking gum and blowing bubbles like a couple of brats. Halfway home, she turns the music low.

"How are Lucy and Ricky?"

"Okay."

"Really?"

"They bitch at each other a lot. Worse since you left, I think. I mean, I'm okay around it, and Toots doesn't understand much. But I think it's really fucking up Roberto's head. Not that, like, his head wasn't fucked up all along."

"Yeah? What are they fighting about?"

I shoot her a glance and am glad for the supershades, because they hide it.

You, I almost say. Instead I shrug like I don't even know, and I speed right through a yellow light before it turns red.

That's when the cop car pops up out of nowhere. Blue and red and white-yellow lights spinning on top, scoops up right behind me.

"Uh-oh."

"Fuck," I mutter.

"Better pull over, Jacko."

But I don't, just slow down and crawl along, hoping in this kind of insane way that it's not really *me* he wants to pull over. Until I see him, through rain spattering the new back window, pull something from his dashboard and hold it to his mouth;

and then, like in some science fiction film, this megaphone voice blasts out for a radius of about twenty miles:

YOU IN THE GRAY BMW. PULL OVER TO THE SIDE OF THE ROAD.

My chest thumps, the way it does near the end of a race. As if I'm about to die. I can feel myself sweat. I pull over, stop. Supershades slide down my nose.

"Oh, shit."

Babe turns the music off, rummages in the glove compartment for the car registration.

"Got your license?"

"Yeah."

"Get it out."

I do.

"Now take those things off, Jacko. You don't want to look like some kind of skinhead moron."

I toss the supershades onto the dashboard. Gray light floods into my eyes—from the raining sky, plush interior, gleam of passing headlights on the wet, fresh gray body of this car.

I tell myself: You have bought it now, Jacko.

But Babe has taken charge, and I let her. Feeling very young. Very small. Still having this weird obstinate kind of absolute faith that, if I do what she says, she will save me, save us both.

"Listen," she says, "don't say too much—let me do the talking, okay? Just act kind of chastened and humble. You know? Like, the basically nice well-intentioned high school jock who got caught playing this harmless trick. And whatever you do, be sure to call him *Officer*, and say *Yes Sir*."

Numbly, I nod. Mr. Police Officer Sir is taking about a million years to get out of his car with the spinning colored lights, and I know it is to play this cat and mouse game with me, fray my nerves even more. When he does get out he leaves his door open, stalks slowly, slowly, heavy-booted and heavy-footed, to the back of the BMW and writes down the license number; then, heavy-booted, with his thick brown matte-textured leather cop jacket zipped just above the holster at his hip, and the gun handle sticking out, and a nightstick on the other side, and rain spattering the one-way mirrored lenses of his round, mean sunglasses, he approaches. Leans down at me through the open window, unsmiling. I cannot see his eyes.

"Any idea how fast you were going?"

"No," I mumble. "No, Sir."

"Take a guess."

"Um—too fast?"

"Yeah." He pulls the shades down his long, stern nose with one brief motion of a thumb. Over the top rim of them he glances at Babe, then back at me. "Good guess. You want to give me your license and registration, please."

It's not a question. I hand both over with shaking fingers.

Babe leans halfway across me. When she speaks, her voice is calm and earnest. "It's my fault, Officer. I *told* him to go as fast as he could. I mean, I just got here, and I haven't seen my family in a really, really long time, and I'm, like, late for Christmas dinner."

He doesn't change expression. He doesn't even look at us again, just down at the registration and driver's license like he's examining them for important clues.

"Who are *you*?"

"Babe—I mean, my name is Mildred Delgado, Sir. I'm his sister."

"You say you just got into town, Miss Delgado? Where from?"

"From a swimming meet, Sir. See, I've been away for a really long time at school, and I'm doing all this special training because I want to qualify to go to the Olympic Trials next year—"

"The Olympics?"

"The Trials. It's where you compete to get on the United States Olympic team. See, here's my—this card—"

She fumbles through purse and wallet for a few seconds, pulls out some laminated thing that is red, white, and blue—an old official swimming association card saying it is okay for her to travel to and compete in certain sanctioned meets—with her name on it, and all her old club affiliations, and date of birth, and our address. Mr. Police Officer Sir looks at it over the rim of his shades, through the open window, without changing expression. Then he waves it away. When he talks, he talks to Babe.

"What event do you swim?"

"Mostly the hundred breaststroke, Sir. But sometimes I do the two—the two hundred—and I'm also on these relay teams, and other stuff—"

"Think you'll make the team?"

"I—gosh, I don't know, Officer! I really, really hope so! I mean, it's sort of what I've been working for since I was a really little kid, you know, like, all my life, and my family has just really been behind me all the way. And my brother here, he runs cross-country and track for Brewer—"

"Brewer High?"

"Yes, Sir."

The mirrored lenses turn my way, merciless and chilling.

"Mr."—he glances down at my driver's license—"Delgado? James Delgado?"

"Yes, Sir."

"They call you James or Jimmy?"

"Um—Jack, Sir."

"Well, Jack. You a good runner?"

I want to reply, but can't. There's this block in my throat. I shrug instead, looking sullen, I know—and I know it's a mistake, but it's all I can do. Babe chimes right in.

"He's great, Officer! He does the mile and cross-country—you ought to see him—he's terrific. They are winning, like, practically *everything* this year."

"Look at me, Jack."

I do. And see my own pale, frightened face, very young and ill-shaven, staring back at me in duplicate from the mirrored lenses of his real cop shades.

"Do you think it's okay to disobey the law?"

"No, Sir."

"Do you know how dangerous it is to speed?"

"Yes, Sir."

"I could give you a citation, Jack, for going twenty miles above the speed limit. And a fifty-dollar fine. Do you think that's fair?"

"No, Sir. I mean—I don't know, Sir."

"Oh, God!" moans Babe, "It's all my fault! Please, *please* Officer, *please* don't give him a ticket! I mean, if you have to, give the ticket to *me*. I *know* he'll never do it again!"

A flicker of a smile softens the hardcore face, then dies.

"What do you think, Jack? Are you going to break the law again?"

"No, Sir."

"Is that a promise?"

"Yes, Sir."

He hands the registration and driver's license back to me. My hands won't lift to hold them; Babe reaches across and takes them instead.

"I won't write you up this time, Jack. You're a lucky guy today. But consider this a warning."

"Yes, Sir."

"The only place I want to see you speeding is on the track, in a race. Got that?"

"Yes, Sir. Thank you, Sir."

"And you, Miss. You shouldn't encourage anyone, much less a family member, to drive over the speed limit. First of all, it's against the law. Second of all, it is dangerous."

"Yes, Officer. I'll never, ever do it again—I promise."

"Athletic family, huh? I think I've heard your name some-where, I forget where. Good luck at the Olympics."

"Thank you, Officer. Thank you *so* much."

"Drive carefully now," he says. And pushes the shades back up his nose, stalks away from the car with gun and nightstick riding his hips, drops of water pearling his leather jacket in the rain.

I don't start up until he's careened smoothly away at a light-ning pace, tearing out of sight around a curve in the road, his white and blue I-mean-business car hugging all the contours. Watching him go, I lean back. The sweat's gushing down my face, over my ribs from my armpits, even soaking through the denim legs of my jeans. Suddenly it seems intolerable to be with-out my supershades any more, and I grab the fuckers off the dashboard, harshly.

"Jack, it's okay."

"Christ, I feel like such a moron. Where'd you learn to pull all that innocent girly jock shit off?"

"From Liz."

"Liz—"

"Liz Chaney."

Oh, I say, and hope that this mention of the name doesn't send her off into her nutsy never-never land again; but it doesn't.

She seems okay. Really. Truly.

Well, almost.

But, for a moment, I remember the way she was—before, long, long before, it seems, even though maybe it was just a couple of years ago—how I used to run up to her at the airport, so happy that she was back for a visit. Like she was my body-guard within the family. With Babe around, I'd stop caring what they fought about.

But remembering too much makes me feel like I might cry. And the truth of the matter is that I've already just about blown my manly cookies for the day. Hunched over the wheel of my mother's new BMW crying, because I almost got a speeding ticket, but didn't because my big sister saved my ass by bull-shitting some cop while I sat there frozen with terror, is not exactly the image I want to present to her—not to Babe, not to myself, or to the world.

I dread this fucking Christmas dinner like I've never dreaded any fucking Christmas dinner before—even though they are all pretty gruesome. I want to warn her somehow, but can't. And I certainly can't save her from it, any more than I can save my own sad ass, because I don't know how to start talking about it, where to begin; because the old Babe I used to run to at airports is only here with me in flashes, now, and whatever else she is or will become is stuff I will never, ever know. But she was my friend, my best, best friend, and I miss her. I miss her.

I mutter a couple of swear words and jam keys back into the ignition, peel off the side of the road setting windshield wipers to fastest speed. I'm careful, this time, to stop at all the stop signs and red lights. Even though, with my supershades on, I want to run them all. And if I was some cyborg robot android headhunter sent from the future, and I was lugging around a sawed-off twelve-gauge and an Uzi submachine gun, I would just hide behind the cool, mirrored lenses and run them all down—all the obstructions: vegetable, mineral, human.

We pull into the driveway. From the salty iced-paved begin-nings I can see that, up near the house, the garage doors are still open, Volvo there but no Saab, which means the old man is not back yet. Long trip for Alka-Seltzer. The trees and bushes are ordered, neatly pruned, dripping water and ice.

"Jack, stop a minute."

I do, edging the BMW's rear end out of the street slowly,

careful not to get much curbside slush on it. I sit there, letting the soft new engine hum, waiting. She glances at me sideways.

"Look, I—um. I dated this guy for a while, up at State."

"Yeah?" And I think, Oh great, now she's going to tell me she's knocked up or she went and got VD or AIDS. So I don't look at her, just wait.

"But I stopped seeing him."

"Uh-huh."

"Jack, I think I'm queer. Or, like, bisexual, or something."

"You mean a homo?"

"Yes. Well, not quite. Maybe."

"Just because you broke up with some jerk?"

"No."

"Why, then?"

"Because of some stuff, you know, stuff I'm—have been—going through. I mean, I just do."

Fine, Babe. What am I supposed to say now? See a shrink? Go for it? Just get laid? What I do say comes out of nowhere.

"So you're a bisexual dyke. So what."

"Oh shut up, Jack!"

I laugh, automatically shift and the car rolls forward through the smooth blacktop puddles. "Come on, Babe, get real. Knock-knock! This is the world, right? not fantasy land. I mean, I saw you with that guy—"

"Kenny."

"Right."

"Okay. But you didn't see the rest of my life. And, I mean, you don't know the rest of what it is now—"

We purr into the garage, a perfect fit. Lights blink on; I press the button on the remote control and, behind us, the right-hand door moves quietly down. Without either of us getting out, or even unbuckling a seat belt, she starts to talk, telling me things that, quite frankly, I would rather not hear and certainly will not repeat and that, truth be told, I have kind of blocked out of my consciousness, because who in hell wants to be told that their sister is not just physically damaged, and mentally stuck out there sometimes where the buses don't run, but a fucking muff diver too?

I do my best to stay where I am, make her think I am listening, really listening. I do my best to make her think that some part of me hears, and understands. But it all really sounds like some kind of sick bullshit to me, and what I really wish is that she'd go see a psychiatrist again and take the right pills or something; because, God knows, I have got other things on my mind. Like Christmas dinner, for instance—the catastrophe that awaits us. And I could use a friend right now; I wish the old Babe, protector and ally, was sitting here next to me. So, muttering uh-huhs from time to time, I really just don't look at her, or say much.

Later, I'd keep thinking that if I'd only been able to warn her somehow, like I'd been warning myself all morning and afternoon, things would have turned out differently. We wouldn't have had all the bullshit we had that day. Which, in some bizarre way, sort of signaled the obvious beginning of things falling apart. Although, if you ask me, things had been falling apart with the whole fucking family, Lucy and Ricky Ricardo and their weird little offspring—but without the on-screen laughs—for a pretty long time.

Only, I don't know how long. Things have to begin somewhere, don't they? But if you asked me how this all began—this bullshit, I mean, this ruin—I'd say: Maybe it began that Christmas dinner. Or maybe it began when Babe's plane went down into the Sargasso Sea. Or maybe, just maybe, it happened somewhere long ago, far away. Before my birth. Before any of theirs.

Maybe that's why I made the call to State. I figured this coach of hers deserved fair warning; to know that it wasn't Babe fucking up, but the family. Then, too, I needed to talk. I needed a friend.

Christmas Dinner

🐬 🐬 🐬

(B A R B A R A)

We grew up thinking it was all going to be more of what we knew.

By that, I mean the New England style: summers on the Cape, the rest of the seasons spent in a variety of places less rustic. But we were tougher than the others, those pallid rich Northeasterners. We grew up tall and large-boned, like my mother's ancestors, rugged Scandinavians who'd settled the Midwest, surviving fever, drought, childbirth, locust plagues, and dust storms to do it, distinguished by our large, quite capable hands and an internal equilibrium that consistently defied all of the world's attempts to ruffle it.

It was a lineage marked by stronger legs than arms. In fact, in the nothing North Dakota town they came to own—through hard work and frugality and a superb business sense, complementing good luck with investments—common wisdom held that once a Johnson began to run, you never would catch him.

Never take a Johnson down!

That is the way my grandfather put it.

And, in the end, the old bastard did compensate somewhat for ruining the lives of most of his available female descendants, early on: He bestowed his excellent physical genes selectively throughout the family; so that, in the particular modern-day unit of marriage and miscegenation to which I had attached myself, to which I had chained my destiny in a fit and folly of romantic love, my son Jack inherited the long, strong legs and reed-slender chest that, deceptively, contains a fabulous pair of lungs; and my oldest daughter inherited the long, strong legs, and the fabulous lungs; and her broad chest and shoulders and long, strong arms from someone less white.

My father's stock was different: a line of genteel Eastern bankers. From him, I inherited delicate lips and lashes, and a willingness to be shrewd when circumstances warranted.

All of these qualities can be seen in Jack.

And all of them, too, in my oldest daughter. Except, perhaps, the shrewdness.

But that—that is the luck of the genetic draw.

My brothers learned sailing and tennis, graduated from Dartmouth, married decently and went into business. I was the youngest, and spent a somewhat coddled childhood learning a mean game of golf. I believe that, in my spare time, I painted dull still-lifes with water color and egg tempera, and dreamed of performing heroic deeds. My bedroom walls were lined with newspaper clippings of the athletic exploits of Mildred Didrikson Zaharias, who was my only hero. I followed The Babe's game closely.

At night, I dreamed of love.

The pale, handsome boys I dated failed to move me. My fantasies were filled instead with dark dashing pirates and bronzed sheiks, forbidden foreign warriors—who traveled the high seas in search of beauty and raw gain, instead of a good closing price. These fantasy creatures were violent and passionate men whom only I could move to tenderness.

In waking life I went thrill-seeking: standing at the edge of high cliffs during our school field hikes and closing both eyes to see how far I might sway; hitching up my skirt to climb fences at a zoo, embracing the bars of the leopard cage; diving into frigid ocean waves at Maine beaches in early spring; skipping school one afternoon to watch a building burn down, while firemen rushed in with their shining tools and ropes and the neighborhood ran screaming, and I stood there in the glow of the flame until smoke blackened my dress and my hair dripped sweat.

* * *

On that long, hot day, I became intimate with fire.

It was the subtle blue light at the core of each flame that fascinated me. I'd have liked to hold it; and I would have, but for my hereditary good common sense. Still, it filled me with a rippling, expansive feeling that made me want to laugh and weep. It was, I thought, what they meant when they spoke of being in love.

But how did *they* know, how could they? all of these grown-ups who would have me marry some straw-colored stockbroker.

And one day, there was Felipe Delgado. Handsome, dark-skinned. Examining me from across the room at a party, with his molten eyes. Then he approached, his smile very white. He was holding a thick book under one arm. Briefly, he made a motion to me of greeting and deference, as if tipping the brim of a great invisible straw hat.

"What are you reading?" I asked.

"I study languages."

"English?"

"No. English I know already. Even though you can't know everything of a language so large, I know it enough."

"Okay. What, then?"

"The language of machines."

"Of machines?"

"Of machines called computers. There are different kinds. They speak different languages. We create new languages to store in these machines. They speak to us with the words we give them. We translate the words of problems into their new languages—we give them the problems, you see; and in their new languages they provide us with solutions. In corporate work, one day soon, I guarantee you, any man who doesn't speak at least one or two of these new languages will be completely out in the cold. Because soon all enterprise will depend on them. And personally, Miss—?"

"Fennelsworth. Barbara Johnson Fennelsworth," I said, figuring that he ought to at least know from the beginning what it was he'd be getting into. But I smiled, to soften the blow. "In other words, Barbara."

"It's a pleasure to meet you, Barbara. Felipe Delgado, *a tu ordenes*. That is Spanish. It means, at your service."

"You're Spanish?"

"My family's from Cuba. Personally, I consider myself to be completely American—"

And I smiled. I remember. But turned away, so that he would not see.

"—And, as I was saying, enterprise is the heart of the American system. It's why my father brought us here to America—for enterprise—"

"Oh," I said—disappointed for the first time, though not the last—"I thought you'd have said: for *freedom*."

He grinned handsomely. "Forgive me, beautiful one, but this is the century of machines. I think that, in *human* language, anyway, there's not much difference between those words any more. Freedom and enterprise are the same thing."

"You're crazy, Felipe."

"Phil. Call me Phil—my American name."

"Fine. Phil, you're crazy."

"Not at all, Barbara. I'm a man of the future."

Thinking what I thought then, I could feel myself blush. His eyes were coal-dark. I imagined them to be Latin, *mestizo* of some sort, with the exotic African danger around nose and lips. Magical. Dominant.

Which, after all, was everything I thought I wanted.

The white collegiate surroundings seemed to spin away then, for a moment. I held his gaze until, embarrassed, we both grinned, and broke, and the pale, pale party came back into focus. But we already had the look of lovers.

Life is full of storms.

Sometimes it comes in unexpected forms. Sunshine, for instance; or the Everglades. I would spill into Miami with him, months later, as if entering a nightmare. Multicolored blinking downtown lights mesmerized me. There was traffic wherever you turned. Heat steamed toward the relentless sun. Lawns were gravel and plastic flamingos, lonely palm trees drooping toward pavement. Jellyfish washed up on beaches to die. I felt cracked inside, instantly, in a way I had never experienced before: riven through with odors of salt and fungus, mosquito venom, plant poison, dripping reptilian fangs. The tropics. Life. Rot of the universe.

It was in a horrid Miami motel room, then—before meeting

the wretched remnants of his refugee family—where everything happened. It had come to this—out of deference for my parents' alarm and disgust; I had made him wait that long. Months and months. It had driven us both half mad.

In this motel room, with cracked shades drawn against the heat, cold water in the bath, cigarette holes riddling the bed quilt, he bowed half naked to brush my knuckles with his lips, kissed my arm to the elbow, glanced up once for confirmation, and I shut my eyes. Then opened myself to him as if we were the last two people on earth. As if survival of the species depended on us, on us alone. In the midst of discomfort, passion, horror. Sun and sea and unforeseen life. And the male-female rot of the universe.

Out of all that came my daughter.

It is our girl María's day off today, so I cook alone. It's all for the best, really—she does fairly well with ordinary dinners and cleanup, but I like to oversee important or special occasions. Potatoes steam. Ham and turkey broil. Gravy smells sift through the air.

Babe was born just past sunrise on the first day of August. The previous few days had shattered records for heat; this one did, too. Outside, the sun scorched leaves and grass. People's shoe soles stuck to the sidewalks.

Immediately, she began to scream. The doctor whacked her some more. An obstetrical nurse sponged the tiny, flailing body of my blood and tissue, and placed it between my breasts. I say *it* instead of *her* because, aside from their genitals, infants really do seem entirely androgynous. So, I think, do swimmers in the water. But that is another story. I remember the remains of tied-off umbilical cord wagging in the air, almost phallic, like a miniature flag. I touched one sweating finger to a tiny cheek that was still silky wet, and sighed with deep exhaustion. It was the hardest thing I had ever done. I had not done it alone.

I believe that, in the waiting room, my husband was gulping down coffee, blinking up at pale ceiling lights. Someone must have gone in there to tell him that his first child was a daughter. I don't know if he was disappointed. The next time I saw him, I noticed that he'd spilled coffee on his shirt. Our daughter was big. Healthy. Perfect. He leaned over us both, smiling, and his eyes lit with tears.

It struck me, over the next few days, how immediately maternity ward nurses come to know an infant's distinguishing features and characteristics. They can pick one out by name from rows of seemingly identical babies. My daughter was tagged right away as a screamer, an attention-getter of epic proportions. *There she goes again,* they'd say, *yelling. There goes the Delgado kid.* She really was louder than the others; I imagined her howls to be a combination of rage and celebration; but perhaps those feelings were more clearly my own, at the time.

Still, her tiny face turned scarlet. Her little hands pounded the air. And, when she slept, it was the sleep of the righteous.

She seemed so ruddy, dark-skinned, boisterous and without shame. I named her Mildred, after my only hero. The nickname *Babe* just seemed to apply immediately.

My husband was a little upset. He'd wanted his daughter named Teresa María, after a favorite aunt of his who had remained in Havana. But I stood firm. I told him he could name his *next* daughter Teresa María. This one would be none other than Babe.

I fill a pot with water. Set it on the stove to boil. In a strainer, the stringbeans wait: fresh-cut, washed, pale green, symmetrical.

Babe grew up splashing through the water off the eastern Massachusetts shoreline. She was a healthy child, and—as long as she got plenty of attention—her smiles lit up the universe. She was big-boned, stocky like my husband's side of the family, and walked early. For a while, she even held a reign of terror at nursery school, collecting every building block in the place and organizing all the other children into a kind of slave colony; she then forced them to build a palace according to her specifications. One of the teachers called me in for special consultation on the matter.

I confronted Babe later with a kind of dread. As often as not, during these confrontations, my daughter would win out. Even now, when she protested tearfully that she had made the others build her palace for their own good, I could see her point: She had simply wanted them to have a beautiful place to play with, instead of the wretchedly ordinary little hovels they usually built when left to their own devices.

"Yes, honey, but you can't make people do something just because you think it's good for them."

"Why not?"

"Because it isn't right."

"Why not?"

"Because it is *never* right to make someone else afraid." I didn't quite know if I believed this myself, but it sounded good at the time—firm, authoritative, absolute.

"Why not?"

I could feel myself losing control. The truth of the matter is that I was certainly not going to engage in any dialogue about beauty and terror with a four-year-old. So I spanked her.

The blows were few and light. Still, she sobbed; and, afterwards, I remember suffering days of self-loathing—I remember feeling, at the time, that if I ever again did anything to fracture my daughter's pride, it would be my own end as well.

But this was a feeling, not a truth. Like all such feelings, it would pass.

The water's boiling. I turn it to low, add a pinch of salt. Slowly, delicately, stir the stringbeans in. I check the ham—bubbling brown sugar—and baste the turkey; steam beads across my face with the effort of lifting, of reorganizing heavy, heated pans, on different racks, in the oven.

"Señorita de mi corazón!"

Every night when he got home from work, my husband would toss her in the air. He'd twirl her in circles like an airplane, dangle her upside down, faithfully play bucking bronco while Babe perched astride him, digging in her imaginary spurs. I was probably a little jealous. I adored them both to distraction. But things were not the way I had imagined. The country, too, was becoming strange to me; much of what I had grown up expecting—all the old traditions—had been smashed utterly over the course of a decade; now all sorts of people were mixing and mingling. And, I suppose, I myself was part of the brand-new stew.

But something about it stank to high heaven.

What I had once thought of as fine and preservable—part of which was, I believed, enduring love—became diluted and faded among the hedges and lawns and ugly gravel driveways of an appallingly *nouveau riche* suburbia, where no one was ever really well-to-do enough, and nothing was ever really pretty enough, to compete with the America I had once known. We did well, I suppose, according to the new classless, raceless standards of the day.

Which, I told myself, was what I had really wanted.

But it seemed, sometimes, that life was spinning along too quickly for me to seize it. And I was pregnant again.

Wearing a white maternity sundress as big as a pup tent, I taught Babe to swim one day when stillness gripped the summer shoreline and the water surface was rippled only by an occasional swell.

I did this by supporting her gently against the roundness of my abdomen—which resembled a hidden beach ball—while my hands locked around her naked belly. I then urged her to paddle rhythmically with her arms, to gently kick. Remembering that, since the age of one, she had enjoyed splashing through shallows, had screamed in ecstasy at the sight of whitecaps, gloried in a roll across the wet sand. She'd always been drawn to oceans, ponds, the rain, sidewalk puddles. Several pairs of shoes had been ruined by this enthusiasm. But I was determined that she learn to float, too, as well as kick up a fuss. It seemed important.

Her response was typical.

"No."

"Yes," I said. "Now move your arms."

"I don't want to."

"Well, you have to."

"Why?"

"Because you have to be able to swim."

"Why?"

"Because," I sighed, "water kills fire."

When I let her go, I was riveted by terror. Sun ricocheted off the liquid mirror, blinding me, sudden swells rose with the breeze and pushed me back toward shore. I opened my eyes and saw my child paddling furiously, several feet away. The smooth dark face was compressed with effort. White froth spun around her little kicking feet. Each tiny hand cupped whirlpools beneath the surface. I beat back every urge to lumber screaming through the water, lift her up and hold her safely in both arms. A wave crested and I almost panicked; then calmed down when I saw Babe's head riding above the crest. Her lips sucked air in a fury of strain and triumph. My eyes filled. As of that moment, I knew, I was no longer my daughter's protector. Helplessly, I watched her swim.

The ham is nearly done. The stringbeans are not. A sugary vegetable smell mixes in the air with a smell of rising bread, dripping meat. From far away I hear the doors, and feet, and suitcases. Not my husband, but my daughter. I can hear the sound of my children's voices—chuckles of sarcasm and delight; the young, husky tones. Squeals as Teresa runs for her. A loud *humphh!*, and hug, as she is lifted in her arms. I stay where I am, and stir.

Jack's birth was, for Babe, a calamity. But Roberto's was much worse. Suddenly, just as things were calming a little, there was another new wailing monkey-like creature at home, consuming everyone's attention.

My daughter sulked with the forlorn contempt of dethroned royalty. She'd just entered second grade, and vented her rage in tantrums that sent other children shrieking. I was notified of this matter by yet another teacher; another consultation was requested.

"Here." I threw the notice at my husband, who was home on a rare vacation day. Roberto howled from his crib. In my arms, Jack screamed. Formula boiled over on the stove. "*You* go for a change, *señor*. I'll meet you there later."

Babe's second-grade teacher was a Mrs. Monahan. A reasonably pretty fair-haired thing, about my age. I am sure that, for these behavioral conferences, she was used to facing mothers. So I imagine that, when my husband walked into the empty classroom, dressed in casual sweater and sports jacket, half-apologetic smile spread over his darkly handsome face, she was momentarily flustered. But, it seems, they got along almost immediately. I imagine that her advice was simple and direct.

It must, I imagine, have gone something like this:

"Mr. Delgado, your daughter is charming and bright. I think

she needs some healthy outlet for her competitive instincts. She needs to learn how to be fair to others. And she'll be just fine." Perhaps she paused then. It was late afternoon. Dull gold afternoon light must have streaked the chalk-clouded blackboard. For a moment, perhaps, she might have seen the yearning that flickered in his eyes. She might have said, softly, "I hope there's no problem at home?"

"Oh," he might have said, "no." And leaned across the desk to kiss her.

At which point, of course, I walked in.

But that is another story.

Two weeks later, my husband took Babe to see the coach at a good swimming club upstate. An expensive place which, we understood, all the best sorts of people with the most talented children went to in the beginning; and the coach came highly recommended.

It was a long drive, nearly two hours. They were on the road at dawn. I was awake too and, between boiling formula, heating milk, stove and sink and crib and den, between one screaming boy and another, I sometimes glanced out the window and saw the sky grow pale yellow over the horizon, thin clouds scatter above the browning leaves of trees.

She places another pot on the stove, turns the burner up.

"You didn't put in too much water, I hope?"

"No, Mom."

"Because they mustn't be soggy, you know. We want them lightly done, almost steamed."

"Fine."

The voice is full of a bored resentment. I recognize it, from before—although this is the first time I've heard it since the hospital—a sullenly careful defiance. I resent it myself; yet, it frightens me. I decide to change the subject, get back on safer ground.

"Tell me—where will you go from here? I mean, with swimming."

She shrugs. Rummages through a drawer for potholders.

"What do you mean, from here?"

"From State. I mean, certainly you aren't planning to stay there? Not with another full year and a half of eligibility."

"Um, I kind of thought I might."

"You thought what?" I echo, though I've heard her.

"That I might stay. At State. I mean, I *like* it."

"Yes, okay, but what about the quality of competition?"

"Hey look, Mom, it's not like I'm so far above any of them, you know." She laughs. It sounds bitter and dejected.

"Nonsense," I soothe, "that's ridiculous."

"No it's not. I mean it. It's the truth."

"Well, if it *is* really the truth—and I can't help but doubt that, Babe—but if it by some stretch of the imagination *is* actually the truth, it is only the truth for *now*. I know you'll be back on top. This slump—it's purely temporary."

"What if it's *not*?"

"Not what?"

She flattens a palm against potholders on the counter, faces me with a glum and resentful expression, hand on hip. I recognize this from before, too: her posture of challenge.

"Not *temporary*, Mom. What if this is the best I can do? What if this is the way I am, now, and the way I'm going to be from now on—"

"Oh, Babe," I sigh, "you mustn't be defeatist."

"I am *not* defeatist! No *way* am I defeatist! I mean, I really think I'm a *realist*, Mom. I am telling you the truth! Does that interest you, or not?"

Steam pearls from the stringbean pot. I face her myself, in a similar stance. "Don't you talk to me that way!"

"Why can't you just *listen*?"

"Listen? *Listen?* I have spent my time *listening,* my dear, for the last twenty-one years!"

"Oh, yeah? Well so have I!"

"This is *ridiculous!*" I can feel the tears swell, but I won't allow them to spill. No. None of them will have that victory over me any more—to fracture me with tears, theirs or my own; and she, for one, must know it.

Because what do any of them understand, anyway, about being a wife? Or a mother?

"I *detest* the fact that it always comes to this, Babe! You walk into the house, you get everyone's attention, and then we're crossing swords—"

"And you think I *like* that?"

"Well, you certainly make it happen!"

"*I* make it happen? *Me?*"

"Yes, you! And I, quite frankly, am fed up with being your punching bag!"

The stringbeans are boiling. The burner knob turned on high—too high—but I won't reach across her to turn it down. She is taller than I, and much heavier. Still, she does look good; even in this anger and this pain I can admit that, can see it so clearly. She is well-formed, muscular, the specific shape modulated almost scientifically for a certain function—which, after all, has been true for most of her life—so even extreme damage could not obliterate that form which, in one way or another, we have all of us, all of us, helped to create. And she is not so unnaturally pale as before, her face is brown, and ruddy with the flush of constant exercise, blood pounds vibrantly near the surface, makeup has made the face look almost pretty, and the haircut—new? for her? for me? for someone else altogether?—layers her dark, thick, shining hair just short of the shoulders, renders her somewhat girlish and almost fashionable so that, despite myself, I approve. But—I have to admit this, too—part of the reason I don't reach across her and risk coming too physically close is her *bigness*. It is repulsive to me. And something else, too: she evokes a kind of fear. But, of what, I really don't know.

This is hateful. Unmotherly. Another extremely good reason to despise myself. But I cannot for the life of me quell it.

She looks at me. The jaw works hard, a strong oval, exorcising anger. Set just above it, the lips are wide and plump and full, almost too full, absurdly feminine. When she speaks, her voice is much softened.

"Listen, Mom—do you love me?"

"What," I hear myself echo. "Do I *love* you?"

"Yes. I mean, do you love *me*—me—" the hands open in supplication; she restrains a motion, a motion to move forward toward me; and her voice takes on a pleading tone. "I mean, *me* the way I am now, right now—or, like, maybe the way I've always *really* been—"

"What on earth are you *talking* about?"

"Or, I mean, if you *don't*, then—*can* you? I mean, can you try? Or could you, some day—"

"This," I hear myself say loudly, too loudly, "is insane."

"Please," she whispers. Then the arms open, spread wider than me, and her, and she is approaching.

Water hisses out of the stringbean pot, spills white and green foam onto the stove. I duck her, turn off the burner, turn it back on to low. My hands are shaking. When I face her she's leaning against the refrigerator, arms stiff at her sides and hands shoved deep into her pockets. I want to tell her, again, that I wish she would change her clothes before my parents arrive. I am so tired of the bad impressions they must get of this family, every visit. But when I open my mouth to speak something salty drips in, then something else, and I realize, without knowing why, that I'm crying.

Her eyes are dark, turned to the floor. She speaks evenly, firmly, with a low alto tone that frightens and maddens me. "You don't, Mom, do you?"

I spit tears. "I don't *what.*"

"Love me. You don't love me. And you can't, unless I'm better than everyone—unless I win—"

"How dare you, Babe?"

"You never have. I had to *win.* Win, win, win. Win, win, win." Her voice takes on a mocking lilt. "Listen to the coaches, dear, they know what they're doing! Win, win, win. Be a *champion,* Babe, a great *champion*—never mind about being your*self*—I mean, nobody could possibly love you for being just your*self,* I mean, for just being *alive,* because it isn't good enough, in fact it is pathetic and disgusting—I mean, what good is just being *alive*—"

"Shut up," I say, "Stop it this instant."

"Like I'm some dancing bear, going through your hoops." She hunches over, hands rendered clawlike in a Quasimodo stance. The face is darker with rage. She growls. "Grrrrr! Grrrrr!"

"That's revolting."

"Grrrrr. Revolting? I'm revolting? Well, *fuck* you! Fuck you! Fuck you!"

I stamp a foot, hear my own voice rising now as if it's detached from me, loud and icy and controlled by a deep agonized fury. "How dare you? How dare you—"

"You *never* loved me—"

"—Speak to me this way!"

"—Not unless I won—"

"Stop it!"

We are both stamping our feet. Pounding our fists on Formica counters, refrigerator doors.

"It's true!" she hisses, triumphant. "It *is* true! I knew it!"

Smoke burbles out around the edges of the stove door. The air is filled with it then: a smell of disaster, of burning meat.

I turn my back to her. Open the oven. A sickening wave hits me—dry, ruined flesh, foul gray clouds.

This, then, is dinner.

I turn the oven off. Turn around, again, to face her.

"Go upstairs," I hear myself say quietly, icily, "and change into some decent clothes. And when you come downstairs, be prepared to behave civilly. We aren't animals around here. We are human beings. And you, young lady—from now on, I expect you to act like one."

"Fine," she says, grimly. "Just watch me."

She walks out, leaving me in smoke, fading steam, open oven, mounds of potholders. Through clouds misting the entrance between dining room and kitchen, I can see her receding back. She is lumbering along the edge of the perfectly set dining table. Looking big, dark, absurd as she passes by the fine lace and china. Beyond the dining room is the living room, dull colored lights on a tree, glittering wrapped packages placed neatly around. Far off, through the clouds of ruined dinner, partway through this large and tasteful house, I can see her putting on her coat, picking up her suitcase.

It occurs to me that she has forgotten to take her presents. It occurs to me that she has forgotten to bring any, too.

Christmas Dinner

🐬 🐬 🐬

(B A B E)

It's that high electric white-light buzz in my brain. I haven't felt
it for months; but now it's like a friend, not an enemy, gives me
strength, makes me capable of moving through the air that is
thick and gray. Christmas tree. Smells of burning food. Reminds
me of something: Ellie's place, in October. Guess I am the jinx
when it comes to cooking dinner.

Dad is nowhere in sight. My hands shake when I kneel to kiss
Teresa good-bye. I don't want her to see, or know why; but she's
probably heard the whole stink, anyway—although, here in the
playroom, with her dolls and all the half-open books and man-
handled plastic vehicles and building blocks, she pretends it
never happened, pretends to shut it out, the way kids do.

"Toots, I'll see you."

"Okay."

She sends a red and yellow plastic truck careening toward her
Barbie doll, which is dressed in a bikini and tiny rubber slippers.
The doll falls under plastic wheels, pink hands in the air.

"Uh-oh!"

"What, Toots?"

"Now she's *dead*. Now we have to do the funeral."

"It's just a doll, Toots—it's not really dead."

"Is *too*."

It occurs to me, on my way out, that maybe she is genuinely

fucked up. It doesn't seem like a normal four-year-old kid would go around killing off her Barbie doll. Maybe Jack's right, and there's something totally rotten about the whole household— which I see as if I'm some kind of visitor, now, for the first time ever: Dad nowhere around, Mom worse than ever, Jack bummed out, Teresa playing hit-and-run, Roberto becoming this dull, pimply, overweight, lifeless cigarette-smoking psycho greaser.

I feel cold inside the coat, hands still cold and shaking inside my gloves. Glad, though, that I didn't unpack. Glad that I did not even visit the bedroom upstairs to deposit my luggage; because here it is in the hall, ready for me to grab without a thought. And here is Jack, lurking, looking nervous and sad.

"Whew. I heard."

"You want to drive me to the train station, Jacko? Or do I call a cab?"

"Where are you gonna go?"

"To see a friend," I say, thinking of it for the first time.

For some reason, though, the thought is calming. Makes me focus. It's what you need, to do anything: a plan. So you can follow through. I am still numb and sweating but the trembling diminishes. I can move better. Things seem momentarily clearer.

In the end, he drives me—taking the Volvo this time, not the new BMW—running out after me still struggling into his leather jacket, which looks ridiculous on him because he is far from being the tough motorcycle bodybuilding type.

Roberto is shivering near a corner of the garage, snot frozen between nose and upper lip, smoking a Marlboro.

"Goodbye, Robo."

"Where you off to?"

"I had a fight with Mom. I'm splitting."

"Yeah?" He blows out foul clouds, tosses the butt end into a dirty wet snowdrift. "Well fucking-bitching-A, Babe. What brought *you* to life?"

"Shut up, asshole." Jack staggers by, swings into the Volvo and warms it, backs it out so I can get in. At the last minute, too, Roberto comes along—slumped in the backseat wiping his nose with his thumb, humming Megadeth riffs; and, I can see from the rearview mirror, once in a while he even smiles.

At the train station I buy a ticket with one of Dad's credit cards. I know where I'm going, I tell myself, yes; even though it's nearly two o'clock on Christmas afternoon, and I am moving with hands and knees shaking all alone through this empty gray weather, my insides scoured out, there is somewhere I can go. Best to save cash. And change, for a phone call.

Some of the streetlamps are busted. Others reflect off black puddles. When the cab wheels roll through, dirty water sprays like blood against the closed windows. We're going downtown—which is actually a downward, downhill motion—on this dark evening, with the avenues much emptier than usual. All the multiple lights of all the square and rectangular windows of apartment buildings are spread out in a sort of looming concrete valley before me, and I'm heading down into it, and below, behind, all around, above, are these shining, shifting lights.

For a moment, they remind me of the candles at Tita's place. But I don't let myself think about that too long, or any of the rest of it.

The cabdriver's Pakistani. Beaded seats. West Asian artifacts hung on the dashboard. His skin's dusky, warm, nearly the same color as my father's; the same color as mine. Christmas evening and he's working; just like any other day, I guess, for him—nothing particularly holy or unholy about it at all—and the cab radio's playing Urdu tunes.

Press the buzzer, she said, and wait for a voice. When you hear it sound outside, that means the door is open. You can walk right in.

I tip the cabbie too much, haul my stuff out and walk across the street, check building numbers, smell cold remains of rain mixing with urine, garbage, car exhaust, hear the slosh of shoes and boots and car tires through puddles, along curbs. Here's the right place; I walk up damp steps. Find the name. Ring.

"Who is it?" crackles a foreign voice. An old voice. Man's or woman's, I can't tell.

Babe Delgado, I say.

"Who?"

"I'm Ellie's friend—"

The buzzer sounds like an insect swarm in my ear, rattling me all over, but I chill enough to push in and rush through the vestibule, past tiny metal mailboxes, push another door open and hear it slam hard behind as I spill into a dim-lit big red hallway. Then, feeling nothing, I move forward. Until the only lights I really see are the tiny, orange buttons on the elevator panel, blinking down one by one, doors sliding open and the old metal insides glinting out for a moment like hands to take me in; then more blinking buttons, gold-white this time, the doors squeak shut, and I'm heading up.

How small.

Weird. But it's the first thing that comes into my head—when they open the door, when I look into the dim-lit place past them, searching for Ellie, then back at them—and, like a chant, it stays there.

How small.

How small th^y are. Little, wizened, grayish-white crooked people. Shoulders bent. Stiff knees, arms, bowed necks. It's as if you took a couple of normal-sized humans and then shrank them a little, somehow—not too much, almost imperceptibly, so that there was something not-quite-normal about their stature at first glance.

How old. For a mother and father.

And, staring up at me, how silent.

"Yo."

I look past them again and, with relief, see Ellie—who is normal height and build, basically, maybe half a foot shorter than me. She's still pale and thin from being sick, but seems to tower above them.

"Hey," I say.

"Zischa, Lottie, this is Babe Delgado."

By their first names, I think; she called them by their first names, her own parents. Bizarre. For a second I feel like my voice has gone. Then I watch myself offer a hand to them to shake. Not firmly, openly, as in days of old, but in the new almost shy, unfriendly way I have now: slowly, in fact, a little reluctantly.

The little whitish-gray people take my hand. Slowly, wanly, a little reluctantly too. Mumbling, in foreign accent, *Well, so, how do you do?*

I can't think of anything to say, and my voice has vanished anyway, so I stay silent.

"Come on in," says Ellie—like she's inviting not just me but her parents, too—and I follow her into a little living room with old furniture and cracking off-white wall paint, and a dark carpet worn thin, window curtains closed against the night. It is tiny, plain, womblike. I can feel myself stooping a little, now and then, as if the ceiling might descend to compress me. In here, even Ellie looks too big; I must look enormous, like some kind of freak. But Zischa and Lottie lock about five locks on the front door, then come into the living room and settle on the worn old sofa, side by side, and motion me to sit. When I bounce into an armchair I don't feel too big, after all; it seems to fit my whole body just right, just right. I grasp the arms comfortably, habitually, like I've been sitting there all my life.

"So," says Lottie, "this is your swimmer friend."

Ellie is standing in the opening between kitchen and living room, arms crossed, watching us all; only Lottie doesn't look at her when she talks, but at me instead. Examining me, she nods a little, impassively, as if I am just what she expected.

"Tell me something. What is it with this swimming? You all do it until you're good and sick?"

Ellie rolls her eyes. "Lottie!"

But I can't stop myself from grinning.

Lottie continues. "You—you look all right. But her—I never saw her so sick! What is it, some kind of indentured service? They work you to the bone?"

Ellie's pissed off. "Lottie! Give me a break!"

"Um," I blurt, finally—like a total, total moron, "you guys don't have a Christmas tree, do you?"

"Christ," Ellie mutters.

Zischa claps his hands once, sharply, and stands. "Swimming, shmimming. Enough with the swimming already. She walks through the door, a complete stranger, and already she's getting criticism. Tell me something, Babe—you like vegetable soup? You like noodles and raisins and bread? Because it's time for supper. And already, tonight, I have heartburn."

Dinner's weird. I try to do things right, and be polite, but I realize I sort of don't know how. For one thing, some of the food is strange: this one dish a mash of cooked carrots and raisins and honey that keeps dripping off my fork—makes me miss the smell of pine trees, I don't know why. For another thing, I keep staring at the numbers on their arms. Lottie's is on top of her skinny, weak white forearm up near the elbow; Zischa's on his arm's underside, right near the wrist. I can tell that, once in a while, they catch me looking. Ellie does, too. But no one says anything. What they do, instead, is basically almost force-feed me—but with words, and somehow I really don't mind—urging me to eat this, at least try that, have some more of this other stuff; and they flash looks of alarm when I pass on a second or third portion. Actually I like it, in a way. The desperation of it makes me believe that they care whether I live or die, and that they know how intimately and seriously this matter of food is connected to other things, like life, and death.

"So," says Zischa after a while, spooning some more potato stuff onto my plate, "your father ran from Castro."

I nod. Sure, I say, when he was a little kid. With most of the rest of his family.

"Why? They were fascists—they preferred Batista?"

"Oh come on, Zischa!" Ellie shoots him an angry, pleading look. "Don't *bug* her, okay?"

But I shrug. I mean, the truth is that I don't know too much about it, just little things my dad or his relatives have dropped, hints here and there, that basically serve to confuse a lot more than to clarify. I tell him I don't know the whole story, really; I always thought Castro was supposed to be the big fascist; and anyway, a lot of the people in my family had some money which, if they'd stayed, they would have completely lost. Plus, some of them were very religious. And Communists hate religion.

"So, Babe. You think it was right, what Kennedy did at the Bay of Pigs?"

"I don't know."

"But you have an opinion, maybe?"

Actually, I don't. But that fact makes me blush. I rummage around in my head—which is basically pretty empty when it comes to politics—and try to figure out what answer he wants to hear. Like I'm coming up with the right team motto for some coach. Then I just blurt out the first thing that comes to me.

"I think it's wrong to fight a war halfway."

"Meaning?"

"Meaning? Um. That, like, those people—I mean, *my* people" — and I feel myself turn a brighter shade of crimson brown, because I have never used these words before—*my people*—and there is something forced about it, something weighty, but also something that feels very nice—"they—um, we—got used. By, like, the Americans, I mean. I mean, not like I have anything against Americans, you know; I mean, this is my country now too, it really is. But I think Kennedy, the American government, you know, sent those people out, and never intended to support them, and felt like it was basically okay if they died."

"They were expendable?"

"Yes, sir. Exactly."

"Hmmm. You think maybe this capitalist system exists because it holds some people to be more valuable or more worthy of being alive, than other people? You think maybe we can sit here eating, right now, because others are sitting somewhere else starving? Because this system says they are expendable?"

Ellie knocks hands into her head, on purpose. *Zischa,* she moans, *please.*

"I don't know." My heart is picking up nervous speed; I'm starting to sweat. What comes out of me are words I never even knew I had inside; at least, certainly not in the form of some coherent political thought. "But *any* system makes some people expendable, doesn't it? I mean, in reality, in the world today. I mean, Castro's not so great either. I mean, he says he's this great liberator, right? but he acts like a fascist, doesn't he?"

"You think, maybe, that Mr. Castro wouldn't be so bad, such a strong-arm, if the capitalist governments of the world didn't carry out a policy of isolating him? And Cuba?"

"Look. All *I* know is that my family lives a lot better here than they would have there. Anyway, Castro set up concentration camps for, you know, some criminals, and for people who have AIDS. You can't tell me *that's* okay."

There is silence. Then, Zischa smiles—a quiet, thin smile traces itself across his pale old face, and fades. He swallows more vegetable mash, shoves taped-together glasses up his nose.

"No," he says, "I can't."

"Enough already," says Lottie. "Enough with your politics. Zischa, pass the margarine and the bread. She needs some more."

I accept more food. Shoot a glance again—I can't help it—at the numbers on his arm. Ellie sees me, and rolls her eyes right up into her head.

Zischa reaches across the table, turns the arm up and holds it there, right in front of me, for several seconds. I get a good look: faded green-gray numbers, tattooed in firmly.

"Shame," Lottie whispers.

"Quiet," says Zischa. "I think it's important. I think it's important to see what kind of a person my daughter loves."

Next to me, Ellie gets even paler.

" 'Holocaust' means 'entirely burnt,' " he says. "That's the literal meaning, a translation, you see." He pulls back the arm, passes me some margarine and bread. "I was in Auschwitz, once, for several months. Auschwitz was amazing! It was an enormous city of factories and slaves and pain. In the winter you could see it from a great distance. Its furnaces lit the sky. It was a city that turned a profit for the fascists. The main business was labor—slave labor, of course, since no one went there of his own free will. And the difference between slave labor and free labor is the fact that slaves are *used* by others—by other people in a system who consider them to be worth less than they are themselves, in other words, expendable—and, when their use runs out, they are discarded or killed and then thrown on a massive junk heap, like pieces of a machine. So it was a great city of endless, mindless, useless labor, and thousands of starving slaves always hurrying, hurrying everywhere, through the mud and the snow, diseased, dying, beaten by drunkards in uniform. Their blood and their pus fell on the snow; they were covered with boils and excrement. They looked like strange, thin insects; they did not appear to be human at all, except for the grief and madness in their eyes. That's what slave labor does, you see, it makes insects of the slaves, because it is about nothing but perpetuating the cogs of the system, of the machine itself; it does not serve life; it leads the human soul to death. And that, that was really the business of this great burning city in the snow, you see: death. It was so busy with the business of death that it ran twenty-four hours a day, it lit up the winter sky for miles with the fuel of its slave labor and the heat of its death. To survive there, at all, you needed to imitate one of the insect creatures. You needed to pretend that you were already dead inside. So. Some of us pretended. Some of us survived. But no one—no one who survived did so without committing many horrible deeds. Even to do nothing—even that was a horrible deed, under the circumstances, you understand?"

Lottie hisses. "Leave her alone! You expect her to understan what is incomprehensible?" She turns to me, for the first time her eyes shining almost kindly in the worn, bland, colorless face. "Listen, the real truth is incomprehensible. We say others can never understand because they were not there, but the fact is that *we,* the ones who survived, will never understand it completely either—not what was done to us, nor what we did ourselves, nor what we did not do. I will tell you one thing, and one thing only: All this about politics—it's all a lie. Political systems are nothing but lies. They cover up the sickness and the rot of people who want nothing but money and power, not for a good purpose, but simply to hoard. When there's hoarding there is waste; and when there's waste, there is cruelty. What matters is not this or that political mechanism. What matters is a kind heart. A heart that does not hoard, and does not waste. There. Now, enough of this already. Eat—here's some more potato—eat now, eat."

I do. Ellie is silent, her hands in her lap folded over a napkin. I look at her once, but she avoids my eyes.

Ellie washes the dishes. I dry them. The dishtowel's a faded Dutch floral pattern—looks old, almost antique. The counter is battered, dented with brown coffeepot stains. By now the lack of Christmas tree and frills and wrapped presents and colored lights has stopped seeming weird to me. After all, I tell myself, the first African slaves they brought to Cuba didn't celebrate Christmas, either. So there, white boy. Thinking this, I can feel myself sneer.

But Ellie is white. And, really, so am I. Well, partly. Pretty soon, I stop being angry.

"Thanks," I whisper, "for saving my butt."

"What exactly happened?"

"Oh, lots of shit. I'll tell you later, okay?"

"Okay. But, look—it's nice that you're here."

"Is it? Really?"

"Yes, Delgado. It's good."

Later, all four of us sit in the living room reading different sections of newspaper. No one says anything. Everyone is basically just a pair of legs, sticking out from sofa or armchair, wide newsprint expanse covering up each torso and head. Once in a while Ellie gets up and walks around, restless. Then she flops back down and you can hear springs squeak, can hear the rustle of thin sheets as she opens up another section, snorts about some political folly or other, mumbles questions requiring no response.

I want to tell her, suddenly, that it is good to be here, too. That—here, in this weird, dim little home, where people rarely speak, with her oddball parents and their damaged bodies and crackpot philosophies and the green-gray tattooed numbers on their arms—I feel, somehow, like I fit right in. Like no one will bother me because they, too, basically just want to be left alone. And maybe it is strange to others, but it feels nice and normal to me, it's the way I am now; and somehow, some way, the way I am now is acceptable here, it is understood here, no explanation is necessary.

Ellie has posters all over her bedroom of swimmers and singers and old movie stars, illustrations of hammerhead sharks she cut out of *National Geographic,* a picture of the Queen of England with a mustache drawn in. I inspect everything on the walls, glance through her books and cassettes. There's a photograph on her dresser, too, framed in this practically ancient tarnished silver frame with floral designs—daguerreotype, brownish matte finish—of an infant, round face hemmed by lace. It's much too old to be her.

"Who's the baby?"

"Oh, that's Oskar—Lottie's son."

"I didn't know you had a brother."

"I don't, really. I mean, he's dead, kaput—he wasn't much older than that when he bought it. They generally killed all the babies and the old and sick people first—"

"In the concentration camps?"

"Right. Lottie was in Bergen-Belsen—that's where Oskar died—I mean, was murdered. Because, I mean, it *is* murder, isn't it?" Her face is matter-of-fact, very thin and pale. Eyes very serious, without their usual sardonic glint, and in that moment I realize fully, immediately, how sick she has been. I want to touch her somehow, somewhere, very lightly, with my fingertips, as if that would bring some comic mischievous light back into her eyes and her face. But I don't.

"Your dad and mom were married before the war?"

"Yeah, but to other people. See"—she bounces onto her bed and sits there cross-legged, right in front of a big black-and-white poster of Dawn Fraser swimming the 100 freestyle in the Tokyo Olympics, 1964. She'd been bashed up in a car crash or something pretty bad the year before, I think, and her neck was all fucked up so she couldn't do flip turns any more in Tokyo; she had to do open turns. Still, though, she won.

Fraser was big. Ellie isn't. For a moment, now, against this background, she looks small to me again, and frail. "Lottie and her first husband had this baby boy, who died—I mean, was murdered—in Bergen-Belsen, and her husband died, too. Zischa had a wife, too, only not Lottie, and he and she had kids, two girls, I think—"

"What were their names?"

"He doesn't say."

"Not even when you ask him?"

She shrugs. "I asked a couple of times, you know, when I was growing up. He wouldn't ever say. So I stopped asking. Once in a while, if they feel like it, they'll tell me things. Sometimes, I swear, it's like I almost don't even want to hear it! I mean, they'll talk about the most horrible, intimate, godawful stuff—and on the other hand, they can be really strange and secretive about details that you'd think would be ordinary everyday kinds of things. It's not easy to understand them a lot of the time. Sometimes, I admit it, I just sort of give up trying. But in a way, I *do* understand. I mean, I'll bet you don't want people pestering you every day with questions about what it was like when the plane went down."

I nod.

"Well, that's sort of the way it is with them."

"They have a before," I say, "and an after."

We both look at each other then, and grin.

"Anyway," she says, "she spent most of the war in Bergen-Belsen, and Zischa was in Auschwitz. They met afterwards. In this camp for DP's—displaced persons. And the rest, as they say, is history. But it's *all* history, isn't it?"

"I guess." I sit on the bed with her, cross-legged at first, but it hurts the knees too much and pretty soon I am lying there, relaxed, head propped up, and she is telling me things in bits and pieces. About growing up with them, mostly, and the way

Zischa would just blurt out some terrible true story at the weirdest times, out of nowhere, about stuff he saw in Auschwitz—things you didn't want to know, even—at breakfast, or dinner, or while you were sitting around minding your own business, watching TV; and this thing Lottie had once about rescuing homeless animals, which she doesn't do any more because of the expense.

"She'd get them all cleaned up, all de-fleaed and de-loused, whatever, and she'd take them to this vet down on Houston Street for their shots—rabies, boosters, all of that. Zischa got pissed after a while—it must have been pretty pricey, and I guess you can see that we don't exactly live in Trump Towers around here—so he made her stop. But you know something, Babe? When she stopped, it left me feeling kind of sad. I mean, all I ever wanted to do, when I was a really little kid, was to *keep* these pets—I'd, like, cuddle them with me on my pillow at night, puppies, kittens, whatever, and I would beg Lottie to let me keep one, just one. And I'd always think, maybe this time she'll let me. She never did."

"My dad brought us a dog once."

"Yeah? What was it like?"

"I don't remember, really—I was really young, I think maybe Jack had just been born or something. It was a big old puppy though, a golden retriever—he was great. All floppy ears, big paws. We named him Paco. But, um, he didn't last long. I mean, he ran into the street one day and got run over. Poor little guy. Like a lot of other living things I've been around—huh? Soon you'll all be calling me Kiss-of-Death Delgado."

She rolls her eyes, sighs with exaggerated exasperation. "God, Babe. You are so hard on yourself."

"Yeah. Look who's talking."

"Okay, but with me it's different. At least, I think it is. I mean, I figure I'm just sort of trying to be the best I can be, and I don't have much natural talent or gift, so I'm hard on myself in that way. But you, Delgado, you—I don't know. It's like Zischa says: There's a lot of pain in surviving—sometimes, maybe, you think it would be easier to have died—"

I tell her to chill, seriously chill; tell her I have had enough of all this talk, talk, talk.

Then for a second, even though I don't want to hear any

more, I want to tell her all the other things: about Liz, and Kenny, and Sager; about what happened. But just the thought of it makes things go far away in front of my eyes, like I'm gazing down a long, dim tunnel, and I can't, I can't.

"Okay, Delgado. Tell me about your *brief* visit home."

I sigh. Remembering it all, I feel numb. Maybe that's why my voice sounds far away from me, too, when I speak; matter-of-fact, like I'm telling her about some everyday occurrence.

"My mom and I had this fight. I don't even want to get into it, Ellie. A lot of the same old shit we always used to fight about, before—just *before*, you know? except this was worse. It was, like, all this stuff about swimming, and how, like, she expects me to be some world record holder again—you know, with *this* for a fucking body!" I pound my chest, a shoulder, a leg. Pull my shirt up over my rib cage, exposing scars. All of which she has seen a million times, of course, in locker rooms and whirlpool and sauna, but somehow I want to reemphasize it again, the hatefulness of it and the ugliness. I don't feel mad, or hurting, but I notice that I'm panting, as if I have been running too far and too fast and am now plain out of breath.

She lays a hand over stitch marks. The palm is cool, dry, light. Friendly and nervous, somehow, but not really afraid or repelled. Then she takes it away. "I don't know, Delgado—I don't think you're in such bad shape."

Thanks for the charity, I mumble.

"And neither did Mike Canelli."

I groan into a pillow cover. Tell her that I really, really, really don't want to talk about *that,* either.

She asks, then, if I want to just pack it in and get some sleep, she personally is pretty tired and thinks it would be a good idea. I realize again how weak she still is, how pale and thin. All the old physical strength of her is gone for the moment; even though she's getting better, it will be a long time before she can do a lot of the stuff we did together—treadmill runs, wall pulley, spotting each other for squats and bench press.

She says she'll get some sheets and blankets for me, and go make up the sofa. I tell her I'll do it myself, she ought to get some rest. And I mean it. But then, without thinking about it, I pull her back down when she makes a move to get off the bed, and she falls so that her back is to me, and I curl against her, just like that, and wrap my arms around her skinny, tired shoulders. My hands meet and touch against the center of her chest. They can feel her heart beat, a rapid patter, and the fading hint of a cough rattle in her lungs and throat. She puts her hands over mine. Her palms are damp.

"What is this, Delgado?"

"Nothing." Skin, hair. Fuzzy back of a neck. She smells familiar. It reminds me of things that are dead now, and gone. So that I still am numb, so numb that if you pinched me with pliers I swear I wouldn't flinch, but tears come to my eyes.

"Well, it doesn't *feel* like nothing."

"Shut up," I whisper, "shut up, shut up."

She does.

I tell her things I have never told anyone before. About Kenny, and Liz. Sager. Angelita.

There's a quilt folded at the foot of her bed, and after a while I sit up to haul it over us before curling all around her again. She lies very still, not turning to look. My hands can feel her breathe.

That is how we fall asleep: light on, door half open, under a quilt, fully clothed, warm and very still, in this small, small place that smells of cooked vegetables instead of Christmas trees. I don't even take off my shoes.

Ellie shows me around the next day—Central Park, Rockefeller Center, Fifth Avenue. I want to go either to the top of the Empire State Building or to the top of the World Trade Center, but in the end it's all this blur of coats and shopping bags and boots and ice, she admits she's too tired, has overdone it a little, and we just head back downtown.

Before we go across town to Lottie and Zischa's, though, we stop off to eat at this cheap little Cuban diner place on lower Broadway. She makes me do it, saying, with mischief in her voice, Come on, Delgado, it's time for you to get it together about your heritage. Sure, I snort, half joking. But we're both half serious, too.

Inside it's darkly lit, framed by storefront windows with Spanish words on them filtering through the gray outside, and it smells of smoke and coffee and sweat. There are a couple of tables of middle-aged guys hunched over cigarettes and empty greasy plates, talking in Spanish; there's a guy behind the counter who looks a little like my father; and a woman—his wife, I think, wiping tables—who looks a little like me. I examine the menu, painted on boards hung on the wall. I had to study a language in high school, and took Spanish, but can't remember much of it at all.

"Ellie. What should I get?"

"Rice and beans. Black beans."

"How do *you* know?"

"How come you *don't* know, Delgado?"

The guy behind the counter approaches grinning, dark skin and neat-clipped black mustache making his teeth glow. His white apron uniform is splotched with red sauce. He speaks to me in Spanish.

"Um," I say. "Rice—I mean, *arroz, con—*"

"*Frijoles negros,*" says Ellie, "okay?"

It pisses me off a little that she seems so comfortable. But, also, something about it feels valuable, precious; this place is warm, and the food is pretty good, and so is the coffee. In my heart I love her for bringing me here.

Christmas Dinner

🐬 🐬 🐬

(B R E N)

Christmas day. I don't know why, but after the boy's phone call I find myself driving around, directionless, then parking, getting out, wandering the campus. Crossing the quadrangled courtyard in front of a library. Walking slowly, methodically, a good-looking, still-slightly-tomboyish woman of thirty-five, authoritative, purposeful, in a fine long coat, commanding respect.

Sooner or later I stop, and glance up to see that I'm here again, in front of the Athletics and Recreation building.

Thinking about loneliness. Thinking about Kay.

Damn you, Kay. Where the hell are you?

I take elevators instead of stairs. Wander down spic-and-span glass-cased halls, past many numbered rooms, to Bob Lewison's office. Not expecting him to be there, half hoping that he won't be. Because what, after all, am I going to say to some straight man coach, in the middle of a shut-down college campus, on Christmas Day? But the door's open; I poke my head around it, tap nervously.

Your Christmas celebrations, Bren. So Protestant and proper. So subdued, dear. Rather Nordic. Strindberg, Ibsen. Ingmar Bergman. Edvard Munch. Hour of the wolf, wild strawberries. Suppression of Freudian feeling. The scream. Beaten with belts, in closets. Locked away in the cold, and the dark. My poor sweet baby. All those centuries spent in winter.

Yes, Kay, you are right about that.

Discipline did what suffering could not: took something tender and tropical from the depths of the heart; stole something away. Yes, love. I know all about winter.

"Hi, Bob."

"Bren." He looks surprised.

"I was in the neighborhood."

"Really? What in the world for?"

"Oh, nothing much. Well actually, something. Have you got a minute?"

"Sure."

"Thanks."

Inside, I sit. Examine his walls. Stuffed bookcases. Good. He isn't even stupid. I remember a few stiffly whispered gibes: Lord knows what a brain like Kay Goldstein sees in her—some callous lady jock; you'd think, if she was going to swing that way, it would be with another professor type. Someone well-read, and verbal. Some soft plump thing, maybe, another sensitive Jew. A liberal Jew in law, or in the humanities.

"Well," he says.

"Well, Bob, we have something in common. We're both alone on Christmas Day. Tell me—is it out of choice? For you, I mean?"

"Shit, no. My kids backed out on me. Janet's boyfriend's unseen hand."

I blurt it, unthinking: "None of the real crap shows up on the surface, does it? At least, not at first. You know it's probably there—you intuit it, anyway—team garbage, family garbage, the sadistic coach, rotten mother, ineffectual father, stress galore, enough to screw *anyone's* competitive ability, never mind *hers*. And it breaks my heart, Bob. I see how hard the kid works, sometimes, just to function."

"Did something just happen? Delgado?"

"Not really. Oh, sure. Her kid brother called." I grin mirthlessly. "Nice boy, actually—maybe you should recruit him, a decent little cross-country runner. Anyway, it seems the family's putting the screws to her. He says she got home—for the first time all season—had a fight with the mother that sounds pretty gruesome, and left. No one knows where. So I calm the boy down, make a deal with him to show up at a meet some time, at least *once* this year. To give her a little support, for God's sake! But who knows what all this will lead to? Maybe a few meets down the drain—I wouldn't doubt it. Well, terrific!"

"Fine, Bren. But you've done all you can, you're not a counselor. Neither am I."

"Meaning what?"

"Meaning that she's been to counselors, right? And a bunch of dieticians. Physical therapists. Psychiatrists. But what she wanted, this year, was normalcy."

"How can *you* know that?"

"You told me."

"She could not have normalcy, Bob, any more than you could pay off your MasterCard tomorrow. Any more than I could have McMullen's job. Or have Kay back again."

There: it is out. Sitting, furious, sweating, I feel relieved, yet also somehow defeated.

If he feels any resentment, he doesn't show it. He says only, quietly, "Listen, Bren, it's what she wants. She's twenty-one. She can drink, she can vote, she can sink or she can swim. Normal or not, she *is* a grown woman." His eyes meet mine. "Now, Coach. What about *you?*"

I sit silently for a second, brooding.

"Rough day?" His voice is kind.

"Oh. Yes, sure."

"I know what that's like."

Sure you do, straight boy.

But out loud, I say: "Okay. Tell me about it. Tell me what you know. Because, Lord knows, I could do with a friend."

Later, I will tell him, he helped get me through the worst part of Christmas. That thin little straight man.

I trusted him, for a change; I don't know why. Maybe because he already knew some of my secrets. Thinking about my life with Kay, about having this known—by even just one other straight person—made me cringe. It felt like a betrayal of Kay, really. But, on the other hand, she was the one I was hopping mad at.

Over a spartan dinner—made of things we picked up at some 24-hour package store—in my house, in the country, he told me about his wife and kids. About women he had dated since. Some of them nice. None of them for him. How the emotional impasse of his life sometimes seemed insurmountable. And the fact that he would never get back all the treasures he'd once *thought* he possessed—but never really had—deadened his heart inside.

Well, Bob, I said. Well, Bob, it's a personal thing, but it's common, too. I mean, we all have problems.

Afterwards, I almost called Chick. But didn't. Instead I drank wine and floated past the fireplace, the drape-covered window. Like a crazy woman, floated. With nothing to give but the wine and the fire. And a touch, a vestige, of snide gay humor; I shared it with him, over wine, and it made him laugh.

He helped me haul in wood from outside—logs and logs. We lit a fire.

I started hauling more things into the living room, stacking them near the fireplace. Boxes of clothes. Boxes of toiletries, and of makeup. Papers. Books.

"Kay's things," I said. "I've kept what I want. Look through the books, Bob. If there's anything you like, please take it."

He looked them over. The fire and the booze made us sweat. Cast bright hot shadows over his face, made him look half-black; probably made me look molten pale, and half-black too. Some of the books were good finds, he said. He took a few. Then asked me what I was up to.

I'm feeling mad, I said.

Crazy? he asked. Or angry?

I didn't reply.

After a while I just crumpled up some papers from the stacks and tossed them in the fire. A flame blazed higher, seared the crumpled little mounds into quick black nothing.

"I'm mad, Bob."

"Deserted?" he said. "Abandoned? Pissed off at Momma? Little girl lost?"

I nodded.

"Sure, Bren. Women. It's like that when they leave you."

I tossed in a book. Then another. Then a few more things that took longer to burn.

After a while I asked my friend to help me. He seemed reluctant at first, then glad. We sat there, burning Kay's things, until Christmas was gone and the fire died.

The Plunge

🐬 🐬 🐬

(E L L I E)

A month goes by, heavy with new courses, make-up tests and papers for the old ones, and increased practice time—which, though I cannot spend entirely in the water yet because I am still too weak and too tired, I must still, as team captain, attend. Babe is solicitous. We spend a lot of hours together—she even comes over a couple of times and cooks some disgusto vegetarian mash with Nan and Jean, and makes me eat it—and I catch her watching me, sometimes, in the locker room; once, when she notices me giving an appreciative glance in the direction of that fine physical specimen, our Coach, she even winks.

Later, that afternoon, we wind up at the Donut Hole and then in her room, side by side on the bed, doing homework.

That's when I take the plunge. Pressing a hand against my stomach, because maybe it will calm the merciless thudding of my heart; while my other hand, like it has a life and a will of its own, creeps firmly up her back, under the sweatshirt.

"Hey! Beat it."

She shakes it off, flaps the soft folds at me. I'm turning to Silly Putty inside. Even my ears are shaking. Even my kneecaps are sweating. But I grin as if I know exactly what I'm doing, and my hand, with that life all its own, inches under the sweatshirt again and presses along her back, touching the tips of scars, caressing.

"Goddammit, Ellie." She jumps from the neatly tucked edge of the bedspread, stands there confronting me, hands on hips, looking very tall, and strong, and bitter. "What do you think you're doing?"

"Hmmm." My fingertips are tingling. "Trying to turn you on?"

"Really? Really? Well, you can forget about *that*. Who do you think you are, anyway?"

"Well, obviously, for starters, I am not exactly a world-class backstroker—"

"Oh, go to *hell*, Ellie!"

"I am Eleanor Josephine Marks. That's who I am. Ugly name, huh? but it's *mine*. Another thing I am, is your friend."

"Yeah?"

"*Yeah*. And I happen to think you're very, very hot." The words tumble out, sounding oddly gentle; I can feel my eyes cross in fun, stick my tongue out at her and wiggle it; I give up absolute control of myself and of everything, resign myself to taking a belly flop after all. Tell myself: fuck it! go for broke! because what, in the whole stupid world, do I really have to lose? Maybe I will gross her out completely, and she'll never have anything to do with me again; but, on the other hand, if I don't tell her the truth, and all of it, I'll be twisting things up between us so that we won't even be friends—and, in either case, I would never have her anyway. I puff out my cheeks and lips, mock pouting. "So *there*."

She seems frightened now. "Ellie—you've got me all wrong."

"Do I?"

"Yes. I mean, you do. I'm not into that any more—"

"Into what?"

"I'm not queer. I mean, not totally. I mean, I'm sorry, I mean, gay—or—"

"Fine," I goad, feeling myself blush, and then I toss it straight at her—this arrow I've been saving all along: "Not even for Liz Chaney?"

"Dammit! I wish I'd never told you *any* of that."

"But you did, didn't you? And it wasn't a lie."

She heads for the door. Through it and through the front room of the suite, past a crystal-clean kitchenette, perfect window drapes drawn against the glass panes caked with winter, obscuring the far-below view of a quadrangled courtyard, a rich kids' parking lot.

"And when you pulled me down on my very own bed, and you put your hands right here"—I pound the center of my chest until it hurts, but don't stop yelling—"I mean, right *here,* Babe, all *night,* right against my tits—that was *not* a lie—"

The bed squeaks as I slide off it, CD blares too loud for a moment when I turn the knob, then shut it off with one quick push. Coughing up remnants of pneumonia, yelling after her anyway.

"And when you watched me watching Brenna Allen today, and you smiled, and winked—*that* was no lie, either."

"Just shut *up,* Ellie!"

"Come on, Delgado—get a *clue!*"

It hurts, leaves me gasping for breath, but I run and head her off at the pass, block the closed door, turn to face her.

Here I am, trying to stop her from running out of her own room. Who *do* I think I am? And where does *she* think she is going?

I'm panting for breath, she's panting in rage and frustration and a kind of fear, and we stare at each other. I watch the panic blaze high in her. Feel it burst open inside myself, like fever sweat, then diminish just enough so that I get dizzy. She has stopped. She tries to say something, but her mouth shuts agonizedly, the large dark eyes search mine. I lean back against the door, spread-eagled.

"No way, Miss Top Seed. Don't run from this."

"Look," she pleads, "get out of my way."

"Dare you," I whisper. "Dare you to stay."

She stops then. Puts her hands in her pockets. For a moment I can read her eyes; there's trouble in them, and a big, dark question. I hear myself talk again, in the voice with a life of its own—softly firm, assured, yes, and oddly, shockingly arrogant—part of an Ellie Marks that doesn't really seem as if she could be *me* at all, because she is so brazen, and big, such a champ, so unafraid.

"No one but queers get to call themselves *queer,* you know."

She shrugs. Her face is sullen. The eyes are still troubled though, looking straight at me. Something rasps in my throat.

"But"—I cough—"*I'll* tell you what's *really* queer. It's going through life without ever being able to love anybody. Without ever really trying your damnedest to reach out and get what you *want.* Or being, like, *ashamed* of yourself, when you try—or when you do."

"You don't know," she whispers, and her voice trembles with rage, with sadness, "you don't know how hard I have worked, Ellie. Not you, not anyone else around here—you can't even imagine it."

She starts to cry. The tears just roll down her face, across her cheeks and lips and chin, and she doesn't blink, doesn't even try to hide them. She looks so strong, then, standing there; so big and beautiful and noble, in a way. Watching her, something inside me shakes all over and almost breaks. The doorknob presses my rear end, hurting. And then I start to cry, too.

"God, Babe, you know, you are so incredibly beautiful. But you walk around like you think you're some kind of freak. Like there's about twenty feet of steel between you and everybody else in the world."

"Well, maybe there is. But how would *you* know?"

I'm angry now.

Because after all, I tell myself, what do I need *this* for?

I lick my lips, feeling hoarse again, almost feverish. There's this part of me, the old Ellie coming back now, that's afraid to continue, but I know I sort of have to—and not just for her, but for myself.

"Look, Babe, I come from a whole *family* of survivors, I could tell *you* a thing or two. Sure, you survived this incredible disaster, and sure, it's a really, really big deal, and it's going to mess you up for a while. Personally, I don't think that's *all* that ever messed you up—and I don't think that's all that ever *will*. But if you want to believe that it is, fine. I mean, it's simple, it even fits. And you can keep telling yourself that things used to be perfect, just perfect, and everything, everything that ever goes wrong in your life is because you got so fucked up when that 747 went down—and because, for once, you grabbed onto something and held on, and you got what you wanted—I mean, what *you* and no one else but *you* wanted, really wanted, more than anything, which was to survive. And to *live*. But if you want to keep lying to yourself about it, if that's really what you think is best, and, like, safest and all, then go ahead, go ahead and lie; about that, and about everything else. Only go do it around somebody else! Just get lost! Get lost *now*, and *don't* come dancing around *me* any more, okay? Please! Do you understand?"

I breathe too hard. Throat constricts with a kind of pain. She's still crying, staring at me with those hurt, complex, naked eyes again, and if I continue to meet their gaze I will come totally undone. I call up one last iota of strength. Then take the plunge.

"Because I happen to be in love with you."

Force a snide grin, an old Ellie grin, through my tears.

"Or maybe just in lust."

Then I can feel the grin disappear.

"But I don't think so."

I look away. At my feet; at the floor. There's this minute, now, when I am sure I've lost. And I imagine myself moving aside, futile and dejected, Babe fiddling with the doorknob that has left an imprint on my ass, Babe stalking out of her own room, walking purposefully down the hall—although where she would go, I don't really know—and leaving me for good. Saying *Adiós, muchacha.* So that I think: Great, *Mizz Mawks,* you have blown it yet again! And I tell myself: Well, shit, why shouldn't she walk around like there's twenty feet of steel between her and everybody else in the world, huh? I mean, really, can you blame her? When once upon a time there was nothing, just totally nothing, between her bare body and death; when once upon a time things were so bad that the only way she could live through any of it was to separate in a way, pretend, hallucinate; say, This isn't really happening after all, is it, it's a bad dream and I will wake up soon, very soon. Who *do* I think I am, anyway—what in the world do I think *I* can offer, little me, stacked up against all that?

I am wrong. Completely wrong. She is right. I should step aside, and go straight to hell.

But when I get the guts to look back at her she hasn't moved. The tears on her face are drying; there's this embarrassed, almost foolish quiver to her mouth, like she wants to smile, or laugh—at me, at herself, I really don't know—and the big, dark eyes don't seem angry any more. She blinks. Then turns slowly, quietly away.

She heads for the CD and cassette deck, inspects the tuner. Stands at the crusted window a minute looking out at a snow-ruined courtyard, dull late-winter sky, looking out at nothing. Reaches with both arms simultaneously, like a bird fanning wings, and with one simple motion closes the curtains. Turns back with a CD in one hand, a cassette in the other, glances at me briefly with this pained, anxious smile.

"Would you like classical music? Something romantic?"

I can feel my eyes narrow uncertainly. I don't reply, just watch her. A disc slots in, flashes rainbow fluorescence. Electronic lights burn silently awake.

Violins weave a warm, piercing cocoon. Gentle minor key. Baroque melancholy. She plays with the volume, adjusts it perfectly. Turns to me, gently mocking.

"Something elegant, perhaps? For a lovely Jewish survivor of suffering and despair?"

"Fuck you, Babe!"

"Okay." She smiles tiredly. "I'm waiting. That's just what I'm waiting for."

I reach behind—to double-latch the door, or to escape by opening it and falling backwards, I really don't know. Metal's cold against my fingers. My toes squirm inside tennis shoes and Thorlo socks. I feel very weak, now, and small.

Across the room she cocks her head. Winks. But I can't tell if she's smiling; I, for one, am not.

"Dare you," she whispers. "Come on, big, big girl. Can you really, really deal? Well then, come on and show me."

It's all one motion: Unsteady walk across the room, not feeling my feet on the floor, sweating, dizzy, everything pounding crazy inside me; and this fumble of hands against hands, though I don't even know if I'm reaching. But, yes, those are my hands, now, on her hips. Those are my hands, now, light and shaking on her shoulders, on the flesh of her neck; my thumbs, strong somehow, and full of want, caressing the lines of her throat. So swollen, she told me once, so swollen I couldn't swallow, Ellie, my tongue was white and stuck out between my lips and it was bigger than both lips put together, I was on intravenous for two weeks.

I pass my thumbs up and down the throat that seems so vulnerable now, so human, shockingly soft. And I can feel her swallow. Breathe. Choke back little sounds.

They're hungry sounds.

Starving, I think. She was sick, and starving.

And then I think: So was I.

But neither of us has to be. There's this difference between fate and choice. In my life, in hers. It's like, biology, genetics, the Holocaust, the plane crash—these things that helped form us, in one way or another—they were fate. The rest of it, though, is all choice. My choice. Hers. To accept what we are, and the tricks fate deals us. But to play them as we choose; I mean, with love or without, with lies or with truth. Because, in the choosing, we form ourselves.

I move my arms around her. How many times have I day-dreamed about doing this? Only, in my daydreams, I was healthy, and stronger. In my daydreams I was taller. And never so afraid. I knew just what to do then. Now, I've forgotten.

Her hips and thighs rock forward, into me, roll back, and I think, *breaststroke*. And begin to remember. But from all the daydreams, really, and nights spent alone; not from what you would truly, truly call hands-on experience—although I guess there is room for debate. Baroque strings pierce the background, change to major key. Her hand moves under my shirt. Circles my rib cage, my shoulder blade and back, pulls me full against her, but slowly, gently, so that this breathless tingling sensation gushes through me, and I think for a second I will melt, totally, then just disintegrate, and I can feel myself move too, without even knowing how: rhythmically, thoughtlessly, rocking into her and back. Now her lips kiss an eyelid. Breathe into my ear.

"Feel good?"

"God, Babe. Is it real?"

"I think."

"Are you sure? Jesus, I'm afraid."

"Of what, Ellie?"

"I don't know," I say. "Of winning."

"Well, *I'm* afraid of losing. But I'll tell you a secret—"

"What—"

"They are both just habits. You know, it's like, behavior mod. You train yourself into one or the other. But you can train your-self out. It's all just what you're used to."

Her lips find mine. I hold her face, feel her sweat, her fear, but sense somehow in the middle of it that she knows what she is doing, yes, knows just how to do this; and I am learning fast. I taste the tip of her tongue, go crazy dizzy again, hear both of us moan.

Time goes by but I don't know how much of it. Maybe just seconds. Maybe hours though, too—my thighs are stiff with fa-tigue when I finish unbuttoning my shirt and let it drop off,

finish unbuttoning hers and move the folds aside to see a
shadow of scarred flesh, then feel the slow, slow hands circling
up past my shoulders, down over my breasts, her hands un-
clasping the stupid, dainty, maddening hooks of my bra with
effort, until it falls to the floor too and my breasts are free,
nipples hard and tingling, each one supported in the palms of
her hands. I lean toward her, pull the dark-haired head down
next to mine. Then I struggle with the bra clasps riding the
center of her upper spine, feel clumsy to break the rhythm
this way, curse them—because there's this thing I want, this
desire centered absolutely in my mouth, on my tongue, to
pull her breasts gently in to me and hold the nipples between my lips and kiss them, just kiss them. The clasps
unclasp and the unnecessary cloth gets pulled away and I
do, I do, and, one by one, I can taste her nipples hardening
into firm tight mounds.

We have covered territory, many feet of floor, half undressed.
She sits on the edge of her bed and looks up at me and I think:
Oh, God. Oh, God. Nothing else.

"Ellie," she says, "you have to do the rest. Don't stop. Don't
make me explain. Please, just hurry—if you stop now, I'll freak."

"Babe—"

"No. Don't even talk, just keep going. Otherwise—"

"Hey," I whisper, "I don't want to hurry."

"—It'll stop," she blurts, "and I won't be able to start it again."

I hold her head against my torso, stroke her hair. "Start what
again, Babe?"

"This. This feeling."

I kneel between her legs, make her stare at me face to face.
Then, when I talk, it's the Ellie I hardly even know yet who
talks, and says words I could not possibly have known to say;
because they're the words of someone who understands a lot,
and is wise, and tender; who is familiar with love, and used to
winning it.

"But it's not just you, Babe. I can start this feeling too. I mean,
I already have." Then, calmly, surely, as if I've done it all my
life, I take her face in my hands and kiss her. It occurs to me,
then, that starting this won't ever be a problem—at least, not
mine. The biggest problem will be trying to stop. But, then
again, maybe I don't have to.

This is what it is, I know now for sure; what the others always talk about in cafés and hallways, in front of mirrors, dripping sweat in saunas, behind locker room doors: this dizzy, wet, electrical moaning feeling that moves you ahead with it, doesn't ask for permission, dripping liquid fire.

Let it happen, I tell myself silently. Let it rip.

Not that I need any encouragement.

I guide her down along the length of the bed, both of us still half dressed. Lie on top of her and feel us move a little, together, back and forth. Nothing has stopped. I'm not even afraid any more. But she told me I must do the rest and so somehow I will, I will. I kneel beside her on the mattress, unbutton her pants.

"God," she says, "I hope that you love me."

I love you, I tell her, I love you, I love you.

And want you, and want you, and want you, and want you.

More time goes by, but I don't know how much of it. Somewhere in the air baroque melodies play, over and over; somewhere there's a light, glowing dimly; she is naked and I am naked, and I'm lying next to her touching all of her scars, thick raw rounded tissue built up around shoulders, ribs, hips, ankles, knees, and she is crying.

Then the whole thing moves me forward, bright wet electricity pounding through my head, and I love her and can't stop it, want her and can't help it, and don't care that I can't stop it, or help it, it feels so very, very good. No one taught me what to do next. No one told me how. I did not find it in the movies, or on TV, or in books. But I am not worried. I am not even thinking. I move over her and across her and caress her and kiss her all over by instinct, and the whole thing of it teaches as it goes, moves me just right, strokes her into a matching motion too until her legs move apart and for the first time I move myself all the way forward, and feel just what it's like inside her, and I can taste her too, and smell her, and it's so beautiful, so beautiful, so creamy and living and good.

Maybe, somewhere, there are voices, telling me this is wrong. But the voices are far away now, small, insignificant, nagging, bleating, piteous. They have nothing to do with this, or with me; I feel sorry for them. And triumphant about what I am moving forward into, becoming part of now—all these pretty, good, living things that the owners of those voices never saw in books, or movies, or on TV.

Because they don't even know what they're missing.
She shudders, presses up against me.
"Faster," she breathes, and I do, I do.

Your left tricep, she tells me, is bigger than your right. And I tell her, Mmmmm, yeah, breathe to my right, left shoulder takes it, faults under water I have never corrected, all that freestyle.

Arms, arms. Everything seems to be arms now: mine around her, hers longer and larger encompassing me, everyone getting snarled in the bedsheets. Even now, at her most vulnerable, she is so strong. It's a big, smooth, firm, fleshy strength that I love, that I want, have loved and wanted all my life. Now, calmer, I can see all the parts of her. Quietly, examine them in detail. There are these veins that run the length of her forearms, crossing over the wrists to pump along the backs of each hand. Tracing them with a finger, I remember how she always worked her forearms so much in the weight room, and I wondered why; then she told me it was this feeling she had, just a feeling, unsubstantiated by science—when she began to work her forearms extra hard, her times in the 50 and the 100 improved a little; and if it works, even just psychologically, you don't question it much, you just do it. I have daydreamed every physical part of her. Now, though, these forearm veins amaze me. I decide, for a second, that they are the part I love best. Then I think: No, I love her breasts. Shoulders. Thighs.

The mattress is unyielding, too small for us both. Therapeutic, she says, I have to sleep pretty flat or before you know it my shoulders and neck and lower back mess up. Too late in the season. Can't risk that.

I run a hand through her hair. She was calm before, for a while, almost drowsy. Now, though, she's begun shivering. It is arousing, a little frightening—to be here, rolled against the length of her body; I've done it all by instinct and, by instinct, my thigh moves between both of hers and is trapped by the flesh and by shivering muscles. I feel the dampness there, warm surge of elation cutting through me. Because I'm sure of her satisfaction; I rode it and felt it and heard it myself, with each muffled cry. But this shivering pains me.

"Babe, Babe. What is it?"

"Don't know." She grits her teeth. Laughs sharply, nervously. "Nothing."

"No way—it's something."

"Yeah." She sweats, mocks Brenna Allen: "Truth is in the body, and the body does not lie—"

"Okay, ace. So tell me the truth."

"You want to know?"

"I want to know."

"It feels like dying. It's like, you lose yourself in this cloud, this light." She sobs, bites her hand. "And, I mean, I told myself, in the hospital, you know, that I wouldn't any more. Never again. Never again. No more flip turns. No more love. I mean, God, Ellie! I don't want to die!"

She rolls away, sobbing and shaking, and I hold her close, stroke her hair and face and back, tell her comforting things, but it doesn't work, she isn't listening. Pain fills me like an empty canteen. What I wished for her, all along, was only joy and pleasure; what I wanted for myself, all along, was to give her more and more—weird and funny, I thought, to start out so full of needing, to wind up so full of giving—like what would really, really thrill me, I found out, was her wanting and her satisfaction. But now she's telling me that it feels like death. Now, it is making her cry.

"Oh, Babe, I'm really sorry."

I whimper it against her back. Then I start crying, too. Until, crying softly, emptied out, dismal and exhausted and drained and confused, both of us doze off, and get some rest.

When I wake up, it seems darker. She is flat on her back holding me gently against her, eyes wide open, gazing at the ceiling. She smooths hair away from my face. Not shivering any more. There's a quiet in her body, calm in each motion. I look up at her, afraid; but she catches my eye, and smiles.

"Your face is so pretty, Ellie. Sometimes, you know, I used to close my eyes and imagine kissing it—you."

"You did?"

"Sure. What do you *think*?"

She grins broadly, fully; there's mischief in the grin, and a big, happy, relaxed joking feel to her that I've never known before. Suddenly, everything is changed. I mean, here I was, a while ago, dozing off filled with misery and desperation and a tangible sense of failure; but now, just because she is grinning, the weight seems lifted. So that I smile, too, and am flooded with pure delight.

"Tell me, Ellie—do you do this often?"

"Sure," I lie. "But only with a chosen few."

She is childlike, winking, teasing. "Well, you *are* one of the chosen people."

"Mmmm. You too. I mean, if I was Castro, I would have *paid* your family to leave."

"He practically did. And at the Bay of Pigs, you know? they fought back to keep us *out*."

"Yeah. You were the Expendables of the Year, right? Like, from everyone's point of view. Nowhere to turn but a raft."

"Not even that, sometimes."

"Havana will never be the same."

"Oh," she says softly, "neither will Miami."

I move away a little, prop myself with my elbows.

"Babe, I lied about this. I mean, I never have before."

"Just wanted to—?"

"Right."

"Well, did you like it?"

"Oh, God." I am humbled now, and blush. "It's beautiful. It's amazing."

She trails a finger across my lips. "Yes," she says, "I think so too."

I want to ask her so many things, then—like what she'd meant before, about freaking, and the feeling of dying, and the cloud and the light, and why it had made her cry, why she hadn't been able to stop herself from shaking, why she'd said she wasn't gay, and who had been the first for her, a man or a woman, and how many had there been since, and which of them had she loved? But there isn't time. She has turned me flat onto my back and is full on top of me—so big and long and fleshed out and strong that, for a moment, I think I'll faint.

"Too heavy?"

"God, no."

"Bumpy. Feel that? I hate all my scars."

"Don't, Babe. Please don't. I want you so much. I think you're so beautiful."

It is a fact: Bodies do not lie. Maybe Coach learned that truth just from swimming; but I doubt it.

She is looking down at me, touching my face, eyelids, hair, falling aside to touch my body with a knowledgeable elegance that feels absolute; and—I can feel this too now and it thrills me—urgency, yearning. She pauses and swallows hard. It's in her face, all at once, twined together—so much want, so much terror. Sweat pops out on her forehead, nose, upper lip.

"Look, Ellie—um, this is hard."

"You don't have to—"

"Shhh," she says, "no, never mind."

She closes her eyes, shakes her head and sweat flies from her skin, her hair. Then she smiles. Opens her eyes like slits and looks far away into some distance I can't even see. Whispers softly:

"No more pain."

"Okay," I say—uncertainly, by instinct.

"Patience, El, patience. One stroke at a time."

"Whatever you want, Babe."

"Whatever? I want?" She laughs. The sound comes out muted, choked, violent. "Just say it's all right. Say you won't leave—"

"I'm here, Babe, I'm safe—it's all right! I won't go!"

The eyes close again, perspiring hands reach to feel the pulse throb in my neck, my wrist, groin, breasts. She presses fingers against it, presses an ear against flesh, eyes shut, listening, measuring. "There. Mmmm. Okay." She's not talking to me, but to herself. "Yes, like that. Okay, okay."

I reach to hold her while her eyes stay closed and she's touching me, put my lips against her ear and speak right into it, telling her things that are light years beyond me, things I didn't even know I knew: that minds lie, not bodies; limitation and barriers, like pain, are only in the mind, but the mind can be transcended, yes, until the body itself is too, until things flow on a different level from your everyday life—automatic, unself-conscious, limitless, free; death happens to the body, but not to the mind; the mind is sheer love—which is different from and stronger than death—eternal, limitless, free. I tell her she has never seemed so strong. So powerful to me. I tell her that, to feel her hold me like this, scarred and delicate and beautiful and powerful and strong, I would endure a hundred qualifying heats, face the harsh, bright barrier of pain many times over, swim any ocean. That I am glad, so glad she survived. And proud, so very proud, to love her.

Don't, she says. Don't say it if you do not mean it.

"I mean it, Babe. I mean it, I mean it."

"No matter what? Won't quit? Sink or swim?"

"Won't quit."

"You have to hold on. Eyes open. Don't let go."

"I promise," I breathe, giddy and tingling wherever she touches, "yes, I promise, I won't let go."

Hold on then, she says. Tight, yes, that's right. Now, don't quit on me. No matter what. Promise. You won't let go. It is easy, you know. Just one more minute. What wait can't you take for one more lousy minute? Real winners don't quit. No pain, no pain. But first, tell me yes. I mean, Stateside. Stateside. Stateside. Stateside. Hold onto me tight. Hold onto me, love. Hold onto me, love. I am taking us home.

We miss practice. Miss all of our afternoon and evening classes. Then sleep when it's dark, wake up in a timeless sort of fog, look at a clock and our watches and realize that a night has passed, it is the next day, late morning—we have missed morning practice, too. Aside from the time I spent sick, I have never even missed a warm-up, or sat out as much as a single stroke drill; now, though, I just really don't care.

Judging from the pleased, half shy look of peace on her face, neither does Babe.

"How you doing, El?"

Fine, I tell her, beyond fine.

"So you still like it?"

Wide-eyed, I nod.

She staggers to the bathroom, bleary, naked, stiff-jointed and lame—I can hear her knees creak all the way across the floor. Then I hear water running, steam seeping sideways out of cracks in the door. Once, I think, I hear her hum a few bars of something foreign and lively. Caribbean, maybe. Salsa. No, not quite. Then:

"God!" she yells. "I feel great! I feel great!"

We miss another afternoon practice, too.

* * *

When we finally do show up the next day, we are late. Warm-up's already started. I feel fractured, frazzled, out of touch, ecstatic. The locker room's empty, except for us. Babe pulls off Ace bandages, pulls on her suit, grabs my head once to rub her cheek against it and heads for the pool without even stretching, half-running, half-limping. I take my time. No one really needs or expects me to swim for them, now. They are all fine without me. As I am without them.

Halfway between shower and pool I run into Etta, who glances at me over the rim of her clipboard, raises both eyebrows.

"Pushing your luck, white girl."

"How pissed is she?"

"Hell hath no fury. But cold, like ice."

Definitely bad news.

Everyone else is pulling and drilling and kicking her way through the end of warm-up. The air's damp, hot. Babe has already hit the water in four and is swimming like shit. I grab a pull buoy, head for lane eight. Brenna Allen notices me briefly out of the corner of an eye, but doesn't change expression. When she speaks it is quietly, her voice impassive.

"In my office after workout."

Silently, I nod. Then I pretend to adjust my goggles, while doom shoots through me.

I follow the program, do what I can. Work as hard as possible—to show her, maybe, that I am still more or less old faithful—and, when I just can't breathe any more, sit out a set. From the side of the pool I watch them all. I shiver a little, wrap my towel around. Smudge soothing cream on the indentations under my eyes. Ceiling lights glint off lane four. Babe is bagging it today. Slack timing, dolphining off her walls, touching in with too much left over, joking around between reps. The whistle blows.

"Swim down," calls Brenna Allen. "Everyone take it easy. Except, of course, for Ms. Delgado, who has already done so, and who will therefore get out of the water and have a chat with me right now."

Etta tosses her clipboard on a bench beside me.

"Mind your manners. She's out there on the warpath."

She starts to gather up kickboards and other equipment, stack it neatly along the opposite wall, and, from across the pool, I can see her shoulders shake with silent laughter. Everyone in the water starts a swim-down except for Babe, who pushes up and out so that light drips from her back muscles, crouches there a minute before standing, stretching, walking to the corner where Brenna Allen is waiting. When I head for the locker room I pass them and briefly catch Babe's eye. Her expression is fierce, intent. I can't see Coach's face. But she is talking in low tones, firmly, quietly; Babe is dripping and listening, once in a while talking too; and they are facing each other squarely, standing tall, hands on hips.

They talk a long time—at least, I think they do. I'm showered, shampooed, dry-haired, clean-clothed, baby-powdered and bright-eyed and hungry for breakfast by the time the first of the team start spilling in from swim-down, Babe nowhere in sight. I want to wait for her, but don't. Instead I evade the first rush, climb stairs and turn corners, pass racquetball courts and weight rooms, tap bravely on the door to Brenna Allen's office.

"Come on in, Ellie."

I do, and sit down, expecting the worst. But she doesn't sound angry. She pushes the edge of the desk and her chair rolls back, quietly. I wonder if I should apologize first, fend everything off and nip it in the bud; then realize that just keeping my mouth shut will be the best policy. Still, I am nervous. Her eyes search the bookshelves. They find me, and smile.

"How are you feeling these days?"

"Better. A lot better."

"That's good. I'm glad. I know that this year has been far from what we planned for you, hasn't it?"

"I guess."

"You must be tired of all the work. I would be, if I were you—all the responsibility, no immediate payback—I'd be ready for some fun, and for a nice long vacation."

"Sure," I say uneasily. "I mean, you know, maybe."

"Well, I can't blame you. The problem is, we don't always get a break when we need one." The chair swivels slightly. Her elbows land silently on the desk blotter, fingers meet. She has nice hands, long and slender. Not thick, the way I'd always thought—my own are just as large. They are smaller hands than Babe's. She leans forward; we lock eyes.

"Tell me something, Ellie—hypothetically, if you want. But for the sake of this team, I really need to know."

I nod. Hold my breath.

"When you—I mean *you* personally now, not some abstract you—say you love somebody. You care for them. Do you also want what is good for them? I mean, not just fun and pleasure— but for them to succeed, say, at doing something very difficult? Something that you know, in your heart, will mean a lot to them?"

Sure, I say, yes.

"Even if they are afraid?"

"Yes."

"Or unsure?"

"Yes."

"Or, for instance, looking for some excuse to stop doing the difficult thing, looking for a way out, maybe without even knowing it? Say you love this person, Ellie—would you help them do the difficult thing anyway? I mean, encourage them to stay on track, stay focused, concentrate, be disciplined, eat right, get enough rest, you know, all the details. Even if, at first glance, there seemed to be nothing in it for you?"

Yes, I tell her, maybe.

"Yes? Or just maybe?"

"Yes," I whisper, bitterly. "Yes. Yes. Yes."

"Good," she says. "It's good to hear that."

I stand. Asking, Anything else? But there is one thing more, she says, waving me back down.

I rock miserably on the edge of a chair, can feel myself blush, wish I was far away and had never swum for this woman, not ever. But she doesn't seem to notice, doesn't seem angry or perturbed at all. She ignores me, in fact, and rummages through a full drawer, paper rustling, objects clanking.

Ah, she says, yes, here. And pulls out a worn little square maroon leather case with metal latch and hinges, rattles it around and holds it to her ear, smiles. Then hands it across the desk to me.

"Go on, open it up, take a look."

I unlatch it and it folds up into a pyramid, old clock face with gold-green numbers standing still, until I turn a side-knob, winding it, and it comes to life, starts to tick.

"That's my old traveling alarm clock, Ellie. When I was a kid they didn't have them on wristwatches. I remember, weekend mornings—well, it got me out of bed. Hang on to it, will you? At least through Divisionals."

She comes around to my side of the desk and sits on its edge, facing me, and shows me how to set it. I test it through two alarms. The ring is almost pleasant—nothing high-tech or shattering.

"Use it, will you?"

"Okay."

"People on this team depend on you. It is *all* time, anyway. If you don't make practice, that sets a bad example."

"Yes, Bren. I'm sorry."

Then I freeze. I have never called her by her first name before; at least, not to her face.

But she doesn't seem to notice, or even mind. She smiles broadly, cocks her head—a rare treat, because it is Coach at her best: bright, knowing, WASPily handsome, engaging.

"And one more thing."

Whenever she says that, my ass will be grass, for sure. My belly sinks. But I snap the clock case shut and rest it in both palms; can hear it, behind worn leather, gently ticking. I try not to let my gaze waver.

"Yes, Coach?"

"I would consider it a favor, a personal favor, if you'd make it your business to see that Babe Delgado shows up for all workouts on time, no matter what. She's carrying a lot—the one and two, and the medleys, and medley relay—well, you know all that, there are plenty of points at stake right there. Just make her work. I mean every day, Ellie. Even if you have to drag her in kicking and screaming. Do it for her. Or for yourself. Or, if you like, you can do it for me. But if you see that through, I'll owe you."

Never, I think. I will never do it for you. Although I might for *her*. Or even for myself.

Anyway, Bren, you already owe me.

"Fine," I say, "okay, I will."

I stand again, slip the alarm clock into a pocket of my coat. She stands too, tells me thanks, and then we shake hands.

Wandering down the hall, dodging notebooks and sweat, it occurs to me that days have gone by. I haven't called home. Nan and Jean probably think I'm some ax-murder victim. For all I know, there's a three-state police alert on. I haven't read, or done any papers, or studied, or exercised much—never mind made workouts—and I couldn't care less.

All I want, now, is her. Her hands. Her taste. Her pleasure. All I want is to see her. I wonder where she is. I just don't want to wait.

And maybe, if I'm lucky, what she wants is the same.

Take that! I yell, silently. Take that, *Bren!* You fucked-up WASP bitch. You dumb frigid closet case. I mean, who are *you*, lady? Who the *hell*? What do you know about suffering? Or passion? Or love?

Partway down the hall is a wastebasket. I caress the old maroon-cased alarm clock in my pocket, consider throwing it in. But I feel the worn tick, and think about time, and I don't.

Like Coach's pet, over the next few weeks I do her bidding. Making sure that I—and Babe—get to every single practice. Sitting with her at mealtime, in the cafeteria or at my place. Making sure she eats. Making sure she drinks enough water. Gets to the weight room often enough. Doesn't overdo it or slack off when she gets there. Like a mother hen, making sure we get to bed before midnight every night and do not stay up for hours, even when she wants to and even when I want to so much I can feel the aching and the wanting everywhere, everywhere. It feels to me like I'm paying back some sort of bad karma or something; like I am paying all of my lifetime adult membership dues into some bizarre club of fate. Acting as if I'm really a good, unselfish girl inside.

She gets the letter just before spring. Final exams are coming up in a month. So are important meets, essential practice; it looks like we're going to get a really good crack at a number-one ranking in the division, this year—a lot of which is due to the presence of Babe Delgado, none of which is due to the presence of yours truly—and so we're destined for Short Course Divisional Championships, in the end.

But all this turns to Silly Putty.

I can tell, when she comes back up to her room on a Saturday afternoon, after going downstairs to get the mail—practice over for the day, nothing else on our minds but a little extremely necessary studying, maybe a walk out to this apple orchard I know about in the country; and, of course, some love.

Something's worse than wrong. Her face has gone that pasty

olive shade it is when she's afraid, or sick, or upset. Her mouth is hanging open, the lips cracked and dry. She's holding this letter in one trembling hand.

Hey, I say, what is it?

She doesn't answer, just leans back on the door to close it. The door thuds, and she does too—falling back like a corpse against it—and I start toward her, to hold her, but she motions me away.

She sighs. Her eyes look red, and damp.

Kenny, she blurts. He's going to die.

Then she shoves the letter toward me, gesturing for me to take it and read, and I do—first skimming, then in more detail. It is signed Tom and Joan Hedenmeyer, although written in what looks to be a woman's hand—Kenny's mother, I guess.

He has for a long time requested that they take him off his life support equipment, she writes. It is something he has obviously considered with care. Our hearts are and have been broken. At the same time, we respect his wishes. We have gone through several months of rather gruesome medical and legal bureaucratic legwork. Now that it is all done, Kenny has decided that he wants the machines unplugged next weekend. He asked me—us—to let you know.

After reading it a few times, I sit on the couch silently. Babe slumps into a chair.

I ask her what she'll do and she says, God, Ellie, I guess I'll go. I'll call them and see if I can. I don't know what else to do.

"But I can't, can I?" She laughs, humorless. "We've got a meet then—we've got tests—"

"Yeah, but so what?" And I know it is the right thing to say, even though it makes me feel immediately abandoned; even though it's completely at odds with Brenna Allen's purpose.

"You're right," she says, "I have to go. Will you come to the airport with me?"

I nod.

"Will you tell Bren for me?"

"No, Babe. You should do that yourself."

She shoots me a look of grief mixed with resentment. We're quiet for a while. I can hear her fighting back sobs.

Okay, she says, then I will.

The Sea of Light

🐬 🐬 🐬

(KENNY)

Off and on, I travel.

Pack your suitcase, Babe. Dallas. Munich. Melbourne. Don't forget the sunblock. Number 15, waterproof. Some of that Bullfrog stuff for the nose. You know what always happens: peel down your suit and there you are, in two colors: pale around the private parts, red or brown everywhere else.

I mean, I get red.

You're brown.

Then I like it, the way it looks together, in the mirror—red and white rubbing brown. And you say: If your hair was blue, Kenny, you'd be the American flag.

They have propped me up near the window.

On good days, they turn my head toward the glass panes and sky, away from the machines. Gravel driveway. Seeded lawn, burned in the sun. Just below, a circle of rocks and wildflowers. My garden. Mom planted it.

For you, Kenny, for you. So you can look out, sweetheart, and see all the flowers.

Planting it, there was tired age in her arms and head. I watched. Stared down at the sunburned red of her neck, beneath the gray hair and a hat. She crouched, digging.

Talked to me, though I did not reply.

What do you think about these? Not exactly tropical, but we'll give them a try. And when it's not too warm, we'll just open up that window. Too much air-conditioning makes the skin stale. Let you feel the air on your face. There, now, that's better.

At first, she ran in every ten minutes. Adjusting dials. Pointing out flowers. Opening or closing windows. Filling food tubes with purified natural products. She plastered the walls with things she thought I would maybe have asked for, before: posters of mountains, of the sea. As if surrounding me with these figments of nature would heal. Would cure. Would make me speak. Or want to survive.

Patience, son, said my dad. It's what she needs to do.

What could I respond with, except patience?

Every other morning he comes in to give me a shave. Dish, lather, towel and razor and brush—like some old-fashioned barber.

Sometimes, at night, he'll sit with me. Stroke the thin remains of my hair. Hold my hand in both of his.

I can't feel it, but I see it.

Perfect vision. Just one way that my eyes betray me.

Sometimes, at night, I will cry.

My boy, he says. My boy.

When the tears drip far, he takes a cloth and wipes them.

Last night, I traveled to the Pan Am Games in Havana. Neat. You could smell tropics in the air: fruit, palm leaves, sea and tobacco. Went to dinner with Liz and Babe—rice and fish and beans, something coconut, lots of bread, flavored shavings of ice chips in paper cups for dessert. Then we walked along a shop-lined boulevard, the three of us, past armed soldiers and rattling ancient cars. Touch of music, somewhere, interspersed with news in Spanish. Laughs. Romance. Dance, I thought, dance. Until there we were on an empty beach, propped up against low grassy dunes sprouting black bushes, watching sunset and the waves. Yawning, burping dinner, whistling out of tune to the far-off radio, me on one side, Liz on the other, Babe in between. Her left hand held in mine. Her right hand, one of Lizzy's. After a while Liz dug an elbow into sand, lay there sideways looking at us both in the red-tinted dark, smiled and ran a hand along Babe's forehead, down her cheek and lips and neck.

"Look you two, I gotta go."

Babe closed her eyes.

"Where to, Lizzy?" I said. "And not alone, huh?"

"Nah, don't worry. Sager said he'd pick me up and haul my rear end back to the dorms—I promised him nine P.M. curfew the night before qualifying heats, he swore he'd make me stick to it—so there you go, guys. I'm stuck."

"Pinned."

"Butterfly on the wall."

She rubs my shoulder and kisses Babe, stands to shake sand off. Somewhere there are lights. A car honks, and she's gone. I nudge Babe's neck with my nose.

"She's fucking him, Babe."

"Who?"

"Sager."

She laughs. "Not Liz."

"How come you're so sure?"

"Look, I just *know*, okay? Anyway, what are you doing?"

Nothing, I tell her, my hand up her shirt. Getting ready for a little romance.

She tells me doing it in the dark on a strange beach with sand up your butt is hardly romantic. I tell her to stop resisting and just love me; which after a while she does—kissing back, touching back, getting naked, all the things she knows I like—with a lot less enthusiasm somehow than I am showing, but with real care and affection. She's had a lot on her mind lately, I know: the battle of wills with Sager, and her slipping times, getting demoted from the animal lane, and all this bullshit she's going through around her family, and around competing; sometimes, I think, it's just Liz and I holding her up in the world so she can walk on her own two feet. But it's not so bad being needed. Even if, most of the time, I cannot make her come. She makes sure I'm happy. We have a good time. I love her eyes, and tits, and long lean belly, and thighs. I mean, I've got no complaints.

That night, though, it bothered me. So that I held her face between my hands and she had to look straight up at me while I moved her knees apart with my own and slowly, slowly, like doing something sacred, I pushed inside of her.

"Keep your eyes open, Babe."

No, she said, don't.

"I love you," I told her. "Stay with me, stay with me, I want to make you happy."

She closed her eyes and I forced them open with the tips of my fingers. She tossed her head out of my grasp; I seized it again, hard, could see the whiteness of her teeth in the dark, and she bit her lip deep and moved her hips up into me, faster, trying to end it all much faster, and I fought against her but couldn't win, finally bucked and pumped and groaned into her, went hot, blank, and came and came.

I opened my eyes against the damp side of her neck. She was trying to push me away, crying.

"Bitch," I gasped, like in a dream, without knowing why, "who else is there?"

She shoved me off of her and rolled away. There I was in the sand, shirt off, pants down around my ankles, and she's staggering to her knees mostly naked, gathering up her clothes, crawling off crying, then running. Hey! I yell. Babe, hey! But she doesn't stop.

When I get back to the dorm all hell has broken loose. She's running down the hall smack into me, sobbing, looking red-faced and crazy, her clothes buttoned on all crooked, still sprinkling sand. Her chin hits my chest. She stuffs a hand in her mouth to muffle the sounds.

"Babe. What is it?"

"No," she says, and runs down some stairs. A door along the hallway slams shut. Liz races out, tying on a bathrobe. It's too long for her and flaps the floor around her ankles. She heads in my direction, and when she comes close I see that her skin is flushed, mouth set anxiously, eyes uncertain, aggravated. She's breathing really hard.

"Where'd she go, Kenny?"

"What's going on?"

She ignores me, pointing. "Down there?"

"Hey." I grab her by the shoulders suddenly, slam her against a wall and hold her there. The bathrobe's not hers. It's Sager's. I can feel sweat drip down my face. Sand in my shoes. Up my ass. I can smell myself—a mean, pungent smell. "Tell me, Liz, why do you care?"

"None of your business."

"No, it really is my business. See, in case you hadn't noticed,

I really, really love her. And along those lines, Lizzy, I happen to be fucking her."

"Funny," she says, her eyes damp and amused, "so am I."

Doors are opening, lights flickering on. People in various stages of undress—from our team, and others—are staggering into the hall, yawning, blinking. Out of shadows at the end of the hall I recognize one larger, older form, heading our way: Sager, jeans zipped haphazardly on, buttoning up his shirt.

"Who else," I whisper. "Who else are you fucking to win?"

"Shut up, Kenny. Just tell me where she is." Sager's too-big robe is open to the cleft between her breasts. Under tropical tan her chest is red, heaving, and for a second I don't blame him for wanting her, but the feeling leaves me pissed off and sweating and empty inside. So empty that I let my hands drop from her shoulders, pull away, and she leans back against the wall relieved. "Listen, Kenny, you don't know the half of it. Why don't you just shut up and swim?"

"Oh, sure I do, Lizzy. I know at *least* half of it."

"But you're not the only person around here with feelings, big shot. I love her too—maybe I'm just more, let's say, ambidextrous. Anyway, it's all for her! I mean, she's the one! She's the one who wanted it."

"Yeah? And you just cheerfully obliged? For how long?"

"Oh, months." She smiles, tiredly. "Since Bart—since Sager told me to."

"Told you to? What are you, Lizzy? Coach's love doll? Some kind of fucking robot?"

For the first time, pain flashes across her eyes. They are empty of the laughter now, empty of the daily, self-assured teasing joy that usually beams out of them, makes everybody love her, makes everybody think they are missing out on something if they are not with her. But she seems to pull herself up and stand taller, clasps the opened flaps of robe together over her chest, and her face sets into granite-hard indignation.

"What *I* am, Hedenmeyer, is none of your business. But just for your general information, I happen to be a hero. America's little sweetheart. As good as you get without drugs, gorgeous, and that means the unacknowledged best in the whole world— you know what that feels like? to be the best? and not be credited with a single world record, because a bunch of dopers set them all? i don't think you do. Go tell *that* to your funny doctor friends—or maybe I am prying into *your* business now. All *I* know is that *I* can walk around the weight room with a clear conscious—I mean, I can do anything I want *by myself*, Kenny—and so could she, if she'd only grow up a little."

At this point, memory blurs. The trip fades. And I tell myself: No, it wasn't Havana, you never made it to the Pan Ams; it was San Juan, Kenny—San Juan, Puerto Rico.

Tall shadows at the door. Babe. Or am I traveling again?

No, say the voices—a chorus of murmurs, whispers—It is really her. So stay awhile.

"Kenny?"

As if there'd be anyone else here. At the same time, I understand exactly why she asked it. It is her voice, yes; same husky, musical, unmodulated tones, meaning to ask: Is there anything left of Kenny here?

There barely is.

But enough of him, anyway, to stay awhile.

She steps into light and I see her now: Still tall, a little heavier, her face looks oddly pale and she's aged, seems a lot older than early twenties; when she steps forward I catch it, the almost unnoticeable limp, vaguely damaged stoop to the shoulders. But she's still Babe, after all. And I want to ask: What did it do to you, Babe? And how have you changed? Almost six months of physical therapy for you, they told me. Never be what you once were. As if that would make me feel better somehow—to know of your misery, your loss. There must have been smart shrinks as well. Could they fix up your mind? Could they fix up your heart?

The machines beep.

"Kenny." I feel her take a silent breath. Watch her face, her pose, as she crosses in the light. Understand the stillness of her expression, because I've seen it before; coming to see me, you prepare for the very worst. Then, at first sight, vaguely human figure resting propped up on pillows amid this clean shiny clicking whirring mass of machines, you recognize something about me and are momentarily relieved; and you tell yourself, Whew, thank God, it's not as bad or as repulsive as I thought. You relax, begin to come closer. And your face grows absolutely still, under the firm fascist hand of self-control, as you realize, after all, that you were wrong. It is every bit as bad. It is much, much worse.

I twist my lips from the tube. "Yo Babe." It comes out garbled. "You look great." Twist them back, and breathe.

She sits right there, on the edge of the bed. Slowly, heavily, as if falling, or shedding a great weight. I am surprised she sits so close. Still nothing on her face. When she speaks it is simply, matter-of-fact.

"Your mom wrote and told me about what you decided. So I came down. She says move the tube when you raise your eyebrows. Right?"

Hmmm, I gurgle, like nodding.

"Okay. It's your life, Kenny. I mean, whatever you want. I'll stay until you tell me to go."

I raise my eyebrows. Slowly, shyly, she pulls away the tube. Her hand shakes a little, makes it tremble near the dimple in my chin.

"Good, Babe. Stay."

She understands.

Open Hand—you called me; I was your Open Hand Boy. Came to you without fingers intertwined. Palms wide, hiding nothing. Strong. Brave. Ingenuous. Heart-on-the-sleeve kind of guy. What you saw was what you got. The only boy you could love.

Liz, you said, was different.

Seemed to hide nothing. In truth, hid a lot. Calculated. Manipulated.

The 200 demands craft, stealth, a smooth, smooth glide. She was sly in that way, you said: that middle-distance kind of way. Liked to play both sides of things. Keep all her options open.

Only pure race, you said, was the 50. No malice aforethought. Just jump in. Swim as fast as you can. Raw burst of power. Thrill. And the fastest thrill wins.

You were right, I thought. It's what Sager said, too. The longer the race, the less you need talent and the more you need smarts and will; but not too much smarts, you have to be crude in a way, have to get things on your side and then not care that you puke all over them in the end; the main thing is will.

Which is why he preferred sprinters. He thought he could

control us better. Talent, he said. Fast twitch muscle. Reflex. Instinct. Don't think; just do. Then go in for the kill. It's like eating. Like slaying. Original art of war.

He was on my side, because I had that—what he said, or so he thought—that speed, that murdering finish. Animal instinct; his favorite words.

He was not on your side, because you had that, that instinct, but contained it like a human; and he knew, urged it out of you, but you would not deliver.

Liz? He just wanted. Because she had what he did not.

Craft. Wit. Will.

Expedience.

All this was in another life.

As for Liz, and her accusations—well, she was right.

The drugs? I took them. I took them all.

Only, not in a malicious way.

It's like this: You work so hard. So very hard. And get so tired. And do so much, at that level, as much or more than everybody else, and they are all taking advantage of every little potential edge, every extra ounce of stamina, every small millisecond that may fall their way; we are all so close in talent and training and ability and times, we all do whatever we can to help our proud, magnificent, limited bodies along. Everything centers around the sport. You sleep for it, eat for it, drink nutritional supplements for it, lift weights for it, diet for it, go to special psychologists for it, monitor your blood with doctors for it, take all kinds of vitamins for it, leave aside a normal life for it; in the end, popping just one more pill into your mouth, going to just one more doctor, handing just one more wad of bills over a counter or a table or a locker room bench, is really nothing more than just one more thing. A little thing. A detail. That you take care of, that you do for the sport. For the win. For the love. It is no big deal.

Not the same as shooting dope or sniffing coke, for instance, to get *away* from achievement, or from pain. It's the opposite, in fact—comes out of the desire, eagerness, will.

Although it hurt me, in the end. Damaged inner tissue. Stopped painkillers and antibiotics from assimilating. Made them hook on more machines.

Not that it mattered, at that point.

I mean, there were other things that hurt me.

I mean, I am sure that, whether in heaven or in hell, Lizzy has no apologies for anyone, and—whatever form she takes these days—no regrets.

Neither do I.

Except for this one memory: Babe. See, I wish I'd loved her better. I wish that she'd loved me.

As a child, Sager told us, he used to take a tiny animal. One for each important race. Because he was fast enough, and good enough, to swim in the animal lane. Guinea pigs. Baby rabbits, hamsters. Trembling, raise its throat up to the razor. In locker rooms, after shave-down. Warrior, he'd say, animals. And sprinkle himself with blood. Hearing this, Babe would wince. Look at the floor. Would not let herself cry. Until the sleeplessness started for her, and the vomiting, and all the weird dieting. She was trying to get out the blood, she said. But her times slipped, Sager started to hate her, and she fell from grace. Tumbled far, far. Out of the animal lane.

"Remember, Kenny?" she says now. And I know it is that—I don't have to ask—I know it is that she's remembering. She crosses herself. I close my eyes. "*Sagrada María, Madre de Dios.* Mary, forgive me. Do you know how I lived, Kenny? I promised the light. That somehow, every day, I would make it up to all the animals—I mean the ones on four legs, and the human animals, too. Because killing to eat, and to win—that's the horror of the world."

A tear slides down her face. And I know that it is my old friend Babe, for sure; that she may sound crazy, but is sane, totally sane. She takes my hand. I do not feel it, but see it.

Listen to me, Babe. When I leave, you'll be the only one. Who remembers. And keeps the secret.

Don't do it.

Tell someone.

I release you. Look at my eyes. Let them break the vow. Dry the blood. Set you free.

Yes, next to me. Turn my head. Pillow drool.

Eyes. Look at them. See.

"Remember the storm, Kenny?"

I raise eyebrows. The tube moves. "Not much. It's all a blur. Like, gray." And breathe again.

"For me, too. But sometimes I get these flashes—of what it was like, you know? And I know then that I know—I mean, know and remember it all, somewhere in here"—she flicks a thumb against her forehead—"or here"—and her chest. "But then it gets sort of gray again. I mean, it's just not on the surface. This one guy in the hospital—this shrink, a Jewish guy—he hypnotized me a couple of times. So I got to where I could remember some stuff. Pretty weird."

"Mind is weird," I gasp.

"So's living."

"Mmmm, Babe. So is dying."

Right, she says. She raises my hand, string-thin and shapeless, in both of hers. Twines her big, long, strong fingers with my useless, ruined ones.

"You want a massage, Kenny?"

She moves the tube. Couldn't even feel it, I tell her. But she shrugs.

"I don't mind."

Oh, then, I tell her, go ahead. That would be kind.

Come here, Babe. I will tell you a secret.

There is barely any Kenny left now. This I that was me is in a way of becoming. Part of something else.

It is hard to explain.

Watch. Listen.

See. Hear.

The way of it—not what you think.

There is no bird's-eye view.

No forest. Only trees.

No ocean. Only waves.

Broad map of it, no; map is not the territory.

It comes upon you like pricks at first. Then aching. Then swells of pain. Until this constant anguish of muscle and flesh. And fire in bone.

But the fire gets cold, does not diminish. Cumulative ice. A deep, deep freeze. Until you are frozen in the pain. And the pain is your life.

Scars, accumulate.

Love, accumulates.

All add to the weight of it. And weight brings you down.

But in the moments racing by, that is not what you know.

You think, only: in this second, I suffer.

Not: I am dying now.

Sometimes, she tells me later, I get this feeling that I'm inside a dream, you know?

I laugh. Gurgle recognition into the tube, which distorts it to a sob. But she looks into my eyes, sees the laughter there, gives me a smile while her own eyes brim tears.

"I feel like it's all some weird, wrong dream. But at the same time I know—I know I'm never going to wake up. I mean, dream or not—this is *it*."

I wink.

"Your legs got really small, Kenny."

So did my dick. But I don't say this.

"And your feet."

She lifts them, one by one. One by one, gently pulls each toe. Faintly, far off, I hear them crack. Release. Odd, not to feel that. Yet there they are—small, translucent, puffy, utterly unused, toenails rimmed with blue, turned up facing me from the bottom of the bed. They are mine. Were. Belonged to the body of a young man once. Blond hair dispersed along the thin, thin ankles. Before a major meet, I would shave all that off. I would clean-shave my chest. My neck, and my arms.

Or, as Sager called it, get clean and mean.

Babe hated that.

He wants to make us infants, she'd say.

Liz would wink at me. Cuddle her head against a belly or a thigh. Oh, just chill, Babe! He wants to make us *fast!*

And, like little girls, they'd laugh.

Tears slide out of my eyes. She strokes them away.

"It's all right, love. Look, Kenny, I'll tell you a secret. I know that you loved me. And I know how much. So nothing else matters, okay? Don't have regrets."

I close my eyes. Time passes. Silence. Open them, tearless.

"Kenny, I have to tell you. I don't know why, it's just been on my mind that maybe it would make you happy, or something. See, I fell in love again."

Raise my eyebrows. Twist mouth away.

"Babe, that's great."

"Sometimes, you know, I even feel good."

"Right," I gasp. "Better and better."

Eyes dull for a second. For a second, then, ears go dead. Blurred vision, in a soundless room. And I know, I know, it quickens now. Continues. Manifestation is fading. Tonight, finish: will vanish.

Babe?

She takes the tube away.

Babe, listen:

"Thanks for the visit."

The tube comes back. I breathe again.

She cries, long, gently, muffled. I watch, helpless.

Twist my mouth away.

"Babe? Let me hold you."

Slowly, gently, she pushes cables out of the way, falls right next to me on the bed. I watch her with my eyes. See her refuse to turn away. Set her head alongside mine right there, right on the pillow. Tentatively at first, then with great affection, rub her fingers along my chin, and cheeks, and forehead. Softly, caress my eyebrows. My nose.

I still swim, she whispers. Kenny, I still do. Only, not to be great any more. Not really. Just to be human.

She closes her eyes next to mine. Falls asleep. I can hear the sounds of her breathing fading in and out of my ears like a shell held up, imitating the sea.

Babe, listen: It starts from the outside in. Death, I mean.

Mine started in the hospital, when I woke up and could not feel fingers or toes. Since then, the lack of sensation has spread, slowly, slowly, inside of me. From toes up. From fingers in. The machines just beep stability. They cannot show this, the real truth: that, lying here, as usual, I am actually traveling far away; and, this time, whatever is left of the young man Kenny will not return.

Babe, listen: This isn't Kenny talking, but a collection of voices into which, bodiless, without personality, the entity who in this life was called *Kenny* will fade.

The young man cannot say this.

So look in his eyes.

We are there, Babe. All of us, unbetrayed, unbetrayable. You saw this once before, while you were dying in the sea. And, because still trapped in body and mind of personality, you imagined it in visual form: a cloud—of light. That hovered close—closer than you imagined seeing it—as close as you are to yourself. For you were not separate.

Kenny, you whispered, do you see it?

He did, but could not reply.

Take me, he told us. Open Hand, he said, dreaming, Open Hand Boy. With every fault and deception. Every action. Every loss, and win. Here, in the water, I am ready. Take me. I loved her. And others. Now, I have given up. Now, I just love.

And there, in the sea, we began.

But you—you were not dreaming. You could still imagine. That you saw with your eyes. Awake. Fighting. Trying to swim.

Kenny, do you see it?

You were enchanted. Also, afraid. And reached toward the light you thought you saw, anyway.

I want, you said.

To live.

We enveloped you. Considered taking you, then. To ease your suffering. To bring you back home. So, again, the journey began. Out of the sea of water, into the sea of light. From which you are not separate, except in the falsity of appearance. Weightless, you traveled, with the light your only covering. Up into the nothing funnel, spiral female male conch shell of the origin and the continuance.

You laughed. Cried.

I want, you said. So much. To live.

Then the journey stopped.

Go back, we said.

You protested. Became the personality Babe again. Saying, Forget it. I *like* being weightless. I mean, this is cool. I can do anything I want.

Yes, we told you, that is why.

Why, what?

Why you have to go back. You aren't ready.

When you're ready, truly and purely conscious, a part of desireless love, non-separate, you will know. And we'll be there.

We'll be you.

Because there is no difference.

But, first, you must know it.

I want, you said. Sobbing.

We conferred. That's it, we decided. It she wants it so damn much, let her have it.

So we threw you on back. Spit you out, spinning wildly, from the whirlwind funnel of light, into the thrashing air, gray wind, and your broken tortured woman's body that clung to life, that tried to swim, into the water and sea.

When she wakes up, the air-conditioning is off. My mother has come in and opened up the window. You can smell the faint whiffs of the flowers she's planted. You can hear cars go by, once in a while; once in a while hear a plane take off, far away, or dog bark, or kid clatter by on a bicycle. Pastel gravel surrounding palm trunks on each lawn. The sun is going down, amid long flat clouds, a vivid purple light in the sky. I can sense but not see my parents at the door. Soon, soon. The doctor will come. And lawyers. Paramedics. Signed releases. Unplug the plugs. Then it won't be long.

For this I am ready like for a big meet: shaved down, focused, drugged just right, all my homework done. Excited and afraid. As much an athlete as ever.

Almost time, now. Yes. I start to shake, to sweat, with terror, with relief. She wipes my face with her hand.

"Look, Kenny. Whatever you want. I mean, I know about tonight, and if you want me to be here when they turn all this shit off, I'll be here."

Raise the eyebrows. Tube removed.

Final words of the entity Kenny:

"No thanks. Me alone."

And:

"I love you, Babe. Now go away."

La Bruja

ᕱ ᕱ ᕱ

(TÍA CORAZÓN)

Black girl, they said, you'd better run. Run now, run girl, or be burned.

They said: Fire in the sugarcane field. It will take down your house. Chickens, goats, die screaming. Better run.

I smelled it before I saw it—the burning, and melting of air. Stood in the open doorway. Made a black and pink fist of my hand, shook it in the direction of the smoke. Saying come now, find me if you can. This black girl will not burn. Here is one with scarred lip and crazy eye, cheated at the altar by that son of a whore, who doesn't care about the curling of the pain, frying of the flesh, skin gone up in ashes, mingling with the clouds. Me, I survive pain. And I don't run.

Animals went insane. Smelling the rot, the heat, before it came, before the sound of the crackling fields. Pulled tethers from deep-dug sticks in the ground. Ran circles around the house, bleating, screaming. Chickens knocked themselves dead trying to escape through the roof of the coop, collapsed in dirty heaps of feathers; cats disappeared, dogs with ears half chewed off whined, pleaded.

Corazón, they said. You with the evil eye. *Como una bruja.* Here's your choice: Sacrifice for that son of a bitch Guillo, that lady's man, suffer for the glory of your soul like a saint; or run away, and live.

Stupids, I told them—without words, in my belly. Stupids. I won't run. But I will live. Watch me. *Como una bruja.*

And to the fire I said, Come and find me. Twist me. Take the broken pieces of this heart. Ghost God, sugarcane gods, gods of all the animals, in mountains, and thunder, and the sea, Santa Barbara and the rest of the Seven Powers, I am too hurt to be afraid any more, I give myself to you, I am broken, take all these pieces as your own.

People sped away screaming, in flat-tired trucks, on donkey back, horseback, driving goats and pigs before them, holding sacks of food, of cloth, holding children's hands, holding chickens and ducks by the legs, upside down, pressing kerchiefs to their mouths and noses against the suffocating smoke.

Somewhere burst the tank of an old army truck, gasoline exploding. It lit the pale sky like celebration. Rotting wood houses caught, roofs collapsed, trapped animals screamed, one by one the structure of the town fell, withered to black ash, fodder for a hundred bonfires. I stood there, brokenhearted, waiting. The bad eye closed. I fell asleep.

They said that I came walking, later, barefoot, flesh hot as a clay oven but unburned by the fire, dress in blackened rags around me, through the leveled fields of cane. That my hands reached before me, arms stretched, in a daze, like they were looking for something. And scarred lip twitched. Crossed eye rolled. That a big black vein along the side of my neck popped close, close, to the surface, pulsed, beat in and out with the beating of my heart. So that, seeing me, some child said look it's the witch, *la bruja*, coming out of the fire. Everyone was scared. And when I reached for them—for comfort, for touching—each body shrank away.

Then someone drove up, in a sparkling new American car. They came from the west. Screeching out of the sunset, like a big, fierce comet crashed to earth. From it stepped a starry creature—a devil, maybe, or angel, or maybe even the son of God. This car was gleaming silver and white, the sides of the tires were white, and the metal on it glowed. It was like a new ship, skidding into port. I reached toward it. Out stepped a man. Dressed in white. Wearing gold. That weak unmarried son of an overseer, that pale feeble dandy of a man, Antonio Delgado, in his ruffles and his rings. The metal jewels blinded me. I stumbled in his way.

There was fire in my hands then, but it was in them for the first time, and I did not know it. I had given myself to the fire, and the Powers, without understanding how they worked—that fire and power would also give itself to me—and I could not feel yet how to sense it, control it, how to use it all correctly.

But there was fire in my hands and, reaching, I stumbled, then fell against the fine soft ruffled white clothes and jewels of this pale, rich, perfumed boy. He caught me. Held me up. He was barely strong enough. I clutched his hands with mine. And heard the crackle, smelled the searing of pale flesh as, within mine, his own hands burned, and he looked at me with his frightened little eyes, his thin ridiculous mustache twitching, and screamed—just once—and sweated with pain, but kept holding my black hands with his own horribly burned ones, and both of us held on, and neither one let go.

Later, it would be the scandal of his family. That one of their bright and pretty sons had wed the daughter of sugarcane slaves. A heretic. Revolutionary. Common black girl whose lip was scarred by a drunken man's knife; whose left eye sometimes rolled straight up into her head; who had been jilted at the altar by some handsome dark laborer and murderer and thief; whose heart had been broken and mind gone mad; who put a curse on things; who walked through flames untouched, and carried the heat of fire in her hands.

I burned his hands; it's true. So badly that he bore the scars on his knuckles and palms for life.

I gave him no children.

But I healed his heart.

He became a man who could breathe, and love. He ate what I fed him. It put strength in his flesh and flesh on his bones. He stopped wearing fancy clothes. Began to build things with wood. His scarred palms grew hard. He smoked, and danced, and swore, and loved. All because of the fire.

They cast us out—but not completely. When a Delgado was sick, or hurt, they brought him or her to me. They knew about the power. They could feel it in my hands, see it in my eye; they detested me, but they were also full of fear and of belief. I learned to use the fire. I healed them when I could.

Old age and Castro came. The brothers of Antonio and their wives and sons and daughters got ready to leave. To America, of course. I told them I would go. But it was not for me but for them that I left; to accompany them to Miami, and be there to heal them. Because I had seen a picture of Castro, and the heat in his beady little eyes, and love of his people in his face—from there, from that, came the fire. I knew he would walk through the cane fields unscathed. He would fight, burning, all the way to Havana. A part of me wanted to stay—to meet him, face to face, to be in the presence of another cunning and terrible witch. But the Delgados were rich—though not for long—and were desperately preparing to flee. And I was a Delgado.

To heal. To heal. *Como una bruja.*
So when the son of Antonio's brother came with his child, it was the worst illness—but not the first one.
Land of liberty. Land without compassion.
It made them all much sicker.
They were bright, and worked hard—at all the wrong things. Because they were pale the way my Antonio had been, before I seared his hands, and put some righteous color back into the man—almost white, almost colorless; and, when they wanted to, they could pass for one of the pale white money-making ghosts. So they did.
Me, I stayed out of it all, especially after Antonio died. In a concrete room in Miami, with my food stamps, and my Medicaid. Did not move. Sometimes shut the crazy eye. With it saw into the heart of the place. Me a ball of fire flying invisible through the streets of this city in the new money country, howling past beaches glutted with tourists, the fake planted palms on white-hot sidewalks, broad flat avenues where old people who had come down here to die hobbled along and barely looked up; barely recognized the fire, and its searing light—they were so used to their fear of it, of the flame and the light that would one day soon come, and signal their own end.
Como una bruja. Fire from the fire. Invisible, burning, I sat in a white concrete kitchen and sent the heart out of me, went flying through the streets of the city in this new land of money and of liberty. Through blinking red lights, past shopping malls where empty grocery carts glinted in the sunlight. White matrons

loaded bags into car trunks, paused to listen as I went by. Purses hung from their shoulders, heavy with the handguns they carried as protection against demented Cuban refugees.

Black girl. Old ugly lady, bent body. Went flying, screaming without sound into the city's core, where buildings squeezed together and streets narrowed. Heat steamed from iron grating over sewers. Lampposts were bent, useless, some with filthy shoes strung from their tops in place of lights. Fire hydrants gushed water along the curbs. In the cool wet rush children danced, twirled hair ribbons, sang rhyming songs in Spanish. Down one alley, men fought with knives—for drugs, and the love of a woman. Their blood flew up to spatter the white undershirts hanging from windows on twine. A terrier barked at them from behind some garbage cans. Boys trying to grow their first mustaches hung from fire escapes, watching, cigarettes dangling from their lips, sweat speckling their chests. Now and then to yell hoarse encouragement to one bleeding man, or the other.

Como una bruja. Invisible, I flew. Burning. From the Powers. From the fire. Like a witch. Black witch. Past an open storefront from which blared the music of a steel band once popular in Havana, before the days of the great witch Castro. Sound of a feeling hot, bouncing, metallic, like the rays of sun gleaming off polished silver bracelets. Irrepressible. Inescapable. It would have you dancing in ecstatic delirium forever, if you listened long enough. You'd leap and spin, reach out for the beckoning, sparkling platinum of moonlight on the sea. Like a fool, try to hold it in your hand.

Past all this, I flew.

To a late afternoon. Shifts changing in a hospital. Cars funneled from the parking lots surrounding it like broad concrete moats. Some drivers still wore nurses' caps, or plastic identification cards on their chest, or stethoscopes. An ambulance took the emergency entrance. Outside waited reporters, and cameras. The story of Angelita's only survivors would make the first edition of the evening news.

Inside this place a large group of witches took over. They did not have the fire, or the Powers, but they did command an impressive collection of delicate tools and magical machines. They could cut into the body of my nephew's daughter without waking her. Sense her life power rise and fall and the inside fire smoke back to life, flickering, flickering, by use of strange wires. Her skin was washed and salved until every ash-colored, swollen, water-bruised inch of it glistened. They put a bag of colorless liquid food on a hanging metal thing beside her, and from the bag came a string, and this string they sank deep into her arm. Her legs, her chest, her head—all were wired to various witch devices. Tubes invaded her nose and forearms. One went right up into the secret part of her. So that she looked like some discarded toy rescued from a puddle: floppy and beaten, internal substance exposed, a vague imitation of something human.

Like this, she slept.

The Delgados came to claim her. They stood around her, sobbing.

I went inside her sleeping head. Burned a flame high to see it all. The water and the waves. Metal and the shattering pain. A demented man who wanted to lead the children, who sought to be a witch, but in the end was merely demented, a boyhood murderer of animals. Smearing himself with blood. Calling it the task of a warrior. He made their bodies strong; he made them ill inside.

Como una bruja. Burned a flame. I saw it all. The boy who loved her. The girl she loved. The water that she loved and hated. And I saw, clearly, that she had traveled into the place beyond life for a very little while; that she had seen it, and heard it, the light, and the thunder, and been afraid. And so had come back—to continue the work of quelling this fear. Such is the way of the Powers: by fire, or by water.

Under the spells and tools of the white-coated witches, she did not know this. She'd forgotten. What she experienced, now, was a vague sensation of rising and of falling. What she heard, now, was nothing but the sounds of her body: an agonizingly slow heart thud that seemed to rack each vein; the suck and pull of precious air into her throat and lungs. She was aware of little else—neither pain, nor thirst, nor hunger nor terror—except of maybe a dim but persistent sense that she was traveling somewhere, somewhere important, and so it was essential to keep moving. She was too ruined, too broken, too drugged, to know that she didn't have to swim any more. So she kept on trying. It seemed important. For this reason, her muscles twitched.

It was like that, for me—when I lived through fire, when I

kept on walking. When my ears heard the thunder and my crossed round eye saw it, saw it, saw the light. Reached for it. Saying, I am broken, take me, I give myself to you. All the pieces of this heart, shattered by love. But the light said, no, Corazón, not yet. Go back, and love more, and suffer. Go back and heal them. *Como una bruja*. Here, here. There is fire in your hands. Live one more life. And learn how to use it.

Watching her, I knew: Here was the one, a child I never bore; and it was time to pass on the power. Felipe's daughter would live. And then, one day, would come to me.

Looking sorrowful, crazy, half drowned again, she is here. About to knock on my door. I'm there before she does, and open it.

"Tita?"

"Sure, child. Come in. You stayed away too long."

With her father's money she's bought things, puts crackling paper bags on the little table in the middle of the square white room. Expensive sauces. Canned beans. Frozen vegetables. Fancy boxes of sugared fruit. Chocolate and coffee. Coca-Cola. An envelope, sealed and unaddressed, which she sets on the table, blushing. I know there's money in it, hundred-dollar bills from a Delgado.

"Dad said to ask you is the air-conditioning working."

"I never use it."

"But it's working? Good. And when you go to the clinic, he said, be sure to take a taxi."

She sits in the still white heat, sweating.

I limp around the buzzing refrigerator. Store food away. Limp around the cupboards. Bent back. Old black *bruja*. Grab tall glasses with colored flowers decorating the sides, crack into them ice, fill them with soda. One for her. One for me.

"You're here alone?"

"Kenny died, Tita."

"His poor little mother," I say, "how can she live now? What a tragedy."

But neither of us cry.

I take her into another room. This one darker, worn, filled with good and magic things—not modern, more humane. Stack of newspapers and old magazines in one corner. Butt end of a

Kool or two in metal ashtrays on the beaten coffee table; I am not supposed to smoke any more, but maybe the child won't tell what she saw. A pair of worn terry-cloth bedroom slippers set near the armchair, stained and molded to the contours of my hardened, crooked feet. One shelf crowded with books, in Spanish. The shelf above it is mobbed with framed photos of the Delgado family: in-laws, nieces, nephews, children and their spouses, and one single old black and white of my slave grandparents, dressed in skin and rags. On a sidetable, a mug from Disneyland filled with pennies. Also a telephone, dusty from lack of use. Placed in the most appropriate spot, next to these images of relatives—who call frequently, but I never respond; because there's something unsound and terrifying about their money, their solicitude, their American way of speaking.

Against one wall, the altar. Feathers. Water. Flower petals, and drops of perfume. Tapestry. Some half-melted, unlit candles. We sit on the torn sofa, watching it.

"Um. I don't know why I'm here, Tita. For Kenny, I guess. And to see you. But, I mean, I really just don't know."

Many flights below, traffic on the streets. The sounds come from far away. Fade into a void. Along with the hum of fans and air conditioners, refrigerators, TV sets. There is silence now. I feel her waiting.

"It's okay, child."

The voice of an old woman, measured and thin, cracked in the middle of each word. Still, it reassures her.

"I went back to school, Tita. I've been swimming again, on this little team there. And I love this—I think, that I fell in love. Except I kind of don't know. I'm still afraid all the time."

"Why," says my old voice, "why are you afraid?"

"I don't know exactly. It's like I'm stuck in this fear. I wake up in the night afraid. Even when I'm laughing I feel sad all the time. Sometimes, when I close my eyes, I can't even imagine anything—the only thing that comes to me is this black, black space. I mean"—the young face struggles—"I want to feel good, really good, you know, like, joy, like other people seem to feel— but I can't. Something stops me."

"How long have you been afraid?"

"A long time."

"What is it about Kenny dying that makes you come here?"

"Angelita," she says. And weeps.

"Why are you crying?"

"I think I'm queer."

"What? Strange?"

"Yes. No. I mean, homosexual."

"Ah. So you're afraid of that."

"Maybe. Of not having children. Or hope."

She forgot the rest, she tells me, what happened the night before Angelita. But now remembers. Sometimes, as she talks, she's enraged, almost taunting, or near tears, at other times sounding calm and dead. Saying, it wasn't Liz who came running downstairs after me, Tita, the night in San Juan, not her and not Kenny, it was Sager.

I listen to her words. I see the man Sager brushing by the young man Kenny, the young woman Liz, shirtless, barely nodding, eyes set ahead, buttoning the top button of his jeans. It was Sager who followed, bare callused feet on cement. He hardly made a sound.

In the room where her things were she locked the door. Light rose faintly from the bedside table, illuminated the bottom half of a bad painting on the wall, graveled beach streaked red, streaked pink. There was sand inside each shoe. She took them off. Shook them out. Breathing hard. Fingers numb. Then a sound like a crack at the door, the latch snapped easily, just like a dried twig, and it opened. There was Sager. She looked up at him with shoes in her hands.

Okay, he said. The voice seemed funny. A cool tenor. She remembered, suddenly, that he was young.

Get out, she said. He shook his head. In the halfway dark she saw a flash of eyes, fluorescent hallway light streaking in from the cracked-open door, almost but not quite a smile. And he said, No, Kitten, you've got it all wrong, *you* don't tell *me* what to do.

"Fuck you, Bart."

Something knocked her head sideways so for a second she didn't breathe. Then twisted it around, smothering, grinding against pillows, and trying to breathe she made a sound. Heard him say, Stupid kid, you've got that wrong, too.

Then her forehead went into a headboard, once, twice. She thought, bewildered: There won't be any blood. Tried to push herself up with arms tangled in sheets. Something ripped. Massive hands around her wrists pulled back, and up, and in the light under the pink-streaked red-streaked gravelly sand she was on the bed on her knees all of a sudden, shoulders wrenched, hands pinned, frozen still, unstruggling, her face in pillows, a throbbing in her head. She told herself: Yell. Instead, froze. What came out were weak muffled sounds. He pulled the hands and arms higher until every ligament in each shoulder strained to the danger point, aching to break. Saying, Big girl, huh? Big animal? Worthless. All that money down the gutter. But remember, Kitten, everything you get comes from me. Every race. Every medal.

He leaned over then to whisper. And every time she fucks you, it's because I say so.

Oh, she thought, inanely, watch out for the shoulders.

As if he caught the thought on air he lowered both her arms carefully, then, to the small of her back, but kept his grip tight around both wrists. For a second, she wanted to thank him. Thinking, as if it mattered: Too many pushups, maybe, baby those joints. Thinking: Time trials, max out. And National Team. Save them for next summer.

Right, he whispered. He spoke softly now, very calm, almost kind. Gold medal deltoids. Million dollar knees. And we don't want to hurt them, Kitten, do we?

He was yanking at her waistband. No, she thought, this is not real. Somewhere, clothes ripped. She could not see. Only feel steamed close air against bare flesh, back, thighs, knees hurting. Sucking air desperately through the pillow cover in her mouth. Between them air, denim, buttons. Then nothing but what he had willed, this piece of him hard and thick and cruel. No, she said, not that, please. But it found what it was looking for and pushed deep inside. Pain burst up through her so that she forgot to breathe again.

Then something left her and went into the aching dull light of the bedside lamp, hovered around bad pictures of gray waves and sand, watching as he did this to her body.

Pain tore up to her body's intestines, but, watching, she did not feel it. For a minute he closed his eyes. He began to move then, harder and faster. She watched from the bedside lamp. Sand seared. Waves foamed down from the bad pink and gray painting on the wall, bubbled like water in a pot. On the floor were her body's torn clothes. On the bed two shoes, partly filled with sand.

Big girl, he said. Big girl, huh? But I'll show you. Stuck-up little mixed-breed bitch.

She watched, feeling nothing. Until her pinned wrists were yanked up urgently, his head tilted back and pale eyes closed, and he jerked forward in a spasm that distorted his face, made him drop both her arms so that they fell numb on the bed, and he groaned once, sharply, plunged some last piece of himself forward, spilled out of her dripping pale drops, dripping blood. Then collapsed across her back, and there were two human beings stacked one on top of the other, still and flat against a ruined bed. She watched, feeling nothing. But her body cried.

Whoa, he said, whoa.

She watched, feeling nothing, as his lips kissed the neck of her body. Then he groaned as if to sob, hid his face against the back of her body's neck, but no more sounds came out. For some reason, or for no reason, the hands of the girl who was her groped forward, pulled pillow covers away from a tear-smeared face, turned the body sideways so that she curled halfway into the shadow of him and was still, crying, and he put his arms around her. She touched a thick white-haired arm with cold fingers. Her voice shook. Incongruous.

Bart?

He was barely there. Gave no reply.

When he stood, he stroked her shoulder. She lay motionless. He stuffed himself back inside the denim jeans and buttoned them up in an orderly fashion, bottom to top, perfectly. He spoke and the words came softly.

See, Babe. He was at the door now, broken latch swinging from its insides, and he opened it a crack then quietly closed it, firmly, intentionally.

See, I can do that any time. Come through any door.

In the light, his back glistened. His face looked tired, a little paler than usual, drained. He turned and was gone.

The body that was hers did not move for a long time. After a while, when tears had dried on the face, it rolled off the bed trailing a sheet spotted with dark drops, and she watched emotionlessly as it crawled across the dusty floor, past rug tassles and spiders, to the threshold of the bathroom; as it paused there, swaying on both knees like a wounded animal, then pulled itself across dirty old tiles to a bathtub that was large and rounded at the edges, colonial style. She watched the bruised wrists swell, watched the hands turn rusted faucets. Watched a young woman climb over into the old white rounded tub while cold water spilled in, puddled around her raw nakedness, and once in a while her body panted in short, repetitive sequence, and once in a while it cried.

She watched, feeling nothing. Followed sparking trails of light from the bedside lamp, from the bad oil painting, fused with stained sand and wet air, watched over her from the light itself and whenever she cried stepped back inside her for a moment, stopping her, saying, Shut up, girl. Saying, I am the brains now, I am the fire here, I am the power. I am the water that puts out the fire. I am the flame that can burn through the water. I am you, girl, I am the thing that will save you. This, here, watching. Take it. Have it. When what happens is too hard to bear. When reason does not matter.

I hold her for a long time.

As she sobs I tell her: Don't worry, child. You didn't create her—the storm, I mean, Angelita. You didn't call her, she was there, long before, and all along, waiting. She took that man away. It was good for him to die. It was good for you to live. And everything good costs pain.

I watch her tears dry. Between us, the silence. Hear the measured breaths of this old black woman. Tragic young face of the young one beside her. Remember the crucifixion statue above a church altar outside of Havana, long ago, dimly illuminated by candles, dark streaks staining the ivory skin of Jesus as he hung there, sadly. But I was never ivory. And neither, my child, were you. There is no pure white sterile beginning to curl back into. Only blood of the innards, in all their difficult mingled pain and joy; hard work, scarred hands covered with dark, dark earth; dangerous, wholesome fire—which, now, you must learn to have and control—from the secret burning part of you. Only forward, is there. Into the suffering, and hope. Into the love. And the terror. The pity. The light.

Old twisted black hands. Crooked joints. Pink callused palms. I offer them to her. Saying, here child, hold these, take what they have to give. Out of this darkness, comes my light. Out of this darkness, yours.

She presses both hands into mine. Eyes glimmer shut. Pale lids over tears. There is fire in my hands. But it warms her, will not burn her. I can feel it come alive, now, in her hands too—after staying inside at the secret dark core of her for so long—the heat, the life. Fire doesn't injure fire. And only dead wood burns.

I tell her it is time.

For what? she says.

To love, I tell her. Use this power for good. Do violence only to protect a beloved. Offer your care and your power to a living creature who needs it. Some child, maybe—one of your own flesh, or of another's, or even a defenseless animal—what matters is that you give up a part of yourself to nurture it. Heal the sickness of human bodies and minds. *Como una bruja*. A big brown witch. Tender woman. Child no more.

The fire courses through us. Joins at the palms. Feeling it fully, for the first time, she is surprised, mistakes its raw energy for pain, and sobs out loud.

Bear it, I tell her. Woman, you must bear it.

For this you came back.

For this, was Angelita.

She grinds her teeth, and between wet gasps tells me about the crash, the sea, the storm. The light that was cold, then warm. Small, then all-surrounding. Gleaming from wrecked metal onto mirroring gems of water. Wanting to take her in.

I tell her of Guillo's child, come out of me too early in a billowing wash of blood. Smoke of the fields. How I walked among stumps of cane. Walked through the miles. Arms outstretched, offering myself. How the flaming ground let me go—though I begged of it to seize me—let me go, and left no burns.

Go back, it said. The water next time.

Later, in sweating twilight, I show her how to touch her fingertips to the wicks of candles. She does. And speckles the room with light.

"I always wondered, Tita."

"What, girl?"

"Why you never had any matches on the altar."

"Sure," I laugh. And snatch a drugstore matchbook out of my pocket. "But you have to keep them around. The Powers aren't yours—they come and go. You're just their vessel. And sometimes, who knows why? the magic doesn't work."

She pauses, unsmiling. "What do I do then?"

"Reason. Use your reason."

Ah, she says, of course.

I boil water in the square place, making *arroz con frijoles negros*. We eat it with bread, and drink more soda. In the electric light she looks younger, beaten down.

"I think my mom and dad are breaking up."

I nod.

"They've just been beating on each other since Christmas. Since before then, probably. It's really depressing, Tita. Jack, and Roberto—and Teresa, she's just a kid—they're going crazy."

"*Pobrecitas.*"

"Jack says they might sell the house."

"Yes," I say, "some things don't last."

"I'm missing lots of tests and practice, just coming down here. I mean, I've like really messed up."

"Ah," I say, "that's not important."

We go back to the room of candles, wiping off sweat with bright kerchiefs. We eat sugared fruit, drink strong black coffee. I search a drawer for hidden pleasures. Smoke forbidden cigarettes.

Tita, she says, show me more things.

In a while, I tell her. Next time you're here.

She tells me that will be in the summer. Kenny's parents are having him cremated tomorrow. No service. No invitations. And buried in the ocean, on his birthday, some time in July. She told them she would come down for that. Go out on the boat with them. Take ashes in her hands.

"So," she says, "I'll see you then, too."

"Good." I wheeze, blow out clouds.

Before she leaves I tell her to give my regards to the family. To eat good food, work hard, be kind to those who deserve it, fight those who are wasteful and cruel, even win more medals if she wants. I remind her about the fire. Patience, I say, use it in love. With age, it gets stronger.

She must go, get on an airplane. At the door our hands meet. Old fire. Young fire. Soon, I'll pass it all to her. Then give myself up completely. To the ending, and the light. And feel my bones grow cold. Inside me, smoke and dust.

When you visit in the summer, I tell her, bring nothing but yourself. Go straight to Kenny's parents. Don't be afraid. Then travel out in a boat with them. On a bright, clear-sky day. With healing in your heart. Dig your hands in deep, and help throw his ashes on the sea. His weightless, well-burned ashes. The pieces of his poor tired body.

Be glad that you were broken, I say. In your body, and your heart. Be not happy, but glad. Which means accepting.

Accept, now, all the love and hate. The father and the mother. And black, and white. Accept, now, the suffering.

Be glad for Angelita.

Finals

ふ ふ ふ

(B R E N)

Delgado does come back, finally, after missing too much practice and nearly all of her final exams. I know, because her teachers complained; word got around to a couple of bigwigs on the scholarship committee; and sooner rather than later—after being tipped off by a maliciously gleeful McMullen—I had a lot of explaining to do.

In the end, though, the kid's rear end is saved, and so is mine. What it all comes down to—as I knew it would, after all the fuss and annoyance—is winning. She has been crucial to our terrific record this year. Her presence is necessary at the Divisional Championships. Number-one ranking is in sight. Alumni contributions are up. Babe Delgado is not expendable.

She doesn't show up for her one-on-one chat, though—she is the only one of the team to miss it—and it makes me feel helpless, more than a little angry, like I have given her too much leeway and now have to pay back the Spoiled Brat Piper. In her appointed time slot, Ellie Marks shows up instead. My irritation cools.

"Babe says hi. She's back."

"Yes," I say, "how are you?"

"Oh, well, feeling sort of like a jerk."

I motion for her to sit. "How so, Ellie?"

"I don't know. It just feels like the year sort of fell apart on me. I mean, it wasn't all bad or anything, not by a lot, but it wasn't what I expected, either."

I tell her that I think I know what she means. Ask her is she ready to swim. Ready to watch, she jokes, half bitterly. No, I insist, to swim. She glances at me uncertainly.

"What do you mean?"

"Well, you're not looking too ill these days during workout. Neither are you tapered, granted. But do you have a four hundred IM in you?"

The young face stares back at me; I examine it for signs of distress or panic. There's a moment, perhaps—when some of that flashes through the eyes, changes the set of her mouth; and I recognize something of myself in the expression: a kind of pained excitement.

"The four?"

I nod.

"What about Potalia?"

"She won't, Ellie. She's pregnant. With some complications. I can't really say that I blame her."

She listens, then, when I tell her what I have in mind. Some paper will have to be shuffled. A couple of lies told. She has never seen this side of me—the sly and manipulative side—openly before, although she has certainly felt it; but a part of her, too, accepts it, knows that I'm presenting it to her as a kind of gift. I could tap Babe Delgado for the 400 IM, if I had to—even though it would be overworking her, even though she would hate it—or one of the good, promising freshmen; but I am offering her a place in the final competition, instead. It is her last chance, anyway. She knows it. Her face cracks into a painful smile.

"I guess I'm, like, suddenly not expendable."

"You never were, Ellie."

I tell her, then, some of what I really think: that she is very strong, and growing into completion, and brave, and deserves a shot at something. That, in the end, there is a kind of detriment to grandeur and to winning, anyway. The bigger things get the broader they are, the more complex; the farther back from them you have to stand to see them; the easier it is to superficially admire and the harder it is to genuinely love—because grandeur in and of itself is incapable of the small, essential effort, the intimate urge to get close, proceed, to survive; it must always be propped up by smaller things.

Oh, she says. Oh, wow. And we're silent.

How are things, I ask her, after a while. How's your life?

"My life? Ah. I think—I mean, it's good these days, really good." And it's obvious, from the hot pleasurable red flooding her face, that she'd discovered love. Watching, I feel like an intruder. But it also makes me quite happy; and the shock of the sensation—happiness, I mean—ripples through me. It has been a long time.

"I'm glad, Ellie. I am very glad for you."

"You are? I mean, you *are*, aren't you."

This is teasing, forthright and tender, surprises us both.

She tells me, then, that she thinks she has known me in a former life.

What? I say.

She blushes. She is taking a class in World Religions, she says. And she likes it. She believes a lot of it. Hinduism and Buddhism, reincarnation. Karma. It's the only thing that makes sense—to her, anyway; otherwise, We wouldn't necessarily be who we are, and love who we love, would we? We'd just be simple products of our environment in this lifetime. But, in so many ways, we are not. And there's so much suffering, so much—if it's all random, in the end, if there's no meaning to it, if through suffering you can't balance some kind of cosmic scales for yourself somehow—then what is the point? So she believes in that stuff, yes. In stuff that does not require faith, really; but only a sort of spiritual common sense.

I don't respond. She doesn't ask me to. Just looks at me now, fully, a little shyly.

"How are *you*?"

"Fine," I say, too quickly. And want to follow it up: Just fine. But I realize I've pressed a hand to my mouth, to hide something, and my face has gone numb, and I can't lie any more.

"Actually," I say, "I'm not fine. Although I *am* getting better." Don't cry, Coach, I tell myself. I don't. "I'll tell you something, Ellie, since you ask. Recently, I lost someone—no, not someone, Kay, I lost Kay Goldstein, my lover of many years, she was very ill, and she died. So, last season and this, I think you can understand now, have been very tough for me. It was quite—it was the most difficult thing in the world. Sometimes, I still don't believe it actually happened. And I think I'm going to be all right; in fact, I know I will, eventually. It's all just a matter of time. I guess that's partly why I believe—about life, I mean—that it's all time, anyway."

I wonder how I can speak these words, now, so calmly, so simply. But maybe the truth is always simple; never as nerve-racking as artifice; and, I know, we should carefully choose our lies, be sure they never own us.

"Your lover," Ellie says cautiously, "must have been a very wonderful person."

"Ah. She was."

Papers rustle under my hands on the desk. My phone buzzes suddenly, insistently. Five rings, six. I let it go unanswered and then it's silent; and we wait, watching each other, little separating us, in this moment, but the years. She stands and puts her hands flat on the desk, leans suddenly across it. I don't think, or pull back. She kisses my lips firmly, chastely. Then she stands apart blushing, and looks away.

I swivel in my chair. Right. Left. Back to center. Finally, I clear my throat for attention, and face her with a stern expression mitigated by vague embarrassment.

"That," I say, "is something that will not happen again. Do you understand?"

"Yes, Bren."

"And as long as you swim for me, you will refrain from addressing me informally again. Even in private. Even face to face. We may some day be friends. But that would be later—much, much later."

"I know, Bren. I mean, okay. Okay."

The mantle of authority remains perched perilously on my damaged shoulders. I can feel us both relax.

I tell her I'm glad we talked. That I expect to see her, and of course Babe Delgado, on time tomorrow morning.

She blushes. Faintly resentful.

"Love and work are the same thing, Ellie. You don't have to understand that right now—just remember it, will you?"

"I guess. I mean I'll try."

She leaves. But halfway down the hall, starts humming—happily, it seems, on key—and, sitting at my desk, I hear it.

* * *

On the bus, at the airport, I'm a nervous wreck but do not show it. The kids have all dressed identically, for a joke: striped gray-and-white pants, gray cotton shirts, white Aerobics shoes. Over the weekend, they have all shaved down. Somehow, too, they have each streak-bleached tailing strands of hair along the backs of their necks and above each ear. I detect the unseen hand of Ellie Marks in this. A cabal, for sure. Passing by on their way to the departure lounge, as Etta and I take count, each says a too-jolly *Hi Coach!* while the next echoes, in turn: Hi Coach! Hi Coach! Occasionally, there is a whisper or a giggle.

When I've taken the right count twice, I sit among them, next to Etta, who is fiddling with her engagement ring. It is a modest, thin band of delicate matte silver with a single, tiny, dainty diamond embedded, and against the darkness of her skin it glows. I notice, glancing at her face, that she seems happy these days— and I am glad for her. This thought crosses my mind: *Next time I'm married, we will both wear rings to declare it.* I don't know where the thought comes from. But although brief, it makes me happy for a moment; for a moment, gives me hope, and a sensation of physiological warmth and comfort that I never believed would be mine again.

They look at me expectantly, with teasing expressions. One of them cups her hands, whispers to someone else; there is another giggle, and then they all watch me with sly grins about to burst, in their matching pants and shirts and shoes, their matching strands of hair.

"Very teamlike," I say, finally. "Nice sense of unity. Love the decor."

One by one, the bubbles of tension prick into laughter that is entirely female, and soft, but tinged with an element of hysteria. I look around at the faces, each flushed and damp. They are all trim, tapered, full of energy and restless calories, ready to burn. They've exceeded themselves over the past few months; and, now, it comes down to this, this attempt at a perfection of readiness, of will, this stillness before action, this waiting.

Then it will be over. And whatever happens is a truth they will have, inside, for the rest of their lives. Some will not surpass it. Some will never redeem it. But others will. And, in that way as well as in many, many ways, all these lives will diverge, continue, crisscross again or not, shrink and grow, and ultimately end.

On my other side sits Karen Potalia. She is silent, fully made

up. Fiddling with *her* engagement ring. I am sandwiched between two straight women with engagement rings, one black,
one white; across from me, feet cluttered with luggage, Ellie
Marks and Babe Delgado sit side by side, carefully not touching,
glancing at each other to share some ineffable sensation when
they think no one is looking. It's amusing—in a gentle way that
is also somehow painful—because here, among this group of
alert young women, whatever they believe they are hiding is an
open secret. As I have been to them, myself, all along: a walking
secret utterly unveiled, an open wound.

Well, probably.

But in some way, maybe, it has made me perfect for this job.
Because I know what it is to love them.

A modulated mechanical voice spills over intercoms, announc-
ing the flight boarding. With sighs and shrieks, all the gray-
shirted, striped-trousered, white-shoed hordes stand. Except for
Babe Delgado.

"Rules, rules!" Etta demands. "No booze, no drugs. Cool it on
the sugar and fat—moderate caffeine." She waves her clipboard—always an implicit threat. "Anyone who doesn't deal
straight with me around this stuff will sooner or later and probably sooner have to deal with Her Majesty"—and she gestures my
way.

There is a collective groan, the fear only partially faked.

They line up to board. Out of the corner of my eye I see Ellie
Marks leaning down, hand on Delgado's shoulder, insistently
whispering. Babe doesn't look up.

I approach. "Let's go, you two."

"She won't." Ellie blushes, agitated. Delgado looks up to meet
my eyes. Everything's written across her face, suddenly: grief,
exhaustion, fear.

"Come on, Babe. What's up?"

"I just don't feel like it."

"Tough," I say, "that's just too bad."

When I turn to take my place in line I can feel them behind
me—gathering luggage and equipment bags, plastic seats squeaking, new shoes scuffing synthetic surface under the constant hum
of inaudible intercom, dumped baggage, traveling sounds. First
one pair of feet. Then another. I turn once to nod in brief
approval. Ellie looks on edge. Babe glares at me, strong and

resentful, icily determined, very angry. As if, touching her flesh, you'd strike sparks.

Which, after all, is just the way we need her to be.

In locker rooms, in the past, I have made these speeches. Today I don't; I just come in and stand near a bench while they sit there in their warm-ups, and wait for silence. But they're already silent; they've been silent, and nervous, for a long time now.

It occurs to me that I don't know exactly what to say. Super Coach would have known. But the woman I am feeling myself to be these days, doesn't really know.

"Is everybody ready? Ready to really *swim*?"

One by one, they nod.

"Good, then. Let's go."

We do and, walking out into a sterile wet damp well of echoing sound, palms on bleachers, announcements and scattered applause, I miss Kay very much, I wish she could be sitting there now to see, and then push her out of my mind. Behind me, the disciplined line breaks at its tallest link. Babe Delgado has turned aside and is gesturing excitedly to someone in the bleachers. A dark-haired, slender teenager, with long hard thin arms and legs, large lips and eyes like hers, reaches down to her, palms open for a congratulatory slap. And there is someone else beside him who she's reaching for, also: a stocky brown-skinned man with thick black mustache, handsome features, ample eyes and lips; he is smiling tiredly, face lined with emotion, waving. Now the boy is leaning over perilously, grasping her hand. She gestures toward me, and he looks my way; then stands, and, for the first time, meets my eyes, and smiles, waves.

The ally.

I nod once, before turning to proceed with my team. Mouth the words: *Hello, Jack.* And give him a grin.

Then, to myself, sing a song of relief. *Thank you, kid, for coming through.*

Delgado turns to follow the rest of us to the tiered benches where we are clustered amid a flurry of towels, equipment, bodies and nerves. Around the big damp bright-lit arena of glistening pastel water, lane dividers float colorfully in perfect tight parallel lines, pool lights gleam beneath the surface. The sloped starting blocks are clean, waiting, empty; there are similar sections of tiered benches, specially set off from the spectator stands, where other teams wearing other colors are taking their places. The spectator stands are dotted, here and there, with individuals or with groups of people—not as few as I thought there'd be, but a pretty sparse crowd just the same. These are qualifying heats, and people work during the day, but maybe they will fill up a little each night for the finals.

Still, the stands will never be completely full. This is not a top division. I'm used to it—and so are most of the kids on the team—but I find myself wondering how it will strike Delgado, after all; she's so used to playing to a full house at big meets—will this be better for her, or a letdown?

This, which is almost the pinnacle of accomplishment for my team, and for the likes of me, may be child's play to her. Something not quite serious. Maybe she'll try to slide through. If I were her, I might.

Standing there, I will her to do her very best, no matter what.

She faces me, gives a thumbs-up.

"My brother's here—and my dad came—"

"That's great!"

"Um. The hundred's *first.*"

I shrug and smile with a calm relaxed confidence that I definitely don't feel. "Good. Get it out of the way, Babe. But there's plenty of time—look, easy warm-up, you know what to do."

She nods, looking terror-stricken. Etta gestures with the ever-present clipboard, taps her shoulder. She has already rounded up everyone scheduled for early warm-up and they stand there nervously, weight shifting from foot to foot.

"Warm-up pool's this way, ladies, let's go. As ever I shall act as your very own personal escort."

She ushers them all in the right direction then, like a domineering mother bird. Turns around, once, to wink.

The next half hour is a daze of damp air, sweat, nerves crackling at each announcement, switching from my role as bad cop to my alternate role as good cop, then psychologist, then big sis, friend, commander general, supplicant. Some of them are mired in the paralyzing agony of taking it all too seriously; which is bad for them. Some of them are too loose, too blasé, too giggly, and don't take it seriously enough; which is bad for me.

I turn around to see Delgado, newly returned, breathing unevenly, her warm-up sweats soaked.

"How'd it go?"

Her face is strained, uncertain. "I don't know. I was just thinking, you know, like, if I blow it, I'll be stuck over in lane eight or something tonight."

"Whoa, whoa. First things first—first, we *qualify*, Babe. Now, remember the plan. Tell me about it."

"Nothing cagey. Even splits. Go out fast and hold it—"

"And?"

"Face down, down, down off the walls. Puh! Stretch."

"Good. Go on, enjoy yourself."

There are announcements. The two massive electronic timers on the walls zero out, blink ready.

First qualifying heat for the women's 100 breaststroke, says a mechanical male voice. And begins to drone off the lane assignments. There is some applause. Then a collective rise of voices; then a hush, in which the sound that has just ceased echoes.

I stand there, arms crossed over my chest, watch her head for a center lane starting block. She peels off her sweats, rotates shoulders and arms and neck, stretches out the legs, torso twists. From a distance, she looks smaller than she is; only the basic blueprint is visible: tall young woman, broad shoulders, narrower hips, lengthy torso, long arms and legs.

From a distance, even one this short, you can't see the fear frozen into her face, the large young dark eyes blinking sadly out; you can't see the crisscrossing lumps of scars around ankles and knees, reaching out across the shoulders from beneath both straps; and you cannot see the rest of the body under the suit, scarred by injury, by surgery—yet, miraculously perhaps, healed enough to move nearly unimpeded, to race strong, and fast; at times, almost, to fly, but through a medium different from air.

She lets the shell of sweatpants and jacket fall away from her. Does not look to acknowledge us. Back turned, for a second, she appears broad and invulnerable. She climbs onto the block.

I watch. I don't move. It courses through me, so much of it, all in a second: How much shit she has been through, and how hard she has had to work; and how much shit *I* have been through, for that matter, how hard *I* have worked; and now—for her, and for me too—it comes down to a little series of efforts, most of them lasting a minute or so.

It is utterly ridiculous. Absurd. Unnecessary.

Unless you begin to recognize it, in your heart, as part of something larger. Of which the minutes and the seconds are mere pinpoint manifestations. A way in which we limited humans, tied to our limiting bodies, can capture and record a sweet, timeless explosion—that, in its potential, is beyond all limitation.

SWIMMERS TAKE YOUR MARKS, blares the voice. Loud. Disembodied. Vaguely distorted.

God's voice, I think.

Then sneer at myself, inside. Because I don't believe in God. Or, rather, I am a skeptic. Believing that, first: if there *is* God, its voice is neither male nor female. And, second: If there is God, it will prove itself—in action, in manifestation—which are the only ways I know. Or, at any rate, the only proofs I accept. A limited human, I can do no more.

But Kay believed in God.

I stare at the starting blocks. Eight bodies, crouching, gripping edges. There is Babe. Feet parallel. She has eschewed the runner's start; maybe it would get her off the block more quickly, she said, but in the end she would sacrifice power; she would rather work on her squats, and her walls—could she? and, trusting her instinct in the matter, I told her yes, of course. She seemed relieved, grateful.

Now, I think.

Even so, the loud echoing disembodied mechanical beep—like the first, suddenly cut-off signal of mortal alarm—surprises me, so that I cannot help but blink, and shudder, and hide it by moving my shoulders raggedly up and down.

"Go *BABE!*" someone screams. Someone from the team, I think at first. But it's a male, teenaged voice and, glancing up at the stands, I see her brother Jack on his feet, hands pounding the air, face flushed and serious.

She's off the block, barely in time—starts always and forever her weak point, I guess. But she hits the imaginary hole in the donut perfectly, and dives right through, farther and deeper than the rest of them, long, powerful kick and fierce pull, and she loops up for air, arching out and forward with the scars across each shoulder already bulging muscle, skin and veins flushed a deep, dark red; and, in that second, lunging in a perfect curve, like a fish, or a wave, out and up but ever forward and over, she looks like a terrible powerful breath-sucking monster, goggle-eyed, hairless, indestructible; of whom, I think with satisfaction, the rest of them should be afraid. But whether they are or not doesn't really matter; they can't catch her, anyway. She is at the wall, propelling in perfectly. Touch and spring, like electric shock you must quick, quick, turn away from. Feet to the wall and big quads flex, and shoot out straight, like an arrow. Puh. Face down, down, down. Reach like a spear. Stretch. Then pull, kick, recover, emerge breath-sucking, almost monstrous. She is now one length ahead. Abnormal, in the 100—to be a full length ahead; and, for a moment, I'm afraid she's gone out too fast. Then I relax. She knows just what she is doing. Her best. And, for a minute and some seconds, as in years now past, her best will be magnificently abnormal—better than the rest.

There is a rhythm that takes over, in this sport: a reach, a roll, an undulation. On good days, it's like a wave you just wait for, poised, and you catch it at the perfect point of entry, immediately in tune with its music and its pace, and, focused not on effort, but on form in the moment, you ride it.

You can also win sometimes when you miss the wave—at these times you race through sheer effort alone—but it always leaves you drained and sorry, takes much more out of you; and, if it happens too often, it makes you afraid. Because nobody likes suffering; everyone works for happiness, in the end—and for these moments of pure rhythm, of ecstasy.

She rides her wave into the wall again, touches and springs off for the turn perfectly; I clock her at the fifty, find her ahead of pace. And worry again—reverse, feet meet wall, quads flex, calves stretch, and like she says: *Puh!*, shoot on, perfectly streamlined, javelin getting ready for the throw—will the perfection stop now? wave dissipate? leave her with nothing but a long, dark look down the barrel of forty or fifty yards of sheer effort, exhaustion, pain? Yet it doesn't seem to stop; there is no catch, no brief cessation of the flow of movement under, and over, always forward. Her walls have been perfect. She is almost two lengths ahead. It's still absurd; embarrassing, frightening, exhilarating. As if she has hidden the possibility of this moment from everyone all along—including me—and, now, can laugh at our surprise.

Reach. Pray. Ride over it. What, at her best, years ago, she had notably mastered: the undulation that is a combination of thigh power and gut power and chest and arms and neck and shoulder power—rocking so fluidly under and over the surface that, deceptively, the motion appears to go up and down instead of perfectly, insistently forward. Clear water. No one is near her. The crayon blue still, unrippled, smooth, not a touch of turbulence to disturb this even, perfect, savagely coiled spring and drive. Into the wall before anyone else. I clock her again, at the seventy-five. Third lap has been a negative split. I let the stopwatch collapse on its string against my chest, bounce there, ticking silently, electronically away; I glance at the big bright silent wall clocks matching it, hear dimly, as if far off, the yells and screams of people watching, and, helplessly, I laugh.

Off the wall, she passes everyone else, in all seven other lanes, going the opposite direction. Now, pulling out a final hint of effort and of manic pride, a few others are hitting the wall perfectly, uncorking some last unimaginable reserve of speed, expanding and stretching each muscle in pursuit. And the pursuit is not of her, but of a qualifying time—which, now, has been thrown up in the air as a wild card, almost out of their league, its only limit the sky—in which anything might happen. I think, for a moment, that it's unfair. Remind myself that, in the end, she will only take up one lane after all.

Approaching the finish she does everything right, pure concentration, no glancing to either side, streamlined straight ahead, kick up pull and over, and again, and she skips a breath, head down, ankles snap together and toes point with a last perfect kick, and she touches right in.

I stop my watch, but don't bother to look.

There is a big clattering swell of human-voice noise that echoes around me and, for a moment, makes me feel like I'll drown in it. As the rest of the field begins to touch in, she is already pulling off her goggles, squinting up at the clock, breathing hard and grinning and then tossing her goggles, ducking in and out of the water as if to cool herself down, throwing up both arms in a big wide gesture of triumph. There are, here and there, the flashes of cameras recording this for college newsletters and obscure swimming magazines; and, somewhere, the silent whir of a very small, very local cable TV channel's video unit. The mechanical voice announces it, with a surprising crack of emotion: she has broken the meet and division records, each by more than five seconds.

Later, timelessly somehow, dripping, veins outlined against the effort-reddened flesh, muscles quivering, still breathing hard, she comes back to us all in our specially set-off tiered section of bench, and for a moment everyone engulfs her in towels, embraces. I stand a little apart. When she looks at me, we both burst smiles.

Congratulations, I tell her. Then send her off to the recovery room with Etta leading the way. Check out the knees and ankles, I advise Etta. She's been limping again. And both shoulders, please. Then bring her back alive. In something dry. But not for too long. That final is tonight.

I turn my attention elsewhere. There are other swimmers to worry about, other qualifying heats; she may be the best right now, but she isn't the only one. I busy myself with the rest of them, being stern or warm as the case requires, going over race plans, double-checking lane assignments, soothing nerves.

Still, I'm proud. In the midst of this new flurry of necessary coaching activity I catch a glimpse of her as she passes by the spectator stands, towel over one shoulder. I see Jack on his feet, fists still in the air, jumping up and down; and Felipe, standing now, reaching to touch her raised hand in passing, and he is crying.

Finals

🐬 🐬 🐬

(E L L I E)

"You didn't come kiss me."

"I was up there on the bench, Babe. I mean, I couldn't exactly parachute over, you know. But I made a big fuss—I blew you a major, major kiss—I *know* that you saw it!"

"Or hold me," she complains. "Like you promised."

"Well," I say, "I am holding you now."

She rolls away, dragging me along. I hold her from behind, my hands warm bunched in the folds of her new dry sweats, and I smell shampoo, clean flesh, powder.

"I'm freaking out, Ellie."

"*Chill.*"

"The knee's about to blow—"

"No way. It's all massaged and whirlpooled and braced and taped up and safe—"

"—I can feel it—"

"Hey," I tell her, "quiet." I stroke her hair and neck and, after a while, I can feel her relax.

Our room is the worst. Squeaky mattress, tag-sale pastel still-life and velveteen landscapes on the wall—I'll bet there are jail cells better than this.

"It's all crap, you know." She sounds glum now, resigned. "Everything they tell you. Relax, it's just another meet, it's just another heat. Bullshit!"

Something's knocking at the door to my brain—something almost familiar. Makes me feel hesitant, a little shy, but also knowing somehow; and I hear myself asking, tentatively: "What exactly bothers you, Babe? About finals, I mean—"

"What do you *mean*, what bothers me? Because it's the real *race*, for God's sake!"

"Yeah, but how come that's so frightening?"

She turns over to glare at me in frustration. Then rolls her eyes. I sit cross-legged on the bedspread, trying to explain—to myself, I guess, as well as to her.

"Look, Babe, it's like, sometimes my parents won't do certain things, you know? Like, Lottie won't ride in elevators. Zischa crosses the street, even when it takes him out of his way, to avoid policemen. And neither one of them will sign a petition, ever. And when something weird like that comes up, I know, I just know in my heart, without anyone having to tell me a thing about it, that it's because of all the shit they went through during the war. So I'm just wondering—I mean, everyone gets pretty nervous before an important race, right? But it usually doesn't ruin your whole life—is there something about racing that reminds you? Of the crash, I mean, of the storm—"

She waves a hand dismissively. And there's that smile again, not exactly spreading across her face but in reality covering it up, hiding whatever pain might be there with the big dumb jock sparkling white shit-kicking grin she pulls out sometimes like a trump card.

"I don't know, Ellie. What is it about Jews?"

"Huh?"

"You're all such a bunch of psychoanalysts."

She laughs, teasing, and I straddle her, pin her arms down at her sides, ride her like a kid playing horse and tell her she is an anti-Semitic rice-and-beans eater, and she tells me so what, I am racist as hell underneath all that Commie shit I get from Zischa. And it occurs to me that there may be truth in what we're both teasing about: maybe she is an anti-Semite; maybe I am a racist; how, in this world, could either of us help having a vestige of each deep, deep down inside? But maybe there is something more to it, too—something that goes beyond this notion of prejudice and hate: maybe, with love, there is this anger—this rage at the separation between us, which is symbolized by our two

separate and different bodies; this rage at the differences themselves, of color, of habit, which act like masks to confuse us
sometimes, and cover up our inner natures, and stop us from
recognizing each other.

Zischa always said: the terrible thing about Nazis was not that
they were so different from people you loved, but so similar.

"What if I'm right, Delgado?"

"If you're right—I don't want to talk about it. Ellie, come
here."

I bend down to listen.

She tells me, then, how tired she feels. How she is looking
forward to the summer, and thinks a lot about spending it together with me; but she has to get through these things first, so
could I just shut up and love her?

Finals can be terrifying, for sure; sometimes you just shut
yourself into inhabiting this numb, mechanically moving body
for the duration: cold flesh and muscle moving through the
damp air, bright lights, sudden enveloping shock of the water.
You are obsessed with small things. Will that annoying fold on
the back of your favorite cap curl up behind? Will you lose your
goggles on the dive, just this once? Or false start? Is your left
buttock dimpling out of your suit, for all to see?

This is the first time I've come to a big meet in really lousy
shape, though; and, somehow, that takes the pressure off. No
one expects me to produce miracles, or even good times—and I
don't even have to worry about qualifying heats for a day or
so—but, for Babe, and for most of the rest of them, it's different.
Maybe that's why I hang back, a little, with Etta and our Coach,
when everyone walks out before the spectators.

I hear the sound of my name being called, faintly, and look
up. It's Danny, watching and standing and waving. For a moment, I want to clamber over all the tiers of heads, and jump at
him, and hold him. He smiles, broadly. There are tears in his
eyes. I wave back, I love him again, and smile. And I notice that
next to him, sitting quietly and stubbornly, with his little blue
eyes squinting behind thick metal-rimmed spectacles, is the
wretched Gary Hesse. I wave at him, too—and he grins, then—
and I blow them both a kiss.

Later, it will not be a blur to me, but a silent, slow-moving
bright-lit room inside a cavern of human sound echoing against

the walls. I'll remember how her face looked, chilly and determined, dripping warm-up water. How she peeled off her sweats, one by one—calmly and steadily, though her hands were shaking—and took some time, a long time it seemed, to fold them, and then handed them neatly folded to me. How I held them against my chest. Their smell came up to me: chlorine and water, a faint hint of this perfume she said her mother gave her once, and the sweet, warm musk of her flesh.

She winked once. Then turned, leaned down slightly, and whispered something to Coach, I don't know what, and Bren nodded and said something back.

She headed for the starting block that marked lane four. Entrance to the imaginary donut hole in the water that, to do it right each time, you must consistently dive through. She shook her head, shrugged to relax her shoulders, before stepping up on it. There was something tired about her, now—about the slope to her back—a tired strength; the strength could not mitigate the tiredness, nor the tiredness mitigate the strength; both were her, inexorably, along with all the other things that she was, to me, to everyone else, to herself. Seeing, I felt tears in my eyes, and closed them.

I wouldn't watch—I felt it too hard and too deep; and, in a way, I didn't have to. It was my race, too.

I could feel the tense shatter of the explosion inside when they went off the block. Glance up and tuck slightly, looking for the hole—and, like it always seems when things are perfect, the seconds slow, there is plenty of time to find it, to reach for it the way a jaguar stretches with its paws for prey, and glide right through.

It was my race, too, and she knew it; she knew it, and I could feel it. Because with the one pumping, gliding kick, reach up and break through, shoulders over the crest of the water, and breathe, I felt the two of us together, and I felt her love me, felt her carry the weight of her love for me, the way she had meant it when she winked, the way she had meant it when she said it that first time—Hold on now love, hold on now love, I am taking us home—only, back then, I hadn't understood from a place in me so close and open but so dug down deep and far away, too; the weight of us both made her stronger, in a way, but in another way slowed her down.

It was my race too this time, and both of us felt it. Here was my chance, blindfolded, moving inside while I stood there still, to swim in a way I never had before: with a big big talented body that had been cracked and damaged but functioned still; with a heart that had been broken badly, and still beat on with love and with rage, giving everything, a warrior heart.

We bounced on the line of electrical energy that flowed down lane four, keeping delicate balance as we rocked and rolled, gasped for breath, puked out air bubbles back underneath water—more difficult now, more exhausting somehow, than in the qualifying heat where a miracle happened; because we were very tired tonight, and had been sick, and hurt, and had had to grow up anyway, but there was no profit without that immeasurable investment of pain; so we just let it spill, and it was like giving, not taking.

As we reached hard for the wall, sprang back reversed and set the bottoms of her feet against it for just that fraction of a second, then powered off, perfect streamlined glide and pull and kick and up, I felt how hard this was for her, for us, how hard she was already fighting for breath. How it was not her conditioning any more, or her strength any more, but her form that took over—not an art, but a craft built up with years of effort, become second nature, consummate enough to hide all the wounds, and then to contain them.

She was carrying me with her, carrying the best part of me: the part of me that was wordless, that beat with a warrior heart. I gave it to her completely now, for safekeeping—because she needed it during the last fifty, more than ever—not in time for the Worlds, or the Olympics, or the Pan Ams, maybe, but in time for her to use it and love it and feel it, yes, for the rest of her life.

I was not afraid of losing it myself. There was plenty more to spare.

I knew, too, that I loved her; not just for the day or the month, but for my soul and for my life. I knew it would not be easy, not if I wanted to love her right, or be loved right by her; but maybe this life was my working life, not a life for ease or relaxation—and there was so much work to do, so far, so very far, to go.

The last fifty was hell. I kept my eyes shut.

At one point, terror and doubt set in. But we smashed it away, said silently, savagely, oh no you don't, fucker. It was around the sixty that muscle spasms lurked, were driven off, came back in a wrenching grip of vengeance when we hit the wall for seventy-five; so that, gasping up and out too soon, we almost came to a complete stop, saw blurs of white wake approaching each side, remembered that we were not alone, there were seven others trying to get to the end first; and, for ourselves, and for each other, and for Brenna Allen too, we had come here to win. Twenty more yards of pain, Babe, I said. What *can't* we stand for a few more seconds? Then the frozen muscles moved, protesting; the brain knew that if we were hurting this bad, everyone else must be, too; the heart opened up, and the guts did too, and the body went forward.

We were careful not to look. To the right. Or the left. Because you never do that in the 100—never.

We made an on-the-spot decision, though, that countered traditional wisdom. We stroked up for one last breath. Sensing that, contrary to what all the coaches said, the breath would help us; that air was good, our human element after all, and to get as much of it as possible gave us power.

Then, all agony, all exhaustion, all focus, we concentrated with our mind and with our heart, and kicked forward, as hard and as strong as we could, forward, glide, touched firmly into the wall.

I opened my eyes.

I could hear her, or thought I could, anyway—beneath the rumble of voices, and applause, the beep of the time clocks, click of Brenna Allen's stopwatch, cheers of women all around me, and the thin, tenor voice of her brother yelling All right *Babe!*— I could hear her sob for breath. Feel her lean her forehead against the slippery cold wet wall. Hands clinging. Trying desperately to breathe. Every rib and chest muscle expanding, throat sucking, and the pounding, lightless, dying feeling the 100 can give you inside.

Out of the water, you say.

Into air. Give me air.

Let me live.

We were separate now; I had my heart back, she her suffering body. She rested it against the wall. Cried because she hurt so bad. Laughed because she'd won.

Left to myself again, in the time between her winning and lifting herself out of the water, I have my comeuppance. I hear the tough, mature, wise voice in my head—the voice that is not quite mine yet—telling me the truth.

Ellie, it doesn't matter that no one expects much of you.

It doesn't matter that you're hurt, and sick.

It doesn't even matter that you qualify.

But, Ellie—if you don't get in there tomorrow and swim that heat as hard and as fast as you can; if you don't dig way down deep and spill out all of your guts for it; if, success or bust, you don't crawl out of that pool with every shred of desire and effort left behind—then, then, you will never be able to look at your face in the mirror again without a mask of doubt; and you will never be able to hear the word Hammerhead again without shuddering; and you will never be able to wear the jacket they gave you, to glory in the dark blood-red of it, with the ugly proud ornate letters over the left breast that say *Captain Marks.*

Fear thuds cold boot soles over my insides. Babe's old fear—of finals, and of qualifying heats—I understand it, deep down, for the first time; but, also, there is something about it that I think I love, that I think I know already. So that, shaking with a joy for her and a terror for myself, I am looking forward to it like some mercenary soldier in the front lines; or a boxer, maybe, waiting for the very first punch.

Babe approaches the bench. She's stopped, for a few seconds, by some anchorman from the definitely obscure cable TV station covering this meet. I see him say something and wave a microphone in her face, see her shrug, reply briefly, turn away.

As she gets closer, I see that she's still breathing very hard. I try to read what's on her face—disappointment? because even though she won the time was slow, slower than her qualifying time, and the seeds in lanes three and five gave her quite a race. But maybe it's not disappointment, or even doubt, maybe it's relief. And maybe not even that, but just pain. Yes. She hurts bad. Coach stands to greet her, and then something happens that I've never seen before: she opens her arms, and Babe steps inside them and puts her head on her shoulder, and cries. Brenna Allen just stands there, patting her back like she's an infant who needs burping. For a second, I am jealous. But then glad.

She sits next to me, dripping. Someone hands her a towel. Someone else smacks her shoulder, someone her other shoulder, saying Nice work, Babe. Congratulations. I realize that I'm still clutching her folded sweats to my chest. She's still sniffling tears and chlorine, chest still heaving, cheeks and forehead flushed with effort. There are veins in her neck, and one across her right deltoid, that still throb, bulging out against the skin. She sets her hands on her knees. Both forearms are shaking. She glances over.

"Oh. There they are."

"Want them on?"

"Sure," she says. "In a minute."

Someone is standing next to us, suddenly, on the deck: a young male, definitely trespassing, in worn jeans and brand-new very expensive aerodynamically designed basketball shoes. A T-shirt displays his skinny arms, over one of which is draped a black leather bomber jacket.

"Yo, Babe. Way to go."

She wipes her cheeks awkwardly. Saying, Thanks. He bends down to kiss her. For a moment I see their faces together: the dark, dark hair and eyes, olive brown skin, West African nose and lips. A beautiful woman. Beautiful boy. Both so obviously part of something that is the same in living flesh and blood, both so beautiful; for a second, surprising me, tears come to my eyes again—tears of a poignant wish, almost envy, as I think: God, she is so lucky, so lucky to have a brother! And Jack's close to her in age. They have opportunity to share a lot, joke around with each other. If Oskar had lived, for instance, he'd be more than forty now—more like a father than a brother. But, if Oskar had lived, if any of the kids had lived, my own existence might not have seemed such an imperative to Lottie, or to Zischa; and I would not be here now, crying, wishing, wanting, loving.

I close my eyes for just a second again, blink the tears away.

Say a silent little prayer inside—for Oskar, and for Zischa's girls, for the lives they started but never really had. And at the end of the prayer I say:

Thank you Lottie. Thank you Zischa. Thank you for making me necessary. Thank you for choosing me over death. Thank you, my mother and my father, thank you for giving me life.

I open my eyes. Babe tugs on the ear of the beautiful boy.

"Jack, this is Ellie Marks."

"Hi." Then he glances at me sideways, a little wary, cocks his head at Babe. "Is she the one?"

Babe nods.

"Oh." He shoves both hands in his pockets and shrugs. "Well, I don't know. She doesn't look like a dyke."

"Jack!"

"No, I mean—Christ, I meant it as a *compliment,* for God's sake—I mean, no offense, okay? but you look all right. I mean, you know, normal. Even, like, sort of pretty—you know, in this Jewish way, I mean—"

"Shut *up!*" Babe hisses, but she's laughing.

I grin up at him. "A little prejudiced, are we?"

"No way! My girlfriend's part Jewish."

I pat a bare space of bench. "I mean about the gay stuff. Sit down, Jack. You're working too hard."

He does. Now I'm sandwiched: a Delgado on my right, a Delgado on my left.

"So," he whispers glumly, "so my sister's queer. So what."

Babe reaches across me to punch his arm. He winces. I push her fist aside.

"Yeah," I say, "so what."

"So. I met you. So what do I do now?"

"Hang out, Jack. Come visit this summer. You'll get to know me."

"Yeah? And then what?"

"Then things get real."

He stares down at damp floor tiles, mutters something I don't quite hear. At which point Coach stalks up.

"You must be Jack. I'm Brenna Allen."

He looks up suddenly, gulps some kind of fear or surprise away. Then starts to say something, but doesn't. I see Coach Allen wink at him. He hangs his head. It's clear they are conspirators of a sort, clear they share some secret; but whatever it is, I will not know. And Babe, blowing her nose into the towel, misses it all.

Bren extends her hand. Jack grips it.

"Nice to meet you. So glad you could make it. But this is an all-women's team, Jack, in the middle of competition. Now get back where you belong."

"Okay."

"You can see your sister later."

"Yes, ma'am," he stammers, and stands, ruffling Babe's hair.

"Jack, cut it *out*."

He grins obnoxiously. Cuffs me on the shoulder. "See you, Ellie. Hope you practice safer sex."

Babe aims a kick at his shin that misses. Then he's gone, waving, climbing back into the spectator stands. Babe blushes. She squeezes my hand apologetically.

"Um, there you go, Ellie—your first Delgado. And, believe me, he's a lot better than the rest."

"No," I tell her, feeling bruised, and mad, but somehow oddly happy, "my second Delgado. My second."

Knowing, without having to say it, that my first one was the best by far.

Telling myself to stay calm, and patient. The worst, the initial contact, is definitely over. And no one who looks so much like her can be all that bad.

Anyway, I have other work to do here.

Finals

ᕫ ᕫ ᕫ

(B A B E)

At night, she sets the alarm clock Bren gave her. Lays out what suits and caps and goggles she'll wear tomorrow—for warm-up, and then for her qualifying heat. Lays out her favorite towel. Her favorite sweats. Her favorite skin cream, and shampoo. Very serious. Very focused. But she's still too pale and thin, still coughs once in a while; sometimes, in practice, will stop in the middle of a set and just cling to the side of the pool, she is so tired. I don't say much. Watching her, my heart aches.

For the most part, though, she seems pretty calm. The only hint of nerves is that she's silent—a rarity—except for clearing the throat, and an occasional question, in monotone:

Should I put out another suit?

For the final, she means.

I tell her whatever makes her comfortable. That I myself always save that for the time after qualifying, because it is less confusing to deal with two sets of things than with three or four.

Yes, she nods, seriously. Usually, she says, she feels that way herself. She calls it the What-I-Deliver-I-Promise School of Modern Swimming Technique. Both of us laugh.

But she thinks that, tonight, she will lay out her stuff for the final. She did that once, long ago, and it worked—well, kind of. She doesn't want to get into it now. But it was a special day, back then; one she'd always remember.

Then she changes the subject. Asks am I worried much about the 200 now, or the relays? Or is it the 100 alone?

My Leviathan? I say.

She smiles.

I tell her I'm always worried. Some people are like that—bundle of nerves; it's the way they compete. Must be, like, all that fast-twitch fiber. But the 100, for whatever reason, gives me more nervous shakes than anything else; even though the 200 leaves you comatose, and so much rides on how well you do in the relays. The 100 is the thorn in my side, the pain in my ass.

Because it's your race, she says.

I tell her Sure, maybe.

No, she insists, it *is* your race. *Your* race. Whatever we do that is hardest for us, is the thing we put our most into. Whatever we put our most into, like our time, and sweat, and blood, well, that is the thing we make our own. Because after a while, it smells like us. It tastes like us. After a while, it calls out our name.

When she talks like that, a part of me thinks it's just bullshit but another part of me falls more in love. I hold her for a while, remembering she promised to do that for me after the 100; but *my* race is over for now, and I don't feel so needy. I wrap both aching arms around her, rest my face against her neck. She usually makes a big deal about how good this feels. Tonight, though, she just sighs, and is silent.

After a while, I feel her sleep.

I turn off the lamp.

It's not the dark that scares me any more. Darkness never did. What scares me is its end, the morning it always brings, harsh bright light in which you choose between the struggle and the giving up, in which you can't help but see yourself too clearly, in which the truth about what you're made of and how you'll use that cannot be hidden.

Calmate, I say. My father's Spanish words, from long ago.

Tita comes to me. There is fire in my hands.

I use it, now, for the first time ever—careful to do it correctly: not for my own benefit, but for her whom I love. Quietly, place the tips of my fingers at her different points of light. Silently sing the magic. Into her heart, and lungs, and belly. Into her head, and arms, and legs. Into the dark secret part of her. Until, sleeping, she shudders, and gasps; unconsciously sweats, coughing out globs of poison.

Then her breaths come deep and calm. And I sleep, too.

I sleep, and sleep. I sleep through the alarm of Bren's traveling clock. Wake up to the day, a soft gray one outside, spring rain pattering through the window and a dull, gentle light through crooked blinds. I gasp, stare at the time. Soft old ticking. It is late morning, Ellie gone. I sit up in a burst of self-horror. Her qualifying heat will be over by now; I've missed it.

Rapid moving. But moving smacks me right between the eyes with reality. Reality of my body—saying, *Delgado, you can't really move so fast or so well any more, or I'll hurt you pretty bad*. I have to slow down. My head pounds with yesterday's effort, groin and belly ache with each stretch. Thighs are sore. Knees, ankles, feel crippled. Arms and even the backs of my wrists hurt, curved inward against the invisible water; my neck and my shoulders are on fire. I sit there on the bed half naked, and start to cry.

Oh God, I say, Ellie, Ellie, I'm sorry. So sorry.

Standing, I pull shit out of a suitcase before realizing it's the wrong one. I dump all of her stuff on the unmade bed, reach for my own suitcase and pour everything out of it too.

Then I stop, suddenly feeling very, very pissed. Because why didn't she wake me? She knows I wanted to be there for her, too; that I wanted to see her swim.

I glance over at the armchair by a bedtable. Two of her suits are gone, but not the ones she'd meant to take. The third one she'd laid out especially for her qualifying heat is still there; only the warm-up suit and the suit she'd planned to use for the final tonight—like there was really going to *be* a final for her tonight—are gone.

I splash water on my face, throw on some clothes and head out, passing a couple of swimmers from some other team in the hall.

"Hey," says one, "nice race yesterday."

I turn blindly. "Look, I'm, um, late for a heat. Are there cabs around?"

"Sure. Ask at the desk."

As I run for the staircase—don't want to risk waiting for the elevator—I hear it echo behind me, bewildered: But it's four hundred IM this morning. You're not even seeded for that, are you?

When I get there, the place looks bizarre for a minute. I realize I've never entered one of these natatorium complexes as a spectator before. The lights always seemed so glaringly, inhumanely bright to me. Now, stumbling through the tiers of stands, they seem just right, illuminating the pool without too much reflection, making things seem colorful and clean and appetizing instead of wet and frightening and clammy. The stands themselves seem shabby, a little beaten, definitely smaller. Always, they loomed enormously around me, screaming judgment from every tier; now they are sparsely populated, the few people seated here and there merely observing, gently and with interest, with knowledge and with dignity—different from the yahoos who usually spectate at most college team sports—and they don't seem threatening at all. Even the pool looks smaller, plenty smaller than it does when you're gazing down its barrel-end from the knife edge of a starting block. Just a contained rectangle, after all, marked off by floating pieces of plastic in tight-linked rows, a basin filled with cleansing chemicals, and with water.

Etta notices me first, waves and smiles.

"Get enough sleep, girl?"

"I guess."

"Then how come you look demented?"

"Etta, where's Ellie? How come nobody woke me?"

"Ellie's fine. Coach's orders, doll—if you could sleep late, you were supposed to."

Brenna Allen doesn't turn around to see me. A few of the team members do, and wave me over, and someone pokes Ellie on the shoulder. She is sitting there with a towel around her upper body, sweatpants soaking through. When she sees me she stands, and grins.

"Hey."

"God, baby! I am so sorry! Why the hell didn't you wake me up?"

She coughs, clears her throat. "Babe, listen—I qualified."

"Go *on!*"

"Can you believe it? I mean, I didn't really think I could."

I start to cry, suddenly, effortlessly. "Oh, Ellie, that's great."

"Yeah. I qualified last, absolutely last, by a long shot, believe me—I mean, we're talking major seconds, and I'm stuck in eight tonight—but, you know, I felt an enormous great big shitload better than I thought I would. So I just went for it."

I am sniffling again, feeling pretty mad, broken somehow, tired; but at the same time so happy for her, and relieved, and unexpectedly sorry for myself, because I wasn't there to see it.

"I wish I'd been here, Ellie. I feel so bad."

"Don't." She shakes her head, suddenly very serious. "You know, maybe I wanted to do this alone. I don't know. I thought about waking you up this morning—I really did, Babe—but you were sleeping so well, and I just thought, what is the point? I mean, she's not going to qualify *for* you, you know—"

"But still—"

"Still nothing. I figured *this* would be my final, Babe—this qualifying heat. So I wore the other suit—you know. But now I've got to do it again tonight—God, I don't even believe it, during the backstroke I really just thought I was going to die—"

"But you did it, baby. I'm so proud of you!"

"Yeah. I am too."

So is everybody else. People are rubbing her back and her shoulders, pounding her chest, telling her to relax so they can massage her temples, stretch out her arms, get her another towel. You'd think she had set a new record, from the stink they are making. I just beam. You can tell, from her reaction, that she's not used to the attention at all. Good, I think, let everyone else touch her—it's good for her.

There is this thing about the magic: You can act as a vessel or a conduit for it, but you cannot really control it. It is just passing through, really, not your own to give.

Also, it only lasts so long. When it leaves, it is gone.

I watch the fire leave her by increments throughout the day, until she begins to cough a little again, and clear her throat, and look very tired—almost too tired, she says, to eat a light lunch; she doesn't know how she can possibly get through it tonight; and she isn't even thinking about winning, or placing, but about finishing, about sheer survival.

Finally, she shrugs. Looking tense and pale, but nevertheless determined. Or resigned. But committed, no matter what. Saying, Well, I guess if worst comes to worst I can *dog*-paddle four hundred yards.

Around us, at the table, people giggle and laugh. She does too.

You won't have to, I tell her; though I am not sure.

I am—or was—a sprinter, clear and simple; even the 200 was stretching it for me. This had nothing to do with aerobic conditioning, but with genetic aptitude.

Not that I had trouble swimming 400, or 1500, or 10,00 meters, for that matter, when I was in reasonable condition—not that my times in distance events were not way, way above average; it's just that, at the sprints, I excelled.

It's this something ineffable that biochemists and exercise physiologists are always trying to quantify: from event to event, a different kind of energy gets expended, and sometimes it varies greatly and at other times just slightly; but it is always different, and the amount of perfection with which an individual can do a certain event, perform the tasks required, varies from individual to individual, too; so that only the people most brilliantly suited to any one particular event will ever really succeed at it on a world-class or national-class level. There is this matter of inborn ability—which no one likes to talk about—but it's true: a fact, a reality, that no amount of consistently superb training can overcome.

On the other hand, it also matters what you do with it.

Or, as Bren likes to say, talent gets you fifty meters; the rest is all just work.

Not strictly true. But true enough. No talent, no wonder drug, will ever substitute for the practice and the work.

I grew up with kids who had all of it together: innate physical talent, mental toughness and desire, a willingness to work. For a while, I possessed all of those attributes, too; and, during that time, I was a champion.

When I gave up the mental toughness and desire; when I let slip away from me just a tiny fraction of the absolute willingness to work; I was no longer a champion. And this is what happened—long before the plane went down.

It's all right. I had other things on my mind and in my heart.

Puberty. Family pressure. Betrayal. Love. A nut case for a coach, who wanted only to win at these games called sport, and who was willing to rape and to spill blood for that, and who was copiously rewarded for his efforts.

When I was no longer a champion, someone else was. Matter always fills empty space, sooner or later.

It's all okay, though I do not forgive, or forget.

I never had a warrior heart—at least, not for keeps.

What I had was an inquisitive heart. One that preferred to observe, and feel, and ask a lot of questions. I know this about myself now.

But what we know is not always what we want to know.

What we know about ourselves is not always what people want to know about us.

That is why, for the time being, I commit myself to swim for Brenna Allen—this year, and next. Sensitive, arrogant, observant scholar that I am, housed in this warrior's body. She—like Ellie—has a real warrior heart. And she's done me some favors. In return, I can lend her team this body, learn from it what I can; I can make it swim another year.

I'll stay at State, stay in shape, swim for the team, finish school. Spend the summer with Ellie—with her and the two funny smart little dykes who already seem middle-aged to me—in that ugly old ramshackle house that has tattered furniture and the warm yellow light.

Who would have thought I'd lust for a place like that? Me, with my trophies, and my Gold Card? Still, it's true. I wanted to be there from the first time I saw it. Wanted to be myself there—no champion, just me—and to be there with her.

Let my parents do their own split-up. Invite Jack, even Robo or Toots, up for a visit if things get too rough. Otherwise, stay out of it. They can't, they won't, help me mourn. They cannot deal. But I have to mourn—for them, for myself, for Kenny, and for everything now lost. Ellie, though—she can deal. And so can I. Not all the time, and not perfectly, but we can.

Right now, I can watch her try her best to compete, to swim. I can ache for her suffering effort, can admire her sheer guts; understanding that this fighting, grinding way is the way she's got to be—her way, not mine—and that it's all just fine.

Because the point is not to exalt one way over the other, but to know which way is your own, your very own.

And later, too, I can hold her.

Understanding these things, making these decisions, I feel suddenly at peace.

Finals

ゝ ゝ ゝ

(J A C K)

It started again with little fights. Just a day or two after Christmas—during which everyone was pretty much comatose and in a state of shock. But Ricky and Lucy recovered. And went back to the ways they had never really abandoned.

Didn't sound like anything out of the ordinary, at first. Standard guerrilla warfare. Nasty snipes. What had she done with his keys to the Saab—ground them up in the Cuisinart? Why had he stayed so long after work that night, two weeks ago—another wild office party for two?

But pretty soon this stuff escalated, until it seemed like whenever the two of them were around at the same time they were yelling at the top of their lungs, saying really disgusting shit to each other nobody wants to even know about—and they were making the house such a fucked-up place to be that, on more than one occasion, I found myself stomping around outside through the snow with Roberto, wishing I could spend the night at Cindy's—not for sex, but to escape—or wishing that indoor practice would last twice as long each day, so I could have more time away.

When they first started to really yell, too, a lot of it was about Babe.

You always rode the kid so hard, Barbara, it breaks my heart! You never really loved her!

Look who's talking! Look who's talking about love! A man who barely takes the time between adulteries to zip up his fly!

Why can't you be a real mother, Barbara? What on earth is wrong with you? Why can't you just be a mother, and love your own child?

Do *you* love her, Phil? All you ever did was shovel money down her throat whenever she won. To the detriment of everyone else around here, may I add. At least *I* tried to instill certain values—

Values? What values? Your cold little privileged white May-flower values?

Privileged? White? I'm the only one around here who is white, *señor*. And nobody around here was ever privileged, really, except you—and her, when she had goals, and a decent body, and a worthwhile life—but you, you, have always just gone ahead and done what you pleased, never mind about the rest of us!

What bullshit! I put in hours of slave labor for you, woman! To buy the house you wanted! With all the things in it you and your stupid parents wanted! To support all those children that you said you wanted!

I wanted!

You!

And so on. After a while, it got so you could tell when things were about to blow. Then I'd grab my bomber jacket and head out for the garage. I'd hang around watching Roberto smoke for a while. Sometimes the two of us would just sit inside the Volvo or the BMW, silently, waiting for the storm to pass. I'd think about Teresa, who was in there curled up in bed pretending to be asleep but really hearing all of this, this nasty bullshit, and I'd cringe. I'd want to go in and take her away somehow, take her away and save her. But, I realized, there is nowhere else to go. And I'm sixteen years old. Barely old enough to drive. How the fuck am I going to save anybody?

Things didn't get better; somehow, this time, unlike all the other times, I knew that they wouldn't. When the old man told me, I wasn't surprised. It was even kind of a relief. But I still wanted to cry and, when no one was looking, I did.

Weird fucking family. Now I am here, this mediocre high school cross-country runner who, let's face it, can't pass for black and can't pass for white, with my soon-to-be divorced Cuban refugee father, watching the Jew girlfriend of my self-admitted queer ex-champion sister get on the starting block for some stupid final or some stupid swimming event in some stupid nothing division.

That's America for you. Bunch of refugees. Makes you feel like you landed on Mars. Makes me wonder if any of us will ever feel at home here. But, what choice do we have—us refugees— I mean, what other home is there? Everyone needs one, has to make one—a home. Me too. Even though I am losing the home I thought I had, and don't know where to go.

The buzzer goes off and I watch, feeling pissed and mean. The whole bunch of them, eight chicks in tight racing suits, sort of smash into the water at once. A couple of them looked really great, standing there—you could practically see their tits. I take off my jacket and bundle it over my lap.

Butterfly, they are doing butterfly. Which I think is pretty cool, I like the way they sort of plunge forward up and out and in again with both arms, like some mad ghost monster attacking something defenseless, pouncing, just pouncing, then kick, and up again, dolphin-like. Ellie Marks is in lane eight, which means she's the slowest, and after a few seconds I swear I don't know why the hell Babe wanted me to watch—I mean, as a swimmer, it's clear that she pretty much stinks. She manages to keep up with the rest of the field for the first lap or so, then starts falling back, and falling back, and it doesn't look like she's ever going to catch them. In fact, by the end of the third lap of butterfly it looks like she's really tired, and slowing down, and when she makes a sloppy turn into the fourth lap I start to blush—I mean, I am actually humiliated for her—and I start to fidget, and wish that I hadn't promised to watch.

The other seven of them all finish up the final twenty-five of butterfly pretty tight together—more than a body length ahead of her already—and, looking very strong, almost inhuman, they all one by one turn gracefully at the wall for the next hundred yards of backstroke.

She turns at the wall last. Still looking sloppy. Looking incredibly, incredibly tired—like the first 100 was about all she could handle.

Her backstroke sucks. I remember Babe's friend Liz Chaney,

how great she looked when she swam backstroke, how once when she visited from Southern with Babe she smacked me on the back and said she'd show me how to do special stretching exercises just for runners, and then got me all twisted up like a pretzel trying to do these stretches, so that my nose was practically up my asshole and I collapsed on the floor like a moron, and she and Babe laughed and laughed. I thought she was really beautiful, though, really hot. And watching this miserable excuse for a swimmer, this Ellie Marks who Babe claims she loves, trying to backstroke, I swear I don't know what Babe sees in her.

I confess: I stop watching; I shut my eyes.

The old man sits next to me like a ghost. I don't know whether or not he is watching, and the truth is that I really don't care. He is the one breaking things up; he's the one taking away my home. But, on the other hand, I don't blame him. I just hate him. And love him. I think of my mother, and I don't know what to even say. That she hates us. And loves us. And neither one of them was big enough for our house, in the end.

For some reason, this sticks in my head: The house, our house, that they socked all that money into, all the land, and the three-car garage—it was too big for them, they were too small to fill it. But somehow, before the plane went down, back when Babe was healthy and world-class and a real contender and kept bringing lots of medals and trophies home to put behind custom-made glass cases on the walls—somehow, then, in this way that is connected to Babe but that I do not understand, somehow then they seemed big enough to fill it, and it seemed like we all of us loved each other, at least on the surface—and like it was a love that worked, and things were almost perfect.

But perfect things don't fall apart.

Thank God, the backstroke is finished. All of them are now light years ahead of her—I mean, like, halfway down the pool already, swimming breaststroke; and, for a second, I think I almost see her pause at the wall like she wants to hang on and stop and not continue.

Stop, I think. Give me a break.

But she dips under water and shoves off the wall—not a bad wall, really; I know that from Babe, who was pretty much at one point basically the best in the world—yes, though I am a moron in the water, you can bet that as her brother I *know* about breast-stroke. And she bobs up, having gained a little, closing the gap between her and everyone else just slightly, closing it ever so much more slightly with each stroke and kick. I mean, no *way* will she ever catch up. But it's obvious that she knows a little about how to swim this, now; and I find myself leaning forward to watch with a vague feeling of interest because, though obviously too tired, and with her timing off too, even so she can pull this part of the race off with a little dignity and grace, and when you see that in sport it's nice, really nice, just to watch, to behold. Another turn. She doesn't explode off the wall like Babe—she doesn't have that kind of agility, really, or raw strength. But she keeps gaining, ever so slightly, closing up the endless gap to maybe about two and a half body lengths, struggling down the 250-yard leg and maybe rushing it again, reaching again with her skull, like she can't wait to get to the wall, and the turn, like she knows that the wall and the turn will save her.

It doesn't. Save her, I mean. Although, after the turn, into the 275-yard leg, she has closed up more space between her and the rest of the field; and looks tired but somehow more on top of things than she looked just a few seconds before; and by the time she hits the final breaststroke turn and pulls ahead more she has narrowed the gap to about a body length. I figure if her freestyle's any good at all, and if she doesn't croak or totally fall apart first, at least she'll be able to finish just behind everyone else, and maybe she won't be totally, totally humiliated.

For some reason, I don't want her to be embarrassed. Or maybe it's myself, somehow, that I don't want to embarrass. After all, I have run a few stinkaroo races in my day. And, while I never came in last, I remember one cross-country race I ran against this team that totally outclassed us; I never was in contention from the starting gun on, even though I ran my guts out, ran much harder than I think I ever had to do before or since; I finished pretty much near the back of the field, and when I crossed the finish line I got down on my knees and puked, and pissed in my shorts, and then I cried. One of those days when you give your best, but your best is nowhere near good enough, and there's nothing more you can do. I mean, it's no tragedy—maybe on some level you can even feel proud—but it is also no fun. No fun at all.

They start the final 100 yards—freestyle—pretty much flat out. There's more spacing between the others in the rest of the field now, too; some of them are fading, looking tired; some of them are battling it out in the middle, not knowing what the hell place they might finish in. Lanes three and two and six are almost neck and neck to the end. The water becomes a slipstream of blue-white turbulence trailing behind each set of feet, and they kick, and kick, and pull, and pull, and pull and breathe as hard and as fast as they can. I watch each flip turn—perfect—I love how they do that. Ellie is trailing badly again. I can tell by the way her head kind of bobs jerkily up for a breath with each stroke that she's exhausted. She seems to make a superhuman effort at the 375, closing a little on the rest, springing off the wall and not breathing for a few strokes, then barreling it down the final lap of the race like a little cannon drooling out the last of its shot, like a toy that's broken but still kind of works, looking weird smashing away at the water, as if she hates it, wants to kill it. Until, many seconds behind the next to last finisher, she touches in.

I'm not even sure who won. I've been too busy watching the loser. Who doesn't even bother to take off her goggles, or look up at the time. She just clings to the wall, bows her head against it. For a second, it looks like she's going to sink.

I sort of sit there, staring at her, ignoring my father, wondering what to do.

But you'd think, from the reaction of her teammates—the most prominent, visible, and embarrassingly vocal of whom is my sister Babe—that she had won first place. They are all jumping around screaming and hurrah-ing, running over to cluster around the block at lane eight and lean over like a bunch of birds clucking over a nest, helping her out of the water and covering her with hugs and kisses. Every once in a while you can hear a particularly high-pitched shriek.

Something you would never hear on a men's team, believe me. Women, females—they seem foreign to me, sometimes. There is no way I could ever really, really understand them; I mean, I know we are all similar as human beings, in a lot of ways, and that, like, we all of us have feelings; but I'm talking about the differences—and I know, I know in my heart, that the gap between me and them is a gap that will always be, that will never close, no matter how much I am in love.

I wonder if it's the same for Babe, and Ellie—do they have gaps? but thinking about *that* is disgusting, so I stop.

Finals

🐬 🐬 🐬

(F E L I P E)

We had to be there, she told me over the phone, had to be there for the 400 IM, even though she herself will not swim it. And watch lane eight. Lane eight. The swimmer in lane eight is her best friend. Someone very important to her. Then—later, after the swimming is over for the night—she and this friend will meet us for dinner. But only then.

She makes it sound like a reward. Her presence, and the presence of this other girl, a gift to me, her father, for doing the right thing. And maybe, in a way, it is.

At any rate, I am guilty as Judas these days, where my family is concerned; a man with no right to object—especially not to the whims of his handsome, spoiled, distraught children. Spending time with them already feels like borrowed time; it feels like visiting rights, hours bowing under the weight of limitation, darkened by grief unexpressed.

Mostly, I don't know how I'll get through them. The hours, I mean; the minutes, and the days. I only know that I will, somehow I will.

The pain is too unbearable to allow itself to be felt. If it did that, it would destroy the organism. I clench my teeth and close my eyes against it. Banish feeling from my day-to-day existence. Skirt Barbara, when she is there—as she avoids me—wander the house like a ghost when she's not, grateful for the freedom, sick to death of everything else. Knowing only that it is what I have to do. And that, later, somehow, I will let myself feel it.

For now, I am a drowning man, on a crowded raft built for one. I must push everyone else off this raft, in order to survive myself; hoping desperately that they, who can swim so much better than I, will swim and not sink, that they will find land or a lifebuoy, or that a rescue ship will pluck them out of the water; but knowing against love itself that if I do not slice them adrift I myself will surely die. And, still, seeing forever the expression on their faces—an expression of anguish, and rage, and betrayal—when I finally cut them free.

I have sat here for some time, now—next to my son, dimly watching my daughter swim in the water. It seems absurd to me, suddenly, this whole practice: her doing, us watching. We have been doing this, for one reason or another, for many years now.

I am proud of her, yes; but, I realize, for something quite other than this: I am proud of her for hanging on in the face of Angelita, and staying afloat in the Sargasso Sea, and coming back to live among us.

There was something, she said last night, after dinner, something important she had to tell me. She held me by the shoulders. Looked into my eyes. I saw dark things in hers; and warm things, like tenderness; and a light. I recognized the light, before I clearly knew it; it was something I grew up seeing, in the sunlight glinting off metal and oceans and fields, reflected in the eyes of Tía Corazón—and, once, long ago, before I was a man with money and too many things, reflected in my own. It is clear, bright, almost frightening. A touch of the Powers. Of madness, and of love.

If you live as if you will die tomorrow, you may keep this light. But if you live as if there will always be plenty of time on your side—time to develop the heart, the spirit, true kindness and compassion for the creatures of the world, time to begin doing the right and just things—then time is what you will lose, in the end; and, in losing it, you also lose the light. It will wither from your hands; it will fade from your eyes. You will chase other things instead, chase them forever.

My daughter is rearing up out of the water now, lifting a fist triumphantly. I see the scars across her shoulders. Buzzers sound. Electronic boards on each side of the natatorium display cumulative team points, there are human voices and the laughter of young women, and yelling, cheering. My son is standing, hoarsely ranting his sister's name, his own name—and mine:

Delgado!

Del-GA-do!

I look at the dark brown backs of my hands.

Mr. Delgado, said that friend of hers, the Jewish girl, at dinner last night—I took them to a fine place, after having to convince Jack, who was for some reason sulking, to dress respectably and come along—Mr. Delgado, I want to tell you something, you have two beautiful, beautiful children. Four, I said proudly, nodding. And Babe laughed then, not in mockery or self-deprecation, but in delight.

Later was when she said it: Dad, look, I have something important to tell you. Inside I could feel the heaviness and the weariness in my chest. I loved her more than ever. And, at the same time, I could not bear another burden—I knew that what she wanted to say was no burden to her, but would be to me. What I did instead of listening was a cowardly thing. I took her hands from my shoulders and held them in my own, and said, I love you, what you want to tell me doesn't matter, please don't. Which was a lie, and a plea; but also, for me, the truth. So that she went away silenced, and relieved, and disappointed.

My daughter's team has won.

Del-GA-DO! yells my son. He jumps down tiers of bleachers, running for her, on the pool deck now, surrounded by a group of women.

They are taking apart the lane dividers. Unhooking them. Floating them sloppily, one by one, until they mesh like clumsy colorful snakes in the center of the light blue contained pool of water—that, under no circumstances, could remind me of the sea, or of Angelita, except for the presence of my daughter.

They are lifting someone up on their shoulders. Multiple hands. Multiple screams and yells, release, laughter. An older, handsome woman. White. Solid. Obviously, that coach. I connect the voice from the phone to her—yes, it fits. They are passing her, hands to hands. Throwing her, fully dressed, into the water.

After You Win

🐬 🐬 🐬

(C H I C K)

Boz and I travel together like old friends, trustingly, knowing each other's rhythms. There's the upper-class freneticism of Cambridge near Harvard, matrix of subway stops, bookstores, expensive alumni gift shops, privilege with something still to prove, and the shifting crowds of wealthy young souls who think they're slumming it in worn, torn fatigues from army surplus stores, indestructible black thick-soled British punk shoes, shaven heads or ponytails, earrings shaped like razors.

We stare coolly out at this, Boz and I, through the windows of my Honda. My turquois blue Honda hatchback with two doors and five speeds—a purchase I agonized over, was later childishly proud of, and which became, in fact, the source of an argument with Bren.

I don't believe you're buying a foreign car, Chick! American industry's going down the tubes, you know—don't you think you ought to be a little more patriotic?

To which I'd replied: American industry's going down the tubes because of poor quality and incompetent management and greed and waste and cruelty and shortsightedness and lies, Bren—not because of foreign products. This is the best car for my money. Therefore, I will buy it. She'd shrugged, mildly disgusted. Gone out and spent thousands more on a Buick. Power steering, plush interior, four doors, heating vents front seat and back, terrible mileage. But warmth and comfort were the big things on her mind that winter, anyway—the car was all for Kay, who had given her the go-ahead to purchase Anything But A German Car.

I press on the air-conditioning. Boz whines with a kind of contentment, his wet nose blotches the dashboard and then my shoulder, and he settles down like one compact muscular circle on the seat beside me. Eventually, traffic thins; the river looms, separating privilege from the other side of the tracks; and we do cross over. Past taller buildings, along poorer, rutted streets. Overspilling garbage cans, water hydrants spewing unhalted while kids dance naked through the spray. Brick and concrete crumbling in this sunny Northeastern spring. Soon long-distance trucks rumble alongside, slowing for highway ramps. I follow one, turn, shift rapidly through all the gears onto a whizzing bright interstate and head north. Away from—or into—the thick of things.

She's sitting out on a lawn chair, shorts and sunglasses on. One arm thrown casually behind her head. A knee up, moving gently in rhythm—to some internal song, I think. But pulling into the driveway I wonder, for a moment, if it's really Bren. The last thing I expected to see was that woman relaxing, un-driven, in the bright daylight of a hot late spring. Coppertone 15 smearing her lips white. She hears the crunch of gravel and sits up to look.

Boz whines a little in anticipation, or anxiety. Lack of fore-knowledge. And I do too, I suppose—only silently. Wondering how this will be. Trying not to wonder.

She approaches barefoot. She's put on a little weight and looks fitter, healthy. She smears sunblock from her mouth with one faintly tanned arm.

"Hey."

When she leans into the window I see that her face is still tired but not tense. The sunglasses slide down her nose. She smiles gently, and I kiss her. There are tiny streaks of gray in her hair, above the ears. Bren opens the door and Boz clambers over me whimpering, flies against her chest knocking her flat, licks her chin in recognition and confusion. I stretch out, sit next to them on freshly mowed grass that oozes pollen, promises hay fever. After a while Boz pants back and forth between us, as if questioning where his allegiance ought to lie. Then he gives up and goes sniffing around newly green bushes, pees on tree trunks. The sun's at a peak; I lie fully out on the ground to soak it in. A ladybug crawls up my elbow.

"Okay trip?"

I nod.

"Hungry?"

For many things, I tell her. "But how are you? How are you feeling?"

"Like David Copperfield." She laughs. Meets my eyes slyly, a little wizened fun sparking her own, teasing. "Ah. You didn't know I read that stuff—right? Kay forced me to. You know, nineteenth century, et cetera."

I read that one too long ago to remember, and say so.

No matter, she says, it's one of those books you really don't have to remember, in the end you just live it.

"Come on, Chick. There's lunch around here somewhere."

Boz! she calls, Boz! He ignores her, snorting through pine needles. Finally I make clucking sounds and his ears snap to alert, he gives his ugly pink dog grin and trots comfortably over.

Bonding, Bren mutters. Leave it to you, Chick.

And, in that moment, I feel necessary.

Whole-grain bread, salad, fruit, some kind of rice and lentil mash served cold—no processed sugar, no salt, no fats. I ask if this is some new dietary obsession of hers. Yes. The right food for endurance. Does it become tasty after you get used to it? I ask. No, she says, but so what. Something about complex carbohydrates, muscular glucose absorption, good fatty acids versus bad fatty acids—what she recommended to the members of her team this spring, and it seemed to work. And as a coach you never instill a practice that you are not willing to attempt yourself. She flushes slightly with pride.

"Those kids really pulled through, Chick. Most of them raced *way* over their heads."

"It must have been wonderful."

Exhausting, she says. And exciting. A feeling it is hard to describe: something more than, and less than, you expect it to be. In that way—she grins, wryly—it's actually a little like love.

"How so?"

"Oh, I don't know exactly." She pours spring water. "Just a feeling I have. You know, you go along feeling like you're totally in control—"

"Right."

"Then suddenly, one day, you find out you're really *not*. Willpower, for instance. It's very important, it can get you through a lot. But in the end it's not the thing that lets you win. Something else takes over—I'm not sure what."

There's a struggle on her face. Words elude her. This interests me, and I toss more lentil glop on my plate and lean forward, questioning. She shakes her head.

No, no, she tells me, you can't really say it. Something deep inside—it surfaces. Things fall away from it, sort of. At least that's what I think. And you move differently, Chick. Like you're not even yourself any more, but an organic part of something larger. You can feel it sometimes—I mean, in extraordinary moments of suffering or of joy. It's hot, and cold, and everything, and so are you. Then you just stop *trying,* and you actually do it. Whatever it is. You live, you die, you win.

She blushes, embarrassed. "Does *any* of that make any sense?"

"Sure. But only in here"—I pound my chest—"and here"—pound my gut. Tap my forehead. "Not necessarily here."

"Oh, well then, screw the mind. That's good enough."

In a way, we are back to a place we've visited, the beginnings of an argument we've had, almost fifteen years ago. I decline to engage in it this time—and, I see, so does she. We serve each other wretchedly unappealing health food instead. Dishing out rice that sticks to the serving spoon, slicing whole-grain bread—*sans* yeast—that is tough as a two-by-four and just as tasty. Forking over apple slices, banana chips, solicitously.

Boz attacks the screen door and Bren lets him in, pours out a man-sized bowl of water, tosses him a handful of biscuits. He gulps the water, eschews the biscuits. I blush guiltily.

"Confession time, Bren. I've been feeding him salami."

"For meals?"

"Just for treats."

She sighs, but with good humor. "Why not steak tartare?"

"Not fresh enough at the butcher's," I say, and we laugh.

She sits on the counter, tanned legs swinging lightly, so for a moment there's something almost girlish about her. But she stops moving, the moment's gone. And she's smiling at me now with an open, odd combination of shrewdness and appreciation.

"I was just thinking."

"What, sweetie?"

"It's good to see you here again. Sitting at my table. With this quiet day outside, and the air blowing in—I don't know, Chick, it feels very nice. It feels very right."

I swallow, hard, and stand to do the dishes.

She snags my arm as I head for the sink.

"Chick?"

I find her eyes, try to break their gaze, can't. Plates, bowls, and rice-encrusted spoons shiver in my hands.

"I think we should find out about that."

About what? I stammer. And focus on the shadows of afternoon outside, gentle coloring of sky that hints twilight.

"About that feeling."

Why? I mutter. Hearing my voice sound from far away, with a kind of cold detached terror.

Because, she tells me, what if it *is* true? And right? Would you want to let it slip? Let the chance to know it pass by? Die one day, and never have given it a try?

"Given what a try, Bren?"

Love, she tells me, just love.

I don't say no, and I don't say yes. But I pull gently away from her and start to wash the dishes, soaping a green sponge thoroughly, rinsing everything in water. I pick up a sopping glass and realize that I'm crying—matter-of-factly, silently, tears dripping past my nose. She stands close behind me, arms around my waist. Once in a while her palms press strong against hips or belly; once in a while her face slides forward alongside mine, rubbing cheeks, smearing tears.

Several tissues later, clean dishes racked, we take Boz along for a walk. It's not quite evening, but the heat of the day seems muffled, broken. And the air's noisy with insects, various flower and weed smells mingling in it like a riotously cheap perfume.

Bren wants to show me the neighborhood—which is mostly winding lanes in need of repaving after their usual winter beating, houses set far back from the roads, plenty of thick hedges, pines, oaks, maples, not a lot of people.

Privacy, Chick, I remember Kay saying once, it's the key to serenity. My attitude toward neighbors and their kids is essentially this: "Howdy, folks! Have a nice life! But live it on the other side of the fence!" She'd winked, taken out an imaginary handgun and aimed, fired, blew smoke off the barrel. "That's America for you, Chick. The ethic of Do It Off My Property, Pal. Land of the tough and the lonely. Lots of individual liberty, general lack of social responsibility. Best there is, though. God, I love this country!"

Yet you're afraid to come out of the closet here, I'd rebutted. Afraid of the consequences of being openly and fully what you are.

Nonsense, she'd sniffed. You're talking to a girl with *tenure* here, Chick. I don't hide my life—I just like my privacy. Besides, not *all* of us feel obliged to go around shrieking about what we do in bed! There are certainly other, more important *issues* to deal with.

The last point had been a sideways slap at me. But the impact, I remember, had been mitigated by the obvious tease in her voice, on her face; a gentleness of tone, an overt affection. Picking up a pine cone now and peeling off a chip, I understand something about her, postmortem: She could love me more fully than I could love her, in a way, because I posed no threat; I had tacitly ceded Bren to her from the very beginning, without any hint of struggle; there was nothing and no one I had ever, or could ever, take from her. From my point of view, the friendship was far more difficult. Maybe I was more than a little infatuated with Kay as well. Rendered defenseless by her subtle, tough, playful femme charisma, lipstick and rouge and perms, acute mind that let no one best it, ever.

I toss the pine cone. Boz, dragging Bren along clumsily, chases it with his tongue gaggling out of his mouth and each fang showing.

All right, Kay, I say to myself, wryly, silently. I was lucky to know you. Queer variation of a Jewish American Princess. Stereotypes can be true-to-life; and sometimes—as in your case— delightful when they are bent or bowed.

"Hey! Cut it out!"

Bren and Boz have become hopelessly tangled by his leash in some scraggly bushes and wild shiny-leafed growth which, on second glance, I hope is not poison ivy. I step into the fray.

Unsnap the leash from Boz's collar. He yelps ecstatically and goes snuffling off through trees, lunging at orange-tailed squirrels that scatter up trunks like soldiers from some army in retreat, his thick fighting-dog paws showering us with chunks of dirt. I help Bren free the useless leash. We are both on our hands and knees in mud, unknotting it from twigs and brambles, faces whipped by branches, hands recoiling from pinprick thorns.

I start to laugh. She shoots me a dark, humiliated glance, and I understand something: This walk was meant to be romantic, a pleasant, seductive pre-twilight stroll through country spring. But I can't stop laughing—at myself, at her—and, in a while, she is sitting in muddy undergrowth laughing too, a big, hearty, healthy laugh that I haven't heard in years. She looks comical and also oddly beautiful, in her rough-cut way—this fiercely uptight, honest, dauntless, handsome woman whose reserve has blown its cover.

"Oh, sweetie! I'm sorry!" But I can't stop giggling. Sitting in the ooze of a milky-stalked weed, hands and clothes grimed, she stares at me in an enraged sort of humor.

"It's never the way it's supposed to be, Chick."

"What?" I gasp.

"Life."

"I don't know. Maybe it's just the way it *is* supposed to be— did you ever think of that?—just not the way we plan it."

"Mmmm," she says, grudgingly. "Well, maybe. I guess."

Boz runs through the brush between us, spattering her chin. There is slime in my hair, sludge smearing the seat of my pants. He goes off in pursuit of something else and Bren looks at me, shrugs, grins. She wipes her face, reaches with the same hand to intertwine her fingers with mine, until both our hands are wet with wet dirt and her thumb caresses my palm firmly, very gently.

"Face it, Chick—you might really belong here."

"Here?"

"Sure. Deep in the mud, with me."

Mmmm, I say, avoiding her eyes. Then look and smile and imitate her, grudgingly: Well, *maybe*. I *guess*.

"Want to keep guessing? Or would you like to test it out?"

"Bug off, Bren. You sound like some slave-driving jock coach issuing an ultimatum."

"So what?"

"So *what?*"

"Yes. That's exactly what I *am.*"

"Oh come on. It's not quite as simple as that."

She takes both my hands in hers, swings our arms playfully.

"Tell me then, Chick," she teases. "Tell me how complex it is."

I pull away, annoyed. "You're a pain in the ass, Bren! Has it ever once crossed your mind that maybe, just maybe, it's not all up to *you?* Maybe *I* need to feel a little power around all this, too! Maybe *I* need to do some of the choosing!"

"Okay," she grumbles, smile fading. "Choose away. I mean, take your time."

She sighs.

So do I.

We look at each other sullenly. Brambles are beginning to pierce denimed thighs, a twilight chill sets in. Boz approaches panting blissfully, speckled with mud, leaves, burrs, thorny twigs. Bren wraps the disentangled leash carefully around her arm and stands. Reaches gently to help me up. My cheek finds her shoulder and for a moment we hug, stand apart, then our eyes meet; we are both frightened and hopeful, I think, and more than a little hurt.

She turns for home, whistles briefly for Boz until he follows, and I do too.

She stops once to wait for me. We walk side by side in softly burgeoning darkness.

Take your time, she mutters again. So quietly I can barely hear it. Take your time. We're on the same side. Good for one, good for all. Team spirit—that's what it means.

I know, then, that I love her still.

DeKuts said once that real strength bends, Bren tells me later, serving spring water with slices of lime on a clean, soft-lit patio. More like a phantom than a barbell. It changes form. Sometimes it masquerades. Masquerades even as its apparent opposite.

"De*Kuts?* That woman-hating old bastard? *He* said a thing like that?"

She nods. "He was rotten, in a lot of ways. But he *knew* some things!"

"I guess so."

Pretty weird to remember it, she murmurs. After all these years. "I don't think I understood the first thing about what he meant, though—not back then."

"Now?"

"Oh, sure. Now I think I understand *exactly* what he meant. Which is probably my pride showing, and not my common sense."

"I don't know, Bren. I'd say common sense is one of your strong points."

"Well, maybe." She smiles a little. "Let's just say it gets me through certain patches of my life. But it's not what gets me to a—an odd phenomenon. Oh, hell. Words fail me."

It's a physical thing with Bren, the turning of thought: a sweating and a grinding, and then a light, playful dance. She'd give up now if I allowed it, and the dance would take place in solitude, go forever unexpressed. I realized long ago that part of what I could bring to her was a catalyzing of expression. She might run away from that now, if I let her.

Insist, I tell myself. Don't let her.

"What odd phenomenon, sweetie?"

She frowns. Then stands so quickly that Boz, encrusted with mud, resting happily on the patio between us, lifts his head and his license tags jangle. Stay there, she urges him. And me. Stay there, I'll be right back. I want to show you something.

We do. I hear her rummaging in the house. The crickets have started to chorus, a high pitch that buzzes, ceases, begins again. There are a couple of stars in the sky, which is not quite night-dark yet. I make a wish. Boz jangles lightly beside me, and sighs.

"Would you like to see Kay?"

Thoughtlessly, instinctively, I open my hands. The urn settles into them. Not as heavy as I'd imagined.

Bren sits on the rim of her chair, leans toward me, reaches gently into the urn's silent mouth until her hand disappears to the wrist, plastic crackles. She pulls it out carefully—a sealed, see-through bag. The patio light makes it gleam dully.

"Here she is." Bren smiles, quietly. "In twenty-five words or less. Here. You can hold it if you want."

I set the urn down, seize and fondle the bag of ashes. They aren't ashes really. Or, at any rate, I'd pictured the substance as being similar to wood ash—fine, dusty, insubstantial, ephemeral material distilled to an almost nonexistent essence. Fragile. Easily dispersed by the slightest breeze. The reality is so different: these are hard, gritty chips, like gravel, heavy shell, pieces of stone. Tangible remains of the physical presence.

We are real, after all. In some way, Bren and her terrible DeKuts were right: Truth is in the body.

But not entirely.

And for a second, I think I understand—in a burst of thoughtless comprehension that is instant, then just as suddenly gone— what she was trying to tell me. Whatever it was—the odd phenomenon, the thing or place that common sense would not take her to, that words would fail to conjure—she had found or seen or experienced somewhere in the land of Not Entirely. Somewhere in that intermediate, limbo state between the truth of the body, and another truth.

I say good-bye to Kay and hand back the remains, murmuring thank you.

Oh, says Bren, you're welcome.

"Will you keep her?" In the dark, I can feel myself blush. "I mean, them? It?" We both grin then. It's hard to know what to call this—death's leavings, packaged in plastic, the burned-down pieces of core material that fire has not destroyed. She sighs.

"For a while, I guess. I'm really not ready to deal with all that. Burial, gravestones, that kind of stuff's *out*. Kay hated the thought of being underground. But there's this point way off the Cape—she loved it so, we went out there once in a boat-for-hire one spring, early spring, and saw whales swimming along slow and graceful as you can possibly imagine, every once in a while they'd spout. I saw one of their eyes, and I swear, Chick, the thing was looking right at me. It was amazing. We took it as a good-luck symbol—for us, I mean—the sighting, I mean—for our love. I guess eventually I'll scatter the ashes there. I think the notion would please her."

She strokes Boz's neck, squeezes a dog ear. He slimes her hand in pleasure. "You know, I kept having this feeling when I'd go to sleep at night, Chick—oh, for months after she was gone. Maybe just a wish fulfillment. I've never told this to anyone else. But I kept feeling she wasn't really gone—she was still with me, somewhere, somehow. I'd talk to her, and everything."

"That's okay, you know."

"I know."

"What about now? Is she still around?"

Bren hesitates. Then: "No," she says sadly, firmly. "Not any more."

"Sweetie, I'm sorry. There's so much loss in that, too."

"Oh, sure. And change. Sometimes I think the hardest thing has been this selfish kind of—I call it survivor's fear, you know?—of having to see, really *see*, that this—life, what we understand, what we do, who we are—none of it is really permanent. But it's easy to take that feeling, that fear, and go into a spin about how nothing really *matters*. I mean accomplishment, goal attainment, any of the markers we use to measure existence. I went into that sort of a spin myself. It was like riding the big snowball straight into hell. Only I realized, after a while, that *permanence* and *significance* are two different things. I mean, ideas. Qualities. Whatever. And I started to feel better. Almost healthy again."

Congratulations, I tell her.

Something else, she says, leaning forward to scratch Boz's neck and chest, to take my hand in hers, and I let her. A sort of self-fulfilling prophesy, she continues. It came to me during the last couple of days, when I was at the hospital full-time—everyone knew she was going fast. I fell asleep in this chair and woke up, I could see how dark it was out the window, night, and I looked over at her. I figured she'd be asleep—they were always giving her these megadoses of drugs, so a lot of the time even when she was awake she was more or less barely there, if you know what I mean. But that night, I don't know why, I don't even remember what time it was, she was completely awake. We looked at each other. She held my gaze for the longest time. Then she passed out again. But it came to me, Chick—somehow I knew—that in some important way I can't even put into words right now she was going to be all right. And I would be, too. And so would we all. If only we could know it.

Wan moths and mosquitoes flutter. Her mouth is waiting for me and I lean forward to kiss it, find it surprised and soft, vulnerable, yielding; and in turn I am surprised to find it so—for the second time in my life, though not the last. Our noses smudge dirt-spattered cheekbones. I touch her lips with a finger and a kind of shiver goes through me. The tips of our tongues meet, very slightly. Tap each other lightly in a soft and indecipherable code. Then we both pull back into patio chairs, separate in the soft-lit dark but this time with the once-sharp, clearly delineated boundaries of separation glowing fuzzily around the edges, pleased, a little shy.

Boz gets a bath that night.

When he hears water gushing into the tub he starts to whine and tremble in a strange, almost frantic, yet subdued kind of ecstasy, submitting readily with bowed head when Bren reaches to unbuckle his collar, standing stoically paw-deep while we pour pots of lukewarm water over him, work dog shampoo through his coat in a lather until the mud washes away and the bathwater's inky, rinse him off from the spout.

Three worn old beach towels later he's clean and proud, scattering around the house like a whirlwind of canine muscle, nails clicking the kitchen tiles and hallway floorboards. He rolls on rugs to dry himself more. Jumps onto forbidden territory: leather upholstery, downy bedcovers. Barks, acts coy, goads us into playing catch with the football-length rubber biscuit I bought him at an overpriced pet store in Beacon Hill. I look at Bren. We're dirty ourselves, tired, our clothes grimed. Pitching the rubber biscuit down a hallway, I realize that the place seems smaller without Kay in it—glossy wood, rustic style and the exposed ceiling beams notwithstanding. Some things are put away. It is Bren's place now. In it, she looks taller, more alone.

Ajax. Torn sponges. We scrub the tub clean of dog hair and dead twigs. The smell sifts up into steamy, fluorescent-lit air, collides with the fresh breezy damp of the night. The manufactured; the natural. Of both elements this human life consists. I resign myself to it: Walking down a supermarket aisle, or walking down a pine-softened, tree-shielded dirt trail, we humans are still creatures apart; never really, fully participating in any immediate environment. Perhaps, in the end, that's what gives us consciousness. Awareness of continual observation in lieu of natural connection. Separate from each other, too—although, for sure, we seem to strive for something different; and, to be sure, none of us start out that way. *Born alone, die alone,* the old saying goes. But it's not really true. We aren't born alone—we come out of the body of the mother. We do die alone, though. And that—

that conflict, between the way we begin and the way we end—that is the friction and the loss, the subtle underpinning of grief, that informs this human existence.

"Bath for you, Chick?"

I nod. What about her?

"Shower. You first, though. Hungry?"

"To be honest, Bren, yes, but not for that health-food stuff."

She grins wryly. "Scored big with my latest fad, I see."

"Yes, you spartan. Is it the sports thing or the WASP thing that makes you so extreme?—tell me. Anyway, let me take you out to dinner."

"Nah."

"Why?" I tease. "Still afraid of running into your *crème de la crème?*"

She shakes her head, gets a look in her eyes that's part mischievous, part serious, part something else I can't read.

"Just for you, Chick. What about pizza?"

I agree. Ask can we please order delivery, like all the college brats? because I'm feeling distinctly childish right now, a little spoiled and regressive? and she tells me Of course, of course, who would want it any other way?

Bath, shower. Baby powder. Fresh scent on skin. I wipe a circle in the mirror and look: Not bad. Early middle age. Growing knowledge of self. Knowledge of self collecting, in fact, like the proverbial moss on stone. Each wrinkle, each deep line that sleep did not put there, that sleep will not ever take away—look at it, woman; look at it hard. Your face. Aging. You have earned all the dents in this fender. Earned every disappointment and desire, every loss, and every win. Which makes me more aggressive, somehow. Assertive. Lets me know more fully what I want. Need. The difference between. What I can do without. And what I must not pass up—or, rather, what I would pass up only at a great unendurable cost.

Cost to what, Chick? To self. And why? Because it would be an avoidance of truth. A banishing of real, raw beauty from my life. Like they say, after all: truth is beauty, beauty truth. Because, in the beginning and in the end, the only truth worth making a big stink about is love. And the truth here is that you love her.

Early middle age. The perfect age to be.

I don't know why I think that, but I do.

Clean clothes, cool night breeze. Two fresh-scrubbed, good-looking women and one fresh-scrubbed, ugly-looking dog in a kitchen, in the country, pulling napkins and platters from cupboards, getting out salt and pepper. When the doorbell shrieks, Boz goes temporarily, protectively mad, and a red-faced teenager stands there shyly while Bren restrains the dog and I fork over bills. He hands back change and a big, flat cardboard box that smells hotly like spiced hell, thanks us for the tip. When he turns back to the gaudy lit sign on top of the delivery car I wonder, briefly, the way I wonder at every momentary human encounter—I can't help it, it comes with the professional territory—whether or not he will have a long life, and what kind of life it will be. Gay? Straight? Full of honesty, or of lies? A life of tenderness and courage? Of pain, violence, love? The headlights flick on, recede down the long, long driveway. I wish him good-bye and good luck. I will never, ever know.

We turn on a couple of soft living room lights, toss cushions onto the rug and set up dinner: a dishtowel, cardboard box open on the floor and pizza mist rising, paper towels for napkins. The fireplace is clean, dark, cold. A simple black mesh grating covers it. I wonder if Bren used it at all this winter—or were flaming Sunday logs, fresh coffee, the *New York Times Book Review*, just Kay's choices really?

"What kind of music do you want, Chick?"

"Something from the late sixties, please, or early seventies. To remind me of my youth. Not that my youth was all that memorable."

She selects a cassette. I watch her move through soft circles of light, through long angular shadows. Her face keeps changing; sometimes it's obscured, at other times gently illuminated, intent, gracefully no-nonsense.

We eat pieces of the thing I've ordered, in what was undoubtedly a mood of childish excess—or maybe just rebellion at Bren's latest ascetic health-food phase. An extra-large deep-pan pizza. Very oily. Double cheese. Onions. Green olives. Black olives. Hot peppers. Mushrooms. I realize it's the fulfillment of a long-term frustrated desire; the kind of pizza I always yearned to order during all the years working my way through a state college to pay for books and food, through the summers to pay off loans, trying to study for exams standing at cash registers or deep-fry vats, through all the lobster shifts and swing shifts of graduate school, pleas of poverty to financial aid committees; always jealous of the rich people who sat beside me in classrooms, envious of those wealthy straight white folk who taught us all—taught us the ways of the mind, gave us an edge in the world which, in the end, was really another ticket into privilege and power. For the people I envied, a way of maintaining the advantage they'd been born into. For me, a way of elbowing into it, once and for all.

At any rate, I've gone all this time without treating myself to anything so frivolous as pizza. It's terrible-tasting, like most wasteful things. I will, nevertheless, enjoy it.

Bren stares at me, smiles.

"You look so happy."

"Mmm. Living well. It's the best revenge."

Revenge for what? she asks. For growing up without a trust fund in America, I tell her. And she nods, knowingly; she has had to work hard too, to hammer out a place for herself.

She pats oily tomato sauce from her lips. "You know, one of the kids on the team told me the other day that she believed in reincarnation." She imitates a husky young voice. " 'It's like, I figure that, like, if I don't, like, do real *well* in this life, I've, like, got a bunch more other *lives* to do *well* in. So, I mean, like, what do *you* think about it, Coach?' "

We laugh, long and loud. Settled flat under the coffee table, Boz cocks his head at us in brief alarm before deciding it's nothing, then curls back to sleep.

"Well, Coach. What *do* you think about it?"

"I told her that I try not to worry about things like that. I figure we're here, alive, in this life, now. And the best approach is to just get on with it."

"Ah," I tease, "but is that what Coach just *says*? Or really believes?"

"Yes, that's what *Coach* believes." She smiles. There are tears in her eyes—from the laughter, or from something else, I'm not quite sure. "As for me—I don't know. Maybe. Although only partly. I mean, in the sense that maybe there *is* something—you know, like an energy force, or an electrical current, or some such phenomenon, that inhabits a form—a human form, an animal form, or plant—who knows? and when the form dies, it becomes no longer viable for conducting the energy, and so the energy, or whatever, travels on and occupies some other, living form. Maybe there's something like that. I couldn't begin to say that I definitely be*lieve* it, in the sense of having any kind of absolute faith in it, you know. Anyway, where's the proof? Okay, yes, these thoughts have crossed my mind—while Kay was sick, and of course afterwards, and probably once in a while before I even met her. But do *I* believe in reincarnation the way I think this kid meant—that is, in the sense that the same person with the same memories, or whatever, gets reborn again and again? No. Absolutely not. I think—I mean, I have this gut sense about it— that whatever might live on has got nothing to do with personality. You. Me. Kay. As *you*, as *me*, we're here just once. Whatever else continues, after our bodies die, it's a lot more impersonal than you, or me. The individual, distinguishable characters that we are, right now, in this life—this is our one and only shot. Maybe some energy survives. But the thoughts and the memories? Talents, failings? All the love and hate that a single person has? I doubt it, Chick. I doubt it." She pauses, a little uncertain now, shy somehow. "Which is why it's important—"

"To work hard and make the most of it, right?"

"Well, yes. Just like that."

Oh, I say, I believe in that too.

Then I lean across a cooling pizza box on my hands and knees, through the dark clean shadow of unused fireplace, just like that, and kiss her.

Some things we remember in detail; others, in metaphor. Maybe that's why, later, it will come back to me as a blur: the long, long time that the kiss went on, became not a kiss any more but an exploration of skin; the beginning of how we touched hair, lips, cheeks, breasts and thighs through cloth; the moment she started to take off my clothes, there on the floor in front of cold pizza and a snoring dog, and I let her do all the work—sensing somehow that seizing the physical initiative was what she needed. There had been something vaguely frightening and unfamiliar about my saying where and when. Her power to control and to please was linked inextricably to her passion; and if I wanted her passion, and mine, I would have to give up a measure of my own control—not something I ever did lightly. But I realized, through a cloud of anxiety and desire, that the control was a much overrated thing I could do without. And, anyway, we must all give it up in the end.

For Bren, I know, the physical look and feel would be remembered with a great deal of clarity. We are different that way. Bodies are ultimately more important to her than they have ever been to me. I can live quite happily in my head; it's the way I am, I really can't help it.

Still, there is this part of me that yearns to know all the ways of my body. And a part of her that yearns to express all the ways of her mind. If, in early middle age, I finally began to know and appreciate the physical channels of being—the electrical currents she had described as being potentially immortal, the dendrites and axions and synapses that conduct the mortal impulses, cause tissue and organ to secrete hormones, process oxygen in blood, make the raw muscle of the heart pick up pace, eyes drip tears, cunt excitement, and tendons attaching raw muscle to bone, the ache and tickle and longing and vulnerability of the flesh—which, she said, was the body's largest organ, *derma,* an entirety into and of itself—I owe the pleasure and the terror of discovery to her. Or rather, to her and to myself; because it was in the combination of us together that the discovery happened. What I began to see was that a part of me that felt necessary to full human existence came alive in her hands. It bloomed in the measure of control I handed over to her. She evoked it; but, after all, it was I who'd made all this happen, and neither of us forgot that.

Talk, you, I demanded, when she stretched naked over me. Stay here, stay. No. Don't shut your eyes, Bren—I want you to see.

See what? she breathed.

Me, I insisted. This. And yourself.

She opened her eyes to look then, broke into sweat.

"God, you're pretty. I'm so afraid."

But she reached to touch me, anyway, where I was softly hot and wet. The fear didn't stop her. Electricity tingled through.

"Tell me how, Chick. I'm out of practice."

Slower, I told her. Like that, yes. Nice and strong and slow.

In the blur of what was, certain things would come back to

me later, the odd detail here and there: that she pressed down and took each nipple into her mouth in turn, sucking with a raw infantile need, as if real milk was about to flow, and her life depended on it. But every once in a while catching herself, pausing to nibble and tease, smiling, when I moaned, with a triumphant sort of slyness; and her hands slid everywhere, fingers slowly, firmly caressing, tortured my belly and thighs and then boldly went inside without an invitation, twisting around, exploring, filling me more and more until I could feel myself swell closer around her, hungry for the intrusion. That's when I got afraid, and had to pause for a while. I told her. So we both were still. She leaned on an elbow and one hand played with my hair while the other stayed motionless inside me, looked down at my face with a pleased and fearless look, and a warm, old kind of wisdom in her eyes. I understood that she wanted to take me to some place that was different in fullness, more truly textured with pleasure than all the lands of perfunctory spasm I'd visited before and called love, and I wanted very badly to be taken; but then wanted to take her, too, and wasn't sure that I could, or that she'd let me. Looming over me like this, handsome and beautiful and nearly all-powerful, she seemed much more than I'd bargained for, and her strength began to scare me.

But on the other hand she was just Bren, after all. My friend of so many years and—who knew? that kid on the team might be right—perhaps of many lifetimes.

The fear dissipated. I could smile.

"Don't stop. Not really."

Oh, she said, I couldn't stop now.

We began to move again, very subtly, a mere simultaneous quivering at first. It took a long, erratic and doubtful time, almost stopped being graceful once and I cried out in a frustration that was tangible—at myself, at my mind that would not shut down no matter what, at this mingling of bodies we'd committed to which was somehow so familiar, yet at the same time near-foreign. I was more frightened than I knew. But in the end what she willed and what I gave over to her will were stronger than the fear. We moved farther and rougher, more extravagantly, she was on me and inside me, moving with me, against me, until there was nowhere else to move into, and I heard myself yell in a bubble of silence, electricity flicker my eyelids, and I breathed faster until, for a moment, breath ceased. Then gave myself up to the surge that washed me against her thighs and breasts and fingers like a wave, jolting me so hard that the wave broke with impact, shattered into successively smaller, sweating currents, then ripples, trickling back now, back, into damp and ragged calm.

Something blocked my throat. More tears. They dripped down my face with the sweat, and her lips smudged them, tasted them. The pain oozed, eased. I breathed quietly, began to feel shy, turned away and she held me with wet arms and hands.

I love you, I said. But the words came out throttled, so that only the middle one sounded, and only its first letter echoed. What? she whispered. I didn't respond. They'd rung pallid and insignificant, clattering in my skull like a bad cliché. Early middle age, and I realized it wasn't exactly *love* I wanted, but love and something more. Truth be told, my own standards were coldly austere in their way, as high as any of Bren's; I wanted nothing less than a magnificently heart-wise fellow traveler in my life to visit new places with in body and in mind, mingle electricity with, abolish unnecessary borders with, see.

I wondered if she'd be all that for me. Wondered what she had in mind herself—was it me she wanted now after all the years, me with all of my chatter, demands, failings, gifts, excessive hidden dreams of my own in which I, too, won what had once been unattainable? Or did she want a stand-in for Kay? an old comfortable and available friend to step into this recently opened slot in her life the way some new recruit might occupy full scholarship position on her team, fill the vacancy left by an especially favored, just-graduated All-American?

And if she wanted none of the above, or all of the above, or some complex combination thereof—which was most likely— what then? If the result was loss of something I'd never had before, and only now just tasted, could I live with that?

If the result was winning what I'd never had before, and only now just tasted, could I live with *that*?

And what if I failed her standards? Or what if she failed mine, was not and would not or could not be this idealized companion of my fantasy cosmos? and offered just herself, with all of her moody silences, rigid demands, failings, gifts, dreams of triumph? Offered mere, faulty love—nothing more? Or less?

"Chick?" Her palm stroked a shoulder, smelled like me, like my own insides. "What are you thinking?"

"That I think too much."

"Mmmm. I could have told you that."

We chuckled. The floor was too hard, hurting my hip and ribs. I turned back to face her.

"What about you?"

She blushed. "I'm fine. I mean, I don't need—this is good with me, right now—"

"Okay, toughie, but that's not what I meant."

Toughie.

She was. We laughed.

"Maybe, Chick. But it's what *I* meant."

"Listen, then, let's just forget about it for now. Take the pressure off—"

"Thanks."

"Off, off, off." And I snapped my fingers, blew something invisible away. I was disappointed, but also relieved somehow; and the look that flooded her face—relaxation, affection—made it all okay. "Talk to me, Bren."

She blinked, confused. "I was thinking about Kay."

"Do you want to talk about her? You can, you know."

She did, in halts and starts. Kay was older by a dozen years, wiser, well-traveled. Beautiful dresser, knew exactly how to wear makeup, when to have her hair done—very femme. With something foreign about her. Maybe the Jewishness. Like something dark, and secret, that no one outside her could ever comprehend; so that, even though she was talkative, ebullient, full of a kind of sunshine—and not just publicly, but between the two of them as well—there was this unspeakably private part of her that had never been trespassed, never would be: by Bren, or by anyone. She hadn't exactly understood Kay, maybe; just given herself up to the feel of things between them, and loved her. Not a perfect relationship. There were plenty of things she did, things that were important to her, that Kay had never understood either, had never bothered to understand. The wordless, deep-rooted thing that made her physical, for instance, that made what she spent her life doing—coaching, training, weights, running around—an indispensable part of who she was, who she'd always be, had never interested Kay. On the other hand,

Bren herself had never been much turned on by Melville, or Hawthorne, or Dickens either. Although Kay *had* made her read *David Copperfield*. Once or twice, too, Bren had forced Kay to come to a swimming meet. Aside from that, their love had been one of acceptance of difference; not an abolition of it.

There were these roles they'd been in, kind of. Bren blushed again. Around sex, for instance. She'd always been the initiator. Always. It was the way things had happened between them, the way things had stayed. Seemed to make them both happy. And she understood how things could be different with other women; that it was all dependent on relationship, anyway, and on how you needed to be yourself—because, in the end, being on top and being more aggressive was never the same thing as being truly dominant. But for her, for Kay, it had worked. And since then, there'd been no one.

"So I'm a little nervous."

"Yes."

"I won't always be."

Take your time, I told her. I smoothed her forehead, gently twisted a lock of hair. Take your sweet, sweet time.

She kissed my nose. Irish, she said. Yes, I told her, that's what I am. Rough around the edges. Not always attractive, or even polite. But real, at least. Sweaty from the guts on out. More than a little warlike. Big fan of mixing it up. Yelling loudly for truth, beauty, attention—and mostly, for justice. Part of my heritage. Though not all of it.

"What's the rest of it, Chick?"

"Of what?"

"Your heritage."

"Oh. Being gay, I guess."

"You really think so?"

"I do. I really think so. Without that, I just wouldn't be the same person—I'd have a completely different point of view about almost everything—I'd have a completely different life. Some of which would be easier, I guess. But some of it would be much, much harder."

"How so?"

Because, I told her, *not* being different in America can lull you, can cripple you—even though it seems desirable to everyone, even though everything in the society pressures you into sameness—it is a handicap in the end. A handicap to live without knowing the struggle of difference—in all of its pain, its fear, its celebration, its compassion.

She thought this through. Gave a skeptical look. Saying Well, maybe, but if that's true it's something she herself has never experienced.

"That's because you don't have gay friends."

"I've never really felt the need."

"But I think the need's there, sweetie, whether you acknowledge it or not. When you don't have that—a small group or a community of friends—not even *friends*, exactly, but people who *reflect* you, who share in or at least identify with your most intimate reality—you tend to feel utterly isolated, almost as if you're the last of your species, ill at ease in the world. As if you *belong* less than anyone else. As if you are *worth* less than anyone else, than all the straight people walking around proclaiming their self-righteous view of normality without even *knowing* that that's what they're doing—because that kind of careless insensitivity, it's so deeply, habitually ingrained, that in a way you learn not to expect anything better from them."

She listened, skepticism still in her eyes. Somehow, though, I am hitting home, and know it. Hallelujah, I thought—and I didn't stop talking.

"But when you more or less surround yourself by a community of queers"—I watch her silently wince at the word, and I smile—"you create a different universe within that seemingly larger whole, a universe in which *you* are the norm, in which *you* are accepted and acceptable. You relax. You laugh, you love, you can suffer loss and openly grieve. Your passions stop embarrassing you so badly! And you begin to see that, in a very profound way, you can be sustained and have a good life with*out* all those straight people! Because the fact of the matter is that *we really don't need them.*"

"You sound pretty separatist," she teased. "Like all those phony feminists."

"Screw the feminists. I'm talking about *lesbians.*"

She laughed. "Good."

"Yes—see? We don't need the straights! Not *any* of them."

"I don't know, Chick. The world's pretty big. I think maybe we all need each other." She ran fingers over my shoulder, my neck. There was a tenderness to her, now, that I'd never directly experienced before; and, for a moment, I got the sense that our customary roles had reversed. She seemed much, much older than me. Kinder. Wiser.

"Another thing," she said quietly. "Not that I want to impede the progress of truth, beauty, or justice, mind you." She smiled. "But when you talk about creating a world in which you are the norm, you forget that norms can be deadening. Most notable accomplishment—I mean in sport, but also in the rest of life— is highly *ab*normal. Winning, for instance—it can never be the norm. *Not* winning, *not* exceeding, *not* being special—those are the norms. And do you really want that?"

She'd scored a point. I told her fine, and accurate, and perceptive—but her world view avoided the whole issue of pride, of self-worth.

"And listen, Bren—don't you want to be proud of what you are? Don't you feel you deserve to be?"

"Maybe. But, you know, I'm not that interested in storming around being *proud* all the time. I know about that, I see it in the kids on my team a lot—when you're that proud of yourself you're arrogant, and when you're arrogant it's because you're afraid—you're afraid because you feel like you have something to lose, and whatever that something is, it's always on the line. You're always defending it, always more or less defensive. Personally, I say, give me the swimmer with nothing to lose. Pride doesn't impede her. And she can experience fear, or pain, but it doesn't stop her—she just throws her guts all out on the table and gets on with things—"

"Win or lose?"

"Win or win. I mean, pride is like talent, Chick—right? It only gets you so far. The rest is work. And acceptance—"

"Of the work?"

"Sure. And of your own little self, doing the work."

She was right. We both were. But, saying all these things, she had looked quite beautiful. I stopped being proud then, and stopped being afraid. Accepted what I wanted. Accepted *that* I wanted. I pushed her down by the shoulders—firmly, but gently, because the joints were aging now, required surgery, would never be the same, and I treasured every ruined inch of them the way I treasured her, and how she'd accepted the pain of them, and of work, and Kay, and me.

Come here, I said.

I am here, she said.

It was true. Then I kissed her with my lips and tongue, as long and as fully as I could, and I wanted to pour myself all over her, wanted to give her every good, blissful feeling in the world.

Now, lady, I told her, let's see just how good we can make you feel.

Oh, she whispered, closed her eyes, opened them. Well, okay.

She pulled me down to cover her like a blanket. I could see a dark fireplace, lamplight, could see a dog tail flick. I kissed her mouth again. She liked it. I told her she was much more than a friend. I told her that I loved her, that I had loved her all my life.

Angelita

🐬 🐬 🐬

Babe called tonight from the Emergency Room. Rough day, she said, worse evening. Patient saturation. She was putting in the overtime because of this last-minute crisis: post-traumatic stress victims, just a bunch of kids really, survivors of a bad, bad boating accident near the Bay that had left two drowned, one in serious condition, the others emotionally comatose—runaways, it looked like, who had stolen a boat. There'd been cameras and reporters crawling all over the paramedic crew, and if I wanted to I'd probably catch it on the eleven o'clock news.

But the real reason she was calling, after all, was to apologize, and complain. She loved me. She was sorry to miss dinner. She was too, too tired, sick of taking care of everyone but herself. But would I tell Kenny that she'd come in later to kiss him good-night?

I love you, too, I told her. It's okay about dinner—I burned it anyway, you know me—so Kenny and I ordered pizza. And I'm sorry you're so tired. When you come home, we will hold you.

I didn't tell her the rest. I figured I'd do that later, when things were safe and warm. She did catch something in my voice, though, and asked Is there anything wrong, Ellie? No, I lied, just twilight blues. Stay sane, Doc. Get your rear end home safely.

*　　*　　*

Kenny and I make a mess. Pizza sauce and cheese and hot Italian peppers all over the counter, the table, the rug, his shirt. TV blares cartoons. Mobile toys turn our hallways into traffic hazards.

Learning to walk put him immediately into Search and Destroy mode. There are protective cases over everything: outlets, phone jacks, extension cords. He's big, like his mother, toppling whatever he does not like, racing clumsily to embrace and slurp over whatever he approves of, gnawing things apart with his full, expressive lips and hands.

My relationship with him is strange—a bizarre combination of substitute mother, big sister, and partner in crime—but, nevertheless, it's affectionate and workable. Often, like tonight, I'm the indulgent baby-sitter; crawling on the floor too, bouncing on sofa cushions, ramming my head into chair edges and crying, placating myself and him with ice cream and sweets. An evening together leaves us mutually stained with tomato paste, licorice, diaper slime. We keep each other company in front of cable TV. Finish up a third dessert. Play horsey and airplane. Trip over bright plastic objects on our way to the bath.

Finally, among miniature bobbing beach balls, floating ships, baby shampoo and white bubbles, he splashes me contentedly and consents to become clean from the strong toe ends of his ample, pudgy feet to the thick, dark, curling hair that crowns him. When the tub drains he cries, suddenly passionate about the water; then stops for a towel-down, tears forgotten.

I read him to sleep in his own bright and busy room. There are brilliantly colored posters on the walls here, advertising events and exhibits concerning things African, Cuban, Hispanic, Jewish, gay. He doesn't understand the book words yet, but likes their sounds, and the deep-colored pop-out pictures that go with them. I have read this particular one at least a thousand times. Something about a cat and a rat. I don't even listen to it myself, but—next to Babe, and baths, and me—it is the great, great passion of his life.

When he dozes off I cover him to the chest, leave two nightlights on. I shove mobile hazards against the hallway walls to clear a path, turn off the TV, dump dishes into the sink, sponge down all besmudged surfaces. I can hear him if he moves, or cries. I can hear a sound outside—a car, or footsteps—and, in the silence, I can anticipate, work, stay vigilant.

Still, confronted with my own presence now, alone, I must face the nighttime differently. Kenny, Babe, eating, bathing—all have been great buffers between myself and this loss. A little afraid, plenty weary, I sit on the couch with just myself and Chick's letter. Open it again, and read through.

Because here, by myself, I can cry.

I do.

Later, I move to the office. It's next door to Kenny's room, across the hall from ours. Shelves are packed with books and magazines; the walls with framed photographs and article headings and book jackets, a bulletin board on which memos and scrawled phone numbers are tacked amid a hanging clutter of age-group and collegiate swimming medals. There are stuffed file cabinets. A hand-held cassette recorder. Two typewriters, one of which works. A computer. A printer.

I turn on specially developed lights—a combination of soft yellow-white and fluorescent that is guaranteed to relieve both writer's block and competitive stress—and sit in a special lumbar-supporting swivel chair at the computer, pressing buttons. Electronic lights beep and blink. I think about Babe's post-trauma kids in ER, and Kenny, and the letter. The day floods through me. I start to write:

Rescue helicopters hovered over the water like great metal dragonflies. Below bobbed fragments of the 747 that had gone down more than two days ago, filled to capacity and carrying with it all the members of Southern University's top-ranked NCAA Division I swim team. No one expected survivors.

It had been one of the worst storms to hit the Triangle in years. Winds gusted to 150 miles an hour and more, swells rose higher than eighty feet, the ocean turned a savage gray color. Meteorologists dubbed the storm Angelita—Little Angel.

Now, though, turquoise swells rippled mildly below, capped with white froth. It was as if this bright calm covered the entire surface of the earth, as if green-blue ocean had always spread everywhere like an undulating mirror of tranquility and always would. Sun seared the tropical sky unbroken by a single cloud. It was hard to believe in Angelita today.

There wasn't much left of the airliner: a few decimated wing parts, some salt-ravaged chunks of material that appeared to be seat cushions.

U.S. Patrol ships cruised the area in their own search. Sometimes they'd launch an inflatable. Navy frogmen went off the sides backwards, hands gripping face masks, lead weights circling their waists. If there'd been survivors after the crash, chances were they wouldn't have lasted an hour in the clutches of Angelita, with or without a flotation device.

But the airliner's demise had made headlines for two nights running, and, back on the mainland, scores of relatives clung to a hope that wouldn't die.

"Gringo to Chico. Over."

In his hovering bubble of glass and metal, Alonzo sighed. "What is it, Stu?"

"I got news for them down there." *The voice crackled harshly from the instrument panel.* "No fins, no bodies. Those Navy boys are a bunch of bozos. They say hammerheads got brains the size of a pea. But how much you want to bet, a hammerhead at least knows where to look? Listen, you want to hear a story? Over."

Alonzo's eyes searched the blue swells. "Not really," *he muttered, but audio never picked it up. Something tugged at his insides. Nausea, maybe, mingled with an odd sense of expectation. Overtired, he told himself. Too many searches futile, too many end in failure, a bad storm at sea is indeed death's little angel—no more, no less—but lately this thought had pierced his logical armor, led him through increasingly frequent moments of black nothingness. These moments had gone unnamed until a recent night when he'd woken in a bath of his own sweat, suddenly knowing the name. Now he scanned the waters below, hot with useless hope.*

"Ever hear the Chinaman's advice to beginning divers, Chico? Over."

"No, Stu. I never did."

"Confucius say, always dive with buddy and always carry knife. If you see shark, take out knife. Stab buddy. And beat it the hell out of there. That's an old proverb, señor. You can tell that to your mama-san. Over."

Sunlight streaked the water a shimmering platinum. It burned Alonzo's eyes and he nosed the chopper down by instinct. One of the inflatables had edged close to something. A piece of material, discolored beyond recognition—one of those flotational seat cushions—he was surprised it had lasted so long. No, it wasn't a seat cushion after all but something that resembled a bloated mannequin, stiff and crusted white with salt. The divers had gone crazy, surrounding it. They'd even sent in a couple of guys with electric prods to buzz off the man-o'-wars.

Encased in his bubble, he watched them ease the thing over the inflatable's edge. He thought he saw it flail an arm faintly, thought he saw it kick. But it was barely recognizable as a human body. Scraps of colorless clothing hung from it, the lips were big as balloons and eyelids swollen completely shut, limbs withered to a clawlike shape. He followed procedure and kept all frequencies open. Seconds passed. The panel crackled silence.

Then, "Jesus," he heard. "Jesus fucking Christ."

One of the Patrol clippers had veered close. The inflatable rocked in its wake, filled with frogmen and the crusted white mannequin thing.

"God," he heard, "is there a doctor in the house?"

Then: "Sure thing, Tarzan. Jesus. Jesus Christ. It's a girl."

I stop. Fiddle with pencils. Scratch my neck. Stand and pace. Outside, it is dark. I see it through blinds: no more twilight, only late night, wind trapped between hills and the Bay, car headlights splintering by, occasional wall-hushed metallic creaks, and lights of the trolleys.

Reluctantly, like a slave crawling back to the temple gods, I slouch into my swivel chair. Adjust the lumbar rest. Save the document, which for easy future reference I name *Angelita*, fret about whether it is a short story or a fictionalized documentary, or a lie, or the truth, or the start of something more and something larger, or maybe just one of those fragments that spins through me, then leaves abruptly, an end in itself. There's not much more I can do with it tonight, in any case. The actions I've chosen today, the news life has dealt, the people I love, have left me too tired. I press more buttons, hear more beeps. Lights flash, red and green. I print it out. Travel on to other things.

Write:

I got Chick's letter today, telling us about Bren. Feels like it has undone me. She was weeding the garden on Sunday, Chick says, fell down, never got up. A stroke, they told her. Uncontrollable blood pressure; medication didn't work. Apparently she'd had the condition for quite some time, and just kept it to herself.

But she went almost immediately. A quick blow. No more pain. Never regained consciousness.

I will miss her the rest of my life.

Stunning wash of grief, Chick said; she is still just beginning to feel it all out. And one thing she knows she'll feel sooner or later is this anger—that she did not have time to say good-bye—but then, how many of us ever do? She knows, after time has passed, that there will be minutes and hours of gratitude, too, for the years of marriage she shared with Bren, and for all the years of love.

Lucky warrior, my Bren, she wrote. To go so swiftly. Do you think, little loves, that she's there with the light?

I'm tired. Too full of a desire to avoid these tears. So I save this other document, shut off the machine, and think about cleaning up—the house, and myself—for Babe. Who will be burned out, cranky, wanting to be touched.

We'll call Chick. Visit her, the three of us. Or, if she'd rather, have her come west for a while. But it's late, now, back east; and the fact that she wrote rather than called implies a need for distance.

We'll call her in the morning.

In the meantime, it occurs to me, there is this story to tell. Of what happened to all of us, and the life that continued for some of us, in the wake of the storm called Angelita.

I remember something Babe told me once, years ago. It was during her residency; she had met a Tibetan monk. He was visiting a terminally ill patient in the hospital—a fellow Buddhist and Tibetan in exile, who had had a very rough life, had seen his entire family murdered by the invading Chinese, had fled Tibet and staggered across the Indian border in the middle of winter, half alive, to eventually lead a menial and impoverished existence, first in South Asia, then in America.

The monk told Babe the tale of his own life, as well: He, too, had suffered in the Chinese invasion and occupation, had at one time been interred in a so-called reeducation camp where he was beaten, starved, and tortured. In fact, during one torture session his interrogators drove a short nail into his forehead. He had the scar still. It had taken a long time to heal. Had become infected, and racked him with fever. For a while, delirious, he was sure he would die.

In this instance, he said, his own religious practices had helped immeasurably. He had tried, as much as he was able in his delirium, to visualize the after-death state, the between-lives intermediate state of *Bardo,* to control his own fear. And, in a moment of feverish clarity, the thought came to him: that the instructions regarding how to conduct oneself during the process of dying, and in the after-death state, were applicable, also, to one's conduct during life.

Then—inexplicably, though prepared to die—he had gotten better. His fever subsided. His forehead wound healed. The Chinese soldiers, deciding he was of no further use to them, let him go.

Babe pressed him for details. It might, she told him, be of help to her in her medical practice. Because, as a doctor, she dealt with diseases of the mind as well as the body; and her patients were more often than not the dying.

How might an individual's life be improved if he or she could abolish the fear of death? Or, rather, of the process of dying? Knowledge of this would be beneficial; too few even thought about it.

Would she, for instance—dedicated as she was to the healing of the body and mind and to the abolition of suffering—know how to conduct herself properly at the time of her own death?

She doubted it.

The Tibetan examined her face for a long time. So long, Babe said, that she could feel herself break into a sweat. His forehead was wide, with a single deep-dug cicatrix left by the nail right above his broad nose, between the small lively black eyes. His age was difficult to discern. His hands were gentle, stroking wooden rosary beads. Finally, he smiled quietly at her.

Oh, you will, he said. You will, you will.

Our lives are short, but also very long. So there's never just one story; there are many, so many. We cannot be the vessel for them all.

I've written about Babe here, and Bren, and others; but there's lots more. The truth is that we haven't always been sharing partners in each other's lives. It's probably more accurate to say that, off and on, we found each other. Sometimes the search was elating; at other times, exhausting. It gave and took.

But that's another story.

I will say one thing: Babe is the person standing in this little room of my life with me.

It is a room that sometimes contracts and seems to crush, sometimes expands infinitely, like the uncontained pool of my long-ago visualized dreams. If she were not here, I would stand in it alone. Which would maybe be okay. Anyway, it would be what it would be. More often than not, I'm thankful for her presence. I mean I'm lucky, and grateful, for the company and the love.

Although, I know, there will be this time when even a lover's companionship becomes impossible.

We have to be alone for final journeys. That way, we travel light.